REAP THE WILD WIND

The Finest in DAW Science Fiction
from JULIE E. CZERNEDA:

Stratification:
REAP THE WILD WIND (#1)

* * *

Species Imperative:
SURVIVAL (#1)
MIGRATION (#2)
REGENERATION (#3)

* * *

IN THE COMPANY OF OTHERS

* * *

Web Shifters:
BEHOLDER'S EYE (#1)
CHANGING VISION (#2)
HIDDEN IN SIGHT (#3)

* * *

The Trade Pact Universe:
A THOUSAND WORDS FOR STRANGER (#1)
TIES OF POWER (#2)
TO TRADE THE STARS (#3)

REAP THE WILD WIND

Stratification #1

Julie E. Czerneda

DAW BOOKS, INC.
DONALD A. WOLLHEIM, FOUNDER
375 Hudson Street, New York, NY 10014
ELIZABETH R. WOLLHEIM
SHEILA E. GILBERT
PUBLISHERS

Jacket art by Luis Royo.

ISBN: 978-0-7564-0456-7

DAW Books are distributed by Penguin Group (USA) Inc.

Book designed by Elizabeth M. Glover.

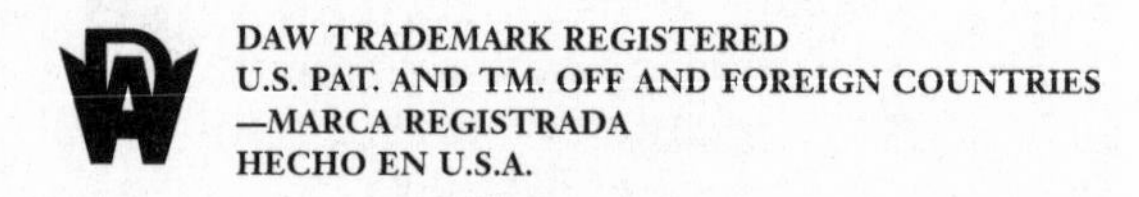

PRINTED IN THE U.S.A.

To Michael Gilbert

There are people you never forget, no matter how long you knew them, or how much time you spent together. They claim their place in your heart, and your life is better for it.

This book, published on the tenth anniversary of my first and prequel to that same story, is the one I've intended for several years to be for such an unforgettable person. Michael Gilbert. Mike, you see, was the first at DAW to read my work. He took it from the slush and recommended it. He opened the door for my career. And more.

I didn't realize then what being published by DAW meant, but Mike set me straight. During my first months as a new, unknown author, he never let me forget I was a new, unknown author. He also never let me forget I was now part of the DAW family, so it didn't matter how new or unknown I was. I'd been adopted. Long chats on the phone, always warm hospitality, and those fat envelopes of wonderful cartoons Mike created—to which I owe much of my knowledge of publishing and fear of long-haired women wielding bats. Or was that deadlines?

It was a proud moment indeed when I earned my own sturdy box (recycled Canadian pulp, of course) from the talented, memorable Mike.

Thank you, Mike.

Acknowledgments

Ten years since I wrote the first of these. Looking back at it? It's essentially the same list today: the wonderful people at DAW, my friends and partners, especially Sheila Gilbert; my family and friends; my colleagues and peers. Luis? For all this time, you've turned what I write into amazing visions. Thank you.

My life and work since has been enriched by more people than I could possibly name. I remain humbled by the response of readers to the story of Sira and Morgan, my first story. I hope you enjoy revisiting that setting. This is, in many ways, for you.

Each book has its own helpers. This has been a more family-oriented project than most. I'd like to thank Bryan, Colin, and Philip Czerneda for advice on metalworking; Scott Czerneda for plot discussions; Jennifer Czerneda for names and my model for hard work no matter what, and my Roger, for the chemistry of combustion, as well as for supporting me in every way, including fresh baked cookies at timely moments. Happy 30th again!

The following read manuscript for me and provided critical

comment: Jana Paniccia, Janet Chase, Jihane Billacois (who also helped proof), Ruth Stuart, and Shannan Palma. Thanks, ladies! I'd also like to thank my hosts over the past year for wonderful events, in particular: Ad Astra, Southern Ontario Librarians Association, CACE-Ottawa, Toronto Trek 20, Armadillocon, World Fantasy Film Festival, Astronomicon, and the Barrie Public Library (Hi Mary!).

Last, but not least. Sir David Attenborough and all those who show us this world's wonders. What . . . you thought I made all it up?

Enjoy!

Prelude

THE M'HIR WIND BEGAN OUT of sight, out of mind. It stirred first where baked sand met restless surf. It became fitful and petulant as it passed over the barrens, moving dunes and scouring stone. Sometimes it sighed and curled back on itself, as if absentminded. But it never stilled.

It only grew.

By the time the land raised its wall, the M'hir was a steady howl, wide as the horizon and heavy with power. Dust and sand marked its leading edge; thunder and lightning heralded its approach. It rushed into the mountain range, screaming through canyons until rock cracked from the sound. But the land would not be denied, forcing the M'hir up and up until the wind became chill and sullen and pregnant with cloud.

Rain came to the slopes; violent, driven rain that carved gullies and tumbled boulders. It washed everything from its path until, spent, it sprawled across the desert as thousands of dark, twisting rivulets that were sucked into the parched earth. Life ignited. For days and days to come, this place would bloom and crawl and flutter, turning the M'hir's grudging gift into color and motion.

The M'hir itself roared up the mountains, what remained of its moisture released in blizzards of white. It ripped clouds as it crested the summits, then plunged.

Stripped of its moisture, heated as its air compressed, the M'hir Wind raced down the far side of the mountain range, faster and faster, its searing breath about to fall on new lands.

No longer out of sight, or out of mind, to those who waited; the first dry hot gusts of the M'hir signaled summer's end and the Harvest.

If you were brave enough to climb.

Chapter 1

OLD, THESE MOUNTAINS. Old and beaten and scoured, until they were more a tangle of sharp ridges than peaks. The ridges plunged like greedy fingers into the swamplands owned by the Tikitik. Those swamplands, themselves an immense grove braided with open water and reedbed, extended from the mountains to the horizon; beyond, should any care, lay the sere plains and parallel mounds of the Oud. For Cersi was a world meticulously divided and ruled.

As it had always been. This was one of three points on which all who dwelled here agreed.

Next was Passage. The Om'ray, third of the races of Cersi, owned no part of this world. Once a lifetime, an Om'ray was entitled to trespass wherever he must over the lands of the others, to reach a mate or die in the attempt. It was an accommodation of instinct which pleased no one, beyond continuing the world as it was.

For that was the final point of agreement: what was and had been must stay the same. Cersi was in balance and at peace. Change was forbidden, for all sakes.

Old, these mountains.

And every summer here ended with the M'hir.

Aryl Sarc stared at the hand near her face. It was hers, the knuckles white with strain beneath smudges of dirt. She eased her grip slightly, looked ahead for the next. She'd never been this high before. Didn't matter. Couldn't matter. She took a deep breath.

"I'm going to fall, you know."

Exhaling the breath in a snort, Aryl twisted to scowl at her brother. Costa Sarc, or rather Costa sud Teerac, might be bigger, stronger, and Joined—thus officially adult and her senior—but he clutched the stalk below her as if to embed himself in its bark. "I'll fall," he gasped. "Any— Oh, no! I'm slipping!" This a howl, as one arm thrashed wildly through the air.

Real fear? He was close enough. She lifted one brow and let her awareness of him become focused, easily breaching the barrier between the acceptable *here-I-am* of Costa and the private *how-I-feel.* It was rude and childish.

So, it turned out, was her brother. "Not funny, Costa," she snapped, pulling free of his delighted amusement.

The flash of a wide, unrepentant grin. "Sure it was. Ease up, Aryl. I thought this was to be fun."

"Only if you don't get us caught," she scolded. A full tenth of the day climbing and they were just at the third spool—the height of five clansmen, short ones at that—from the wide bridge suspended below. Below that support, it was a drop of twenty or more to the dark water glinting its menace between root buttresses and trunks. Young Om'ray were encouraged to drop scraps from such safe heights. The resulting boil of activity made this a good object lesson, for the Lay Swamp was home to many things; what didn't have leaves, had teeth. Om'ray learned not to fall.

Rarely, anyway. Aryl pointed down. "Next time you feel the need to slip, dear brother, aim for the bridge. I'm sure Leri would love to help heal a broken leg for her beloved Chosen." She lowered her voice to a fair imitation of Haxel Vendan, Yena's First Scout. " 'Mark my words, young Om'ray. If you miss,' " she growled menacingly, " 'you'll be eaten before you drown.' "

Costa chuckled. "Leaving you to explain to the family."

"I'll do anything if it makes you hurry, Costa! We don't have time to waste. The M'hir's coming."

At this, his grin faded. He stared up at her, beginning to frown. "You keep saying that as if it's true, Aryl. The Watchers haven't called. You're no—"

"They will soon," she interrupted, unwilling to discuss the source of her impatience. Costa's strange little sister kept such *feelings* to herself. This inner anticipation—half excitement, half dread—was never easy to interpret when it arrived. But she'd learned it meant change.

Change, today, could only be the M'hir.

"When the Watchers call," she continued, "we'll already be in place. No one will have time or breath to argue." Aryl tucked her toes between the long, sturdy fronds and pushed higher. Until now, the passage had been easy. No need to use the ladder scars coaxed from the straight stalk. Besides, she thought, running her fingers through the soft gray down that coated the underside of the nearest frond, no one knew the lower reaches of this great old rastis as she did, her favorite of all those that towered in the Sarc grove.

Each of the great families of the Yena Clan had a rastis grove to hold its name and the essence of those who passed beyond flesh. So the Adepts taught, though Aryl couldn't see how this possibly applied to lowland Om'ray, who certainly had names but would have to trek for a full fist of days to reach the nearest vegetation taller than their heads and had no swamp to take their smelly dead anyway. She didn't raise the question aloud. If she did, she'd probably keep going. Several teachings of the Adepts failed to match Aryl's observations. Not that she worried about the discrepancies; there were many truths clutched by the old the young could ignore.

Like who could climb to the top of the rastis to meet the M'hir. She was as good a climber as any; better than some. Aryl slipped between fronds and reached for the next spool, pulling herself up. "Hurry—" She closed her mouth over the words, tilting her head back as she tried to see through the latticework of fronds and leaves and branches.

They weren't the only ones who'd guessed the wind.

"Oh, no," she grumbled. "Ghoch's here."

"Where else would he be?" Costa puffed noisily, as if to prove he was doing his best.

"I mean right here. Above us in the grove." She pursed her lips and blew a curious, bright-winged *brofer* away before it landed on her nose. Most of the smaller life high in the rastis took cover before the M'hir. It was one of the signs the wind was due—as well as the only time to climb without wearing every possible protection. A rastis had its earnest defenders and Om'ray flesh suited that vast array of biters just fine.

Costa pulled himself to where she could see his sweating face. And broad grin. "Naughty Aryl. This would be why no one plays climb and seek with you, little sister."

Aryl grimaced. "I'm not a child."

"You know what I mean. Who else can name anyone from a distance? Hmm?"

He sounded proud. She shot him a disturbed look from under her eyelashes. "Hush, Costa. " Their mother constantly warned her to be discreet; here was her brother, babbling at the top of his lungs.

She didn't want attention. Any new Talent had to be examined by the Adepts—which could take years; only after agonizing debate would their findings be voted upon by Council; and only then, she fumed to herself, would that Talent be declared either so subtle and innocuous as to be unlikely to upset the Agreement and allowed—or, much more likely, Forbidden, just in case.

However harmless or convenient or hard not to use that Talent might be.

What they didn't know she could do, Aryl told herself, they couldn't forbid. She liked knowing who was who.

Costa leaned back to swing from one arm. "You started it."

"So I'm stopping it. I've no desire to be sent to the Adepts."

His big hand wrapped around her ankle, squeezed once, and let go. "There's no need to fear your gifts," he said mildly. "This one could be allowed."

"Or Forbidden," Aryl dared say. "I'm happy to be unnoticed, thank you."

Her brother coughed. It sounded suspiciously like a stifled laugh. "This would be why you talked me into spying on the Harvest," he pointed out. "Good thing I've you to blame for the trouble we'll be in by supper."

"We'll only be in trouble if we're caught at it. Hush!" she urged again, then tilted her head to look up, eyes narrowing as she tried to see through patches of overlapping green, yellow, and brown. There might be no sign of anyone else in the giant rastis or its neighbors, but she knew better. Ghoch and the rest were not far above now. She *felt* them, as surely as she felt the great plant between her hands, as surely as she knew the direction and distance to her home, or to the Cloisters where the Adepts dwelled, or to the very edges of the world.

For the world of the Om'ray was shaped not by mountain or

grove or sky, but by the Om'ray themselves. They felt their place within it from birth. Direction was the first awareness. Newborns would move restlessly in their sleep until facing one or another of the six distant clans, then still, soothed by knowing their place in relation to all others. This late in summer, the sun rose between Clans Amna and Pana. It set in line with Grona. If Aryl put Grona to her right hand, she would face Tuana, with her back to Rayna. Vyna lay directly beyond Rayna.

Distance came next, a sense honed by age and experience. Very young Om'ray couldn't climb beyond their awareness of their mothers. Too far, and that tight comforting bond began to thin, sending the child back to safety as quickly as it drew the anxious mother. That bond loosened with age, replaced by the deep, constant awareness of those close by, the family and friends of one's Clan, amid the faint comfort of those more distant. Aryl knew, as all of the Yena Clan, that Rayna and Amna were closest, Vyna farthest.

If she had to, she could find any of her kind.

So it was for all Om'ray. Those above would *feel* her presence and Costa's, though not who they were. Om'ray were never lost or truly alone. Clans stayed where they were, defining the world. Only Passage sent an Om'ray from home, to seek and answer the call of another Clan's Chooser. Such strangers were welcome, though they rarely made it to Yena.

No strangers here. Not now.

Of course there were no strangers. She, of all people, could tell. Aryl shook her head.

More than where, she'd always known *who* was nearby, "nearby" being a nebulous measure she'd found increased with effort and practice. Costa was right. Oh, how it had bothered her playmates when she would call out their names, sight unseen. She suspected it troubled her elders even more; they buried their thoughts deep behind shields around her. Not that it hid their flavor in her mind, should she *reach*.

Now, to Aryl, the canopy above glistened with more than sunlight. She *felt* the seventeen permitted to be there and knew every one.

Including—she bit her lip and climbed faster—Bern Teerac.

It wasn't Bern's fault he'd been selected this M'hir and she had not. That they'd trained and climbed together for two seasons preparing for this day, neither besting the other, made no difference to the will of the Council. Afterward, he'd stammered all the things a heart-kin who was as thick as an Oud might say until Aryl had managed to escape.

She hadn't spoken to him since.

She might not—for a while, at least.

Costa didn't touch her feelings—she'd have felt it—but he didn't need to. Her reason for this illicit adventure wasn't a secret. "Aryl," he said quietly as they resumed the climb, "being passed over the first time you're old enough doesn't mean anything. You're not like me, too heavy for the ropes, slow as a pregnant *aspird*."

Thinking of the fat creature, which hung upside down for most of a season without moving while eggs warmed on her belly, Aryl's lips twitched. "An aspird's faster."

It was true, not everyone could participate in the Harvest.

But Aryl couldn't fathom why she hadn't been picked, if Council considered Bern ready. They were reflections of each other. Closer than kin, in many ways. It was only a matter of time. . . .

She felt her cheeks warm and silenced her thoughts. "We're almost there."

"How can you—" Costa's words were swallowed by an undulating moan, so loud it vibrated through the stalk holding them both. It was as if the mountains themselves had cried out. The sound diminished, only to come again.

"The Watchers!" Aryl shouted to be heard. "I told you. The M'hir is coming now! Hurry, Costa!"

She lunged upward. Her brother would have to follow as best he could. Her left hand closed on an *irka* vine, its edges slicing through the skin, the tiny barbs taking hold on flesh beneath. A trap for smaller prey. Aryl tugged her hand free, leaving a splash of red along the green, and continued upward.

The higher she went, the brighter the world became. Patches of blue blossomed like flowers through the canopy. Sky. She'd seen sky before. A rastis older than memory had fallen last M'hir, tearing a hole to admit the hot blaze of Cersi's sun. At firstnight, she'd glimpsed tiny lights, as if when it left Yena, the sun pulled a gauze screen over its face against the biters and peered through that mesh. A few fists later? The tumble of cloud, the flash of lightning, the sun and its curtain were hidden again behind the rush of new growth that filled the void. The Adepts claimed the grove kept the Om'ray safe.

Aryl had felt betrayed.

But not now, she told herself fiercely. Nothing was going to keep her from seeing sky again, seeing what lay above this place.

She pulled herself past the final spool of giant fronds only to find herself stopped. Ahead, the single great stem thickened into a bulb: the underside of the rastis' crown. She couldn't see past it. Worse, a dense collar of vines feathered downward, some bearing the yellow galls that warned of stingers hiding within, others pale and white with the sap Aryl knew to be glue and poison in one. Even without these hazards, none of the vines could support the weight of an Om'ray child, let alone an adult.

She wedged herself into the topmost spool, leaning back to study the problem. Flitters flew by, their small brightly colored bodies revealed by their clear wings. Her kin hadn't flown up there. Aryl frowned, eyes searching the vines. There had to be a way.

Suddenly, she sensed her brother had moved above her. "Costa?"

"Here!" His call was triumphant. Aryl pulled herself to a stand to look for him, careful to keep her head well below the reaching tips of the vines.

At first, she didn't see him, then glimpsed his brown tunic in the midst of the vines and stifled a cry of her own. Remarkably, Costa wasn't waving off stingers or trapped in sticky vines, despite being halfway around the stalk and three body lengths higher. "How did you get up there?" she demanded.

"Here," he repeated, this time pointing straight down.

Aryl worked her way around the spool until she was beneath where her brother so mysteriously hung in what should be midair—with vines. She looked up and laughed in surprise.

Mystery solved. Costa stood on a ladder of slats and braided rope. It hung free from the bulb, leading—she tilted her head—past the broadest portion. Any vines that might touch a climber if shifted by a breeze were carefully tied back, not cut. She assumed they'd be released after the Harvest, to hide the way up and protect the rastis' tender crown.

To any Yena, such a ladder was as easily run as a flat bridge. Aryl's brother eased to one side to let her rush past, but she stopped beside him to claim a quick one-armed hug. "I knew I brought you for a reason."

Costa laughed. "Remind me later."

Later, Aryl didn't remember climbing the rest of the ladder, or the moments it took to pry open the door leading through the decking above.

For once she did, she was in a world none of the stories or shared images could have prepared her to experience.

The crown of the rastis—this one and those to every side—grew a grove of its own. Tall, slender stems rose upward, uniform and so densely packed Aryl couldn't have forced her body between them. They sprouted dull-gray and straight, so thin her fingers met around them.

At waist height, they changed.

Aryl followed one of the stems upward with her fingertips, to where it thickened. What looked smooth to the eye felt woven, like cloth. No, not cloth, she decided, but a rope of the most tightly spun thread imaginable. The texture deepened into a spiral that wound up the remainder of the stem, its line traced in crimson that spread wider and wider until, overhead, the stems were vivid red and thick, edged in orange. They appeared taut, as if ready to burst.

The Watchers moaned again, the deep vibration rattling the decking that was as much coaxed from the living rastis as fastened to it. Costa clung to the doorframe as he climbed through to join her, his eyes wide. "Aryl!" he mouthed.

The moan died away; the world steadied. It was temporary, she knew. "Hurry, Costa."

The decking curled around the flattened top of the bulb for several steps in either direction. It held more than a door. A large sling-and-pulley array was fastened to one side, its precious metal chains padded with cloth to protect the rastis during use. Costa walked over to the other feature, a sturdy plank ladder slanting up and into the stalks, wide enough that three could climb at once.

The stems obscured the top. The ladder was partnered by another set of cloth-covered chains. Aryl put her hand on one and looked up. "This must be how they bring down the ripe *dresel*." She put her foot on the first rung.

"No!" Costa grabbed her arm to haul her back. "This is far enough—too far, Aryl. We'd only be in the way." His free hand waved at the roof of gently swaying stems. There was more blue between them now. "There's no room. Stay—"

"There's all the room in the world." She shook free. "I want to feel the M'hir for myself. I want to touch the sky. Don't try to stop me, Costa. Wait here if you must."

He lifted both hands and stepped aside, automatically wary of the deck's edge. When Aryl felt his weight hit the ladder below her as she climbed, she smiled to herself.

The first twenty rungs plunged them deep within the strange aerial grove of the rastis, until Aryl couldn't see in any direction but straight ahead to the next slat of wood. The stems brushed against her and one another. They didn't feel like plants anymore. They moved without wind, as if impatient. With each upward and inward step, she could see the stems swelling, enlarging along their spiral indentation, turning slowly as they did.

There were always scents in the grove—decay from the shadowed water below, blends of musk and sweet and sour from the creatures who moved and climbed. Above all, the rich blend of growing things, the perfumes that changed with the seasons as flowers opened, ripened to fruits, and fell into the water to rot.

Here? Aryl had smelled dresel all her life, but that faint clear spice was nothing to the heady draught now entering her nostrils. She felt as though she climbed through fragrance, warmed and pierced by shafts of brilliant light.

The ladder met two others at a triangular platform, unexpectedly small. As Aryl stepped up to it, her head cleared the top of the rastis stems at last.

The world exploded away on every side, roofed in blue, carpeted in red-orange, punctuated by taller growths with their clusters of green leaves. *Nekis?* They had to be, though Aryl had trouble connecting these full, lush tops, filled with flitters, to the spare, hard-to-climb trunks that stretched their pale columns from the water below.

The vegetation released her gaze and she moved, mute and

staring, to give Costa room beside her. She pointed to the strange harsh line against the sky. "Costa. Do you think those are mountains?"

"I think I'm going to be sick." He shaded his eyes with one hand. Aryl followed suit. "Yes. They have to be. The world, Aryl. It's too small."

"This can't be all of it," she reasoned. But the same dismay kept her voice low, too.

The red of the rastis extended only so far. The seemingly vast groves of the Sarcs, the Teeracs, the whole of their Clan—from this new perspective they melded together into a smallish mass, one bounded by wild stone and by a darker, more twisted foliage that itself gave way to an expanse of glittering light. Aryl squinted. "Is that the ocean?"

"It can't be. The other Clans are between us and the sea. That must be where the Tikitik have their crops. I've heard they need water open to the sun. They have ways to control what will grow in a place. An understanding beyond any Om'ray . . ."

Costa sounded wistful. He loved growing things; as far back as she could remember, his room had been crammed with bits and pieces of life collected from the groves, tended with care in an assortment of pots and baskets. He would coat himself in ointments and silks to fend off biters in order to harvest strange wizened seeds from plants no one knew, only to spend futile fists trying to coax them to sprout. Thinking to help, Aryl had once suggested he ask the Tikitik for their secrets. His frustrated anger had startled her, for Costa was the gentlest of their family. She'd understood later. Only the appointed Speaker for the Clan Council spoke to the Tikitik; then, only to answer questions, not ask them. It was the way of the world.

Though Costa went to live with his Chosen as was proper, their mother had left his room as it was. Whether she wanted the plants to stay or roots had made their way into the flooring and she couldn't be bothered removing them, Aryl didn't know or care. It brought him home again, regularly, to water and fuss while listening to her latest stories. He stayed part of her life, something Aryl hadn't known could end when she'd been younger. For Costa might have decided to take Passage, leaving Yena behind to find Choice and a new life within another Clan. For her, it would have been as if he died. Those who left never returned; they were never heard from again.

There was a darker side to Passage, whispered behind hands when eligible unChosen gathered and talk turned to their futures. Some didn't survive the harsh journey, it was said—perhaps why so few came to Yena. Others failed its purpose. Three M'hirs ago, Oryl Sarc had drawn one such with her Call: Kiric Mendolar of the Tuana. Floods had delayed him; he'd arrived to find Oryl already Joined to Ghoch.

Aryl had watched him—from a safe distance, or through the gauze of a window. Strangers weren't to be trusted, not until Choice made them kin. And this one had moved oddly, always too slow and with a hand to the nearest rail or rope. He preferred to work inside, cleaning dresel with the elderly. Aryl herself couldn't imagine a worse fate.

She'd decided this Kiric was sick, perhaps dying—a tragic, romantic figure—and had enjoyed her version until Costa had quietly explained that this stranger had come from a place without rastis, where Om'ray lived on flat, dry ground. He'd wanted her to feel compassion for someone so lost and alone. Aryl had thought this a clever new story for Costa to make up for her and repeated it, with suitable embellishment, to her friends at every opportunity.

When no Yena Choosers ripened by the next M'hir, Kiric the Stranger had stepped off a bridge and disappeared into the black waters of the Lay.

Older, wiser, Aryl understood her brother was one of the

lucky ones. He might have little time to spare for his young sib, but he'd found his life partner among his own Clan.

Where his sister could still entice him to climb with her.

As well as Costa, Aryl *felt* the others, knew where they were; with the slightest effort, who they were. Her head turned to seek them. "Costa. Look. There. They've strung the lines."

Her eyes fought the bright sunlight until she could make out what she hadn't before. The rastis groves were covered in ropes, as if a weaver bigger than any imagined in a nightmare had used the strong nekis trunks to support its looping web.

Figures were moving into the open along that web, bare feet sure despite the rope's bounce and sway. Arms were extended, for balance and to run fingers along support threads too fine to see from where they stood. Almost flying, she thought with an envy close to pain.

That could have been her. *Should have been her.*

Aryl could see the pattern they made as it took shape, here and in the distance. Each Om'ray was running to his or her place along a curved line beyond the rastis groves, downwind.

Flitters launched into the air, as if disturbed. Instead of wheeling and crying in protest, they plunged without sound into the canopy, disappearing from sight.

They fled the coming M'hir. She knew it. Could almost *taste* it.

The Om'ray had found their places and stopped, waiting. Aryl saw flashes as hooks were freed from their belts and held ready.

Watchers moaned again. This time Aryl could tell their sound came from the mountains. As would the M'hir.

Costa's fingers locked around hers as the world seemed to take and hold an endless breath. He pulled, urgently, and Aryl obeyed, dropping to lie beside him on the small platform. His arm went over her. *Hold on!* she heard, not words but mindspeech.

As she grabbed for her own hold on the platform, she twisted her neck to see.

The crimson stems nearest her face trembled in the silence. Trembled . . . then bent ever-so-slightly. No, they weren't bending. Aryl's eyes widened as the stems began to twist open.

Costa stiffened beside her, lifted up as if compelled to look closer. *No!* she sent, reinforcing the warning with a grab at his hand, determined to hold him safe.

Then there was no need for warnings.

The M'hir struck.

It was like the opening of an oven. The next breath she took was searing hot, dry, and full of a chokingly fine, acrid dust. Aryl coughed and quickly closed her mouth, but the air stole the moisture from her eyes and nostrils, took the sweat from her skin until perversely she shivered.

The first fingers of wind tore her hair free of its braided net, whipping the strands against her cheeks. The stems clattered against one another as if excited.

The wind's force continued to build, steady and irresistible. Below, far below, Aryl had experienced the annual M'hir as little more than a rustling overhead that warned of bundles of dresel to be opened and stored. The rastis supporting their homes might lean slightly, disrupting dishes left on tables. Torn leaves and shredded bark would whisper and float its way into branch and crevice, making piles and obstructions to be pulled from ladders. Fine powders would rain down as well, reds and yellows and orange streaking the walkways and clogging screens. Another glamorous chore for the youngest and those not in the Harvest, sweeping and sweeping and sweeping until the black water below grew a skin of rare color.

Up here? The M'hir moved everything.

Including the crown of the rastis beneath them. As it began to shudder and shift, Costa tightened his grip until Aryl could barely breathe. The great plant *groaned,* a deep, tormented creaking. She waited for it to snap, her heart in her throat. Instead, it bent, crown bowing to the M'hir.

The platform went over with it, tipping to one side. Costa shuddered with strain but held on. Aryl's own hands were clenched on the thick edge. Her toes found a gap in the planks and she forced them in . . . if they tipped much farther they'd be shaken off . . . they'd fall . . .

The rastis stopped bending, though the M'hir now howled and gibbered on all sides. The platform rocked back and settled, no longer level, but safe enough.

They might be safe . . . what of the others? Aryl raised her head, fighting to see through the wind-whipped stems.

The webbing strung between the stiffer nekis trees held, though along its strands the Om'ray danced in the wind like leaves trapped against a billowing curtain. Each leaned forward, body and face wrapped and obscure, hand gripping a guide rope, hook ready.

Aryl sorted through their *tastes* to find Bern. *There.* She could just make out his wildly swaying figure.

"Bern!" she shouted. The M'hir ripped away her voice. She concentrated, trying to *reach* him with her thoughts. Child's play when touching, a minor skill at arm's length, demanding more and more Power with distance until impossible. She'd never reached as far as this—he was barely discernible, a toy in the wind—but she fought to connect, to send his name—

Hush. Don't distract him. Costa's mindspeech filled her thoughts, calm and sure, though she could feel his excitement. *He has to prove himself.*

I should be there! she sent back, frustrated beyond reason. *That's where I'd be, Costa. I'm unChosen, too! It's my right.*

It's too dangerous.

I'm unChosen.

Everyone knew the unChosen were the expendable members of any clan, not yet Joined to a life partner, not yet mature. Free of expectations or even a sure future.

There are Chosen up there. A flash of fear. *Only the best of them dare. That should tell you the risk.*

Aryl hid her pity from Costa, burdened with the responsibilities of another life. He'd worry and play it safe for the rest of his days, for Leri's sake. She'd take freedom while she had it. Freedom like those Om'ray tethered in the face of that raging wind. To be part of the sky, part of something larger than life itself. To fly . . .

Aryl dug her elbow into her brother's conveniently broad ribs. *Don't tell me you're sorry you came.*

Ask me if we get down again.

The bent stems had continued to twist. Suddenly, they snapped open along their length, releasing clouds of red to the M'hir.

The odor of ripe dresel intensified until Aryl found the only way to breathe was to keep her bent arm in front of her nose, her lips close to the skin. She'd taste it forever. She'd probably smell of it just as long.

Light-touched red surrounded them. It filled the sky, each separate piece growing wider and wider until the whole overlapped like the glistening scales of a flitter.

And like a flitter, the red took flight.

She'd learned this. She'd never imagined the reality of it. The red—Yena called it the dresel's wing. Now each piece continued to expand as the wind tugged it free of its tight wrapping. She could see through it, as if it were the finest window gauze, immense and growing, billowing and snapping in the wind. On the ground, flattened, it would smother other growth in favor of the rastis' own. In the hands of skilled Om'ray, the material could be soaked and teased apart, its component threads rewoven into any thickness. The clothing she wore, the ropes they'd climbed, the gauze of their windows, all came from this source.

She dared let go with one hand to touch the nearest wing,

but its softness eluded her. It came free of its stem, pulling with it real treasure—moist chains of dresel, the length of her arm.

Having cleaned her share, Aryl knew most of the light fragrant pods contained already sprouting seeds, as well as dresel itself, the soft purple flesh that would nourish the seed's first explosive growth. All three—pod, flesh, and seed—had value. The waterproof pods covered Yena roofs and graced their tables as elegantly carved dishes. The dresel was a staple on those dishes, delicious fresh and easily dried for later use. A small portion of a harvest would fill Yena pantries until the next M'hir, and well it did. Though they gathered other foods, an Om'ray could exist on dresel alone.

Yena Om'ray could not exist without it. Unlike other clans, with the luxury of growing all their bodies required in the ground—something Aryl couldn't imagine—the Yena lived where no other food could fill their needs.

The rest of the dresel, and the sprouts from each pod, were bundled for the Tikitik. Whether their neighbors couldn't climb the rastis, or collect enough intact pods from the grove edge for their needs, whatever those were, Om'ray didn't ask. They simply took the power cells, glows, and other items the Tikitik provided in return.

Some pods had other contents. There were a host of tiny riders who schemed to place their offspring with the rastis' own. Costa collected them in small jars; Aryl avoided those. A very few would contain a more lethal invader, *somgelt*, its puffy white threads deceptively innocent as they frothed outward from a carelessly opened pod. All, like the Yena Om'ray, timed their lives to take advantage of the dresel's flight.

For flight it was. Despite the risk, Aryl willingly rose with her brother. They held each other as well as the now gaunt and bare stems, to watch the rastis send forth the next generation and Yena begin the Harvest.

The M'hir was hot, dry, and steady. It was a hand brushing

over the world, taking with it whatever chose to go. Aryl watched, amazed, as the red fluttering wings rose higher and higher, only their load of dresel keeping them from the wind-ripped clouds overhead. The pods themselves hardened almost instantly, their brown taking on a dark rich gleam.

Aryl's cracked lips parted in a surprised smile. The drying pods rattled and clicked against one another, like the clumsy chimes made by children and hung from fronds. As the sky filled, the various rattles and clicks blended into a wave of lighthearted percussion, as if the rastis sang their children to their futures.

It wasn't an easy or sure one. Some wings were immediately torn by the M'hir, or shredded by collision with the sharp twigs of the nekis. These folded and dropped in great twisting loops of crimson, caught in branches where flitters and climbers quickly claimed their hapless pods. Most wings continued, sailed higher and farther, but they weren't free yet. There were those waiting to reap the wild wind.

Already, hooks were flashing as Om'ray snagged wing after wing from the air. The goal was to collapse each over the nearest guideline, ideally in neat folds that might still catch the wind, but not be taken by it. Those with a few Harvests behind them took their time, avoiding those wings which were already tangling in the air in favor of sure catches. Aryl frowned as the tiny figure she knew was Bern flailed after everything in reach.

She'd have done better. Though he did calm down and improve.

The growing load of hanging wings and their pods gave stability to the lines. The Om'ray began moving along, chasing streams of red.

They weren't the only ones.

A shadow whooshed by overhead and Aryl flinched, startled. Another. And another. Costa shouted in her ear, as if too excited to concentrate on a sending. "*Wastryls!*"

The giant creatures soared in with the M'hir, a confusion of black and white set with bright yellow eyes that caught and flashed the sunlight. Aryl had only seen a dead one before, and that damaged. These, very much alive, plunged at the dresel wings, their great claws out and ready, tentacles poised.

They weren't a threat to the Om'ray, being unable to maneuver in tight spaces and wary of the lines. They were mountain dwellers, drawn to the canopy by the M'hir. Like that wind, the wastryls passed by, taking what they could grab. Aryl saw how the claws snatched wings from the air, then tentacles plucked free and held the pods. This first flock—there had to be dozens in it—came and went like the brief shadow of a cloud. She watched them tumble and wheel about, turning toward the mountains with their treasure.

Red drifted down below them. It would smother new growth along the grove edge, but there would be no seedlings to take advantage.

A second flock arrived, larger than the first. Aryl laughed when two wastryls clutched the same wing and screamed their outrage at each other. The battling creatures almost fell before letting go. Their loss was another's gain. A ready Om'ray snared the falling wing, adding it to the growing harvest.

A glint that wasn't eye or sun caught her attention. Aryl tugged at Costa. "What's that?" she shouted, risking her hold to point.

He stiffened as he saw it, too. *I don't know.*

Whatever it was, it was coming closer. That wasn't what dried Aryl's mouth.

It was coming closer against the wind.

Chapter 2

NOT ALIVE.

Aryl nodded at Costa's mindvoice as she studied the strange object in the sky. The howl of the M'hir, its steady, deadly shove, its choking dust, the now-stripped crown of the rastis—these belonged. She did.

This didn't.

A device. Tikitik or Oud? she offered, the words colored by the wary distaste they used for whatever involved their neighbors.

The object could have been one of the clear globes Costa used for seedlings. Much larger, Aryl judged, and filled with something that sent out sharper glints, as if its insides turned to present new surfaces to the light. Without wings or other means of moving through the air, it continued to fly toward them. Toward the harvesters. It dipped and rose, out of sequence with the wind or what drifted through it.

Not Oud. An image filled her mind: a large ovoid half buried in a rock slide, its surface gray and edged with black protrusions, most of those broken. Nothing like the dainty thing floating in the wind. The Oud device had two flat arms, long and bent. Wings, she realized. *One of their fliers,* Costa told her.

Probably tried to cross the mountains during a M'hir and crashed. Leri saw it the summer she helped clean the Watchers.

With the ease of practice, Aryl shielded herself from the rush of heat that flowed beneath the name of his Chosen; the recently Joined were indiscreet at best. "Tikitik, then," she shouted aloud.

"Why?"

Good question, she acknowledged to herself, stretching to keep the object in sight. The Tikitik, cued by the Watchers and the M'hir itself, would be coming for their share of dresel. Why distract the harvesters?

The object, as if oblivious to its surroundings or too curious for sense, dropped lower and lower until it collided with the stream of red filmy wings still being released by the rastis grove. It disappeared and then reappeared as the billowing masses simply slid over its surface. It slowed and seemed, if such a thing were possible, now to be watching the Om'ray.

Had Bern noticed? Aryl sought and found his figure among the rest. His hook was out and working, a small but respectable line of wings and their pods hanging from the nearest web. Their practice together had paid off. Then she scowled, remembered she was angry. *It should be me up there,* she sent full force, not caring if the oaf heard or not.

The M'hir gave the crown an extra push and Costa's arm tightened around her waist as the rastis swayed in response. "It's not bad, being Joined," he shouted in her ear, half laughing. "You'll find out when your time comes."

Aryl felt her face burn under its coat of dust, hoping against hope this was Costa being annoyingly old and not some veiled warning. They'd been careful, she and Bern. They'd made sure to be alone before slipping inside each other's thoughts to forge their inner connection, delicious and secret. They would be *heart-kin* forever, able to reach each other's minds more easily, closer than siblings. It was the bond of the best of friends, but they intended more. They'd touched trembling fingertips, made breathless promises in the dark. When Aryl's time came, there would be no other, for either of them. Her Choice was made, despite her age.

Even if Bern Teerac was the single most obtuse and irritating—

A shadow swept over them, fast and cold. The next flock of wastryls. Aryl twisted to watch and tensed. These weren't flying as before, spread apart and claws ready. No, this flock moved as one, claws aimed forward, intent on the gleaming intruder.

Costa's mindvoice was amused. *This should be interesting.*

The wastryls keened their defiance as they dove to attack. The M'hir, as if on their side, sent another sudden gust against the rastis. Wings whirled and twisted, caught and tore. Costa and Aryl slid to their knees within the stems and hung on. Her arms ached with the effort but she kept looking.

The wastryls struck.

Thunder and lightning shattered the open sky. A blast of hot air slammed into the rastis from the opposite side, against the M'hir, and Aryl was blinded and falling. Her hands grabbed and held. Her body slammed into whatever it was—a stem that broke—then the ladder—which didn't.

Everyone was still falling, leaving her behind!

Bern?! She didn't need eyes to find him. Her mind rang with his terror, his horror as he dropped.

No!

He had to be safe. He had to be . . . the bridge below, the safe, solid bridge. Aryl *wanted* Bern on the bridge, safe. Bern had to be on the bridge. *NOW!*

Something inside Aryl *pushed.*

The crown shifted back; the M'hir reclaimed the sky. She sobbed and clung to the swaying ladder, unable to climb up or down. She could smell burning. Wings and wastryl, caught by fire, being swept clear by the wind.

It was over.

"What have I done?" Aryl whispered. "What have I done?" But she knew.

Bern was on the bridge. Safe, if terrified.

The rest of the harvesters, the cream of the Yena Om'ray, were gone. Aryl had felt them fall through the canopy, the lucky ones impaled on branches, the rest plunging into the black waters of the Lay. She'd felt those who'd survived that impact, their minds afire with pain that was extinguished as they were eaten alive.

Oh, she'd saved Bern.

Aryl pressed her face against the braided rope of the ladder. She closed her eyes. She shut down every other sense, withdrawing deeper and deeper, wanting *away* until she found herself in a darkness that surged and flowed with the violence of the M'hir itself. A perfect place.

A place where she couldn't feel Costa die, too.

Interlude

THE SHOP'S BIN SAT EMPTY within the latest pile of metal shards. As usual, the Oud who delivered the leavings during the night had missed the bin—or the point of the bin. Enris Mendolar had yet to hear anyone sure on the question.

That the Oud brought the metal was more important.

Out of habit, Enris picked up a loose, green-tinged shard from the packed earth near his feet and tossed it on the pile. A dozen *iglies* scattered from their hiding places with bright flashes of alarm, jointed legs working almost as fast as their jaws as they scampered for deeper shadows. Once safe, the tiny creatures made wet smacking sounds, a bravado sure to impress other iglies, if not beings inclined to squash them flat.

Enris dipped his cart forward on its front wheels and shoved it into the tallest part of the pile as hard as he could. Pieces sharp enough to cut flesh spilled over, striking his well-wrapped legs and booted feet, but the cart was full. Load number one of the day.

He tugged the cart free and turned it, heading home again. He took it slow. The path, though smooth, rose in steep twists. Ordinary Oud only came this close to the surface; Om'ray would only go this far from it. His steps were sure and steady, his breaths deeper with effort but unlabored. He was strong for his age, with a last spurt of growth that left him larger than most Chosen in Clan Tuana. His hands were callused and hard, his shoulders already bent from cart and shovel. Though Council agreed with his family's pride in his skills, Enris privately believed he was most useful here, pushing the cart, collecting the wonderful metal of the Oud.

Maybe one of his younger cousins would grow.

The glowstrip along this section dimmed and then brightened. They'd need to power it up, Enris noted absently. Not that he couldn't find his way in the dark. Anyone could. Up was toward that warm presence, the rest of his kind. Down was away from it, and dangerous. The Oud didn't care for company. They begrudged making room over their lands for those on Passage.

The Om'ray didn't care for the Oud. Made it even.

"Enris!" The call echoed down the tunnel, followed by the rapid thud of boots.

Startled, he sent without thinking. *What's wrong?* He quickly silenced his inner voice. Not down here, this close to the Oud. Never this close. "Ral?"

His fifth youngest cousin burst around the turn ahead, catching himself before he stumbled into the cart and its sharp contents. "Enris! There you are. The most amazing thing's happened!"

Loath to waste momentum, Enris didn't slow his steps. "What is it this time?" The other Om'ray could enthuse over a rainbow.

Ral dodged and kept pace with him. "Naryn. She's done it. In front of Council and the Adepts and everyone. Except you," he added. "I had to come and tell you!"

Bowing his head, Enris leaned into the cart. The next turn led to the final, steepest section.

Ral trotted along. He didn't offer to help. The last time he'd tried, the cart had toppled sideways and spilled its load the width of the tunnel. His strength lay elsewhere, when he could settle long enough to use it, designing ways to bring water to their crops.

"C'mon. You know you're impressed," his cousin suggested slyly. "Wasn't it you who said she'd never dare?"

Enris thought of Naryn S'udlaat and shook his head, dark hair tumbling across one eye. "I said she shouldn't," he growled. "I knew the fool would."

He didn't have to ask what she'd done. The willful daughter of Adepts believed herself a child of destiny as well, one with great Talent about to show itself any day. Unfortunately, it had, and at him. When he'd refused to let her take her pick from their shop's display, Naryn had used Power, not her hands, to launch a hammer at his head. Her amazed triumph had been somewhat dampened by his refusal, having dodged the hammer, to relent. When she'd failed to repeat her accomplishment for anyone else—Enris himself bluntly vowing he'd never testify for her without mentioning her attempt to take what wasn't hers—he'd hoped that was the end of it.

He hadn't been the only one. They'd tried to hide their relief, back then, the Adepts, the older ones, but Enris had felt it and understood. The Tuana Om'ray lived a fine line between Oud and sky. Troubling those underfoot wasn't wise; their Clan had paid the price before this. But there'd be no stopping Naryn now.

The vast expanse of tunnel behind him seemed to listen to his thoughts. Enris felt the skin of his neck tighten, *tasted* change.

The Oud didn't care for that either.

Chapter 3

BELLS TOLLED ONCE, THEN AGAIN. Aryl heard each deep mournful sound; felt it tremble the bed, crawl up her fingers. She counted . . . ten . . . eleven . . . then lost track. Tears leaked from her closed eyelids. Which had been for Costa? She should know, shouldn't she?

A breeze lifted the hair stuck to her forehead. She shuddered and drew herself into a ball under the sheet. She couldn't find Costa. She couldn't find anyone. That couldn't be. No one was alone. The world was Om'ray, given shape by their presence.

Where was she, if there was no one else?

Aryl. An identification more than a name, shrouded in grief and worry. She clung to it without understanding. She was alone. How could there be a voice?

The sheet lifted, leaving her cold. She squirmed and whimpered until a gentle hand rested on her forehead and granted her sleep.

Low, passionate voices. They belonged to no one. There was no one else. Aryl lay still, wherever this was, and heard without caring.

"We don't have time. Wake her."

"I would if I could. This is more like retreat than sleep."

"She's unChosen. A child. I thought only Adepts could disappear within their own thoughts."

"Truer to say only Adepts first learn how to return by their own will." A sharp breath. "Aryl is no longer a child. We must bring . . ."

The voices left.

Or Aryl stopped hearing.

"Can she hear me?" Warm, worried.

Aryl buried her head within her arms, pressing their bare, cold flesh over her ears. *Not that voice. Never that voice!* She hummed inwardly to drown it.

Aryl?

The mental voice was worse, rippling with its own grief. Aryl did her best to shut it out, too.

How could she hear Bern, sense his mindvoice, yet not *feel* his existence? He couldn't be here and not here . . . but where . . .

The wrongness overwhelmed her—she slipped toward a darkness of her own. It was so close. She knew exactly where to find the seething black cloud. *There.* She had only to let it take her, pull her from whatever kept her in this empty, soulless place.

ARYL!

The Other was there, this time not to offer the surcease of sleep, but to force her back from that edge. No matter how Aryl fought, she couldn't evade it. She tried hiding in memory—

the Other refused that comfort. She thrust out her pain and fury—the Other took it and gave back something that offered peace.

Peace . . . but she was still alone. So terribly alone.

Instinct reached for the first bond, the oldest. *Mother!* Aryl cried. *Why have you left me?*

HERE. The word rang like a bell. *We are* all *here. Come back, Aryl. This is the way. Follow me.*

Where? I'm alone!!! This with all the despair and longing in her heart.

I know. But you can come back. I know how. I'll show you.

She knew that sound . . . a *wysp,* trilling the arrival of truenight . . .

Costa brought it home for her, its eyeless head seeking shelter under his big arm. A fragile creature, pale and long of wing. Aryl thought it ugly and refused to touch it.

He insisted she stay with him, with the creature, refusing to explain. Over her protest, he disconnected the power cell from the room's glows, glows that would otherwise shine their soft, steady light over panel wall and rail, that made the bridges leading between homes safe—if prone to attracting everything else that loved light. In an alarming, unfamiliar darkness, Aryl twitched and fidgeted and wished her brother normal. Finally, bored, she almost dozed.

Until the wysp began to trill. Sitting up, she tried to see. Costa's warm hand found and covered hers, comfort and an urge for quiet.

The trill continued—it was as if three singers lived within that slender throat, each with its own range and tone, competing to see who could make the sweeter sound. She held her breath, afraid it would stop if it heard.

It sings to greet the real dark, the truenight, little sister, he sent, along with a vision of strange tiny lights against a black void. *Without eyes, despite the canopy's shadow, it knows when the sun has truly left us and when it returns.*

Aryl listened to the song, then frowned anxiously. *Where does the sun go?*

To Grona Clan, to give them daylight while we sleep.

The singer increased its volume, lovely but loud.

Aryl yawned. *Who could sleep through that?*

Costa's laugh silenced the wysp. That night, Aryl dreamed of chasing the sun over the tops of the rastis, her arms become wings . . .

She blinked, once, twice, slowly realizing she'd dreamed a dream. There was no trill. There wouldn't be. Soft beams of sunlight filtered through the window gauze.

Midday.

It was abruptly important, why she couldn't say, to pay the utmost attention to her fingers and toes, to straighten one leg at a time, to ease her body slowly from its curl.

Gah, stiff all over.

She licked her lips. And thirsty.

That sensation aroused others, each cautious. Her eyes were dry and sore. Aryl rubbed at them, feeling grit on her lashes. Her hair was loose. Her hands—she stopped and sniffed. Dresel.

Everything smelled of it.

She found herself on hands and knees, staring down at a wrinkled sheet, her mind helplessly seeking its place within an empty world . . .

. . . and suddenly, wonderfully, finding it.

Her mother. There, nearby. Above, in her room.

Aryl *reached* farther, her inner sense touching those warm spots of life that marked the Yena. But they were frail lights, afloat in a seething, churning dark. Now afraid, she struggled to see nothing but those lights, denying *that place* even as part of her responded to its call and wanted nothing more than to . . .

She fought and won, head hanging between her shoulders. Shudders of relief racked her body. To be whole again was what mattered, to feel the world and her place in it. Aryl clung to that, wanting to know every Om'ray. More carefully now, avoiding that eager darkness, she searched for them all, adding the faint glow of distant clans to the steady warmth of those close and dear and known.

Too few.

And some of those had become—strange. Five. She sought them, found them. Not where they should be . . . but farther away, all together.

The Cloisters? But that was where Adepts lived, apart, honing their Power. Where they sheltered the mindless and the lost.

Aryl *tasted* their names and finally understood. When Chosen Om'ray died, the loss was always more.

She dimmed her perception and lay flat, curling into a ball, tears soaking the sheet.

She sensed her kind again. She'd regained the world.

And remained alone.

Chapter 4

"I DON'T REMEMBER."

"Try again."

Aryl slumped forward, elbows on her knees, and covered her face with her hands. It felt as if they'd been doing this for tenths. She remained mute, beyond argument. Not that arguing with her mother was likely to work. Taisal di Sarc, Adept and Speaker for Yena, back down first?

The world would end before that happened, Aryl thought bitterly.

"You must."

She didn't move.

Aryl.

"No!" She *pushed* the mindvoice away with all her strength. At the soft, pained breath, she looked up through her fingers. "You can't make me."

Taisal laid her long hands on her lap, then adjusted the fall of her robe. Adepts wore the formal garment when journeying to or from the Cloisters, as well as for ceremony. The white fabric was thick with fine embroidery from shoulder to floor, its pleats a sign of rank and power. Not worn to impress her, Aryl knew. Her mother would act as Speaker tonight.

The Tikitik were coming.

"You can't make me," she repeated wearily, sitting back. Her own hands were restless, plucking at an imaginary splinter in the wood of the bench. As if any of the well-polished furnishings of the Sarcs would have splinters.

"Then open to me. Let me see what happened."

"You know what happened. That device exploded. All the webbing ripped or fell apart or—" Her voice shattered. "I should have held on . . . been stronger . . . He shouldn't have . . ."

A single tear sparkled on her mother's pale cheek. Taisal turned her face rather than wipe it away. Light touched lines of fire from the chainnet that held her thick black hair; only metal could contain the willful locks of a powerful Chosen. Aryl's hair, pale brown and fine, obeyed ordinary braided threads. Most of the time. At the thought, she poked an errant strand back in place and waited.

Composed again, Taisal continued her argument, growing stern. "We must learn how Bern saved himself, Aryl. All he remembers is thunder and flame, a moment somewhere dark, confused, then finding himself on the bridge in time to see—to see the others fall past him." Gentler. *Aryl.* "You're the only witness we have. You must try to remember. Anything, everything."

No, Aryl thought. She would forget it all. Afraid her mother could sense this rebellion, she closed her mental shields even more tightly than ever before. "Why does it matter?" she sighed. "Can't you be grateful at least one survived?"

"Two," Taisal corrected, gesturing gratitude with a lift of her hands. She gave her daughter a keen-eyed look. "Enough for now. Council can wait."

"Council?" Aryl echoed, then was ashamed of the quiver in her voice.

"A new Talent is the concern of Council, Aryl. You know that. Bern's ability must be understood and dealt with, for the good of us all."

Power shivered between them, as if a knife had been half drawn to glint in the light. Almost as quickly, the sensation was gone.

Her mother's lips curved in a tight smile, while Aryl's eyes widened in dismay. Not at the unspoken threat . . .

Because she wasn't sure who had made it.

The Adept rose to her feet. "Until tonight. Rest."

After her mother left, Aryl scowled at her bed. Rest? She went to the window and pulled aside the curtain. The view through the gauze panel was improbably ordinary. From here, she could see six other homes, like hers wrapped around the main stalk of a rastis or a nekis' trunk, like hers with white walls open to light and air through ceiling-to-floor panels of thin gauze. The remaining panels were so tightly woven as to be opaque, their surface watertight and private. Doors were the same, but bore unique patterns imposed by unbleached threads. The vivid red undulations and blobs might make sense to Tikitik, who had made them, or they might not. They didn't to the Yena Om'ray, as far as Aryl knew, but—she squinted at a neighbor's—some were prettier than others.

Narrow slatted bridges led from each door to the main bridge, though as many sloped up to that destination as down. Their homes were where they were, given their living supports grew at different rates. The main bridge was wide and strong, spanning air from the meeting hall—the one place large enough to hold all of Yena, if the unChosen were banned to feed biters on the outer deck—to the varied workplaces and warehouses. Those were the simplest structures of all: roof, window panels and doors, floor. Following Harvest, they'd be full of tables where most of Yena would open pods and sort their contents. There would be others washing and teasing the threads from dresel wings for the waiting weavers, and those stacking pods to dry for carvers. Above all, those packing bundles of fresh dresel and sprouts for delivery.

Any other Harvest. Aryl knew they'd sit empty now.

Nothing was solid. When the M'hir blew and the rastis swayed, the entire Yena village swayed, too. Children learned early to secure their toys or see them fall.

She watched the few Om'ray on the bridges, their steps easily accommodating the occasional shift in wood and rope. Some carried small bundles; she guessed they were supper, perhaps last M'hir's dresel. Others hurried by on their own business. Most would be inside, midsummer's habit, when the afternoon brought a heavy, cloying heat interrupted by sudden downpours, and evening was preferred for socializing. The M'hir had begun to clear the air, if only for a brief while. Soon enough the Om'ray would change their ways to suit. The drier, less oppressive feel meant time to pull vegetation from the undersides and roofs of homes, to replace panels, to inspect bridges for rot before the rains returned. What grew here was intent on erasing the Om'ray, or consuming them.

Like now. Determined biters swarmed the gauze, climbing for her face as if they could somehow bite through the fabric. When they blocked her view, Aryl tapped them into flight with a finger, not admitting she was looking for someone.

Bern . . .

Guilt killed the questing thought before it was more than half-formed. Not the familiar sly guilt of having played a good trick on someone. Not the embarrassed guilt of having spied on another's mind for an answer, or of having followed Bern to where a newly Chosen pair fumbled with each other's clothing in the shadows in a way she'd thought hilarious and he'd . . .

Bern . . .

Aryl flinched and turned from the window. This guilt? Every thought of him cut. She was vaguely surprised not to bleed.

She left her room for the half-oval of the main hall. It was the largest space in their home, indented on one side by panels to protect the stalk of the living rastis. The floor of polished nekis wood incorporated and revealed the whorl of carefully cut and sealed fronds that supported the building. The resulting lovely pattern of grays, yellows, and rich browns was a pride of the Sarcs.

Her father, Mele sud Sarc, had filled this hall with his booming laugh. Now, her fingers touching this and that, Aryl wondered if laughter could die, too.

Here was the long burnished table they'd used as often for games as meals, set for only two. There were the pulls to bring the yellow sling chairs from the ceiling beams; easy to spin an unwary brother with the flick of a wrist. A pair were now anchored to the floor, unable to move. Other slings, these for storage, filled the ceiling like the clouds she'd seen for herself. The cupboards, sleek and elegant and old, had held hidden treasures—as well as a certain small sister at times.

She opened one at random. Empty.

Taisal lived here less and less, her duties as Adept calling her to the Cloisters, many of her possessions taken there as well. Costa—Aryl moved before her eyes had to fall on the closed curtain to his room, but not before she thought of Leri, his Chosen.

When a pair Joined, both changed. Everyone felt the new bond between them, strong and permanent, closer than that between a mother and her newborn, or heart-kin. There were outward changes as well. Over a span of days both finished maturing in body, ready to be parents themselves. Since this change was greatest in those who would be mothers, they spent that time alone with theirs, receiving the special knowledge they would need to understand the new workings of their body and the demands to come. Her impatient partner would be distracted by friends. It was a time of joy and celebration.

To Aryl's profound annoyance, it was also a time when everyone else got jokes she didn't.

But if one of a Joined pair died, the survivor changed again. Everyone could sense it: Chosen, but not. Om'ray, but not. When her father, Mele, had succumbed to a wasting fever, Aryl remembered flinching from the stranger who should have been her mother, comforted by Costa and others until she'd accepted the peculiar, hollow feel now bound to her mother's presence. Once, maybe twice a generation, those left somehow drew strength from their loss, gaining in Power. Taisal, already in line to become an Adept, had been such.

M'hirs later, once old enough for the truth, Aryl had learned how close she'd come to losing both parents. Most survivors became lost within themselves, their inner voices fading, minds forever childlike. The rest? Died within heartbeats of their Chosen's end, as if there could be no life apart.

She would be like that, Aryl decided, taking her lower lip between her teeth. If anything happened to Bern, she would have no reason to exist. A sudden, dramatic death. No more of this bell tolling and grief. No more being alone.

She scowled at the table. "Death is better."

"Than supper?" Her mother pushed through the curtain from Costa's room, a tray overloaded with bright red sweetberries in her hands.

"I—" Aryl focused on the fruit. "They're ripe? Leri—" The words died in her mouth. The sweetberries were Leri's favorite. Hard to find before the flitters, difficult to pick even then, Costa had finally coaxed several vines to take root in his window's gauze—keeping them as much of a secret as anything could be between Chosen. "Are you taking them to her?" she managed to ask.

"She won't know what they are." Taisal's voice was absurdly normal, as if she didn't hear what she was saying.

"But—" Aryl choked back whatever else she might have said. To exist yet be mindless? Never, she swore to herself, shields tight. Never that.

Taisal took her silence for concern. "Don't worry about Leri. She and the others are safe."

"Safe," Aryl repeated, and swallowed bile. Her voice rose. "Never to leave the Cloisters, you mean. At best, a—a servant."

"She lives. The others live. Of the seventeen killed at Harvest, eight were Chosen, daughter. Be thankful only three more died."

The world, to Aryl's inner sense, still held spaces where—she made herself think their names—where Oryl, Teis, and Ilea belonged, where all the others should be. The Yena Clan had been decimated *while she, while she* . . . she trembled, the truth a poison she had to spit from her mouth or die. "I should have held on," she began, her voice low. "It's my fault they died—that Costa died and Leri and—"

"No! No, Aryl. Never think such a thing. It was an accident—a terrible accident. There was nothing—what if you—" Without warning, Taisal sank to the floor, her elaborate gown bending in stiff awkward folds as if uncertain how to cope. Berries fell around her like drops of blood. "Oh, no." With faint despair, "Costa's sweetberries."

One rolled to where Aryl stood, frozen in dismay. It stopped short of her toes, rose ever so slightly from the floor, and followed its own shadow back to the tray on Taisal's lap.

She sensed tendrils of Power reaching out. Berry after berry silently obeyed, rising, *moving*, their lush red surfaces gleaming when they caught the light. "What are you . . .?" she breathed, then couldn't say another word.

Eyes down, Taisal tidied her tray with short, fussy movements. When done, she held it out. Aryl took it, careful no more berries would tumble and tempt her mother to . . . to . . . She put the tray of flying fruit on the table. "What did you do?"

"I *pushed* them," Taisal answered, matter-of-factly, as if she wasn't on the floor in the middle of the room. Tears slipped from her eyes and ran down her cheeks. She sniffed.

Her mother never sniffed. This final oddity, of all the rest, drew Aryl to kneel beside Taisal, though she didn't dare touch her. Not with Power still pulsing through the air and tangling her thoughts. "Are you all right?" she asked, disturbed by this reversal. What could she do? "Should I get another Adept?"

A too-wise look. "Please don't, for both our sakes, Daughter. I'd hate to explain why the Yena Speaker, of all Om'ray, was using a Talent Forbidden years ago. Especially—" a pause as Taisal accepted Aryl's help to rise to her feet in the cumbersome robe, "—while on the floor." Standing, she wrapped dignity around her like a cloak. One hand found the moisture on her cheek and she shook her head. "Forgive me, Aryl. These past days—I should be stronger than this. Must be. The Clan needs me tonight. You do."

While this was true, Aryl looked into her mother's sad eyes and her confession stuck in her throat. Tomorrow, she promised herself. She'd find the words; she'd make things right.

Before the silence grew louder, she blurted, "This *pushing* . . . is it what you think . . . is that what Bern did? To save himself?"

"Sit, please."

Once they faced each other across the table, Taisal chose a single berry and placed it on the polished surface. "It's a little thing I can do," she began. "Most who become Adepts possess unique abilities. I tell you this, Aryl, because I expect you will join us one day."

Be an Adept? Spend the rest of her life in study, tending the ill and dying, never to climb on her own? Aryl pressed her lips together and held her shields firm.

Taisal didn't pause. "Within the Cloisters, we share what we can with each other, practice what may in time be useful for all. It is how we learn more about the Power and ourselves, how we decide which abilities are safe to spread through Yena. Outside the Cloisters, beyond Adepts, such abilities are safer Forbidden. Why?" She waited, an eyebrow raised at her daughter.

"You might be seen," Aryl supplied at that prompt. "By the Tikitik."

"Or by non-Adepts. Yes," she asserted as Aryl frowned, "there are Yena—impatient or careless—who underestimate how very closely we are watched. They would risk the Agreement for their own gain. No. We can only afford changes small enough to go unremarked, or abilities that appear gradually, as if they always existed. That is our safety, Aryl. As for what you saw?" Taisal smiled slightly. "Pushing is Power applied thus . . ." She gave the tiny globe a nudge with one finger. It rolled toward Aryl, then slowed and stopped. "The object moves through space as though touched. It never disappears. Is that what you saw at the Harvest?"

Trapped by the question, Aryl stared at the tiny thing. Safer than meeting her mother's steady gaze. "I didn't see what happened," she mumbled. It was the truth.

"The scouts report the Tikitik delegation should arrive shortly after truenight, Daughter. I may have to explain what happened. Don't make me expose Bern's ability to them."

Aryl's eyes flashed up. "What do you mean? By what right—"

"Don't play the child with me," Taisal warned, her face pale and stern. "You know who supplies the light and warmth to our homes—who built these homes for us. The bargain struck by our forebears forbids fundamental change within any race, to protect the peace that is. The Tikitik have every right to ask questions about this disaster and be satisfied by the answers, no matter the cost to us."

Aryl flattened her palms on the tabletop and leaned forward. "They should be asking who sent that machine to spy on us!"

"The Oud are not our concern."

"But Costa said it wasn't theirs—" Too late, Aryl closed her mouth.

Taisal surged to her feet, nothing soft in her eyes now. "You do remember more. Show me what happened, Aryl. Now." Her Power *pressed* against Aryl's, demanding to be allowed through.

"No!" She tightened her shields, tried to hide within. "No! Let me tell you!" She wanted to explain—make excuses—not this.

"Not this!" Aryl sobbed, even as the Adept's trained strength ripped her shields apart as if they were gauze.

And forced her to relive it all.

Interlude

ENRIS BRUSHED HIS FINGERS along the row of slender punches until he found the finest tip. The wristband was waiting in the grip, its pale green surface polished until the intricate designs might have been water as it curled over stone. Not that he'd seen such a thing for himself. The memory of stream and stones had come with his grandfather, who'd taken Passage from Grona Clan, and Enris liked it.

It was the inside of the wide band that concerned him now. Taking his favorite hammer, the one with leather wrappings worn to the shape of his palm, he sat at his bench and carefully punched tiny indentations into the smooth metal. First, an outer square, no larger than his smallest fingernail, open at one corner. He thickened its lines slightly before moving inside to shadow it with a thinner one. After a moment to stretch and rest his eyes, he returned to work, painstakingly hammering a pattern within the squares. Random dots, to those who never went outside in the dark, or looked up; precisely placed, to someone who did.

These were the first stars he'd ever seen for himself. Two were bright—and hammered deeper—three the same in a line below, then another below these and to one side, faint and blue, invisible if either moon shone. He marked this last with the lightest possible dimpling, unconsciously holding his tongue between his teeth until done.

Enris ran his forefinger lightly over what was a familiar face. Through the seasons, he'd watched them slip around the night sky as if on Passage themselves. Unlike the Om'ray, the stars stayed with their Clan as they traveled; unlike the Om'ray, they always found their way home again.

At the thought, he sent a possessive look around the shop, its benches and furnace generations old. This was his place, all he wanted in the world. Not even for Choice would he leave it.

The metal band grew warm, reclaiming his attention. Enris let a strand of his Power touch it, explore it, know its elegant shape. He would remember this piece. His smile widened. As it would remember him. Hammering his signature was duty to his family and expected, but to him, unnecessary. Everything he made and touched with Power *sang* his name back to him. Not a Talent of use, since he'd yet to find another able to feel it, but it pleased him.

A quick buff with a polishing leather, and the wristband was ready for its owner. Enris wrapped it carefully and locked it in the concealed drawer beneath his father's bench. The Oud expected their scraps to be turned into useful things—blades and hooks and fasteners—not adornments for the Om'ray. This close to Visitation, it was prudent to tuck such gauds out of sight.

His lips twisted in a grimace. If only he could tuck Naryn and her followers in a drawer. That would solve a few problems. But the unChosen were rarely asked their opinion. He shrugged on his longcoat before making his rounds. The furnace was already set for the night, its bellows now blowing heat away from the melting vat and throughout the village, carried by pipes embedded within building floors. The air outside Tuana's homes chilled rapidly after sunset. During the day, the furnace vented to the sky and they worked shirtless.

Sunset also brought *lopers.* The sly little thieves loved anything with a sparkle, and would carry off whatever fit their paws. For something brainless, they were disconcertingly good with fasteners. He'd had to design locks for the ceiling vents and windows. He tested these now, one after another, ignoring his stomach. Supper could wait; their livelihood lay within these walls and he didn't take chances.

On that thought, Enris took a moment to check the interior of the shop. The Oud rarely entered buildings; that didn't mean one wouldn't this time. The door would do—it passed the wide cart well enough—but the well-swept shop floor was split into two narrow aisles by this summer's new bench, a wonderfully solid structure positioned beneath the main sky vent to catch the natural light. His idea.

Against the far wall with it, then. He gave the massive wooden structure a tentative push. It didn't budge. Taking off his coat, Enris flexed his arms, planted his hands on the bench, and leaned into it with a grunt.

It still didn't budge.

He frowned.

Need he care? If an Oud wanted in tomorrow, the bench would move out of its way, all right. In pieces.

"Not good," he muttered. Intact, this bench matched all the others. Broken, the pieces would reveal its wood had been used before. Solid beams like this were reserved for tunnels, Oud tunnels. Granted, these came from an abandoned spur and the Om'ray had permission to use what they could take, but all such within Tuana territory had been picked clean before he'd been born. Wood was something precious in his generation, traded for other goods, reused, or hoarded by Council decree.

With Enris coming of age, the shop's workspace had been increasingly cramped, his father doing his best to share with his son. That son? Enris wasn't sure if he'd lost patience, common sense, or both—but he'd wanted his own bench.

To get it, he'd traded with runners.

The tunnels beneath the Om'ray stayed as they were. That was the Oud's side of the Agreement; theirs was to stay where they were. Go outside Tuana territory and Oud tunnels were no longer reliable. For no reason shared with Om'ray, a tunnel would lose its light and heat, remaining empty and unused, a temptation of wood and metal and other supplies. A day might pass. Or a full set of seasons. But the moment would come when, without warning, the Oud would remember this tunnel and violently reshape it, collapsing ceiling and walls, smashing the floor. A tunnel could fill in seconds, obliterating everything within, or restored lighting could reveal new openings, a different direction or slope. There was no knowing.

Except that an unlit tunnel was a trap.

Runners dared go beyond where Om'ray were tolerated. Never to trespass on the Oud—no one was that stupid—but where no others would go. Everyone knew it. They gambled they could glean from such tunnels before their reshaping. Questions weren't asked, by Council or those seeking what they had to offer. Runners weren't of one family, or one Talent, though those with the ability to sense imminent change were persistently if quietly courted. They were risk takers, not fools.

Enris laid his hand on the innocent, so-useful bench. The Oud didn't care if Om'ray took wood. They didn't care if they died trying. What provoked them was an Om'ray stepping beyond agreed boundaries. This much new runner wood in one place would be proof.

There was nothing else to do. He lowered his barriers to let his inner sense explore the village, finding the warm lights of his Clan. Without making contact, he couldn't tell who was family, friend, or acquaintance, but he cared more for privacy. No one was near or approaching.

Good enough. He pulled back into himself, raised his shields, then concentrated.

The tools on the bench began to vibrate.

Blinking away sweat, Enris *pushed* harder. The bench shuddered, then *moved*. The legs left gouges in the floor, but when he was done, the bench, with its incriminating wood, was safely out of the way against the far wall.

He retrieved a jar of polish that had rolled off and replaced it, then scattered sand over the gouges, grinding it in with his boot until the marks were no longer obvious. Satisfied, Enris picked up his longcoat and turned off the lights.

Chapter 5

"TAISAL?" THE DOOR PANEL SHIFTED, as if whoever had come three times already in search of the Adept had lost patience. Shifted, but didn't turn open. There were firm understandings among Om'ray. Without permission, you didn't touch a person. You didn't open a door.

You didn't enter a mind, Aryl thought numbly.

Unless you must. The words slipped among hers, layered with emotion. Remorse was there, and pity, but over and through all pulsed determination. *Do not regret this sharing, Daughter. You'll need every protection I can give you.*

Was the fear drying her mouth hers, her mother's, or something they now shared? Aryl didn't look to where Taisal continued to pace, back and forth. She laid her hands on the cool table and moved them in small, light circles. She could feel the wood grain through generations of polish. Tikitik didn't work thus in wood; they wouldn't take carvings in trade. No one knew why. "Syb's at the door," she said out loud.

Power surged and Aryl pulled her head between her shoulders in reflex. Not directed at her, she realized. "He'll wait," her mother stated with confidence. "But we don't have much time." *You've touched the Dark that waits inside us all, Daughter. Seen it. Used your Power within it. Few can.*

So it was real. Aryl pressed her palms flat, the old table's tangible strength a comfort. *Where is it? That other place.*

Puzzlement. *Place? Why do you think it's a place?*

Because she'd sent Bern through *somewhere,* Aryl almost replied, but quickly buried the thought. Her mother was the Adept. *I don't know what it is,* she sent instead.

Taisal's hands swept up as if gathering air. *To touch that which binds us all mind-to-mind is like walking through the rooms of our home. Safe. Understood. To touch the Dark . . . that is to step outside in truenight, without glow or guide. Yes, it holds Power, or is Power manifest. But it holds danger above all. Know this, Daughter. I was caught there once. Part of me remains—lost there with him—* The memory of her father was a maelstrom of grief, longing, and emptiness. Aryl gasped, trying to keep them away. Instantly, the emotions vanished behind Taisal's restored shields.

If that was how it felt to outlive your Chosen, Aryl told herself, it was another reason to die first.

She hadn't hidden the thought. *So your Chosen suffers instead?* her mother's tone was scathing.

He'll want to die, too! Aryl sent wildly. *What's the point of surviving alone?*

Answer me when you have children, came the searing reply. *Quickly now. What matters is you are in danger, Aryl. Avoid the Dark. It will call you, tempt you to explore it. The Adepts know the risks, you do not. The Dark is an abyss that will consume your mind if you allow it. Promise me!*

Aryl shuddered. *Never. I'll never touch it again.*

Be sure, Daughter. I'm not the only Adept Council has watching. The others will know if you do. For now, they'll believe it was Bern Teerac—the Dark left its touch on him. I felt it.

It wasn't Bern's fault! We can't let them believe that! Aryl protested. *I won't.*

Taisal stopped near a gauze panel; its soft curtain lifted in a breeze, whispered against her robe. After a long moment, she nodded. *Best to keep attention on the cause, not the result.* She drew the image of the airborne device to fill both their minds. *It wasn't Oud. That we know.*

For the first time, Aryl was glad her memories of that day rested behind her mother's eyes, too. She relaxed slightly. *What can I do?*

Be unnoticed. Taisal lifted the curtain and gazed outside, speaking aloud as if this she wanted heard. "Council sent lookers to collect salvageable pods as well as any remains of the device. With luck, they'll bring something worth showing our neighbors."

It was an uncommon, but highly valued Talent: the ability to precisely sense what was new or didn't belong in a place. Lookers were always scouts, marking fresh *stitler* traps—not all biters were small—and other hazards. Aryl might sense when something around her was about to change, but such inner warnings were too personal and vague to be useful. Adepts warned against trusting them.

Hadn't she believed she'd sensed the M'hir coming? Instead, it had been disaster.

"If they don't?" she asked with an effort, pulling out of memory.

"You have skill with ink. Can you draw me the shape of it, any details you recall?" Under the words, caution. *We don't dare send this memory mind-to-mind. They'll know what you did.*

Aryl stared at her mother. *What did I do?*

"I'll get a pane for you." This time, beneath the words, a thrill of fear. *What no one ever has. I'll search the records. Make discreet inquiries. But it doesn't matter if this is a new Talent or a rediscovered one, Aryl. This is no little* push, *easily hidden. Worse, it involves the abyss we rightly fear. What you did threatens all Om'ray, let alone the Agreement. The Tikitik must never know. Do you understand?*

Aryl swallowed bile and managed a half nod. She'd never do it again. Didn't that count? Shouldn't it be enough? Questions she didn't dare ask as her mother went to the door.

"Now hurry and do as I've asked. Truenight will be on us soon."

Aryl waved her hands over the finished pane, wishing there was a Talent that dried ink. It would probably be Forbidden, she thought morosely. She ignored the shift in her sense of place as more and more adult Om'ray descended from Yena. They made their preparations for the pending Visitation. This was hers.

Not bad, she thought, passing a critical eye over her work. The process of putting splinter to fabric had brought details from her memory she didn't recall seeing, yet trusted. She added a symbol at the top, a tiny curve and dot she imagined as her name, as if names—the essence of an Om'ray—could be captured in mere ink.

The drawing didn't portray anything dangerous, unless the series of disks on the underside could be dropped on someone's head. Aryl studied it more closely. *How did it fly?* There were no engines spouting flame, such as she'd heard lifted the Oud's machines. And no wings.

She waved the pane again, feeling the draft it sent through the air, like a wingbeat.

Wings were necessary, weren't they?

Not the way she'd sent Bern to the bridge . . .

Aryl gagged and almost dropped the pane. Her mother's warnings, her fear, didn't matter. What she'd done—it had made her forget her brother, made her pick one to live over others. Remembering how it had felt to do what she'd done made her sick inside. It brought the churning wildness of the *Dark* up behind her eyes until she had only to close them to be lost in it. Her mother was right. It was dangerous.

"Wings," she told herself, keeping her eyes open. "I need wings."

To go where?

Her hands wanted to tremble as they cleaned the splinter she'd used, then resealed the ink pot. It was a simple question. Reasonable. Why did it feel . . .

About to put the pot in its cupboard, she hesitated.

. . . perilous. That's how it felt. Not one of her inner warnings this time, but as if she stood too near the side of a bridge and stared down at the Lay, about to lose her balance.

Her mother had brought five panes, each white woven panel framed in strips of pod wood. She'd only needed one. Now, feeling foolish but determined, Aryl picked two from the stack and held them out at arm's length. Slowly, she moved them up and down, imitating a flitter.

She didn't rise from the floor, but the growing draft caught her finished pane and sent it skittering along the tabletop.

Aryl pumped her arms faster, putting real muscle into it. Glow strands swung back and forth, spilling shadows over the floor.

The curtains along the far wall lifted from their bottoms, curving inward toward her until the nearest billowed and snapped like a dresel wing. Aryl stared at it, her arms stopped at shoulder height. The fabric settled. All was normal again.

Her shoulders complained, but Aryl paid no attention. She didn't need force, she realized in awe. She had that, so long as the M'hir blew. "All I need are wings," she breathed.

To go where? whispered something at the back of her mind. She paid no attention to that either.

Aryl filled the remaining panes with drawings of something quite different from the mysterious device. She did her best to recall the dresel's wing, how a single strip of material unfurled and filled with wind to lift the pod, how the pod had dangled below. The shape of a wastryl's wings filled two more panes on both sides, requiring her thinnest splinter so the ink wouldn't soak through. She found she remembered how the wings curved differently if the creature maintained height or was diving after a pod. Beside each drawing Aryl added lines to remind her of the wastryl's speed and direction, muttering under her breath as she overlaid those with more vague recollections of the M'hir itself. Thick lines for fast and powerful movement; thinner when slow.

If she knew the marks the Tikitik used, she could put words, here, safe from prying minds. But only those on Council were given that knowledge, to maintain clan records of greater import than the flight of what was, after all, a harvest pest.

She shook her head and concentrated. The glows outside sent slanted beams of light across the ceiling. Truenight was close.

The last pane she filled while absently chewing a strip of dried dresel. She'd regained an appetite, if no interest in finding a proper meal. She toyed with fantastic designs. Wings made of baskets, of rastis fronds, of panes tied together, of wood and rope. She inked a pod dangling beneath each, a pod which, in her mind, wasn't a pod at all.

"Aryl. Aryl Sarc."

At the summons from outside a window, Aryl grabbed her panes, leaving the one of the device on the table. "Coming!" she called, rushing in the opposite direction.

Where to hide them? Her room was hopelessly tidy, trunks and mats secured in this season when rastis might bend without warning. She dumped the panes on her bed and tried to lift the mattress, but it had been fastened through the base to the floor. Gathering her drawings again, she ran to Costa's room, pushing through its curtain.

"Aryl!"

Only her cousin, Seru Parth, could instill one word with that much drama. "You want me dressed, don't you?" Aryl protested over her shoulder.

Here were hiding places beyond count, so long as moisture didn't wash away her ink. Avoiding tables draped with greenery, Aryl rearranged a row of unused pots near a back wall panel, then tucked her panes in the space behind. It wasn't perfect, but in a room full of distractions it would do.

Distractions such as the heavy scent of flowers, and overripe fruit, and the drying black goo Costa valued so highly for his plants that he'd regularly risked the Lay's inhabitants to pull the stuff from water-soaked buttresses.

Where he belonged, where he should be in her mind . . . Aryl found herself *there,* facing only that unreal, churning waste. The Dark, her mother had called it, knowing it, too. She pulled away.

A wysp trilled. There was no time left. As she headed for the door, Aryl scrubbed moisture from her eyes, only afterward thinking to check her fingers for ink. At least she was already dressed, her hair neatly bound, her arms and legs wrapped against night biters. On top, she wore her second-best knee-length tunic, the one her mother liked. The cut was old-fashioned, and its yellow thread made her look a child. Still, tonight being thought young might stop hard questions.

She lifted the gauze cowl from around her shoulders to loosely cover her head and ears. Any biters aimed at her face she would swat herself, with great satisfaction. And there would be some. She didn't need the faint whine and beat against the gauze panels to know. Most of those who lived in the canopy's uppermost level moved down for safety while the M'hir blew. Unfortunately, they were then drawn to Yena by the glows.

Another bitter gift. Was there any place without the M'hir? Aryl tucked the drawing of the device under one arm and snorted. If there was, she assured herself, it would have its own problems and things after Om'ray blood.

"Finally," Seru exclaimed. "What did you do? Bathe?"

Aryl made sure the door turned fully closed. "Why the hurry? Are they here?"

Her cousin wrinkled her upturned nose. "The best seats will be gone if we aren't first. You know that."

By "best seats," Seru meant where they could see the eligible unChosen, and be seen. This preoccupation of those who would be Choosers was encouraged by their elders and the subject of lively mocking by those too young to care. Aryl had teased Costa at the last M'hir; this one, she'd planned to savor having Bern look only at her.

"We don't want to be obvious," she told her cousin.

Seru frowned and sent a faint questing thought. Sensing it, Aryl offered a layer of cheerful anticipation. A smile lit her cousin's face. "You're right, Aryl. We'll be oh-so-mysterious. I know just the spot. C'mon!"

Burying her shame, easily from Seru if not herself, Aryl let her cousin lead the way. The Power was uneven in the Parths; they produced few Adepts and no healers or scouts. It wasn't right to use their weakness against them; Power existed for the benefit of the entire clan, for all Om'ray.

She'd make it up to Seru, another time. It was only that she couldn't face *him*. Not this soon and not there. Especially not with the Tikitik and secrets to be kept.

They walked the bridge to the meeting hall and joined the line of others waiting to climb the ladders dropped from its broad deck. Glowbeads wrapped the ropes, a decoration that illuminated the rungs and climbers and, more importantly, protected the area below from truenight's hunters. Thorn-laced vines, normally encouraged to grow beneath Yena buildings, had been tied back to allow safe passage.

Aryl had secured the pane to her back, careful to keep the face of the drawing hidden. With any luck, her mother wouldn't ask for it. She moved forward a step with the others, smiling a welcome to various relatives. Her best effort, now she was here, seemed little better than a child's scribbling, her memories of the device meaningless.

Seru was looking around with interest, waving to friends. "I don't see Bern," she announced. "Where is he?" This in a too-loud whisper. Seru knew full well why her cousin always won at seek. Though she kept the secret, she wasn't above borrowing that skill.

Aryl flinched; Seru didn't notice. "He's always late," she managed. Involuntarily, her deeper sense *reached* to those nearby, tasting their names and emotions.

The result made her misstep and bump into one of the Chosen. Stammering an apology, Aryl shook her head and pulled back.

Despite the smiles and nods, she was surrounded by fear.

Why?

Her hands found and grasped the guide ropes. Like the rest of the Yena, she descended facing outward, her feet sure on the wide rungs, her pace determined by those ahead on the ladder. After one quick look into nothing, she lowered her eyes to watch her knees and Seru's head.

Truenight. The grove's shadows had fused to utter black. Other hunters grew bold now, including those that swarmed from the waters of the Lay to seek the unwary. Only once a M'hir, after the Harvest, did the Yena willingly leave their homes and well-lit bridges to descend this late, without the sun. They took with them bundles, lowered by pulley and chain beside the ladders—the Tikitik's tithe of fresh dresel and sprouts. Aryl glanced left, then right.

She saw only one, two ladders over. One chain, one bundle.

Was this why she'd sensed fear? She frowned, confused. Surely there was no blame to the Om'ray, who'd died trying to collect the pods.

They moved down, the sound of creaking rope and footfalls from twenty ladders louder than breathing. Only those who sheltered in the Cloisters were excused: the Lost, the infirm, the ancient. Babies and crawlers were secured in carriers. Their total lack of mental control—there was nothing as agonizing as the brute *HUNGER* of a newborn—was shielded from other Om'ray by their parents. For the moment, their big eyes were bright and alert through the fine gauze of their hoods, their expressions content. Most smiled. Like all Om'ray, even the youngest took comfort being together, in moving as one.

But not safety. Aryl remembered Om'ray falling and her hands clenched on the ladder rope, though she didn't stop.

The ladders ended at another, much different platform. This was solid, as if rooted to the ground beneath the water. Young Om'ray exclaimed over the odd feel of it, staggered, and pretended to be dizzy. Their parents kept them close.

Aryl took a steadying breath, fighting the urge to turn and climb. Not that she could; every ladder was filled by those coming down. She hated this place. She'd tried to explain to Costa, M'hirs before, how she felt crushed by the weight of the grove above, how she felt imprisoned by the limits of light, sickened by the cold, damp rot that clung to the very air near the Lay Swamp. He'd teased her about loving the sun and air above.

He hadn't, she thought sadly, been wrong.

The platform's shape echoed the deck of the meeting hall directly above, though wider to allow the ladders to be anchored at their base. Its wooden surface had been repaired and cleaned beforehand. Today, during daylight, the ever-present slime had been scraped with metal rasps to make the footing secure. No one wanted to slip into the water, too close at hand.

That water was further spanned by three long, narrow extensions from the platform, like flat arms reaching out. Each arm was traced by ropes of glows. That light reflected in the water, not from ripples but from eyes—eyes as far as Aryl could see, disks of white and red and yellow, some paired, some clustered, some alone.

None moved or approached any closer. She heard distant splashes, as if more were coming or busy with easier prey, but knew they weren't a threat tonight. The respectful distance meant the scouts had poured toxin made from *somgelt* into the water. They would have soaked the edges of the platforms with it, too. As if in proof, small corpses rolled and bumped against the wood, their bellies bloated and white. The larger, more dangerous hunters would avoid the taste until it wore or washed away. Fortunately, the M'hir meant no rain, for now.

She slapped at a biter and drew her hood farther over her face.

"Move, Aryl. You're blocking the others." Seru's urging was hushed; she seemed to respond to the tension everywhere. The Chosen were coming down the ladders and in a hurry—impatient, Aryl decided, as well as anxious. The Council and their Speaker, her mother, would be last.

To the right was less crowded; the two headed that way, moving around the massive buttresses that rose up through the platform to support the rastis itself. The flattened outer sides of those roots had been draped with fabric laced with toxin; in front of the fabric hung thick benches supported by rope. Most were full of Om'ray, sitting cross-legged to give their neighbors below more space. Seru glanced up and stopped abruptly. "Wila saved us seats!" Without waiting, her cousin climbed from one bench to the next.

Aryl ducked her head and pretended she hadn't seen. She slipped through the milling crowd, seeking anywhere alone.

As she passed where a buttress arched overhead, a figure stepped from its deep shadow to confront her. Her inner sense knew it was Bern even as her eyes saw a stranger, his normally cheerful face pale and set in grim lines, his hands clenched at his sides. There were red marks—burns—on his cheek and neck.

"What did you do to me?" His voice was wrong, too, high-pitched and hoarse. "Tell me!"

"Hush," Aryl pleaded, appalled. A quick glance over her shoulder showed no one paying attention, but she slipped into the shadow he'd left, relieved when he followed. "I don't know," she told him, quick and quiet. "I don't!"

"I shouldn't be alive." It was an accusation. "You did something. I felt your Power, Aryl!"

"I couldn't let you fall—" she began.

"So you brought me back to life?"

He was making less than no sense; the glint of eyes was all she could see of his face. "What are you talking about?"

"I died, Aryl," he said. "I was gone. You—somehow you brought me back."

"You think you died?" she repeated, stunned. "That's ridiculous." Everyone knew what made them Om'ray faded to nothing once the flesh died. Adepts waited for that moment before allowing the husk to be discarded. There was no putting the two back together.

"What else could have happened?" His anguish filled her mind until she feared it would betray them before their voices. "I was in—it was dark . . . moving . . . cold—I wasn't real—"

Guessing where his mouth was, she put two fingers across his lips. "Listen to me, Bern. You didn't die. I—yes, it was something I did, but it was a—" she hesitated, loath to use Taisal's description, even to repeat it, "—a *place* I pushed you into, trying to keep you safe. Not death. All I could think—" She was aware of his turmoil, of the tension and fear of others, suddenly aware of too much, as if Bern's closeness weakened her ability to keep *what-was-Aryl* separate and safe. A wave of guilt, sickening and strong, surged up through her. She tried to contain it, but couldn't. She heard him gasp.

I wished you safe, she sent, giving up the struggle. *You, not the others, not Costa. I wanted* you *on the bridge and you were. That's what happened.*

Bern's arms came around her then. She leaned her forehead against his shoulder; he was taller than she remembered. The unChosen finished their growth in spurts. Maybe she'd be taller next.

Aryl. Heart-kin. I'm so sorry. Images of Costa flickered past under the words, of her curled on a sheet looking—looking dead?—then of those falling past him, one after another . . . the shock . . . the grief . . .

Fighting back tears, Aryl *shoved* Bern's thoughts from hers. "Enough!" Pulling free wasn't as easy; he kept staring down at her without moving, his fingers pressed into the flesh of her arms. Did he see her or visions? She took another anxious glance. The crowd was thinning as those left climbed to the benches, but they were still unnoticed. "Bern, you great oaf," she said gently, quietly. "Let go. I'm not a branch."

His hands opened and she rubbed her sore arms. "Why keep me from your thoughts till now? Avoid me. Why? What have I done? Live?" Louder, almost petulant. "That's not my fault, Aryl Sarc. It's—"

"Hush!" this time backed by a flick of Power.

"Ow! Aryl—"

She touched his arm, apology and a final plea for quiet. "Bern, please. This isn't the place or time. Trust me. The Adept said—"

"Your mother." Harsh, but thankfully a matching whisper.

"Did you know she's letting them believe it's something I did to myself? Did she tell you she threatened me with Council Sanction? It's true. I'll be exiled if I so much as lower my shields and think about what happened where someone else might 'hear.'"

"No!" The drawing she carried—had Taisal ever meant to use it, Aryl wondered bitterly, or had this been her plan all along? "I won't let her blame you for what I did. You know I won't."

"How did you do it?"

Did she even know? "It doesn't matter," she told him. "I'll never do it again. Just forget it, Bern."

His arm went around her shoulders, then; he rested his chin lightly on her head. She felt him sigh. "Heart-kin. I'm very glad I wasn't dead, believe me, and will be very happy not to be exiled, but it's not that simple. You can't forget something like this."

"Why not?"

"Because—"

A shriek pierced the night, drawn-out and moist as if something suffered and died. Another.

They startled apart, both looking out to the water. Murmurs from those on the platform mingled with the echoes of the shrieks.

The Tikitik.

"What matters now," Aryl said quickly, staring into his shadowed face, "is keeping this from the Tikitik. That makes it simple. If you're asked—say you struck your head when you fell, that you don't remember anything more." With all the urgency she felt, she sent, *Words, heart-kin. Tikitik use words. They can't sense the truth.*

Adepts can. Council will.

"That's my problem," she countered aloud, trusting her voice to sound more confident than she felt. "Bern, trust me. I won't let anything happen to you."

"You didn't, did you? Sweet heart-kin." He bent and kissed her, a brush of dry cool lips against hers. "Thank you."

Aryl felt herself blush. It might not be the first kiss of her dreams, but it was, nonetheless, a kiss.

And truenight was young.

Chapter 6

ONLY THE SPEAKER COULD BE on the platform when the Tikitik arrived. Aryl and Bern weren't the only ones hurrying to climb to seats as a final shriek reverberated over the water.

Like candles extinguished by a breath, the floating eyes disappeared. They reappeared at a greater distance. Curious, with caution.

The first thing Aryl did once seated was put her drawing on her lap, facedown. The pane was small enough she hoped no one would notice, though Bern gave it a questioning glance before doing what everyone else was doing—watching for those who approached.

Aryl's attention was caught by her mother, standing alone where the central arm of the platform began. In profile, Taisal di Sarc looked calm and confident, the image of a Speaker. Everyone relied on her for their safety. Having seen her collapsed on the floor in those same robes, Aryl abruptly wondered where Taisal could turn for protection. Custom held the Speaker inviolate and blameless, but there had been Speakers who failed Tikitik expectations in the past. All Council had done was appoint another, quickly.

The Council: if she leaned recklessly forward, she would see that row of six seated above and behind Taisal, one from each Yena family: Sarc, Teerac, Parth, Kessa'at, Vendan, Uruus. Although all were in the robes of Adepts, white and stiff with thread, only two were of that order, Sian d'sud Vendan and Tikva di Uruus. Council seats went to those of greatest age and experience within a family, not Power.

Unlike the rest, their heads were bare to the night, but Aryl knew from her mother's preparations that their hair was liberally anointed with a rare oil to discourage biters. The dignity of Council would hardly be served by them flailing about to protect themselves from clouds of small annoyances. It didn't work as well as somgelt toxin, but helped.

The Speaker's Pendant, heavy and narrow, rested between Taisal's small breasts. Having heard from playmates that Tikitik couldn't tell each other apart, let alone Om'ray, a young Aryl had guessed they used the ornament to know who her mother was. Taisal had smiled at her, saying only that it was easy to underestimate those who looked different. She'd let Aryl touch the pendant. Its markings weren't like those the Tikitik wove on Om'ray door panels; the metal itself was equally foreign, pale and green as if a leaf had hardened. It was the oldest object among the Yena, of forgotten origin.

Now, Aryl knew the pendant was more important than the individual wearing it. No meeting could take place between any of Cersi's three races without the pendant of each Speaker present and displayed. There were, she'd noticed, a great many such incomprehensible rules, minded more by Council than ordinary Om'ray.

To be fair, when not in their robes and wearing implacable expressions, those on Council were, in Aryl's experience, ordinary enough. Old and inclined to make pompous announcements, smell funny, and pat her on the head, but that was to be expected. That had been her opinion before this M'hir and the Harvest. Before she'd done what she'd done. Now, the six looked dangerous, a threat to her and to Bern if the Tikitik weren't.

They'd probably always been dangerous, Aryl decided morosely, her fingers restless on the pane—they wanted to slip between Bern's for comfort, and she refused. Was this growing up? Realizing what their kind of power could do? Sanction. Exile. They'd been words before. Now they were real.

"There. There they are." The whispers came from all around them. No one dared mindspeech; no one gambled they knew everything about the Tikitik.

She could see them now, three narrow forms taking shape at the limit of the glows. An angled limb. A curve of neck. A broad foot plunged into the water; a final movement that sent ripples outward. The watery rings captured light before they wrapped around the platform's varied edges and crossed to darkness.

Aryl focused on breathing through her nose. There were cries from children, quietly hushed. Someone nearby gave a nervous laugh. Another coughed. The benches creaked on their ropes.

The Tikitik waited. They were aware of the profound confusion their physical presence caused Om'ray; it was unlikely they understood it. Though intelligent and capable of speech, to Aryl's deeper sense they were *not-there*. It was like watching a drawing come to life, or having a table answer a question. Impossible and disturbing. You couldn't prepare, Aryl knew. Only work your mind around to belief.

It took a moment for the Om'ray to settle. Once they did, the Speaker took a step closer to the platform edge. "We see you," she announced, the words clear and loud.

Even as echoes came back, the Tikitik were moving.

Eyes winked out, leaving a swathe of dark water to precede

them. Respect and sense both. There was only one sure mode of travel through the Lay Swamp, and the Tikitik owned it.

And rode it. Their *esask* mounts rocked forward on six thin, armored legs long enough to find secure footing during flood. Although they were the largest inhabitants of the Lay Swamp, their bodies were narrow—tall and long rather than wide—allowing them to easily pass between the dense columns of buttress and trunk.

The upper half of those bodies was covered in shaggy hair, dyed white and red in more of the Tikitik's inexplicable patterns. The lower half was protected by black overlapping plates. The head was carried low on a twice curved neck, and constantly in motion, swinging side to side to check for danger. That head was ably equipped, boasting four large eyes, paired open nostrils, and an upstanding brush of hairs running from neck to snout that could, Aryl had been told, somehow sense movement.

While esask could move silently, these lifted and drove their broad feet into the water, splashing a warning to would-be predators. A warning they'd heed, for esask were hunters, too, with twin rows of needle-sharp teeth. Once they spotted prey, beneath or on the surface, it rarely escaped.

These had full pouches sagging the first neck curve, implying they shouldn't be hungry. Aryl still felt uneasy as they came closer and closer. The concept of an animal servant was difficult, let alone trusting something that would normally eat you. Costa's seeds and clippings were the closest any Yena came to bending other life to their will. Had the esask agreed to their servitude? Made some trade with the Tikitik? Since they made no sound, and she sensed nothing from their minds, it was hard to imagine how that could be.

The things were huge. As they stopped beside the platform's arms, she leaned back in order to see their riders. The two esask on the left bore clusters of Tikitik. She couldn't tell how many of the black creatures clung to each other, but guessed three on each. Their beasts were festooned with the body-sized gourds the others used instead of bags or baskets, tied on with woven ropes. Some of the gourds would contain power cells and glows; others, metal objects: blades, chain, rings, fasteners; while a few, hopefully, would be heavy with the sweet, fragrant *oba* juice Om'ray prized and Tikitik provided at long intervals. All would be emptied and refilled with fresh dresel and sprouts.

Aryl winced. There were a great many gourds.

The esask to the right carried a solitary rider. Aryl couldn't tell if this was the same individual who had come last M'hir—suddenly embarrassed to realize this was the first visit where she hadn't cared more about whispering to her friends about unChosen—but it didn't matter. This would be her mother's counterpart, the one who would speak.

Not that she would see its mouth. Aryl unconsciously leaned into the solid comfort of Bern's side as she stared at the strange being.

The Tikitik rode astride, its pair of long, thin legs a match to those of its mount. From a distance, there were similarities to an Om'ray's form as well, but only from a distance. There were two arms attached to a body, but the body was concave and gaunt, its surface covered in small, knobbed plates instead of skin. The arms were too flexible and bore short spines from wrist to shoulder. The shoulders, though flat and broad, met at a too-long neck that curved forward and down so the head was held in front of the chest.

Aryl's stomach protested.

The head was triangular, widest at the back, and framed by two pairs of eyes that reflected cold white disks from the glow-light. Each eye sat at the tip of a cone of flesh. The hind pair were large and aimed forward; the front pair were tiny, their cones kept constantly in motion as if a Tikitik worried about its surroundings at all times. To make it worse, in Aryl's opinion, the small eyes moved independently of one another unless the Tikitik was interested. Then, all four would lock into a forward stare.

The mouth was obscured by fleshy, fingerlike protuberances, pale gray and of unknown function. Tikitik could hear, but no Om'ray knew what passed for Tikitik ears. Or nose, for that matter. It wasn't because their bodies were hidden from view. They wore no clothing, though they wrapped their wrists and ankles in cloth patterned with more of their symbols, and used belts to carry longknives like those they traded to the Om'ray.

Their Speaker wore its pendant attached to a broad swathe of plain cloth that went from right shoulder to left hip, ending in long tasseled braids that swept down the side of its mount. Aryl couldn't tell, at this distance, if its pendant matched the one around her mother's neck; she had no desire for a closer look.

"We see you," Taisal said again. She managed to gaze up at her counterpart without losing her dignity, even though beast and rider towered the height of three Om'ray over her small form. Aryl felt a sudden fierce pride.

The Tikitik bobbed its head, twice, a sharp motion involving the joint at the neck, not the shoulder. Taisal raised her hand slightly, the signal for those carrying the bundle of dresel to approach. The two Om'ray eyed the esask warily, but the beast did nothing more than widen its nostrils. They put down their burden, opened it to show the purple lumps of flesh within, and backed away.

There should have been a steady stream of more with bundles, accompanied by those with empty baskets to take away the contents of the gourds. There should have been Om'ray waiting to transfer the dresel into the gourds.

Instead, there was a moment of awkward, outward silence,

while to Aryl's inner sense, Om'ray tension made it hard to breathe.

The Tikitik grouped together made hissing sounds. The Speaker's head bobbed again, once, and they quieted.

Then it spoke, the words and voice shockingly normal. "There is less, Yena Speaker."

"There are less of us," Taisal replied.

It seemed to notice the gathered Om'ray for the first time, swinging its head slowly as if counting. "How are these observations related?" it asked when done. "Has an independent faction taken the Harvest to establish themselves elsewhere?"

This brought an unhappy murmur from some of those assembled. Aryl didn't say anything, but then, she had no idea what the creature meant. She suspected it was stupid.

"There was an accident. Caused by others." Taisal beckoned a second time to bring the First Scout to her side. Tall and white-haired, her features hidden behind gauze, Haxel held a curved piece of something that wasn't metal or wood in her gloved hands. Aryl leaned forward for a better look, but her neighbors had the same idea and blocked her view.

Before she could object, everyone sat back as if startled.

Easy to understand why. Against all custom, the Tikitik Speaker had dismounted. Water rained from the plates of its esask as the beast rose from its crouch. "What is this?" the Tikitik demanded, taking too-quick strides to loom over Taisal. "What is this?" again, as if she were deaf, but it didn't reach for the piece, only stood and looked at it with all eyes.

Haxel had taken a half step back, but not her mother. Slim and straight, Taisal stood within arm's reach of the tall creature. "This is part of a flying device that exploded in the midst of the Harvest. Seventeen Om'ray died then. Three more—"

"Making you less," it interrupted.

Stupid and rude, Aryl decided, frowning.

"Yes. We—"

The Tikitik bobbed its head twice, then turned its eyes to stare at Taisal. Lit now by glows from two sides, Aryl could see its knobby patches of skin were actually concentric rings of very small, even bumps, the whole having a fine texture almost like coarse cloth. Ugly cloth.

"Where is the rest of the Harvest?"

Anxiety flashed from so many minds at once that Aryl shivered violently. She felt Bern's hand on her back, then, warm and strong. Through the touch, he sent reassurance.

Which might have worked better if she hadn't sensed his fear, too.

Taisal gestured to the single bundle. "That's all there is."

The Tikitik Speaker didn't bother to look. Aryl took slow breaths, waiting with the others. "No," it said at last. "That is all you have brought." The pronouncement drew more hisses from the other Tikitik. "We require more. You will bring what you have stored, now."

For the first time, Aryl heard an edge to her mother's voice. "We're entitled to keep a supply to last us until next M'hir."

The Tikitik uttered a soft guttural bark, a sound echoed more loudly by its fellows. Aryl feared it was a laugh. "You are less," the creature observed, "thus need less, while our needs remain unchanged. Keep one third. Bring us the rest. Now. Or we will leave. What is your choice, Speaker?"

More murmurs from the Om'ray; words of unease slipping from mind to mind like a chill gust of rain. *One third wouldn't be enough . . . not until the next M'hir . . . they'd starve . . .* Aryl's fingers clenched the sides of pane.

Taisal's fingers were carefully positioned at her sides. She offered no threat to the Tikitik. How could she? Aryl thought desperately. Her mother's white-gowned figure was dwarfed by the black creature. Taisal's Power could likely *push* it into the swamp but not influence the empty space that was its mind.

She couldn't make them free the gourds from the esask. Without their contents?

The Tikitik were no fools. Each M'hir they brought sufficient power cells to last the Yena, with care, only until the next Harvest.

Without power cells, water pumps would fail, food couldn't be cooked, the night chill would penetrate. What mattered most, however, was light. Glows needed to be powered as well, before homes and bridges turned dark.

And deadly, Aryl thought, now thoroughly frightened. There were things that hunted the canopy during truenight, things only kept from the Yena by light.

"For everything you've brought, we will share half the fresh material from our stores," Taisal answered, stressing the word "share."

Another bark. "Unacceptable. Two thirds for us. Two thirds of what we have brought for you. Or nothing. You cannot survive without our technology."

"We can't survive without food. As for technology?" Taisal's sudden smile was the most forbidding thing Aryl had ever seen. "There's always fire."

"Fire!" The Tikitik flung up its head with a quick snap of its flexible neck as if avoiding an attack. It looked painful. The others did the same, staying in that posture. Their gigantic mounts dozed, oblivious to the distress of their riders. Aryl thought that just as well.

"You may not!" the creature continued, its voice shrill and loud. "You may not! Fire is dangerous! Burning is Forbidden! The Yena agreed never to use fire!"

"We didn't agree to sit in our homes and die." Taisal spoke quietly, but with emphasis. "If we run out of power, we'll do what we must. Do we understand one another, Speaker?"

Slowly, as if grudgingly, the Tikitik lowered its head. Aryl let out the breath she hadn't remembered holding and relaxed her death's grip on the pane. "One half of your stores," it said, "for one half of what we brought."

"Of our choosing," Taisal countered quickly.

The Tikitik raised the tip of one of its three long fingers. "Of your choosing," it agreed, "in return for that." The tip bent to indicate the piece from the flying machine. "We share an interest in the cause of our mutual problem."

"Done. Fetch the dresel."

Taisal didn't confer with the Council seated behind her, not in any way Aryl could see or sense. The Speaker's authority, here and now, was unquestioned. Perhaps, Aryl thought, their leaders were preoccupied with the future and how they would manage. She certainly hoped someone was thinking about that. Her stomach growled.

Several Om'ray immediately ran up the ladders, heading for the warehouses. Taisal took their evidence from the First Scout, passing it to the Tikitik. The creature raised the fragment of the device to the fleshy protuberances where its mouth should be. They wiggled and fussed over the pitted curve like busy fingers.

It was, Aryl decided, the most disgusting thing she'd ever seen.

The inspection, if that's what it was, was thankfully brief. "This belongs to the strangers," the Tikitik announced, tucking the piece within the band that crossed its chest. It stuck out at a funny angle, but Aryl didn't laugh.

Strangers?

She wasn't the only one taken aback. The word passed from mind to mind, laced with confusion. Even Taisal looked puzzled. A stranger was an unChosen from another Clan. The only way a stranger could arrive was by Passage; he remained a stranger only until Choice. There was no other meaning, not to Om'ray.

Who were "strangers" to the Tikitik?

Interlude

JORG SUD MENDALOR RAN A finger along a benchtop, then scrutinized its tip with great care, his thick gray brows almost meeting with the effort. "Well done, Enris," he pronounced at last, giving his best apron a tug to align it properly. "I'd say we're ready."

The younger Om'ray hid a smile. His father didn't mean the not so dust free though tidy surface or the racks of well-oiled tools. But neither of them would mention the strategic relocation of the bench itself. Jorg was aware of his son's abilities; it was he and Enris' mother, Ridersel Mendolar, who had stressed the importance of keeping them private. Tuana's Council was tolerant of new Talent, if kept from the Oud.

At that thought, Enris lost his good humor. He opened the nearest side window and gazed out at the street. Shopkeepers had lifted their awnings, but only a trickle of customers hurried between. Few ventured out when a Visitation was imminent. "She's going to try something," he growled. "You know it as well as I."

"Naryn?" Jorg came to stand beside him. "Don't worry. She'll behave."

Enris couldn't remember when he'd first seen over his father's head, but now the other's mass of curling silver-gray reached no higher than his shoulder. Jorg's own shoulders, though strong, were curved from seasons of work, his neck permanently bent. He felt a surge of protectiveness as well as pride. His father was the best metalworker the Tuana had ever had, known as much for his kind heart and generosity as the beauty of his creations. He would, no one doubted, become a valued member of Council when Enris' grandmother passed on.

Just thinking of Council made Enris frown. "They can make all the edicts they want. She'll disobey. Council can't control her."

His father chuckled. "Which would be why Naryn and her friends were invited to the Cloisters for the day."

"How—" Enris answered his own question. "Council offers those scatterbrains a chance to become Adepts."

"Oh, they might pass tests of Power." At Enris' offended huff, Jorg patted him on the back. "They'll never have your control, so don't worry. You're far more likely to—"

No, he sent, horror coloring the denial. "I work with these," he said aloud, holding up his callused hands.

Jorg patted Enris again, firmly. "And well you do." It was his turn to glance out the window. "If they come today at all, it won't be till sunset. Would you like to help me with a casting? There's a bit of a trick with this one. I could use your knack with puzzles."

"You're trying to stop me worrying, aren't you?" Enris complained as he followed his father to the vat.

Jorg took up the partly finished mold, examining its reversed shaping of a gear-to-be. His eyes were bright with mischief as he glanced over it at his son. "Is that possible?"

Enris started to protest, then the corner of his lips twitched upward. "Show me the problem, and I'll let you know."

Chapter 7

THE TIKITIK SPEAKER SEEMED TO grasp that it had confounded the Om'ray Speaker, if not how. "The material," it declared, "is from another world. It must have come with the strangers."

Someone snickered. Bern was shaking his head. There was, of course, no such thing. The world, as everyone could feel from birth, was defined by the seven Om'ray Clans. There was nothing beyond them. How could there be? If you could somehow move farther than that connection could reach, you would be nowhere at all.

But Aryl thought of the Dark. She could sense its churning without effort. It was where she'd somehow *pushed* Bern to move him to safety, where she'd felt drawn in her grief. Her mother denied it was a place yet admitted it was real. Bern had described it as if he'd seen it for himself.

Was this what the Tikitik meant? Another world beyond this one—unseen but within reach of Power. Could something *not-there* to her inner sense feel it, too? She felt on the cusp of grasping something vital . . .

"Aryl Sarc."

Bern nudged her and she started, only then realizing she'd heard her name. "What—?"

"Are you asleep? The Speaker wants you. Hurry!" Sure enough, Taisal was beckoning impatiently.

Cheeks warm, Aryl hopped down from the bench, careful not to drop the pane. That would be all she'd need.

Her steps slowed involuntarily as she entered the long crossed shadows cast by the Tikitik. The creature towered overhead like a nightmare. It watched her approach with that disturbing all-eyes' focus, and Aryl forced her own gaze to the planking underfoot. She walked forward until she could see the hem of her mother's gown, then stopped.

She smelled something musty, like a blanket left too long in a chest, and yet sweet, like the juice from one of Costa's plants. The combination roused memories of her grandmother's tiny figure, huddled deep and motionless within faded cushions. An Adept had come each morning for the full five days of a fist before pronouncing the body an empty shell and ready for disposal in the Lay beneath the Sarc grove. Until then, he'd claimed something of Unnel Sarc's Power lingered, as though by outlasting her Chosen, she'd locked her mind's grip on the world.

Dresel laced this scent as well. Aryl slid her eyes sideways. The Tikitik had blunt claws on the ends of its long toes.

"The drawing?"

Aryl jerked to attention and met her mother's almost imperceptible frown. "Yes, Speaker. Here it is."

Taisal took the pane and passed it to the Tikitik without a glance at its surface. "This is a representation of the device. Do you recognize it?" She'd apparently decided to avoid strangers and worlds altogether.

Aryl agreed wholeheartedly. She eased back, hoping to be unnoticed.

The small homely pane looked wrong in the Tikitik's hands.

Aryl swallowed a protest as the creature raised it to its face. To have something from her hands being groped by those gray—*worms?* Her mother gave her a sharp look, and Aryl tightened her shields to keep in her thoughts.

The creature used its eyes to examine the drawing, that was all, tipping the pane from side to side as if seeking the best light. It was so normal a scrutiny that Aryl relaxed, very slightly.

"Who made this? You?" Four eyes aimed at her. "You were there. What else did you see?"

Aryl wanted to sink into the wood. No one but the appointed Speaker could address a Tikitik. Clearly, the rule didn't hold in reverse, which wasn't fair. She looked to Taisal for guidance and received another warning frown.

"This shows the device," her mother repeated, avoiding the issue of the artist too. "It was observed to move against the M'hir, to hover in place. When wastryls collided with it, there was a release of light, fire, and noise, like a lightning strike. We don't know if it was by accident or—"

"Not an accident," the Tikitik interrupted, eyes back to Taisal. "This disrupted the Harvest, causing us hardship. Making you less." It bobbed its head once, then added, "We will endure. You may not. Do you have a death dispute with the strangers?"

Not stupid, Aryl decided. Insane. From the swell of outrage pressing against her shields, she didn't think she was the only Om'ray reaching that conclusion.

Taisal clapped her hands. Those lowering bundles to the platform froze, the pulleys and chains swinging gently with their loads. "It is against the Agreement, Speaker," she said over the faint creaks, "to use terms without common meaning."

The other Tikitik had been untying gourds from their mounts and passing them to waiting Om'ray on the dock. They halted, too, hissing to themselves.

"What do you need defined?" their Speaker asked. "I can simplify. Is this," it lifted the pane, "trouble of your making?"

"Of course not!" As her words echoed across the water, Taisal made a conciliatory gesture Om'ray would understand, if not the Tikitik. "How could it be?" she reasoned. "You talk of strangers. Yena has seen only two such in the last handful of M'hirs, Om'ray on lawful Passage. You talk of another world." Here her voice showed strain. "We know only this world." Her hands lifted to indicate those behind her, then dropped to her sides. "You have what evidence there is of a device not of our making, a device that has cost too many Om'ray lives already. It's your puzzle to solve, Speaker, not ours."

Drawing conclusions from part of this, at least, the Tikitik tucked Aryl's drawing inside its chest band, to join the fragment. It bobbed its head twice, a signal that sent the others back to work. Taisal hesitated, then nodded to the Om'ray. As the sounds of effort resumed—the slide of chain, the dropping of bundles and gourds, heavy breathing—Aryl felt the tension ease.

She took advantage of the moment to move away from Taisal and the Tikitik, one step. Two. When neither paid attention, she turned and almost ran to her seat.

"You're shaking," Bern whispered as she settled into place.

"You would be, too," she retorted as quietly. "I don't know how my mother can stand there like that."

They'd be finished soon. Couldn't be soon enough, in Aryl's opinion, an impatience felt by all around her. Once the exchange was complete, the Om'ray would ascend to the safety of their homes. They could forget these *not-there* creatures existed until the next M'hir.

Which suddenly seemed impossibly distant. There were two hundred and seventy-seven Yena left, between the Cloisters and those here. "Did you hear? Half the dresel is all we'll have," she whispered to Bern, afraid to send. "We'll starve."

She wasn't sure what starving to death would be like; she'd rather not find out.

"Of course we won't. Council will have a plan. For all we know," his breath tickled her ear, "they've hidden supplies against just such a day."

Aryl kept her doubts to herself. Fresh dresel rotted within days. After each Harvest, the Om'ray pressed their share into flatcakes, dried over heat and kept in sealed casks. To be eaten, the cakes were remoistened and baked—Aryl's favorite treat was baked dresel with sweet sap—or more usually ground to a powder and combined with other foods as a spice.

Tikitik wouldn't touch dried dresel, considering it ruined. There wouldn't be any left anyway. As always, the Yena had feasted while they waited for the Watchers to signal the M'hir, using up the last supplies before Harvest. It was tradition, to make way for fresh new stores. Which now seemed a very bad idea, to Aryl's thinking—though in their defense, there had always been more dresel harvested than Yena could ever use, more than enough for the Tikitik as well.

Council would meet tonight, Aryl knew, trying to shake off her fear. Their combined wisdom was beyond that of mere un-Chosen. Bern was right. They would know what to do. They knew everything.

They didn't know about her, something deep inside countered. They didn't know about the *Dark* the M'hir had shown her.

"Aryl." Bern's shoulder pressed against hers. "Cheer up. We'll be all right."

Heart-kin, she sent, grateful for his dependable warmth, and he smiled down at her in a way no one else ever had. The guilt she carried faded like morning mist. They belonged together, Aryl knew. Whatever was to come, they'd face it together.

And when she was a Chooser, Bern Teerac would be her Choice.

Chapter 8

ARYL AWOKE THE NEXT DAY to a bedlam of footsteps and voices. She jumped from the bed and rushed to the window panel, pulling aside its curtain.

The bridges were bustling with Om'ray, but only those who, to her inner sense, were connected by unseen bonds, some to one another, others to those left in homes. The Chosen.

Adults were always, in Aryl's opinion, in a hurry to do the incomprehensible. She yawned, rubbing her eyes.

They were burdened, she noticed curiously. Some carried wooden chests with ornate carvings, awkward to manage on the more narrow bridges. Family heirlooms? Others had bags or objects wrapped in cloth. She couldn't guess. Whatever they carried, they were taking it to the meeting hall.

After a quick wash, Aryl pulled on her tunic and shoved her hair back in its net. She wanted breakfast and answers, not necessarily in that order.

Her mother would know.

Her mother, it turned out, had left for the Cloisters. Meanwhile, her mother's sister, Myris Sarc, and her Chosen, Ael sud Sarc, arrived to take Aryl's home apart. They claimed consent but wouldn't explain. So Aryl sat at one end of the Sarc table, scowling so fiercely her forehead hurt, and took her time chewing the last bite of the tiny portion of cold breakfast she'd been allowed.

"You could help instead of glaring," Ael suggested after a while. Like many Kessa'ats, he was dark of hair and slight. He was an excellent climber—only a still-healing ankle had kept him from this M'hir's Harvest. Myris was a younger version of Taisal, fair and given, normally, to irrepressible giggles. Aryl adored them both.

Until now.

She scowled harder.

She watched as her aunt and uncle opened every cupboard and pulled out the contents, piling these with care on the table until she had to lean to one side to keep an eye on what the pair did next. They pulled down the storage slings, dumping their contents with less care, as if running out of time or patience. Piles began to grow, on the counter, before the window panels.

More pointless tasks. Myris went on hands and knees, running her fingertips along the floor's finely fitted planks as if hunting dust. Ael, having rolled the carpets, pulled the sling chairs up to the rafters one by one, scrutinizing what was underneath. He freed the fastened one at the table and did the same to it.

Then he eyed hers; she didn't move.

With a shrug, Ael headed for Costa's room.

Stop!

Both adult Om'ray looked pained.

Aryl covered her mouth with her hands, as though she could take back that fierce inner shout.

"We've a job to do," Myris said gently. "It's no easier for us."

Aryl hurried to the door, where she put herself in Ael's path. "You can't touch Costa's things. Not—not without my mother here," she added forcefully, feeling on more solid ground. "If there's something you need, tell me. I'll bring it to you. Just—wait. Please."

They exchanged looks. "We don't know when she'll be back, Aryl," sighed Ael. "She's busy with the—"

Hush!

Even Aryl felt that. She narrowed her eyes, and looked from one to the other. "Busy with what?"

"There are lists to be prepared for Council. Using symbols in ink for things." Her aunt stopped there.

"I know," grated Aryl, "what a list is. Lists of what things?"

They looked at one another again. If anything passed between them, it was on that deeper level Chosen used with one another. Ael made a clear gesture of protest before walking away. He went into Aryl's room, where she could hear him opening trunks. Her trunks.

Oddly, she didn't care. Her attention was on Myris, who looked suddenly much older than she should. "Lists of what?" Aryl repeated. "Please, Myris. What's going on?"

"Last night. The Speaker did her best. But we've half what we normally need until the next M'hir."

I was there, Aryl thought impatiently, but didn't say it out loud. Adults rarely liked correction from unChosen. "What does that have to do with—?"

Rip!

The loud sound came from her bedroom, followed by an alarming: *creak . . . SNAP!* "What's he doing?" Aryl protested.

Whatever it was, he was happy about it. Ael's triumph flooded her mind. "Found it!" he shouted.

Myris almost ran, Aryl at her side. They stopped in the doorway to stare. For Ael stood inside what was left of—

"My bed? What have you done?" Aryl demanded. The sheet was on the floor and the pad beneath had been sliced open with a knife. Flakes of stuffing drifted through the air, tumbling in the light breeze through the window. As for the rest? A line of connected planks stood upright in the middle, as if startled awake. Their ends were splintered and broken. And it wasn't just her bed—this had been Taisal's, her grandmother's, her—Aryl couldn't remember how old it was.

Clearly, no one would sleep there again.

"I'll fix it," Ael promised, though she couldn't imagine how. "Look what I found! This has to be your great grandfather's gear." He held up a strange-looking bag by its straps; the brown material was stained and faded, but intact. The bag itself bulged in several directions, closed with more straps and metal buckles; a rope of some odd woven fiber was fastened to one side.

Ael dropped the bag to pounce on something else in the ruin. "And supplies!" He straightened, both hands full of small pouches. From their look, they were of oiled leather, not woven as was normal.

Which great grandfather? She had, Aryl frowned in concentration, four. No. Eight. Who . . . then it dawned on her exactly what Ael had found inside her bed, what they'd been hunting. "That's traveler's gear," she accused. "For Passage."

Myris nodded. "These belonged to Dalris sud Sarc—Dalris Sawnda'at. He came on Passage from Amna."

Unnel Sarc's father; her mother's grandfather. Aryl wrinkled her nose, unsure what offended her more: the destruction of her bed; that her family would hide dirty old belongings in it; or not finding them first. She settled for all three. "Then they're mine," she declared. "That's my bed."

Ael stepped over the bed frame, bringing the pouches and

bag with him. "And I will fix it, Aryl. But these? They go to Council."

And that was all either of them would say.

"Why do I have to put everything back?" Aryl muttered. She'd been tidying the main room since Myris and Ael left with their discovery; the piles on the table, floor, and counters remained daunting. Who knew adults could make such a mess? "And where did they find it all?" she complained, knowing full well but enjoying the freedom to speak her mind with no Chosen about. She left the storage slings hanging like surprised drapes in the middle of the room, their ropes swinging loose. The cupboards had been virtually empty; she might as well fill them. It was besides the point that it was easier.

"Most of this isn't even mine. Anymore," she qualified with surprise, holding a tunic better suited to be a shirt against herself.

Why hadn't Taisal given this—all this, she thought, spotting more too-small clothing that had to be Costa's—to some other child? The Om'ray passed such things between families. They always had. Unless it had further use . . .

"It can be a hat!" Laughing, Aryl plopped the dress on her head and spun around, keeping it in place with both hands. "Everyone will want—"

Her inner sense told her she was no longer alone. She froze, her back to the door. "You should knock," she said archly, whisking the little dress into a pocket before turning around. "As you can see, I'm very busy."

Bern grinned at her. "Is that what it's called?"

Aryl opened her mouth, ready with a cutting reply. She shut it again. Something wasn't right. *Heart-kin?* she sent.

Bern's pale eyes slipped away; he answered aloud. "This

isn't the only mess," he informed her, giving a loosened chair a gentle push to set it swinging. "They're tearing through every home. It's been going on all day." As he spoke, he prowled the room as if following a trail—or too restless to stand still—moving around the hanging slings. "Only the Chosen, mind you. They're taking what they find to the meeting hall." A glance through her bedroom door made him purse his lips and whistle softly. "Ouch. What are they after?"

"Things on lists," Aryl offered. "Myris said the Adepts made lists for the Council. They must be gathering what's on them."

He paused beside the rolled-up rugs as if she'd surprised him, one hand taking hold of a dangling sling rope. "Like what?"

How should she know? Aryl wanted to say, but something about him subdued the impulse. For the first time, she paid attention to what Bern wore: his favorite heavy tunic, woven from cunningly supple braid, reinforced down the back and front with inlaid slices of polished dresel pod his father had bleached white. It was excellent camouflage within the dappled canopy light. His longknife and hook gleamed at his belt; a fine rope and a set of tightly rolled nets crossed his chest from either shoulder. His legs and arms were sheathed in fresh bindings of gauze; his gloves and hood hung from their clips. She frowned at his boots. They looked scuffed and old, though sturdy, and she'd never seen them before. Buckled instead of tied? What a waste of metal.

Dismissing the boots and Bern's air of gloom, Aryl focused on what mattered. "You went hunting without me?"

Bern shook his head. He'd left his hair loose and it tumbled, as always, into both eyes. "I've been summoned to Council. I should be there now." He hesitated, then a word slipped into her thoughts. *Heart-kin.* "I had to see you."

At first, this made no sense at all. Which fit the day, she decided.

Then it made too much. "Passage." The word fell out of her mouth. She fumbled for the table, found a grip. Strange time for the rastis to sway, though nothing about the world was as it should be. "That's silly," she said desperately. "You're not old enough."

Bern shook his head again, this time slowly. "No, Aryl. You aren't."

His shields were up, so she searched his face, finding shadows beneath his eyes, harsh lines beside his mouth. There was no fear in it, only a sad resignation. He looked, she thought abruptly, like the stranger, Kiric.

The stranger who'd died.

There was a way to keep Bern here, where he belonged. Aryl surreptitiously rubbed her hands against her thighs, making sure they were free of dust, if not truly clean. She licked her lips, then walked up to him. "We can—" her voice broke and she coughed, avoiding his eyes, her own shields desperately tight. She placed her left hand on his chest, palm flat over the cool lines of inlay. The rope scratched her wrist but she didn't flinch.

Aryl, no.

She shook her head fiercely to silence him, trying not to feel his pity. She lifted her right hand, hoping it hadn't started to sweat—her palms grew damp when she was nervous, she couldn't help it—and captured his. She took a deep breath and said the words.

"I, Aryl Sarc, offer you Choice, Bern Teerac."

Then waited.

Their hands were callused from branch and rope; his was warmer.

That was all.

Finally, Aryl had to look up. "Am I doing it right?" she whispered.

"It doesn't matter. You can't." Bern's eyes glistened. "It's too soon for you, Aryl."

"No. No. It's something I'm doing wrong. Tell me how. What do I do!?" she pleaded, tears in her own eyes. "You're all I want. You're all I've ever wanted. You can't—you can't leave."

His wavering smile was a terrible thing. "You're all I've ever wanted."

"Then stay!"

His hand cupped the back of her head, gave it a gentle shake. "You have so much Power, Aryl. I'm not surprised you're the one to have this amazing ability—can do what maybe no Om'ray ever has before. Me? I'm nothing special," he told her. "But I'm unChosen and male. We feel the Call of Choice when we're ready. I feel it. It burns . . ." his voice became hollow as his head turned right ". . . in Grona . . ." left, ". . . in Amna . . . and Tuana . . ." this last looking into her eyes. "But not here. Not in Yena. Not this M'hir."

"Wait for me." Aryl rose on her toes, pressed both hands on his chest. "I'll be old before you know it."

Heart-kin. Bern stepped away. "It's not my decision to make."

Aryl stood very still, feeling the blood drain from her head and shoulders, sensing the wild *darkness* as if another eye opened without her willing it. His shields didn't protect him in that realm. Suddenly, she could touch Bern's innermost thoughts, share the pain so like her own.

And the anticipation. The *lust.* He might not know it yet himself, but she did. "You want to go," she accused.

She'd shocked him; she could see it, sense it. Then, with characteristic honesty, he lowered his head. It wasn't quite a nod. It was, nonetheless, an admission. "I've been ready since the last M'hir," the words said so quietly she almost didn't hear. "I waited for you, Aryl. I was sure—it doesn't matter now. Something in me . . . I'm empty. I need . . ."

He never did know when to stop talking, Aryl fumed to herself. "You need someone else, is that it?" she snapped. "Then go."

Bern gave her a stricken look. "We'll always be heart-kin—"

"Find your Chooser," Aryl interrupted haughtily. "I hope she's stupid and afraid of heights!" She turned and stormed into Costa's room, closing the curtain behind her.

Once there, she sagged against the wall panel, her fist in her mouth to stifle the sobs shaking her body. She sensed Bern's sending brush her shields—no words, just an anxious, lonely touch between heart-kin—and retreated inward until she couldn't.

She'd saved him.

She listened to his footsteps; they grew faint, then were gone.

She could *see* Bern now, safe on that bridge, and knew she could make the vision real again. Her Power was waiting, ready to use, if she dared.

But she wouldn't see him, not where he was going.

Were there even bridges?

Aryl slid to the floor and buried her face on her knees, letting despair shudder through her.

How could she save him there?

Interlude

THE DRUMS OF THE WATCHERS announced their guests, that heavy beat vibrating through lungs and hearts as well as floors. Enris lifted his bowl from the table, making a quick grab to capture a mug about to bounce off the near edge.

The drums stopped, but his mother, his height and youthfully slender despite birthing three, hadn't been quick enough. She glared at the resulting mess. "And what's wrong with a bell, I ask you?" she muttered. "Worin, get those, please." While her youngest cheerfully scrambled beneath the table to retrieve errant tubers, Ridersel collected the pieces of what had been her second favorite platter.

Enris met his father's somber gaze. It wasn't a question waiting an answer. The Tuana used drums, set into the ground, because they suited other ears than theirs. "I should get to the shop," he said apologetically. When he went to scrape his share of supper back in the pot, Ridersel intercepted him.

"No need to starve," she said, taking his bowl. Cutting open a dumpling, she spooned the contents, a rich stew, inside, then wrapped the whole in a square of food cloth.

"This time, don't forget it by the vat," Jorg advised around mouthfuls. "Lad gets preoccupied," he reminded his Chosen. Ridersel smiled fondly.

Enris could feel the warm bond between his parents. Not everyone could, he knew. And not every Joining produced such a resonance between its partners, although it was more common now than in his grandparents' time.

Kiric, his older brother, had felt it, too. That was why he'd taken Passage so eagerly, hoping to find someone to complete him, as their parents completed one another. Those he'd left behind believed in his success. Belief was all they had.

Except for Enris. He'd never told his family how he'd been roused from sleep, night after night, to his brother's pain. Night after night after night until . . . it stopped, torn apart by inner screams. He never hinted he knew the truth.

That Kiric had died of loneliness.

And Passage was a lie.

"Don't listen to your father. Keep it warm," Ridersel urged, pressing the bundle into his hands. She paused, her eyes searching his, then her silver-streaked black hair stirred from its peaceful fall over her shoulders and back, locks reaching toward him.

Though thick and lustrous and the crowning glory of a Joined Chooser, that hair was prone to opinion. It could also be sensitive to the moods of others, and Enris backed away, very slightly, to avoid its silken touch. Ridersel restrained her hair with what appeared an absent sweep of her slender white fingers. Unlike some, she scorned metal clips. When younger, Enris had argued this was an unfair advantage; his father had only laughed.

"Thank you," Enris said with unconscious dignity. "I'd better go."

Worin peered over the table's edge, blue eyes gleaming. "Do I get your sweetpie?"

"I'll meet you there, Enris." Jorg ruffled his youngest's hair. "With your pie."

"Be well," his mother added. Words formed in his mind. *Be careful.*

"I will," he said, to both.

Chapter 9

LIKE SO MUCH IN OM'RAY LIFE, there were customs and traditions to be followed when sending an unChosen on Passage. Most made a certain sense, Aryl thought numbly.

The family would search their home for anything that could help their son's journey. Dried fruits were a popular choice, easy to carry and lasting. Flasks with wide mouths to catch raindrops were another, given the waters of the Lay were not safe to approach, let alone drink. A precious glow and a power cell, for the light to keep hunters at bay.

Finishing with a handsome new shirt, to wear when meeting his new Clan and, of course, to favorably impress the Chooser who waited.

Not in Yena, Aryl reminded herself bitterly.

She hadn't cried long; perhaps she'd used up her tears already. Now she felt light-headed, almost dizzy. Seru kept giving her worried looks, her own eyes red and swollen. Taisal di Sarc had slowed and nodded gravely as she'd passed Aryl during the processional, but hadn't stopped.

There was no need, Aryl thought. Yena itself bled today. What was her pain, to that?

In the history of their Clan, there had only been five M'hirs when two unChosen left on Passage at once. In many, including the last four, no one had left at all. Never, to the whispered dismay of those gathered now to say farewell, had all gone.

For that was who stood in line, receiving gifts of dried fruit and flasks, glows and handsome shirts. Every eligible unChosen male, the ten who hadn't died in this M'hir's deadly Harvest. Their names were those of friends and playmates, cousins and brothers.

And heart-kin.

Aryl's gaze slipped to Bern, standing with the rest. His gifts were being carefully packed into an older bag, with metal buckles. It could be the one Ael had found hidden in her bed, though there were several such being filled. The lists—they must have been of supplies like this. Preparing one to leave was a task. Preparing ten?

No wonder they'd scoured every home for relics.

Bern wasn't the oldest, though most were younger by a M'hir or even two. Seru sniffled loudly and Aryl nudged her to stop. If their families could stand proud and silent, those who'd flirted and dreamed of being Choosers one day had no right to weep.

Once the bustle of gifting ended, the families moved back to join those surrounding the unChosen. The panels of the meeting hall had been turned open, letting the overflow spill out onto the deck and bridge, granting access to all. No one paid attention to the biters who took rude advantage.

Taisal stepped forward, again—or still—in her ceremonial robes. Councilor Sian d'sud Vendan accompanied her, his hands full of metal disks. She stopped before the first in line, Yuhas Parth, and bowed her head to him.

"Receive this token, that you may Pass unhindered to Choice." With this, she took a disk from Sian and pinned it to Yuhas' tunic. "Find joy," she finished.

Was it hard, Aryl wondered, for her mother to wish them what she'd lost?

There was no wasted motion or delay. Daylight was the only safe time to travel; they'd gathered at dawn for this ceremony. The odd wysp trilled its farewell to truenight, a fitting sound. The unChosen had been brought back from the Cloisters, where they'd been given what memories there were of the landscapes beyond Yena. There were Adepts who collected such from each who arrived on Passage, though few made it this far. None had crossed the desert between Yena and Pana, though secondhand information came from other Clans. None had come from Vyna either. The routes to Amna and Tuana were freshest in memory, being the most recent to arrive, but the latter crossed the vast plains of the Oud, alien to Yena in all ways. Those to Grona and Rayna, remembered only by the oldest, would be dimmer and less accurate.

They *knew* where to go, Aryl assured herself. It was innate. The world was the Om'ray; they could never be lost in it. As for what waited along the way? She suppressed a shudder. Not all were as experienced as Bern; in truth, only he and Yuhas climbed with admirable skill. Some had barely started training, a few seemed bewildered by straps and hooks.

The tokens glinted as their wearers began moving out of the hall, the rest of Yena making way. The existence of enough tokens for all was a surprise in itself. Aryl was glad of the distraction. Had this many come on Passage in the past, leaving their tokens with Council? Or was there a store of new tokens in the Cloisters?

She sighed. Not that it mattered.

Heart-kin. Fingers brushed hers in the crowd. She felt the warmth in his touch. *Be well.* Then he was moving beyond her.

I didn't mean it, she dared send, keeping it focused and tight, hoping their connection would protect them among so many. He had to know. *About her. You'll find someone wonderful.*

Faint . . . so faint . . . *I did.*

Heart-kin. Her lips trembled as she tried to smile. *Be careful.*

Aryl's wish was being echoed throughout the Yena as the unChosen took their leave. By custom, they would travel separately, to better listen for their Chooser's call. By plan, they would seek in different directions, aware no one Clan would have so many Choosers to spare. A couple would try to reach distant Vyna, despite the mystery shrouding that path.

It seemed a morning for impossible goals.

She went with the others as they spread along the bridges, looking up to watch Bern climb. They'd use the canopy for their road as long as they could. It had the best light, the most food.

It was marginally safer.

The figures moved quickly, sure on familiar paths, disappearing between one breath and the next. Aryl struggled to see through the crisscrossed fronds of rastis, following the climb in her mind's eye, knowing each step and reach and pull.

Hear me, Yena.

At the summons, Aryl turned with everyone else to face Taisal and the Council. They stood, shoulder to shoulder, in the main doorway to the meeting hall, their expressions determined and dignified. She would have been comforted, if her inner sense hadn't felt apprehension from all sides.

"Our unChosen face a difficult trial," Taisal said. Though it carried well, her voice was hoarse, as if overused. "But by taking Passage, they stand a better chance of survival."

A startled murmur that died immediately.

"Only those on Passage may leave Yena," Taisal continued. "The rest of us must stay. That is the Agreement. Neither Tikitik nor Oud will suffer our breaking it. Our Chosen have collected every scrap of dresel, every bit of preserved food, from our homes. Combined with this M'hir's Harvest, that resource will be shared by all. It cannot sustain all." She paused, as if to let that sink in, then went on. "We must do whatever we can to find more. Glean what we can from the groves, hunt what comes near.

"Above all," she said, her voice now loud and sure, "above all, we must preserve the strength of those who will reap the coming M'hir for us, or Yena is doomed."

"Are you sure this is what you want, Aryl? To stay here alone?" Taisal sat with hands neatly folded in her lap, but she looked distracted, as if already gone. "There's no guarantee how long this bridge will last. Myris and Ael have room for you."

The diminished stock of glows and their power cells was another problem facing the Yena. Council had responded by reducing the area to be lit through truenight. Which, thus far, had meant cutting free bridges and ladders leading to already empty buildings.

They'd been more populous once.

The next step would move people from outlying homes. "Sarc joins the main bridge," Aryl pointed out. "It's more likely I'll need to find room for them. Don't worry. I'll manage."

Her mother's mind came back from wherever it had wandered, her eyes warm. "Yes, you can. You've grown, Daughter."

Just not enough.

Taisal gestured understanding. Aryl shrugged and collected their dishes. She took them to the basin, automatically reaching for the fastener on the water pipe, but stopped herself in time. Water pumps consumed the same cells that powered glows; Council had decreed only those essential to fill the communal cistern remain in use. Everyone was to retrieve water from that source in gourds or flasks or whatever was available. Already, weavers were busy making biter-proof covers for roof collectors, though the rains wouldn't start until the M'hir blew itself out.

"Take my room," Taisal said, rising to her feet. "If my sister decides to move in, her Chosen can fix your old bed." There'd been a clever catch-and-hinge arrangement to lift the frame after all, something that would have saved time and the bed, had any living Sarc known of it. "I wish I could stay longer," she finished.

"I know." Her mother's duties in the Cloisters now included searching records for any forgotten sources within the canopy with the virtues of dresel. That those duties also included tending those who would weaken first as their rations were cut was an unspoken, but tragic truth. "I'll be busy myself," Aryl added more brightly. She was to climb the canopy tomorrow and join the urgent hunt for still-edible pods. Council may not have picked her for the Harvest, but at last they acknowledged her skills were too great to waste plucking fruit with other unChosen.

"Be successful," her mother said soberly. "A pod means a fist of life."

Aryl swallowed. She hadn't thought of it that way. "I will."

"I expect nothing less." Taisal appeared to hesitate, then nodded to herself. "And be careful. Aryl, this is important. Do not let any Tikitik see you."

She blinked. "I thought they couldn't climb." And she wasn't planning to go down to the Lay before next M'hir either.

"Don't confuse assumption with fact," Taisal frowned. "We've never seen one climb. That doesn't mean we know what they can do or where they can reach. If one comes near you, hide any pods you've found. Don't tell it what you're doing."

"Tell it?" Aryl echoed faintly. "You mean it would talk to me? I'm not a Speaker."

"They want dresel. If they suspect we've more than we've said . . ." Taisal stopped and went on more calmly. "Between us, Daughter, no further." At Aryl's nod she continued. "You were brought to their attention—there was no help for it. But Tikitik aren't as rule bound as Om'ray. They have their factions; these sometimes disagree. A representative from one or another will not hesitate to approach you if it finds you alone. And ask questions."

Aryl remembered long arms and a repulsive mouth. "Do they—would it try to eat me?"

"Child's tales." Taisal shook her head with reassuring promptness. "Harming an Om'ray is against the Agreement. So long as we stay within our groves, we're safe—from our thinking neighbors at least. Now, I must go. Is there anything else you need?"

What she needed was for life to be the way it was, with Costa bringing his armloads of dripping, smelly greenery through the door, and Bern being annoying.

Without the awareness of the *other place* always beneath her senses, and a guilt that weighed her heart.

Since none of that was remotely within her mother's Power, Aryl found a smile. "Good weather in the morning."

"That, the Watchers promise," Taisal smiled back. *Be well.*

Alone, Aryl found herself doing what her mother or Costa used to do at the end of each day: checking the fit of gauze against biters, testing and replacing cells in the household glows, making sure the door panel was latched in place for the night. They were familiar tasks—when Taisal stayed at the Cloisters, they were hers anyway. But this was the first time she'd done them aware this was her home now.

Growing up wasn't what she'd imagined, Aryl mused as she dimmed the light within the bedroom. Instead of jumping on her parents' bed, a romp that typically resulted in doing dishes for a fist, she'd done the dishes without thought. Now, she slid between the sheets and lay as she was, too exhausted to shift to a more comfortable position. Not that more comfort could be imagined, she groaned, her eyes closing against the light from the bridge glows that snuck between the curtains. There was a sensation as though the bed turned under her—a not-unpleasant dizziness.

Though her body was still, Aryl's mind began to race. Plans for tomorrow's hunt: equipment, where she'd try first. The Sarc grove would have been scoured already. Teerac's? She veered from that train of thought to a closer problem: what to do with all the clutter now filling her old bedroom. It could go back into the storage slings, pulled up to the rafters.

No. She didn't want old things, their things.

She'd host a gathering—her very first—and invite her friends to take what they liked. There couldn't be a proper supper. Council had ruled that each Om'ray would receive only what he or she needed for the next day's meal, brought to the meeting hall each morning. That was fine with her, Aryl decided. No dishes.

Picturing herself dressed in something much more mature than yellow, Aryl drifted toward sleep. Her dreams took over from imagination . . .

. . . . She found herself waiting at her open door, a flower in her hand. One by one, her friends arrived, dressed in their best, their faces gaunt and hollow. They begged her to feed them and she refused, though she smelled fresh dresel on her clothes, hands, and hair.

Next came those who'd fallen into the Lay, their bodies swollen and putrid where the flesh hadn't been torn off in jagged bites. They dripped on her floor, and begged her to free them from the water. Costa was at the front, the stumps of his arms outstretched to her, and she told them they were dead.

Her party ruined, she tried to close the door. A hand

stopped its turning, then another, and another. They pulled it open again, pushed through, their arms and legs wrapped in gauze, their booted footsteps loud. Their mouths were open, screaming without sound. They were burned . . . broken . . . bitten . . . starved . . . yet moving . . .

She *pushed* them away, into the darkness, only to find herself going with them. It was like drowning in black water . . . she had nowhere to go . . .

Aryl found herself sitting up and shaking. Beams of light barred the walls, cracked by shadows. The shadows were of curtains, wall panels, and the gently moving tips of rastis fronds.

Nothing more.

She wrapped her arms around her middle, holding herself in place. Dreams were . . . they were just dreams. The Adepts said so; they should know.

This—it had been more. She wasn't sure why she believed it, but she did.

Aryl doubted she was the only one having this particular nightmare tonight. Some of those Joined were rumored to share dreams, though there was no need to invoke a mental connection to explain common fears after the events of the last—was it only three days?

But hers—it was more.

Now as restless as she'd been tired, Aryl swung her legs over the side of the bed and padded to the window, her fingers gathering a fold of curtain to let her see out.

There wasn't much to see. Only scouts would be awake, armed with longknives and watching the bases of the few ladders left connected through truenight. Every building and bridge was strung with glows. She'd delighted in them once. Now, it seemed her world ended at the limit of light.

Bern and the others were beyond, in that darkness. Aryl's fingers tightened. Few had her *reach,* whispered something inside.

Everyone knew it was wrong to try and contact those on Passage. They were gone to whatever fate awaited them, as good as dead. A Clan must rally around those left and ready a welcome for any who might arrive, though without Choosers to send their call of longing, Yena would see no strangers this M'hir.

Aryl rubbed her cheek against the cloth. Who would want a stranger?

Was it wrong to try? After all, it couldn't be done. Once away from the grove, the unChosen were beyond a sending. Weren't they?

Few had her *reach*.

And heart-kin shared a bond, the closest possible other than mother/child or between those Joined. She had only to listen to her inner sense—*there!* Aryl's head snapped left and up. He was there. The others were flickers, as if seen at the corner of an eye, but Bern's mind was like the sun breaking through the canopy.

Maybe she could touch his thoughts if she—

Aryl stopped herself, remembering her mother's warning. The Adepts watched for Forbidden use of Power. She didn't know how, but it wasn't worth the risk.

She opened her hand and let the curtain fall in front of her face. With one finger, she traced the fold for a short distance.

Bern wasn't far, not yet.

Aryl went back to bed, her mind full of plans.

Chapter 10

BY MIDMORNING, THE SUN had become an enemy, this high in the canopy. Aryl's eyes ached from its unceasing brightness, and she sought shadowed branches as her road wherever possible. It was cooler there, too, however slightly. She could almost wish for the rains to hurry and start again. Almost.

Short-lived as always, the M'hir had diminished to a cantankerous trickster, no longer able to sound the Watchers, muttering to itself through the canopy. It blew in strong, fitful gusts that swept the sky clear of cloud and the air of moisture, then would abruptly die to a breeze—luring the incautious to trust slim branches. While she begrudged the time it took, Aryl kept to wide, strong stalks and those branches unlikely to sway.

She'd found three pods since entering the grove. One had been torn open and emptied. She'd let it drop, listening as it slithered and smacked through fronds until out of sight. The others were whole, hard, and promisingly plump. She'd put both in one of her harvester nets, left that hanging in the open from a straight, bare nekis branch. The nets were impregnated with a foul-tasting compound, the same one used to coat the undersides of bridges to slow rot. It wouldn't keep all potential thieves at bay while she was gone, but it would discourage most.

As she climbed, her eyes roved the greens and grays, hunting the rich brown of more pods. She was going in the right direction. The rastis in this grove, Teerac's, had been blown clean, their crowns barren tufts. Downwind lay a wide swathe with red wings draped forlornly over other growths, or waving from threads caught on thorns. It was as if the canopy had been decorated for a party, and then no one had come. Most of the pods were missing, lost below or taken by wastryls and other harvesters quicker to take advantage than Om'ray.

Still, she'd collected two, and the day wasn't over. Aryl found herself repeating her mother's words: "a pod's a fist of life." Somehow, they made her climb faster than ever before.

For it was a race. Once a pod cracked open to light, its seedlings would grow with incredible speed, sending fine rootlets through the soft dresel to digest and consume it. If a pod landed in shadow, it would stay closed and its contents quickly spoil.

Aryl had already encountered a third possibility: an intact-looking pod vigorously defended by a swarm of stingers, intent on drilling their way into its wealth. Aware they'd be as willing to drill into her, she'd given them a wide berth.

Only when she couldn't take another step without trembling did she hook one leg over a bare branch and rest—after checking the area carefully—with her back against a trunk. Dying nekis, free of leaves, were best for the long view; she'd discovered she couldn't tire of gazing into the light-touched expanse. She took slow, deep breaths, waiting for the burn in her legs and arms to subside. Thoughtfully, she pulled one of the wads of dresel wing she'd collected from her belt. The red material was torn and dirty, but smooth between her fingers.

It had flown, once.

The dull stone of mountains was behind her. Ahead, between canopy giants, was the line where the grove became something else: a deep textureless green broken by brilliant flashes of light. Costa—she put her lip between her teeth—Costa had said something about the Tikitik, sun, and water. This must be more of their holdings.

Bern would reach it soon.

Aryl tasted blood and steadied herself. He was making good time. He was alive. Three of those who'd left hadn't survived their first truenight, their presence in her mind gone; without reaching outward, she didn't know who. It was better, she decided, that way.

Except Bern. *Heart-kin.*

"What am I doing here?" she whispered, feeling the old trunk shudder as it resisted the M'hir's rude push. It might not fall this season or the next, but it would come down, making room for other growth. "I can't—"

Can't what? answered that something deep inside, something wild and rebellious that answered to the freedom of this world above the world. Patches of blue interrupted the grays and greens. Every so often, something would fly across them, disappearing, then reappearing. The canopy, the Lay Swamp? Nothing to such creatures.

While they trapped the Yena.

Aryl pulled a shred of bark free and let it go in the next gust. It soared, twisting and turning. She watched until it hit a frond and dropped, then looked up consideringly. "Should have a hat," she told herself.

Before moving on, she took careful sips from one of her water flasks but didn't bother to eat. She'd make do with less now, when she could satisfy her hunger easily; later she might not.

Her eyes hunted the best path. Vines promised an easy swing to the next major stalk, but no Om'ray would trust that road. An assortment of creatures relied on ambush, let alone vines with resins or hidden spines to trap the unwary.

There were, Aryl knew, many ways to become what satisfied something else's hunger.

Any horizontal branch that could hold her weight bore its own more permanent guests. Aryl stepped over those low growths she knew were safe, avoiding *thickles* and their white-tipped thorns. Touch a leaf or thorn, and those weapons were launched in a wide arch. Their poison was more nuisance than threat to a body her size, but Aryl wasn't fond of pulling pointed objects from her skin at the best of times.

When her way was blocked by an exceptionally large thickle, she cut it free from the branch with her longknife and sent it toppling.

She found her next pod a tenth or so later, glimpsing its red brown stuck within another familiar cluster of thorns. That protection had likely kept a flitter or other creature from taking her prize.

After carefully prodding the pod free with her longknife, and taking a few thorns in her arm wrappings for the effort—her mother's ability to *push* objects, however Forbidden, would have been handy—Aryl managed to get it on the branch with her. She bent forward eagerly, only to stop in surprise.

The pod was empty after all. It had been neatly sliced open, like any left on a counter after a meal.

She spotted a small trace of purple inside. Absently, she freed it with a fingertip, then savored the taste on her tongue. It hadn't been exposed to air long. She was catching up.

Of course she was. She'd beaten Bern every time he'd challenged her.

Aryl stood, balancing on the moving branch with ease. Her eyes flicked past vegetation, shadows, bars of light; ignoring the normal, wary of threats. "What am I doing here?" she asked herself again.

She could feel Yena, the pull of minds that marked home. Returning was always faster—she'd learned the path, though she must be wary of those who'd remember her, too, and lie in wait.

If she turned back soon, she'd be home in daylight. She'd be a success, with two pods to show.

Dried and carefully shared, they would carry Yena two fists closer to the next M'hir.

Bern would leave the Om'ray's portion of the grove soon; she couldn't catch him before truenight.

There was a glow in her pack. No one traveled without that deterrent to night hunters—though what protection a small light could afford was open to question.

Her blood quickened. Was she willing to find out?

Urges buffeted her like gusts of wind—constant pushes to follow that each time died away, leaving her confused.

Aryl took a step, then another. She stopped and looked down, startled to find her feet making a decision. "What if he doesn't want me?" she asked them.

The childish part of her knew that wouldn't matter, that if she caught up to him, and it was too late for her to safely turn back, he'd take care of her; knew that if she insisted on following, he'd keep her close. That was Bern Teerac.

Not because they were heart-kin, she realized with a jolt. But because he was older. Because he knew Om'ray took care of their own.

Standing there, between swamp and sky, Aryl found herself accepting the truth at last. The person she'd clung to as friend and playmate would never be more. "I suppose that makes me older," she told the sleepy aspird hanging overhead.

She had to take care of her own.

"Time to go." Aryl swung around to retrace her steps and burst out laughing.

There, hanging in a familiar net, were four plump pods. They'd been hidden from the other direction by a bent frond.

A parting gift and a message she couldn't mistake.

"Oh, sure," she complained as if Bern could hear, wiping moisture from one eye even as she smiled. "Make me carry them home."

Interlude

THE DRUMS HADN'T LIED. The Oud came down the street with ponderous grace, chased by the long shadows of the setting sun. They were also pursued by clouds of brainless, winged things, brown and the size of a child's fist, that whirred and clicked through the trails of dust. Pest or sycophant, they appeared when the Oud appeared. No Om'ray knew why or cared; they were merely grateful the noisy creatures left with the Oud as well.

There were three Oud this time; not an unusual number, though most often only their Speaker made the arduous journey from the access tunnel to officially pay a visit to the Tuana Om'ray.

These three traveled one behind the other, a procession necessary since the main street of the village wasn't wide enough for two of their massive vehicles, not if shopkeepers were to keep their windows intact. Slow, steady, and methodical, the treads of their machines grinding, the Oud would eventually reach the meeting hall where the formalities of Visitation would take place. Along the way, however, they were prone to stop where and for how long they deemed necessary. On rare occasions, an Oud would heave its bulk from the flat top of its carrier and enter whatever building it chose.

They didn't ask permission; there was no need.

The Tuana Om'ray kept their distance. Those not watching from the doors of businesses or homes waited with Council in the hall. Only those unable to stand—or otherwise confined to the Cloisters—were excused from this duty. Their names were inscribed on a list.

The Oud were also prone to keeping count.

Standing with his father in the shop doorway, Enris shared the unease of his Clan as their visitors approached. Some of it was simple distaste. The Oud were unpleasant at best; Worin described them as uncooked dumplings and that, in Enris' opinion, was being kind. Their rotund bodies were long and tapered to points at front and rear; the flesh beneath their garb moved as though soft. That garb, featureless and faded brown, more resembled a tent or wrapping over a cart's contents than clothing. It covered every part of the Oud's body, save for a transparent dome over the front end. For convenience, the Tuana assumed that was the head, though there were no visible features to prove it.

Oud had an uncounted number of limbs under their bodies, of varied shape and function. Most supported the body's bulk, but to speak to Om'ray, an Oud must lift its "head" to expose a concentration of appendages. To Enris, these looked more like tools from his bench than parts of a living thing.

To complete the first impression, Oud smelled, at close range, like the spent oil from their own machines.

Far worse than their outward appearance, to Om'ray, was what could be sensed inwardly. The Oud had no self, no mind; they were nothing, bizarrely still able to form understandable words. This, the Tuana had learned to accept.

But once in a while, where an Oud's thoughts would be if they existed at all, was a *disturbance*. Touching it was painfully disorienting. Children would cry; Adepts be left incapacitated for the better part of a day.

This was why shields were locked in place; those most capable almost disappearing from the inner sight.

Did the Oud feel anything in return? Enris wondered, not for the first time. Were they uneasy outside their tunnels, watched by silent, unmoving Om'ray? Or did they enjoy the open air and the company of creatures with only two legs?

He had no idea how to tell.

The first vehicle passed them by, silent except for the crunch of tread. Whatever powered the machine was beyond the technology granted Om'ray. Enris felt a familiar frustration. He wanted a look; he knew better than to ask.

The second vehicle passed, the head covering of its rider coated in fine dust from the first. Enris hoped it didn't need to see to drive.

"You were right. We're in for it," his father whispered as the third and final vehicle slowed to a stop in front of their shop. Clouds of whirr/clicks settled with the dust around it, milling in dizzy circles and climbing over one another as if lost. Abruptly, they rose as one to follow the still-moving Oud.

Small mercies, Enris thought, having been ready to slam shut the door if the things tried to fly inside. Which, he realized wryly, would probably not be the welcome their visitor expected.

The Oud moved by humping its body in the middle, thus bringing its limbs into position to thrust it forward. Despite this awkward-seeming process, its size meant every thrust covered significant distance. Enris found himself half running to keep up as it entered the shop.

It stopped in the middle of the open floor, lifting its front to a position slightly higher than his head, thankfully not threatening the skylight. The two Om'ray stood before it and waited.

The creature used one appendage to brush off its head covering. The dust covered Enris' boots and he spared a moment to be glad he hadn't bothered trying to polish them. He fought a sneeze as he stared up at the Oud. He'd never been this close to one before.

"Metalworker." The voice was husky and low-pitched. It originated from the cluster of black moving limbs, but Enris, despite his proximity, couldn't find a mouth. "Metalworker are you." It wasn't a question. "Both are?"

That was.

Enris glanced at Jorg, who frowned, sending a message with his eyes. They had a problem. Any Om'ray could answer questions from the Oud Speaker.

This wasn't the Speaker. With the dust cleared, they would have seen the pendant affixed to the front of its "head." He could see the consternation in his father's face and almost let down his shields. Almost.

The Oud's limbs stilled except one, which tapped a rhythm against the joint of another, for all the world as if the creature fidgeted. "Both are?" it said after a moment.

Its body almost filled the shop. Enris was amazed it hadn't knocked into the benches on either side, but it did appear aware of where the rest of itself was. He tried without success to imagine a face within that oblong cluster of black fingers, claws, brushes, and what might be a sponge.

"Both are?" This louder, as if they were hard of hearing. It shifted back, cracking a support beam. "Both are?"

"Yes," Enris told it. He shrugged at his father. It was answer, or risk damage to the building.

"Goodgoodgoodgood." The body stilled again, but the tapping accelerated. "Metalworkers. Best are?"

Like a customer preparing to haggle, he thought, dumbfounded. "Yes."

"Goodgoodgoodgood." A small bundle wrapped in the same cloth as its body appeared at floor level, then was passed rapidly forward from limb to limb until it reached the cluster with the voice. "What is?" the Oud demanded, turning the thing around and around. "What is?"

"I can't see it like that," Enris protested.

The bundle was thrust at him.

He didn't need his inner sense to know Jorg was horrified. No Tuana engaged in direct trade with an Oud, if that's where this was going. Though having broken the conversational taboo, he found it worried him less to take the thing.

And he was curious.

Metal, by weight. He parted the wrapping, conscious of the huge creature's rapt attention, if perplexed how it could watch him without eyes.

Seeing what he held, Enris pursed his lips and whistled.

"What means?" The Oud reared, knocking its head on the skylight, which rattled but didn't break. "What means?"

"Don't be alarmed," Jorg said quickly, holding out his hands as if calming a child. "It's a sound of—of—" he faltered.

"Surprise." Enris lifted the object, holding it within its wrap. "This is—I've never seen anything like it. What does it do?"

"What is," agreed the Oud. "You best." Seemingly satisfied, the creature lowered itself to the floor. With a deft hump and thrust backward, its rear patently as adept at leading the way as its "head," the Oud left the shop.

When it was gone, Jorg came back. Enris had already laid the object on a turn plate on his bench and sat to examine it. He pulled a work light close.

"'What is,'" his father repeated, leaning over to take a look. "Does that mean what it's made of—or what it does?"

Enris grunted something noncommittal, busy making a sketch. The outward details were straightforward. The stubby cylinder, two hands long, was metallic, its golden surface brushed rather than shiny. A row of small indentations marked one side, with another, larger, on the opposite. Its inner workings were visible, a mosaic of tiny crystals, but not by intent. "See here?" He indicated the ragged edges to that opening. "Some of the casing was removed by force—or broken."

Jorg spun the turn plate a quarter and adjusted the light. After a moment's inspection, he said, "Looks more as if it had been attached to something else, then snapped off."

"Have you seen anything like it?"

Bringing over a stool, his father sat beside him. "No. This metal—those crystals? It's not Oud."

"Or Tikitik." They traded somber looks. What had the Oud left them? "The work is incredible," Enris added, almost wistfully. Answering to impulse, he picked up the cylinder in one hand.

His fingers and thumb covered the indentations exactly.

"Impossible," Jorg whispered. "It can't be."

Enris raised his eyes to meet his father's.

This is Om'ray.

Chapter 11

THE BRIDGE CROSSING THE VAST spans within the Sarc grove had never looked so welcoming. Aryl lowered the nets to its wood slats before climbing down herself, vaguely pleased to be able to stand. She'd thought she'd known the limits of her body; training with Bern—competing, to be more honest—had spurred them both to wilder and more dangerous climbs.

This was different. She stretched, hissing between her teeth at the sharp aches that answered. Not far now. She picked up the nets with their precious contents, ignoring the pain of blisters under her gloves as she secured her grip.

Aryl counted the bridge slats touched by her shadow. Eight. If she wasn't quick, she'd be outside the Yena glows at firstnight. There would be sufficient light to see her way.

Just not enough to see what might be out for an early hunt.

"Faster it is," she told herself.

The bridge system through Sarc consisted of five major sections, each meeting at the greatest rastis of the grove, and three lesser, leading to nekis used for the Harvest. They were convenient passageways for more than Om'ray, and Aryl kept watch for anything not on two legs as she walked. She didn't bother with her hood, preferring to see her best. Biters were an accustomed torment, and there were fewer in the open, where the M'hir still stirred the air. The bridge swung gently underfoot, its soft creak no more than strong rope and wood welcoming her confident steps.

Until she started across the third span. Despite the need to hurry, Aryl found herself slowing, her free hand seeking the rope rail. She looked up and saw only the undersides of fronds and branches, the tips of hanging vines, but she knew.

Here.

It had been here.

Involuntarily, she stopped, leaning to shift some of the pods' awkward weight from her shoulder to a hip.

And below.

She wouldn't look down. That much grace she gave herself, in this place where Bern had stood to watch Costa and the others fall to their deaths.

Where she'd *sent* him.

The wood was improbably solid underfoot; the braided rope taut under her fingers. It might have been a dream, except for the lives lost that day and threatened now.

Except for the Dark. Aryl could *see* if she looked just so, a *place* that billowed and surged and snapped as if the M'hir had wings of its own . . .

. . . Like the great wind, the Dark had no boundaries, only irresistible force. Like the M'hir, it stole the breath from her mouth and hammered against her skin until . . .

Aryl shuddered and blinked herself free.

Free of what?

Her fingers still gripped the rope, the knuckles white. The grove filled her nostrils when she inhaled, redolent of ripe fruit and rot. She hadn't gone anywhere.

Had she?

"Enough," she told herself, letting go. It had been a long day. Her body said so; as for the rest—the less thinking about that the better.

If all this was her fault, Aryl vowed, the only way to atone was to stay away from the Dark and, she gave the nets a settling heave, help those she still could.

The lights of Yena were in sight between the stalks, the inner glow of her kind a magnet, when Aryl first heard the sound.

No, she decided, stepping into a shadow and holding still. She'd heard it before, when she'd stopped on the bridge within the grove. The canopy was a noisy place, day or truenight; experienced climbers learned to ignore what wasn't a threat. But hearing it again, she knew what it was.

The hissing Tikitik made to one another.

Sound bounced from wood, softened against frond, carried over water. It was why Om'ray Scouts and Harvesters relied on mindspeech. Aryl listened as intently as she could, but over the ambient squawks, whirrs, and buzzing, couldn't make out a direction. Not close, she thought, unless the faintness was an effort to speak quietly because they were close.

Which meant they could be right below her.

Aryl felt the weight of the pods on her shoulder. Her mother had warned her not to let the Tikitik know. They'd demand their share of what she held, that at least. Or they could want it all. She didn't know or care what they used dresel for—she only knew they couldn't have what she'd carried all this way, what Bern had left.

Six fists of life.

Weary and sore, she assessed her options. There was the path ahead, the one she'd planned to take. Straight along the wide bridge, around the platform ringing the next rastis, down the ladder to this end of the village bridge, from there, a handful of steps to where the glows marked safety. There might be a Scout on the platform, certainly one at the ladder's base. At truenight, once all Yena were safe, they would remove several rungs and replace them with false steps, some coated with poison and spikes, others weakened to the breaking point. No friend to Om'ray climbed in the dark.

If she took that straightforward route, she'd be walking over the platform and dock—and be visible from the waters of the Lay below. She had time yet, Aryl decided, to take another way home.

Taisal di Sarc had never remarked on her daughter's constant climbing, except to insist on a tidy and prompt appearance at supper; Costa, well, he'd had her pick plants for him he couldn't reach on his own. But the Teeracs, Aryl remembered vividly, had taken a dim view of their eldest son, as they put it, chasing that Sarc scamp through the canopy when he should have been learning to braid rope like his kin.

To be fair, she hadn't been the problem; Bern didn't like braiding rope.

Or anything else that involved sitting still for five breaths, unless it was to eat. His parents had been forced to make Bern promise not to walk the bridge from their house until he did his share of the work.

He'd braided for a full day and his parents had been cautiously happy. They were less amused when they discovered this diligence had produced a rope ladder that Aryl secured to a branch over their home so Bern could leave without breaking his word.

They'd eventually given up. Bern had eventually become dutiful enough to braid every day, at least until Aryl climbed down the ladder to wave through his window. A ladder that still waited, wrapped in toxin-soaked cloth.

As she left the bridge and climbed the rastis itself, Aryl half smiled. Even Bern's parents had grudgingly admitted they were perfect for each other.

Had been perfect.

Feeling empty, Aryl moved as quietly as she could with the nets. She crossed between rastis by balancing on their overlapped fronds. A child's trick, not without risk. Old fronds could crack at their base from the main stalk, young ones were supple and bent unpredictably under the weight of an adult-sized Om'ray. Especially—she staggered once and caught herself—one carrying an extra burden. But she couldn't be seen from below and there were more reasons than a daring Om'ray for a frond to sway, including the M'hir.

Firstnight had arrived, the sunlight now diffuse and rapidly losing to lengthening shadows. As she climbed, well above the Yena rooftops, spots of warm yellow light peeked through openings between the fronds. Their glow turned the world upside down, as if she walked with her feet to the sky. She fought the disorienting sensation as much as the gloom. This path was as familiar as the floor of her bedroom.

Of course, now she had a new one, Aryl told herself, forced to slow her steps to keep her direction as everything turned dim and strange.

She started as something soft and unseen brushed her face. A nightflier. Harmless, but something had flushed it from its perch.

She didn't want to know what.

Truenight was almost upon her by the time Aryl reached the ladder. With feverish haste, she tore off its wrappings and tossed them aside. The braided rope had held Bern; she had to trust it could support her plus her load. There wouldn't be time to lower the pods first.

The steady splashes from the Lay below gave warning—the hunters were out and on the rise, tracking by scent and heat. She could hear their stealthy, clattering movement on every side, claws digging in as they climbed, muted clicks as they shoved one another for best advantage. No screams rent the air yet. They would soon. These hunters killed by eating their prey, swarming in such numbers they fought each other for room to bite.

No swarm would eat her, Aryl vowed. She pushed the ladder over the branch, starting to descend before it finished unrolling. The weight of the nets made her unbalanced, threw the ladder into a swing. She didn't falter, hands and feet flying from grip to grip. She not only had to get herself down, she had to make sure this ladder wasn't left as a road for what pursued.

She let go at the third last rung, landing on her toes, unable to believe she'd made it. Shrugging off the nets, she grabbed the retriever cord twisting in the air beside the ladder. With both hands, leaning her whole body into the pull, she drew the ladder back up to its resting place. Release and pull. Release and pull. Om'ray ladders were meant to be removed; Bern had known his craft, however much he detested it. One more. There.

Out of habit, Aryl bundled the loose cord and tossed it over that very convenient frond above the Teeracs' roof. She spotted a cluster of Om'ray running in her direction and raised a weary hand in salute.

She didn't move at once. Her body wasn't inclined to do anything beyond taking deep, shuddering gasps, now that she was safe.

Safe. Her mouth twisted. Here, on this bridge in the midst of well-lit and protected homes, encompassed by the inner warmth of her kind, she could close her eyes without fear and breathe, imagine cleaning the sweat and dust from her skin and hair, plan supper. Sink into sleep.

While Bern and the others remained out there, alone.

They'd each huddle over a glow for truenight, their bodies

wedged between branches as high as they could climb. They wouldn't dare sleep until dawn, though the Lay's hunters rarely ventured into the sparse open growth of the upper canopy. There were other dangers, things that flew over the rastis crowns by starlight, hunting the hunters. Things that wouldn't mind plucking a careless Om'ray from his perch.

Council had sent them on Passage; she'd felt their grief. The Tikitik had made it impossible to do otherwise; she couldn't blame them for needing dresel, too.

Whoever sent that device to spy on their Harvest, she thought, that's who was responsible. Aryl felt a sudden fierce anger, deeper than any she'd felt before.

It lacked only a face.

She picked up the nets and went to meet her welcomers.

Chapter 12

"SIX PODS. ALL BY YOURSELF."

Aryl nodded, again, doing her best not to slouch. The pods in question had been taken immediately, their precious dresel to be dried and stored—most within the security of the Cloisters. She, on the other hand, had made it only these few steps from the sorting table toward the meeting hall door. The door through which she had to pass to go home. Her skin itched from bites and thorns, her muscles ached with fatigue, but none of these were as taxing, she discovered, as trying to keep her temper.

Evra and Barit sud Teerac, Bern's parents, made no such effort. They blocked her exit, their angry voices collecting more than a few looks of disapproval from those working here. It wasn't Om'ray to confront one another. It wasn't Om'ray to shout either.

They'd lost their only son. Aryl found a little more patience.

"Did you steal these from Bern?" Evra demanded, again. "Leave him to starve?"

So much for patience. She straightened with a jerk. "I told you—I found them—"

"Don't lie!!!! You followed him!" thundered Barit. He raised the net in his callused hand and shook it in her face. "We made this for Bern. Did you think we wouldn't recognize it?"

At this, Haxel Vendan broke away from the discussion she was having with two of her weary scouts to stride over to them. When the First Scout scowled, it twisted the deep puckered scar that ran from her left brow to the corner of her wide mouth, a reminder that she was one of the few Om'ray to survive a stitler trap. She was scowling now. "What's going on here?"

"Aryl's obsession with our son!" Usually placid, Barit's face was flushed and his mouth worked between the words. "She put his Passage at risk—"

"She's no Chooser," Evra broke in, her contempt slamming against Aryl's shields. "She'll never be. Look at her. Pretending to be adult, as if this is some new game. Any proper Om'ray would have matured by now." At the appalled hush around her, she paled, but stumbled on. "Everyone knows it. Being the Speaker's daughter doesn't give her the right to destroy our son's chance for happiness."

How could Bern's mother believe that? Aryl felt the words like a blow. How could anyone? She tried not to hear the sendings speeding through the hall: *thief . . . violator . . . how dare she! . . . Forbidden.*

Haxel sketched a gesture of appeasement, the movement of her hand brusque and almost impolite. "Control yourselves," she ordered. "Aryl," almost gently. "The truth, now. How did you get this net? Did you find Bern's body?"

Evra gasped and whirled to press her face against Barit's chest. He glared at the First Scout, his arms around his Chosen. "Our son isn't dead! Ask her!"

Haxel turned to Aryl. "Well?" Pursing her lips whitened the scar.

There were over thirty now-silent Om'ray standing or sitting in the meeting hall. None were working, too intent on the unaccustomed scene. Anything she said would be heard by everyone here; shortly after, by everyone else. The only choice was the truth.

Her heart hurt.

"I picked Teerac grove to search for pods. I did find two there, but that's not the only reason I—I went," she confessed. Barit and Evra glared at her and Aryl shook her head. "Not to stop him," she protested. "I knew Bern would travel through his family grove one last time. He—I—I just wanted to spend time where he'd been, that's all. Bern must have known I would. I believe he left the pods for me to find. Yena needed them, and he trusted me." The thought made her smile.

"Nonsense," Evra snorted, pulling free of her Chosen. "Bern's on Passage to his Chooser. Why would he think about you?"

"I'm sorry you've never approved of me or our friendship," Aryl said, weary beyond caution, "but we were friends. Dear friends. I would have gladly been more. I would follow Bern Teerac across the world, if I believed it could be. But it can't. My place is here, helping Yena survive. I don't know what else I can say."

Haxel nodded, as if this confirmed something she knew. She faced the Teeracs and gestured gratitude. "Yena thanks your son for his gift." The gesture was repeated by everyone present, including Aryl. Then the First Scout fixed her difficult-to-meet gaze on Barit and Evra. "Without Aryl, his gift would have fed flitters instead of Om'ray. Remember that, if you ever again think less of their friendship, or her skills as an adult."

Glows vanquished truenight's terrors, or at least held them at a forgettable distance. Aryl walked the bridge to her home, that safety lulling her into a pleasant numbness. The day's triumph, the Teeracs' accusation, Haxel's unexpected intervention—she let it all fade to a blur. None of it mattered as much as rest.

When other footsteps matched hers from behind, she *reached* to sense the First Scout and hoped it was coincidence. Haxel could be on her nightly rounds. There wouldn't be anything further asked of her now, especially conversation. She'd be lucky to make it to her bed without falling face first on the floor. Finding something to eat? Taking off her filthy arm and leg wraps? She couldn't imagine that effort.

Once at her door, she unlatched and turned the panel, hand almost trembling.

"Aryl Sarc."

Groaning inside, she looked around. "Yes, First Scout?"

"Could we talk?" Haxel walked through the opening without waiting for an answer.

Holding in a sigh, Aryl followed and closed the door.

Haxel stopped by the long Sarc table, her eyes sweeping her surroundings as if she checked for an escape route. "You're here on your own." Her shields were impeccable; her voice revealed even less.

With an arm that protested the motion, Aryl pulled down a sling chair. She motioned to another. "For now," she nodded. "My mother's sister and her Chosen may join me soon." She eased her body into the chair; the relief of sitting made her close her eyes for an instant.

"This won't take long." Haxel had her hand on the chair rope, but didn't pull it. Instead, she studied Aryl. "Few Om'ray climb with your skill."

"Then why wasn't I selected for the Harvest?" The accusation—for that's how it sounded even to Aryl's ears, startled them both. She gestured apology at once. It had to be the exhaustion. "Forgive me, First Scout. I meant no disrespect."

"You know your strengths. That's good." Haxel frowned

slightly, the scar twisting her brow. "I did select you. Council overruled me."

"What?" Aryl leaned forward, holding the chair still with her toes on the floor. "Why?"

Haxel pulled down her chair at last, sitting with care as if she distrusted the sling. Or, Aryl thought, was more used to branches than civilized furniture. "I believe they chose not to risk your special Talent," the First Scout said. "I find I agree."

"What Talent?" Aryl asked in her best "who me?" voice, the one that had worked, most of the time, to shift blame to her brother. With luck, her face was too dirty and swollen with bites to show her dismay.

"You played with my nephews." Haxel gave a thin smile. "I'm curious, Aryl. Do you always know who an Om'ray is? Or does it take conscious use of your Power to identify someone?"

That was why she'd been passed over? Her outrage faded as Aryl thought of Taisal and the sweetberries. Another small and harmless—even useful—Talent; her mother, afraid to be caught using it outside the Cloisters.

Was Haxel one of the careless Yena her mother and other Adepts feared?

"I cheated at seek," Aryl said calmly. "Better than some of the others. That's all."

Haxel raised one eyebrow, the scar resisting. "Then why did Council overrule me?"

Easy to sound petulant. "Taisal didn't want me to go. Maybe they listened to her. She said I was too young, the Harvest too dangerous. Mothers are like that." Not hers—Taisal had alternately encouraged and ignored her adventures—but Haxel wasn't to know.

She wasn't someone to underestimate either. First Scout was a position of merit. No Om'ray climbed with Haxel Vendan's skill, none approached her ability as a tracker and hunter. Yena slept well at night because of the rigor with which she trained those she chose for scout duty. No fool studied Aryl through those narrowed eyes.

She checked her shields and smiled back. "Was there anything else, First Scout?"

"Yes. I want you to join us."

"Me?" Aryl echoed, her voice cracking on the word. For a moment, she actually considered it. Scouts were the most disciplined of Om'ray, responsible for the protection and defense of Yena. Superb climbers all, they built and maintained the bridges and ladders that made movement through the canopy safe for every Om'ray.

Only a child thought it a glamorous life, she thought. The reality was mapped in scars like those on Haxel's face. When a scout did his or her job well, no one noticed. That part, Aryl found unexpectedly appealing.

What did it say about her?

"I'm not old enough," she evaded desperately. "I don't know how to track or build." Aryl frowned to herself, unhappy with that list. What was she to do? Be the Speaker's daughter until Choice? Become an Adept and leave freedom behind?

She hadn't expected to need those answers so soon.

Haxel's lips quirked to the side. It wasn't a smile. "Scouts were lost in the Harvest. Most of those training with me left on Passage. Council will allow me any recruit I can find, believe me. Your ability—to cheat at seek, that is—could be useful." She hadn't fooled the older Om'ray for an instant, Aryl realized with a shiver. Suddenly they were playing an adult game, where you used words because you didn't dare share thoughts and the truth.

"How?"

"Council's sending everyone who can climb and carry with us to gather whatever we find that's edible. I can't argue—" from her sour tone, Aryl guessed she'd tried, "—the rains are coming. By tomorrow I could have fifty such helpers scattered through a grove, a quarter barely able to *send* beyond their noses. You could help me keep track of them. Know who's heading toward trouble; who's close enough to help." Haxel lifted a callused finger lacking a nail and drew a short line in the air.

Aryl chewed her lower lip for a moment. The First Scout waited, her eyes hooded, her shields as solid as before. She knew the Agreement forbade change that might be noticed—which meant new Talents. Everyone did. The difference, Aryl decided, was that Haxel didn't care—not when that Talent could offer an advantage.

Adult games. She could play them too. Aryl stood and swept her hands in the gesture of gratitude. Her mother used it regularly to end a discussion. "Thank you, First Scout. I will keep your offer in mind. Be well."

The other rose, too. There were courtesies when visiting another's home; departing when told was one. "As I'll keep you in mind, Aryl Sarc," Haxel said with a nod, then pulled her gauze over head and face. "Thank you for your time."

After she closed and latched the door behind her visitor, Aryl listened to her heart pound. There was no reason to feel she'd just made the narrowest escape of the day, here, in her own home. No reason, she scolded herself. Being a scout was an honorable profession; better suited to her solitary nature, she admitted, than most. Yet . . .

It was the *taste*, she realized. Something was about to change. When she'd first sensed it, she'd assumed it meant the arrival of the M'hir Wind, then the disaster of the Harvest. Maybe even Bern's leaving on Passage.

But the feeling had never left. It lingered, deep inside, as real as the glowlight making its way through her windows and as hard to hold in her hands.

There was worse to come, Aryl shuddered.

Now she feared it would come from within the Om'ray, not without.

After a night and a half's sleep, broken only when Aryl woke long enough to fumble out of her filthy clothing before plunging back on the mattress, the ominous warning in her mind seemed . . .

"Nonsense," she assured a nodding flower. "I was overtired. People weren't letting me rest. I ask you—was that nice, considering all the pods I brought home?"

The flower wisely kept silent. Aryl finished pouring water into its pot, careful not to let it overflow on the floor—not that Costa's floor was in any shape to care—and looked around for more to do.

Leaves on some of the plants were withered and pale. She wasn't sure they were dead. After all, her brother would hover protectively over desiccated sticks, claiming they would grow. To be on the safe side, Aryl poured water into every container she could find.

She wrinkled her nose when done. It hadn't improved the smell.

Now what? Her muscles were too sore to trust with another climb this soon. She'd washed her skin and hair, using the same water to soak her wraps. For the moment, she wore only a knee-length shift, loose and comfortable. Breakfast had been slivers of dried fruit, quick and easy to eat with fingers. No dishes, she thought with satisfaction.

The sweetberry vine had conquered one window gauze and was making a concerted effort to reach the nearest rafter, tendrils waving in the air. A gleam of red between its toothy leaves caught her eye. A last few berries. About to pick them, Aryl withdrew her hand.

It hadn't been her imagination.

Something *was* wrong.

Haxel's position as First Scout didn't make her the Speaker's peer. Nor, Aryl realized, did it give her the right to summarily dismiss a Council decision in front of the Speaker's daughter. Om'ray could argue and disagree—she and Bern had fought constantly—but never about matters of Power or its use. Never about what Council declared best for all.

Haxel wanted Aryl to use her Talent—despite it being secret, despite no Council permission for its use. It hadn't seemed to matter that she'd no proof the gift was real, she'd wanted it. The First Scout must have realized Aryl would tell her mother—she hadn't said anything to stop her. It was as if she wanted Taisal to know. Why?

Aryl touched a sweetberry with her fingertip. She'd never paid attention to relationships between her elders, other than knowing who was a close enough relative to require her to do dishes during a visit and whose conversations could keep her mother preoccupied so she could slip away and climb with Bern.

All of Yena were relatives, of course. The six families crossed and blended with one another based on Choice alone, though it was rare an Om'ray was called to Join with anyone closer than a full cousin. Those who arrived on Passage brought new blood, their stranger names left behind at Choice, "sud" to a Yena Chooser. Adepts made their cryptic records of births, part of their duty to the Cloisters and Council. Presumably there was a reason, though the only record most cared about was who was Chosen first, since the First Chosen in a family took over the household responsibilities—and the home itself.

Aryl had only a dim idea of how Haxel Vendan might be related to Taisal. There were, she decided, tugging the berry free, a few Uruus and probably a Teerac between.

But they were close in age. She was struck by a novel

thought. With few young Yena each generation, Haxel and Taisal must have played together, like she had with Seru, Bern, and others of their age. Climb and seek in the canopy. Giggles and secrets.

They might not be friends now; they had to know each other well, nonetheless.

Aryl tossed the berry on the floor and watched it roll. Did Haxel know about Taisal's Forbidden Talent? Was all this to send her mother a message—that the First Scout rejected the Council's restrictions and wanted the Speaker's support?

Having clean knees, she left the berry where it was and picked another to pop into her mouth. The sweet tang burst against her tongue.

Support to do what? Aryl shook her head, feeling as though she climbed a ladder made of threads, not wood. The Chosen were supposed to worry about such things. That's why they had wrinkles. The thought made her run a palm over one smooth cheek and she grinned. None yet.

The grin faded. She was young, not stupid. What she'd done to save Bern was of an entirely different order than *pushing* a berry or sensing identity. She didn't want to do it again—ever—but that wasn't the point.

Taisal feared her revealing this Talent above all. Aryl found herself wondering if her mother was more afraid of the Tikitik learning of it—or other Yena like Haxel?

She rubbed cold arms and went in search of warmer clothes.

There was nothing she could do about the chill in her heart.

Interlude

THEY RAN OUT OF TIME before questions, and Enris reluctantly locked the object away in a hidden cupboard only he and his parents knew existed. Locking it out of sight, if not from his thoughts.

Om'ray technology to rival that of the Oud and the Tikitik?

What did it mean? How was it even possible?

"Don't drag your feet, Enris," Jorg said from the door. "They'll have other business first—you know our current Council—but the Speaker will read the roll of unChosen soon. You don't want to miss it."

Enris froze in place. "Me? Why me?"

His father smiled gently. "Because you're finally ready. Did you think your mother couldn't tell?"

Yes, since he couldn't, Enris grumbled inwardly. He didn't doubt Ridersel's ability—but shouldn't he be the first to know? Feel different? Care about Choice more than the puzzle locked in that cupboard and burning in his mind?

"Come, come. This harvest's Choosers-to-Be will be named as well."

Giddy cousins, noxious neighbors, and dull little strips—to become Choosers, the most desirable of their kind?

One of them to intrude on his time in the shop?

Aghast at the mere notion, Enris followed Jorg out the door, waiting while he locked and checked it, trailing behind all the way to the meeting hall. Like his father, he avoided stepping in the tread marks from the Oud.

Unlike his father, he wasn't in a hurry. His mind had stuck at "eligible." Shouldn't that be up to him?

In too few steps, the meeting hall was in sight. Like the other buildings lining the Tuana's main street, it had been made from materials at hand—a cobbling of salvaged tunnel wood, scrap metal, and flat bricks made from a mix of local sand and *surry*, a syrup refined from *nost* peelings that dried clear and hard and impenetrable.

And, like the other buildings, Enris thought with pride, the hall had been built with care and an eye for beauty. The sunset's glow reflected from intricate brickwork that both bound the structure to the earth and rose past each corner to touch the darkening sky. Precious wood, rich with carving and hand-polished to gleaming smoothness, met the brick. Metal bands, scorched and strained to reveal rainbows of fantastic hues, formed curves and angles. Last, but not least, sheets of surry formed broad windows to admit light.

The Oud vehicles were lined up outside, their attendant whirr/clicks resting in uneven piles. Jorg was about to climb the steps to the open doorway when Enris stopped him with a hand on his arm.

"Wait," he pleaded.

Though Enris kept his shields tight, Jorg's smile faded as he looked at his son. "What's wrong?"

"Last Harvest. During the Visitation. Everyone seemed to know who they—they just knew."

Jorg looked relieved. "And you don't," this with a nod.

"Of course I don't!"

"Maybe—" a wink, "—someone inside does."

If his father had wanted Enris struck dumb, he couldn't have done better. Jorg seemed to realize it and made a gesture of apology. "It's harder for you," he said quietly. "That's my fault. I kept you working when you could have been making friends, getting to know the Choosers-to-Be. I didn't think."

"You didn't make me work," Enris protested. "I love the shop. You know that."

"I know. But while others were—" Jorg paused and shrugged. "What's done, or not, is done. Relax, Enris." His voice lightened, as if they discussed tomorrow's tasks. "It's only your first eligible Visitation. UnChosen often wait for their second or third before finding a Choice that suits."

Enris raised a dubious eyebrow. "How often is often?"

His father laughed. "I'm sure at least once before. Come on. Think of them as customers."

As they went inside, Enris shook his head. "Stop helping me," he half-joked. "Please."

* * *

The Tuana meeting hall, like those of other Clans, had started as a simple room, large enough to hold those in attendance. There had been some modifications. To safely host their visitors, the floor was now of metal-reinforced brick. To accommodate a steadily growing population, for Tuana was a prosperous Clan, stairlike seating had been added along its three windowless outer walls. Several times. Today, they sat crammed shoulder-to-shoulder, children in laps, and there was barely room on what floor remained for Council, the unChosen, and their guests.

Enris had heard talk of tearing down the back wall or removing the roof—anything to expand the space inside. According to Ridersel, similar schemes had been brought to Council in the past. All collided with Oud sensibilities. Other than the Cloisters, this was the largest building they would tolerate above ground. The Om'ray were welcome—even encouraged—to dig if they needed more room.

The Tuana Om'ray politely declined to enter the realm of the Oud, and pressed ever closer to their own kind.

Though shields were up, Enris felt the pull of so many together. He didn't need to look to see where the families were. There was a pattern, as old as the village, and only those who would be the focus tonight stood or sat elsewhere than expected. Jorg gave his shoulder a hearty pat before leaving to squeeze his way up two stairs to where Ridersel and Worin waited with the rest of Mendolar.

The three Oud were gray-brown hills in the middle of the open space. In front of them stood the Tuana Speaker, Sole sud Serona. Behind him stood the six who formed Tuana's Council, also resplendent in white, embroidered robes. One, Mendolar, leaned on two canes, but her bright eyes flicked to Enris as he passed, her lips pressed thin in disapproval.

Grandmother didn't miss much, he thought ruefully, hurrying out of range with what dignity he could.

Enris knew where he was to go. The lines of eligible unChosen, suddenly his fellows if he believed it, stood to the right of the door. He nodded a greeting to Ral, somehow not surprised to see his younger cousin; he deliberately looked past Mauro and Irm. The Lorimar brothers viewed themselves as above working with their hands, and enjoyed sneering at those who did—not that they didn't want the results for themselves. Just as well. Enris wouldn't trust either with a tool or the responsibility to use it.

The only place left to stand was in front and there was, of course, dust on his boots. He resisted the urge to comb his fingers through his hair. It was thick, black, and almost as unruly as—Enris stopped there.

The unChosen weren't the focus of the Visitation, not yet. The

Speaker was reading numbers—the yield lists, from the sound of it. Enris took a couple of deep breaths and tried to relax. It didn't work, though it gained him a sympathetic smile from his neighbor, Traud Licor. Traud was quiet and reserved; like Enris, he had little patience for the few their age who didn't earn their keep. The Licors were crop tenders, as were most on the stairs. Making those Traud's numbers, too, Enris thought, sure the other must be enjoying this moment. It had been, everyone knew, an exceptional growing season.

Traud leaned close. "Isn't she beautiful?" he whispered.

Not the numbers. Enris looked where he carefully hadn't to this point, at the assembly of potential Choosers: a blur of colorful beadwork and gauze, topped by improbable hair ornaments. "Who?" he had to ask.

"Olalla, of course."

Another cousin. "Lucky you," he said, grateful that shields were considered appropriate tonight. Olalla Mendolar, whatever her beauty to Traud, had crooked teeth and a tendency to hiccup when nervous. Which was, he recalled, most of the time. When she wasn't humming off key.

He couldn't think near someone like that, let alone work.

As for work, he thought, they'd have to be careful. He and Jorg had discussed the next step. Before anything drastic like removing crystals, they'd do more precise measurements and test the metal of the outer casing. They couldn't risk the object. They had to assume the Oud wanted it back, and in the same condition.

Which Oud had it been? Enris studied the creatures with new interest. The Speaker was obvious, centermost and facing—or the equivalent—its Om'ray counterpart. Its pendant was affixed to that end, anyway. It crouched in its front-end-up position, ready to talk in turn. The other two had their heads down.

Maybe they were bored.

Bored, he understood. He was bored. And anxious. And,

above all else, he didn't want to be here and they couldn't make him—

Traud glanced his way and Enris checked his shields for leaks. "Beautiful," he whispered quickly and was rewarded by a bemused smile.

Were all the other unChosen that hopeless?

Other than his location at its focus, this Visitation continued like all the others Enris could remember. Om'ray liked tradition; the Oud didn't like change. First came the good news: the amount of *nost* drying in racks; the number of fields freed of various scourges—the most repugnant plants had their pests and Tuana scouts were always busy while the crop ripened; lists of those born and their immediate relations; lists naming those arrived on Passage and any others Joined since the last Visitation—which always produced a rumble of approval from the assembled Om'ray, though Enris doubted the Oud cared; and so on. There would be lists of the productivity of various trades, his and Jorg's shop among them. In short, all that had been improved by their village's existence.

After that came lists related to the village's impact on the Oud. The area of land used to grow food for Om'ray; the amount of that food harvested; the number of warehouses required. The number of power cells consumed and glows to be replaced; the quantity of other supplies used, from water to cooking oil. The number of blades broken; accidents to equipment; damage to buildings.

And deaths. When their Speaker reached this list, the Tuana hushed and held their children. They were six hundred and sixteen strong this Visitation, their greatest number in memory. But there had been losses. It was a source of dismay, that the Oud wouldn't leave the dead in peace, though they didn't ask for names. They demanded cause, and the Tuana Speaker gave it, his voice flat and even. Ten lost to age. One found ravaged by nocturnal hunters in a field. A child succumbed to wasting fever. The worst—a Chosen who had died during childbirth, the final cost three lives.

Eryel S'udlaat and her unborn son, followed at once by her Chosen, Mirs sud S'udlaat. Mirs Eathem had come on Passage from Amna Clan, drawn across the world to Eryel's Call, entranced by her kindness and mirth.

Enris forced himself to look at the Choosers-to-Be. What would it be like? He tried to imagine being lured, to imagine finding his life's partner. He made the effort to imagine dying at the loss of his Chosen.

His imagination wasn't good enough, he decided. All he felt was queasy.

All too soon, it was time. The Oud Speaker had begun its statement on the balance between their two peoples, a fancy way of agreeing to supply its share of the predicted needs of the village for the coming seasons, be that power, water, or seed. The Oud had made those calculations while listening to the Om'ray Speaker. It was always accurate, if never overgenerous. A cagey but reputable customer, as his father would put it.

Soon would come the moment Enris dreaded. With the Oud as witness, the Speaker would reveal those eligible unChosen who'd asked to take Passage and been judged fit by Council to do so. Next, he'd announce those who would be Choosers before the next Visitation. There was, Ridersel had told her sons privately, a fair amount of guesswork involved in the matter, but it let official courting begin.

Last, and most unnerving, in Enris' opinion, would be the naming of those already committed to one another, to the joy of all present. The resulting swell of emotion pouring from mind-to-mind had been known to inspire otherwise sane unChosen to bolt across the open floor and fall on their knees in a fit of suddenly discovered passion.

That was not, he assured himself after another wary glance at the crowd of costumed gigglers, going to be him.

Startled dismay flooded Enris' mind. What had the Oud just said? He'd stopped paying attention.

Apparently, he wasn't the only one who needed to hear it twice. "What did you say?" asked Sole, their Speaker. In no pleasant tone either.

"Too many," this with emphasis. "Send away."

"Our Council decides who takes Passage."

"Who decides Om'ray. More decides Oud." It nudged the creature on its right. "More tokens we. Decide who."

From the anxious murmurs behind him, Enris wasn't the only one taken aback. What was happening? He looked for his family on the stairs, found his father first. Jorg gave a helpless shrug. Ridersel was holding Worin so tightly he should have been squirming. Instead, the youngster stared down at his brother, his face the color of ash.

"Decide who!" This louder, with that abrupt, agitated body shift Enris remembered all too well.

Sole was an intimidating figure, well suited to his role, but now he seemed fragile. He glanced back at the Council members as if for help; they looked equally shocked. Turning back to his counterpart, he gave a slow nod. "We will, " he told the Oud. "But we need time—"

"Decide who! Tokens we!" This with a hard shove against the one next to it.

As if the blow was a signal, the abused Oud humped toward the assembly of potential Choosers.

Every Om'ray rose to their feet with a shout, outrage surging from mind to mind. Enris found he'd taken a step forward with the unChosen, his hands now fists.

"What are you doing?" Sole shouted. "Those are Choosers! Get away from them!"

The Oud might not be able to tell Om'ray apart, but it understood the shout. It immediately humped backward until Enris was staring at its dusty rear. Then it turned in place, little feet drumming rapidly against the brick, and stopped. It rose to speak. "These are?"

It looked and sounded like the one in the shop. But he couldn't tell them apart either.

"Decide who!" bellowed the Oud Speaker, thrashing its body from side to side twice. The Om'ray on the floor scrambled to get as far away as they could, which wasn't far. Some climbed the stairs, helped by family.

The other Oud endured what had to be bruising contact without moving.

Hear me, Tuana! The sending from their Speaker quieted the room. Sole bowed to Council before coming to stand before the unChosen. His face was pale and set. After a moment, he bowed to them, a respect that dried Enris' mouth.

The Speaker moved along the front line of unChosen, his gaze touching each in turn. The silence in the great room was so profound Enris feared the pounding of his heart could be heard.

Sole sud Serona paused before Irm, then spoke at last.

"Irm Lorimar shall take Passage."

The waiting Oud rose slightly higher. Its limbs rushed in the tidy waves Enris remembered to ferry an assortment of packages from underneath itself. Most were immediately carried back down in a reverse flow almost too quick to see. Sorting through its pockets, Enris thought wildly. Too many packages were caught by limbs near its head and held ready. How many of them had to leave?

Tuana sent at most three or four on Passage, always those who, like Kiric, had petitioned to find Choice outside their village. Everyone knew who they were. There was time to prepare, for farewells.

It wasn't done like this, not by ambush in front of their families.

Sole took a package from the Oud, opening it to reveal a metal disk. Though smaller and plain, the style resembled that of the pendant around his neck and the one affixed to the Oud Speaker's head.

Sole fastened it to Irm's tunic. "Receive this token, that you may Pass unhindered to Choice. Find joy."

The unChosen looked ready to faint. Mauro, his brother, didn't hide his relief when the Speaker moved past him.

Next to receive a token was the eldest son of Serona, who smiled and tipped the disk in his hand to admire it. Obviously, one of those who'd asked for this fate.

When his turn came, Enris tilted his chin, prepared, he thought, for anything.

He wasn't prepared for the grief in Sole's eyes; his own widened in response. It couldn't be . . .

"Enris Mendolar. Receive this—"

The Oud, showing unexpected reach and quickness, snatched back the token. "Decide other."

The Tuana Speaker's mouth worked without sound for a moment. He looked from Enris to the Oud and then back. "We decide," he said.

"Yes. Decide other." The black claw thrust the token at Traud, who frantically backed into those standing behind him to avoid it. There was a faint squeal from the area of the Choosers. "Decide this."

"No!" Enris protested and grabbed the token. It was cold and hard. He closed his fist over it and stared up at the Oud. "I'll go."

"Stop! All of you!" The now-livid Tuana Speaker brushed a hand over his pendant, as if to remind himself and them of his rank. Enris could sense the Power he used to shield his thoughts—which was, he decided, just as well. "You make a mockery of our ways," Sole said to the Oud, his tone nothing less than forbidding. "And you—" only fractionally milder to Enris, "—remember who speaks for Tuana." To Traud, who had resumed his position, shaking so hard Enris could feel it. "Your Chooser awaits you here," still with that edge.

Back to the Oud. "We decide who."

The creature was unimpressed. "Metalworker this. Decide other."

Sole drew himself to full height. "No."

The remaining tokens began a rapid journey back down its limbs. "Decide none. Goodgoodgoodgood."

Enris wasn't sure what that meant. From his frown, neither was Sole. The Oud Speaker rested its head on the brick floor, either lacking an opinion or deferring to what they'd all assumed was a servant.

Servant, Enris wondered, or had the Oud brought their version of Council?

This had to be the Oud who'd come to the shop.

And the object it had brought was somehow worth risking the Agreement between Om'ray and Oud, that had stood since the world began.

At least it was to the Oud.

Chapter 13

"SIX PODS." SERU'S LIPS POUTED as she whistled. "No wonder Haxel wants you for a scout."

Aryl lifted the spoon, checking that the purple powder came only to the mark carved on the inner curve of its bowl. Perfect. "Not interested," she muttered, tipping the spoon's contents into a fold on the square of waxed gauze, one of a stack before her. Taking the gauze, she twisted it into a packet, then secured it with a thread. No dresel cakes this M'hir. The powder was being divided to the last grain. Each packet contained a day's serving of dresel for an adult, scant but in the opinion of Adepts, enough for survival. They'd feel the effects over the coming fists: growing weakness, aching in their joints, diminished appetite. Two packets for each child—otherwise growth would be permanently affected; half a packet for the very old, a decision they'd made for themselves. No one said it aloud, but everyone knew. Even so rationed, there wasn't enough for all, not through to the next M'hir. A store must be reserved for the harvesters, Yena's only hope for the future. When the time came, rations for everyone else would be cut.

Seru had started with a similar stack. It was now substantially lower than Aryl's, the other unChosen being as quick with her hands as her opinion. "Why? Father's all for you being a scout."

"He is one," Aryl pointed out. "And they need more."

Seru changed tactics. "You're the best climber—you love it! You could be First Scout one day. Besides," she noted, "you hate jobs like this."

"I don't love climbing," Aryl informed her cousin. Not anymore, she thought. She did her share; the soreness of her muscles reminded her of that. This was another rare day of rest, crucial, if her body wasn't to betray her in the next climb.

She gazed around the room. "What's wrong with this?"

The heady spice of dresel filled the air, muted from the fresh but able to mask the scent of the flowers nodding by the window panels. They sat at one of several tables gathered at this end of the meeting hall. The click of spoons in gourds, the low murmur of young voices—for this was a task given those who weren't out hunting meat to be dried in the kilns—the constant flow of Om'ray through the doors, bringing their finds to be sorted by the older, more experienced Chosen at the other end of the room . . . Aryl felt as if she soaked in a warm bath, secure and comfortable, free of demands.

Every Om'ray was busy: here, in the warehouses and kilns, out in the canopy. Only the looms were silent. Without fresh clean wings, the weavers were set to repair and patch. Aryl suspected they'd all soon wear layers; she hadn't a shirt free of holes.

The end of the M'hir would bring the return of the rains, carried on hot heavy air from that part of the world marked by Pana and Amna Clans. Added to the need to repair rooftops and bridges was the new urgency to gather seeds and fruits, to hunt game before climbing became treacherous and the biters hatched anew in their hungry clouds. If they were to put away enough food to last until the M'hir's return, it would have to be now.

"Wrong?" Seru gave her an odd look. "Nothing, if you like gossip and sitting all day. Which you don't."

"People do grow up," Aryl said absently, lifting her next spoonful.

Her cousin put down her packet and turned to face her, her eyes aglow. "Aryl. You feel it, too?"

Though Seru was capable of being excited over a new hair-net, for some reason Aryl was uneasy. "Feel what?" she asked, spoon halted in midair.

"The dreams. The burning. The urges!" In case anyone in the meeting hall had possibly missed her passionate whisper, Seru thrust her right hand out in dramatic emphasis.

Aryl grabbed her cousin's wrist and yanked it back down; the blush burning her cheeks deepened as she heard giggles from the Vendan sisters at the next table. "Stop that!" she snapped. "What are you—" Then her eyes widened in shock. Her inner sense had *touched* Seru.

And there it was. The wild, exotic Power that flared from even the weakest among them when ready.

A Power with but one purpose: to summon an unChosen and bind him in Choice.

The irony escaped no one. Council had sent away all their eligible unChosen and, within a fist, Seru and the Vendan sisters were declared Choosers, their inner Call reaching out across the world. It was possible they'd lure back some of their own, but unlikely. Once Passage was begun, an unChosen picked one Call to follow. The one, Adepts promised, that touched closest to his heart.

Which didn't, Aryl fumed inwardly, say anything about the shortest distance or most sensible route. There had to be a better way.

She'd cleared the end of a table in Costa's room for her work, propping her drawings against pots. It was the brightest room.

It was the one place left where she could imagine nothing had changed.

Along with their other tasks, scouts now had to watch for those on Passage to Yena. No one said aloud what everyone knew—that the coming rains would make the difficult impossible. The waters of the Lay would rise to flood the platform below. The higher water meant its creatures could swim among the lower branches; many spawned in this time, trumpeting their warnings to rivals. The high route of the Yena would be the only one.

But other Clans lived on flat ground; they couldn't climb.

"There's a better way," Aryl declared, studying her latest creation.

She'd cleaned the piece of dresel wing she'd collected as best she could. Yena didn't use the wings intact—the natural material was tight and strong at first, but naturally broke apart when exposed to moisture and light over time. Weavers cleaned and soaked the wings in vats of soapy water until individual threads became swollen and loose. They'd tease them apart, collect and dry the thread, and only then weave the threads into fabric. Treated this way, cloth made from dresel wing was long-lasting yet soft.

Aryl's piece was intact. She'd cut it into various shapes; this triangle was the latest she'd tried. By trial and error, she'd come to use dried hollow stems for supports, and sacrificed old clothing for threads to secure the wing to them. More threads dangled below, attached to a splinter of wood. The wood had little eyes and a mouth inked on it, all shown wide open as if alarmed. "Ready, Fich?" she asked it, grinning at her own joke.

Hook-nosed Fich, now Chosen and above children's games, had been a thorn in Aryl's side in M'hirs past, especially once he discovered she had the ability to sense identity from a distance. She had no sympathy—his favorite trick had been to sneak up and listen to private conversations, then tattle them to anyone he could find. He probably still did—just not hers.

And, rare among Yena, Fich wasn't fond of heights.

She compared it to her drawing of a wastryl's wing. The proportions looked right, but there was only one way to find out.

Aryl gently pushed aside a lively vine and turned open a window panel. Leaning out, she held her creation over the black waters of Lay. "Good luck, Fich."

She let go.

Ignoring the biters attacking her arms and face, Aryl watched the red triangle eagerly. It tipped, slipping rapidly sideways toward a bridge support. She held her breath. At the last moment, it righted and the material billowed into a shape she remembered, slowing its descent. Wooden Fich swung gently beneath.

She lost sight of it in the shadows, but thought she heard a splash. Followed, inevitably, by several other splashes as what lived below fought to see if what had dropped into the water was remotely edible.

The drumming of rain in fronds overhead was enough to make her pull in her head and close the panel. Drops began to land on the roof. It always took a while for rain to get through the canopy.

And, Aryl thought with distaste, it would take even longer for the canopy to stop raining. This wasn't the start of the rainy season, but it was close. She needed more materials. Tomorrow she'd go out.

She went back to the table, gathering a handful of dried stems and another "Fich." There was enough wing left for one more model. That initial tilt and slip were a problem. She frowned. Perhaps if she used a wider triangle . . .

Aryl.

Her mother. Out of reflex, Aryl glanced at the doorway, but the summons had been inner. She *reached* to find Taisal, and the stems fell with a clatter from her suddenly numb fingers.

Impossible. It was impossible.

By direction and distance, Taisal was still at the Cloisters. Too far for Aryl to *hear* her mindvoice. Too far for her to *sense* despair in her mother's thoughts.

Despair?

That, unexpected and alarming, was more important than how. Aryl found herself on her feet, hands braced on the table. *What's wrong, Mother?* she replied. It seemed to take no effort at all, beyond what was normal to create the words. She was afraid to wonder why.

Aryl? Recognition followed by confusion. *What are you doing here? Who let you cross the bridge? You shouldn't have come. I'm in Council Session. Go home.*

I'm— Aryl shied from the truth, that she wasn't at the Cloisters. If Taisal couldn't tell, she doubted it would help her mother's distraught state of mind to know. She began to suspect her mother hadn't called her, not on purpose, and carefully reinforced her shields to project only calm concern. *I felt something wrong.*

Of course something's wrong. We're trying to keep Yena alive. Stop distracting me and go home. I'll see you tonight.

Beneath the rebuff and dismissal, Taisal's emotions again betrayed her. Aryl sensed something forlorn, desperate. A need.

A need for her?

Raindrops hit the roof. Vines twisted slowly in the breeze through the window gauze. Leaves whispered to themselves as the air stroked Aryl's cheek in turn.

It should have been impossible to *hear* her mother, to *send* back.

She straightened and closed her eyes, somehow unsurprised to find the *other place* waiting there, its seething darkness so close at this instant it could have been the breath leaving her mouth.

That was how. Her mother's distress had found her through the Dark, as easily as if they touched hand-to-hand. She'd used it, too, without intent or plan.

Whatever it was, it connected them.

Aryl shuddered and opened her eyes, relieved by the light, then gave a brusque nod. She couldn't ignore her mother's summons, even one made unaware.

She'd worry about the details later.

Chapter 14

UNLESS AN ADEPT OR MEMBER of Council, an Om'ray visited the Cloisters only three times in life: as a newborn, to be dutifully—and quickly—added to the Yena records before being returned to waiting parents; as one of a Joined pair, that union to be affirmed by the Adepts; and to end their days in peace, granted none of the many hazards of the canopy ended it sooner.

Aryl squinted at the tower. She hadn't thought of it before, but the Cloisters was, beyond doubt, the perfect place to drop and test a model. Had she known she'd be coming . . . not that she had, but still.

Such thoughts were easier than imagining why her mother needed her here, of all places.

There were other reasons a Yena might come here, of course. Those sundered from their Choice and Lost . . . those of damaged mind . . . maybe even those who'd tried to hide a new Talent, to be investigated by Adepts and punished?

Aryl concentrated on planning to fly a fich.

The Cloisters rose from the waters of the Lay on its own gray-green stalk, thick and straight, with three flat sides that met at crisp joins. The canopy closed overhead, but not around it. The nearest rastis set buttress roots well away from its artificial neighbor, though smaller plants had less respect. The lower portion of the Cloisters' stalk was coated in a thick growth of vine. The growth ended where six clear panels, parallel to the stalk, jutted outward at angles. There was no apparent reason why vegetation shunned these protrusions; why no flitter would perch there and no biters flew close.

Above the panels, the stalk widened into a perfectly shaped crown, as if a rastis after all, but this crown, from below, looked like two giant bowls, one nested within the other. From higher in the canopy, Aryl remembered, the structure looked more like an opened flower: two high-walled platforms encircling an inner curved core, itself topped by a series of overlapped white rings.

The core was a building of two floors, each opening to one of the encircling platforms. The building's round outer walls were broken by a series of tall wide arches. Within each arch were three smaller ones: the centermost a door, the outer two filled with the same clear material that somehow guarded the stalk from living things.

Inside . . . she had no idea. Aryl straightened her best, though mended, tunic and checked her hairnet. Till sud Parth, the scout guarding the bridge platform, leaned against the stalk to regard her thoughtfully. "I don't know about this, Aryl."

She'd hoped for someone who'd be impressed by her being the Speaker's daughter. Instead, she had Till, Seru's father and someone who'd bandaged her knees more than once.

As she feared, he pursed his lips, then shook his head slowly. "No. You go home. I'll keep the drawings here. Contact someone from the Cloisters to fetch them. That's best, Aryl."

She pulled the bag of panes closer to her chest, trusting he wouldn't become suspicious and demand a look. "I drew these for the Speaker," Aryl said truthfully. All Yena had witnessed her giving a drawing to Taisal for the Tikitik; a minor, if crucial detail that the art she now clutched had been done years ago by a much younger Aryl, and involved more ink than skill. "She'll have questions about them." Definitely true.

His keen eyes left her to scan the rain-shadowed canopy, why she didn't know. Having less of his attention, Aryl took a small step closer to the bridge, slinging her bag over one shoulder, then another. Till didn't appear to notice until she was almost there. Then, he frowned at her.

Aryl gave him her best smile and patted the bag. "These shouldn't stay in the rain, Till. Let me go, please?"

"I suppose you'll be the one in trouble." With a resigned snort, he waved a hand in dismissal, again intent on whatever he watched.

The Cloisters' bridge was a marvel in itself. Not wood, but metal slats. No rails, but true sides and a curved roof, themselves of such closely woven metal threads they really did block the rain. The bridge was attached to that normal platform of wood, girdling a great rastis. Above were other platforms, older ones and no longer of use. A new one would eventually be built to replace this one, as the rastis continued to grow and lift the platform and bridge with it.

For the Cloisters was older than the Lay Swamp, so the Adepts taught, and its remarkable bridge had once reached dry ground.

Aryl started across the bridge, listening to her footsteps' light echo. She'd always scoffed, to herself, at the stories of its age. What ground? The waters of the Lay had always been below. The grove might change, but it was as old as the world.

She'd believed the Adepts—her mother included—made up stories to keep everyone in awe.

They didn't need to, she thought, fingertips brushing the smooth metal. Unlike other bridges, this didn't sway with her footsteps. Unlike others, it felt cold to the touch.

How had her ancestors made this place? Aryl asked herself for the first time. Or, was the real question, why? Every Clan had a Cloisters, like enough to this one to be instantly recognizable, although she'd heard Grona's Cloisters sat directly on the ground, either lacking a stalk or with it buried out of sight.

Why weren't their homes like this? Why did Yena sit in fear, protected only by the glows the Tikitik gave them, if Om'ray could build this? Only Adepts and the infirm were allowed to spent truenight within the Cloisters. Even members of Council returned to their homes. So it had always been.

The bridge led to the lower of the Cloisters' two platforms, ending in a massive pair of doors. These were metal—there had to be enough here to satisfy the needs of the entire world—worked in intricate patterns. Not the plain gray-green of the bridge, but a surface ribboned in color to rival any flitter or flower she'd seen. Not ink or paint. Something in the metal itself. Aryl stretched her hand to touch it . . .

The leftmost door turned open without a sound, and she dropped her hand hurriedly. A figure in a plain brown robe stood within the wide gap, face shadowed beneath a hood.

"Welcome to—" The greeting died away as the Adept saw her. "Who are you?"

Aryl was about to ask the same when she recognized the wrinkled face peering from the hood. Pio di Kessa'at? Had it been that long since her great-aunt last left the Cloisters? "Aryl Sarc," she replied. "Taisal's—"

"By Mele sud Sarc. Yes, yes. I know the lineage. It's quite interesting. There are expectations—why are you here? You haven't Joined." Aryl felt a deft touch explore her shields. "You aren't even ready. Go home."

Expectations? Refusing to be distracted by the old Adept's rambling, she braced herself to argue. "I was asked to bring—" she began, hand on her bag.

"No, you weren't. There's been no messenger." The Adept shook a crooked finger at her. "We play no games here, child. Go home." She began to turn the door closed in Aryl's face. "Children always try to sneak inside," she grumbled to herself. "Don't hurry your life away!" This to Aryl, who found herself speechless.

Without pausing to consider, she put out a hand to stop the door. "This is no game, Pio. My mother needs me. I know she does." She let her shields weaken, hoping her worry for Taisal, her sincerity, would accomplish what words could not.

And received a stern flash of anger back. "Impudent!"

"Desperate, Aunt." Aryl removed her hand and gestured apology. She restored her shields but stayed where she was.

Pio's eyes were bright spots within the shadow of her hood. "Your mother was the same at your age. A troublemaker. Bothersome as a biter. She matured into a thorn. Will you?"

Another of those questions better ignored than answered, Aryl decided. "Please. Let me in."

Pio didn't answer immediately; she didn't close the door either. Aryl waited, feeling a draft of warm, moist air from the bridge behind her, making herself as small and insignificant a mental presence as she could.

Then, the Adept stepped back, turning the door wide open with no obvious effort despite its thickness and height. "You can't wander around alone, you know," she cautioned as Aryl gratefully stepped through to the open platform beyond. "I'm the gatekeeper. I certainly can't take you." Pio finished turning the door closed, its inner colorations aligned perfectly with those of its partner. From this side, Aryl saw that the doors curved inward at the top, that curve matched to the one defining the low wall that edged the platform. "You stay here," the Adept emphasized. "Right here. I'll find someone."

"I won't leave," Aryl promised. "Thank you."

The old Adept's wrinkles creased deeper. "I'm sure you won't. Only an Adept can unlock the Cloisters' doors. In or out."

Aryl didn't move from the shelter of the great doors. Though the deserted platform swept intriguingly away in both directions, and windows in the wall beckoned, she wouldn't risk disobeying Pio di Kessa'at.

Plus, it was pouring. She stuck her hand beyond the overhang to catch drops for a drink. There were no real puddles. The platform sloped to the inside, the water disappearing into a series of channels. She wondered if it rained down along the stalk from there, or was collected.

Aryl had run out of such questions by the time two figures appeared in the archway across from the doors. They were faceless in their robes, robes colorless through the curtains of rain. She swallowed her curiosity and didn't *reach* for their identities. One hurried toward her; the other followed at a more deliberate pace, as if the deluge was beneath notice.

The one in a hurry was Pio. The old Adept tossed back her hood, showering Aryl with drops. As she blinked to clear her eyes, the other pointed. "I brought a guide."

The second figure was dressed in dull red, without a hood. As she stepped from the rain into their shelter, she spoke, her voice oddly flat. "I will take Aryl to the Speaker."

A familiar voice, nonetheless.

"Leri!" Aryl greeted Costa's Chosen with a glad smile, a smile that died on her lips.

At first glance, Leri Teerac looked as she had before the

M'hir, save for the plain red robe that smothered her from neck to ankles. She was still slender and tall, with those high cheekbones and startling green oblong eyes. But Leri's thick golden hair, Costa's particular joy, was no longer secured in a metal net. It lay sodden and limp over her shoulders and back, as if what gave it life had died.

It had.

Costa's Chosen beckoned. "I will take Aryl to the Speaker." There was no impatience to the gesture, no expression to her face. Her features might have been composed by an artist who worked from corpses. As for the inner sense . . . Aryl withdrew instantly. All she felt where Leri stood was that familiar roiling *darkness*. Involuntarily, she stepped closer to Pio.

Lost. Aryl swallowed bile. She hadn't known it meant lost in the Dark. Was this what her mother had somehow escaped, while remaining connected to it?

What did that make her?

Pio didn't seem to notice anything strange about the other Om'ray or Aryl's reaction. "What are you waiting for, Aryl?" she demanded querulously. "The rain to stop? You won't melt. I've wasted enough time. I'm today's gatekeeper. Go."

"I will take Aryl to the Speaker." The same words; the same beckoning.

"It's Leri," Aryl said helplessly. "My brother's—it's Leri." As if repeating the name would help the Adept understand.

"I will take Aryl to the Speaker."

Aryl wanted to cover her ears. "I heard you—"

"I will take Aryl—"

"Stop saying that!"

"—the Speaker."

"Pio!" Aryl turned to the Adept, who shook her head.

There was no amusement on her face this time, only a weary grief. "She'll stop when you go with her, child," Pio explained.

"There's no talking to the Lost, you know. Well, you can try, but it doesn't get you anywhere."

"I will take Aryl to the Speaker." The beckoning. The horrifying precision of that repetition.

"But she knows me," Aryl whispered. "Doesn't she? She says my name."

"She doesn't know herself. She's saying what I put in her head to say. Follow where she leads. Go now. But don't expect more. The Lost are empty."

"I will take Aryl to the Speaker."

Aryl took a deep breath and stepped into the rain with what had been Leri Teerac.

Despite her unease, Aryl followed Costa's Chosen through the door in the archway, along a series of hallways, and through rooms unlike any she'd seen before. Instead of glows, light emerged from the curved join of ceiling and wall, soft and white. It hadn't failed in Om'ray memory, though there were no cells to change. Instead of wood or mats on the floor, they walked on some resilient material for which she had no name, pale yellow and smooth. The damp hem of Leri's robe whispered as it brushed that surface. She no longer spoke.

Aryl studied her surroundings, to avoid looking at her guide. Frames hung on the walls every few steps, frames that held clusters of disks and lines. These were of metal; most bore markings that reminded her of her mother's pendant. None formed pictures or shapes that made any sense. Why were they here, in a place where only Om'ray could go?

Though Aryl found little to prove this place was home to her kind. A display of wooden bowls caught her eye; they were lined up along a clear shelf, their carving a match to those on Aryl's table. But beside them was a tall cylinder of pale green, seamless and smooth; she couldn't guess its purpose. The air held a hint of dresel, but stronger was a crisp, clean tang, as if there'd been a storm indoors.

There were other Yena here. Aryl was aware of their existence as they would be aware of hers—they were Om'ray after all. She didn't dare *reach* to know who was who, not here. There would be the Adepts; Yena boasted thirteen and all lived here. A trio in ordinary brown had hurried past them, their heads close together as they spoke in silence. There would be the elderly. A long, low seat before a windowed arch had contained a pair of sleeping Om'ray older than Aryl believed possible, small and wizened, taking such slow, soft breaths that only her inner sense of their presence assured her they lived.

As for the rest . . . she didn't want to find more of the Lost.

Each step with Leri eroded days of healing, made the past real and urgent again. Aryl's eyes stung as she found herself consumed by the memory of Costa slipping away again, reliving the agony she'd sensed as he died.

When her guide finally stopped before an arch, curtained reassuringly like a door at home, Aryl abruptly realized she wasn't reliving her own memories, but Leri's. She firmed her shields at once, staring at the other's passive face in horror. Was all she was an echo of Costa's death?

Not even her own?

"I will take Aryl to the Speaker," Leri intoned. This time the beckoning gesture was reversed, indicating the closed curtain.

Aryl restrained a shudder and pushed the thick material aside. She'd loved Leri as the sister she'd never had. Now, she couldn't wait to be away from her. She'd been right to believe death would be kinder.

The curtain had fooled her into thinking she would enter a simple apartment. Instead, Aryl found herself in an immense curved expanse, standing on a metal floor awash with more of those exotic bands of color.

At first, she thought the only furnishing was a narrow raised dais centered on the longer wall, with six tall-backed seats of the same pale green as the cylinder on the shelf. The wall behind the dais was lined by those windows, three times her height. She guessed they'd offer a spectacular view of the canopy, though now all she could see were gray sheets of rain. Yet no drops marred the clear material.

The Council Chamber. It had to be, though Aryl was astonished by its size. All of Yena could fit in here, with room for a hundred more. Why? The meeting hall, with its benches and tables, was where Council met the rest of Yena. This space was a waste for six alone.

She'd come through a discreet entrance to one side, perhaps the Councillors' own. The proper, ceremonial doors were at the far end. Leri's mistake or Pio's instruction?

"Let be. I don't need a healer!"

The weak, strained voice made a lie of the words. Aryl found its source.

To her left was a cluster of unusual, though comfortable-looking, chairs, set before one of the windows on a simple woven mat that might have come from any home. There were low tables between the chairs, some crowded with mugs, others with piles of what looked like pod-wood trays, only silver. An Om'ray sat slumped in one chair; six others stood around him, their postures indicated concern. No one turned to look at her or otherwise indicate they knew she was there.

Which, of course, they did.

Until officially noticed, Aryl didn't dare take a step or make a sound. She glanced desperately around the room. Austere, empty, and utterly lacking in places to be inconspicuous.

Her mother was one of those standing. She'd know her anywhere. From here, she couldn't be sure who the stricken Om'ray was, although this was Yena's Council. The Adepts were easy to spot; Tikva di Uruus and Sian d'sud Vendan wore brown robes twin to that of Pio's, as did Taisal, the gleam of her Speaker's Pendant muted against the fabric. The rest looked ready for a climb or day of work, their tunics and wraps as oft-repaired as Aryl's own.

Why would her mother bring her here?

I didn't.

She winced. No one else reacted to Taisal's aggrieved sending. Aryl checked her shields, trusting they'd work, and considered whether she could sidle back through the curtain or if escape at this point would only make things worse.

One of the six did turn, then. Her mother. "Aryl Sarc." Her name bounced from the distant walls. "Come here."

As Aryl warily obeyed, her feet making their own too-loud echoes despite soft-soled boots—at least she'd remembered boots and wasn't slapping her way across the magnificent floor barefoot—the others straightened to watch her approach. One kept her hand protectively on the shoulder of the still-hunched figure and glared at Taisal. "What's the meaning of this, Speaker?"

It was Morla Kessa'at who chided her mother while comforting the sufferer. Who was, Aryl recognized with a delay that startled her, Yorl sud Sarc, her mother's great-uncle and acknowledged head of their family. She'd bounced on his knee, learned to draw at his table.

She'd never seen him in such pain, his arms held tight to his chest and his face beaded with sweat and sickly pale. Here was the reason for Taisal's distress.

"You know what drew her," Taisal said, beckoning her daughter.

Aryl went to stand by her mother; she couldn't take her eyes from Yorl. The clinking bag of old drawings on her shoulder now felt anything but clever. She shouldn't have come. What had drawn her here was nothing she could help.

"The child can't help," a too-accurate echo from Morla. "She—"

Yorl's head lifted, and he reached a shaking hand toward her. A slight turn of the wrist indicated the broad arm of his chair.

Aryl moved to take his thick, chill hand in hers without hesitation, though she sat cautiously. It might be wood, beneath its burnished black finish, but the furnishings here weren't Yena-made.

She braced herself to share Yorl's pain across the bridge of their hands, then was startled when all she felt was the dimmest glow of his existence. It was as if his Power had been drained by whatever hurt him.

No, Aryl corrected, abruptly understanding. Yorl's formidable Power was somehow focused inward; a struggle no less real for taking place out of sight. He fought to heal himself, to strengthen some failing part of his body.

Was such a thing possible?

Aryl *sensed* another presence and glanced at Morla in surprise. "Perceptive, indeed," the head of Kessa'at said, her stern expression softening. The weave of family with family showed in her large, wide-set gray eyes, a match for Aryl's own. She was the smallest here; standing, her netted white hair wouldn't reach Aryl's shoulder. Unwise to judge her by that—Morla had ruled her close kin for many M'hirs. One of Yena's most accomplished woodworkers, she was first on Council as well. "Let her stay," Morla decided. "She may comfort him."

"Yorl should go to the healers," Taisal's voice had an edge, as if she'd pressed this for some time without result. "Aryl can go with him."

The words hardly penetrated. Aryl found herself fascinated by what she sensed within Yorl. Some Om'ray healed from wounds or illness much faster than others. The difference must lie in this Talent.

But it was costly. She could feel Yorl weakening with each labored breath. He wasn't eating enough dresel, she fumed to herself. He'd been stinting himself, like all the older Om'ray. She cupped her other hand over his. *Why won't you go?* she sent, hoping he could hear. *You're worrying my mother.* As if she wasn't terrified for him, too.

His reply was whisper-faint, almost imagined. *We decide Yena's future, here and now. Your future. Sarc must always have a voice. Help me, child.*

How? As she asked the question, she *felt* its answer. Something began draining from her to him. It flowed from shoulder to arm to hand, the sensation of a rapidly moving fluid so vivid Aryl stared stupidly at her wrist, expecting to see blood pumping from a wound.

She began to gasp; Yorl to take easier breaths. Dimly, she heard voices, angry and upset. She heard Yorl answering. She reeled and would have slipped from the arm of the chair if not for his now-strong grip on her hands. She . . .

ENOUGH!

. . . Aryl was pulled free and pushed, almost roughly, into a chair. She curled within its unfamiliar shape and closed her eyes, hoping the world would stop spinning like a loose ladder in the M'hir.

If it didn't, and soon, she was quite sure the Yena Council would not appreciate the result.

"— Yorl's right! Admit it!"

Aryl realized she'd been listening to the heated debate for a while, listening but until now without hearing the words or caring who said them. She cautiously cracked open her eyes, unwilling to remind those nearby she existed.

Not only that, but her head pounded. The light made it worse. The nausea was gone, but she doubted she could stand without tipping over.

What had Yorl done to her?

The others had taken their seats, leaving those to either side of hers empty. Aryl was happy to be excluded. Fighting a shiver, she drew her knees to her chest and wrapped her arms around them. Did it feel the same to her elders—that being huddled together on this homely mat offered little protection in this vast exposed space?

Why, she wondered again, did they use this place? Old people and their habits. An unmistakably deep voice drew her attention. Cetto sud Teerac.

"—we've sacrificed, there's worse ahead, much worse," he was saying. "We all know." Cetto was Bern's great grandfather and Leri's grandfather, a strong, thoughtful Om'ray whose abilities had always rested in his hands, not his Power. His green eyes tended to water when he was weary or emotional, or when the young ones sat on his lap to tell him stories. Aryl noticed they glistened now.

She also noticed Yorl sud Sarc was sitting straight up in his chair, his face flushed with healthy color. He was watching the others, his eyes hooded; Taisal watched him, her expression one of bewilderment, as if she didn't know how to act.

For the first time, Aryl was struck by how young her mother was in this company, how out of place.

"Cetto—" Morla began.

"We all know," the head of Teerac repeated, refusing to be interrupted. "There's no time for despair or pity. Not if Yena is to survive. We must prepare." He patted the stack of odd metal squares on the table near his hand. "The inventory lists will be of use to Haxel and her scouts. She'll need an Adept to read them."

The lists were pieces of metal? Aryl longed to see one up close.

"Prepare?" Sian steepled his fingers and regarded his fellow Councillor over them, as if over the rail of a bridge. "Surely premature, Cetto, since we still debate Yorl's original proposal."

"Then I say end the debate!"

"Oh, on that we agree." Sian said sharply. Aryl *sensed* tension between the two Councillors. The slender head of Vendan was elegant compared to Cetto, his skin darker and less worn, his long black hair streaked with bands of silver, not totally gray. She'd always been a little afraid of him. Sian used words the way others used tools, to split ideas apart and rebuild them, and had little patience. On the rare times he left the Cloisters, he spent more time in the Sarc hall arguing with Taisal than he did with his own Chosen. Given warning of such visits, Aryl would escape to climb with Bern.

"Peace, both of you." Yorl leaned forward to catch the gaze of each of his fellow Councillors in turn, avoiding Taisal. "Yena can't endure a second year of famine. We can't risk the future on the hope the coming M'hir will be free of disaster or that our few starving harvesters will reap sufficient dresel for us and the Tikitik. You've heard my proposal. All of Yena must seek a new home while we have strength and supplies left. We must leave the grove as soon as possible."

Aryl's hand flashed to her mouth, smothering the gasp she couldn't stop. Leave? Yena was the grove! No Clan abandoned its home. Was it even possible?

"Nonsense!" protested Adrius sud Parth. Oldest on Council, his voice had rotted into a loud rasp, interspersed with spit. The joke was that standing in front of old Adrius when he spoke would get you as wet as the rains. Aryl no longer found it funny. The rasp made each word hook-sharp. "I'm going to die right here," the head of Parth vowed, bouncing in his chair. "Right here! I've earned it. Here, I say!"

"Die, then," Cetto countered harshly. "No one's stopping you."

"Think of our unChosen, Adrius," Yorl urged, gesturing a tactful apology while giving Cetto a quelling look. "We sent them away to help them survive. How is this different?"

"You know how," Morla answered before Adrius could. "They had tokens. A place to go. As it is . . . another perished, Yorl. Four of ten failed, despite being young and healthy, despite the best supplies we could provide."

Aryl felt a wave of guilt-laced grief. It might have come from any or all of them. Or been hers. She knew how it felt to have picked who would live, only to face the consequence of who did not.

Morla continued, "You suggest that our entire clan take Passage—can't you see it's impossible? Even if the Tikitik should permit us to move through their groves—"

"It's impossible to stay. We'll arrange permission," Cetto rumbled, his cheeks flushed with emotion. "The Tikitik like to trade. Speaker?"

Aryl shuddered, remembering a mouth of finger-things and moving eyes.

"They do, Councillor," Taisal agreed, then held up her empty palm. "But we have nothing to offer."

The head of Teerac looked triumphant. "Yes. Yes, we do." His strong hand smacked the arm of his chair. "This place. They've wanted it for generations. I say we trade the Cloisters for Yena's freedom."

From the ensuing pause, during which her breathing—and Adrius' wheeze—were the loudest sounds, Aryl knew she wasn't the only one shocked. But was Cetto wrong? she wondered in the safety of her own thoughts. True, the Cloisters was a remarkable structure, but what use was it to everyday Yena?

None, so far as she could tell.

Sian pursed his lips. "The Cloisters," he said in a reasoning tone, "is the heart of Yena, as it is for each Om'ray Clan. As well talk about abandoning who we are."

"There's our heart," Cetto rejoined, twisting in his seat to thrust a finger at Aryl. She tried not to shrink away. "There.

Our young. Our families. Our future. All to starve if we stay here."

"By the next M'hir—"

"And how many of us will be alive when the Watchers call?" This time it was Yorl who interrupted with passion. "Every day we grow weaker, Sian. Soon, we won't be able to leave."

"The time to act is now," Cetto agreed. "While we can all still climb. Beat the worst of the rains; look for a place in the mountains."

"And do what? Die on the rock? It's too dangerous—"

Several began to talk at once; underneath, emotions spilled past their shields. They were like biters, jostling for the same scrap of exposed skin.

Aryl was appalled.

Yena's Council: the venerable and respected heads of the six families. Yena's Speaker: a powerful Adept, selected for rare skill with words and diplomacy. She'd come here believing they could do anything, Aryl realized, as if being responsible for the entire Yena Clan somehow made these individuals more than ordinary Om'ray.

Had that been fair?

She'd believed until this moment they could save her, save everyone; that the rationing, the hunt for more food, the heartbreak of sending away their unChosen were parts of a well thought out plan to keep them safe.

Wasn't it?

Or was this the truth in front of her, in their bickering? Cetto's desperation. Yorl's conviction. Sian's fear. Adrius' selfishness.

The dread none of them—Yena's eldest and wisest—could fully hide.

Was there no future?

No need to be warned of consequences if she repeated a word from this meeting. If it upset her to hear all this, Aryl couldn't imagine how Seru or others might react.

Tikva di Uruus, hitherto silent, lifted her hand to catch Aryl's attention along with the rest. Two of her fingers were wrapped together; from the purpled tip of one, a break. Despite her rank as Adept, the wiry head of Uruus had been among those out hunting before the rains.

"Before we climb to the unknown," she said, the words crisp and sure, "I suggest we look closer for our salvation. To the Power that lies within us all."

NO!

That denial slammed through Aryl's mind, ripping past any shield. She winced. It wasn't Taisal's. She found herself staring at Sian d'sud Vendan, who'd surged to his feet.

Not Taisal's sending, but her mother rose as well, her expression equally defiant as the two faced their fellow Adept.

Tikva raised one brow, seeming unaffected by their protest. "It's *Council's* duty," she stressed the word, "to consider any and all means to save our people." She deliberately looked away, focusing on the four Councillors who weren't Adepts.

Aryl was puzzled. Adepts didn't acknowledge a leader among themselves, but Tikva acted like one. Did they answer to their eldest member after all, like families? If so, she grimaced, they were lucky Pio di Kessa'at was a season younger.

Then she hurriedly checked her shields.

No one appeared to notice. Taisal and Sian sat back down, though they looked no less angry.

"An option that divides Adepts?" Morla asked. "Now I'm curious."

Yorl frowned. "And I hope you aren't wasting our time, Tivy."

Aryl tried not to squirm at the nickname.

"Then let me be quick," Tikva said smoothly, "I propose we increase our chance of survival here. Thus." She lifted her hand once more.

A carved mug floated from the table to meet it.

This demonstration was greeted with an astonished wheeze from Adrius, narrowed eyes by the other Adepts, and a dismissive shrug from Cetto. Aryl wasn't sure if she should try to look surprised; her mother's great uncle certainly wasn't.

Morla remained still, then her white brows knotted. "A skill of Adepts," she observed.

"One we can teach." This with a confidence that rang through the immense chamber.

Aryl couldn't take her eyes from the mug in Tikva's hand. This was her mother's Talent. If she could learn it . . . breakfast in bed, she decided without hesitation. Doubtless more significant and important uses would follow, but that first.

"Teach to who?" Cetto growled. "Everyone? Or those with the most Power?" Another shrug of broad shoulders, still well-muscled from a life of climbing. "How many could learn this, Adepts? Do you know? Can you?"

"We know." Sian glanced sideways at Tikva, as if asking permission. When she did and said nothing, he continued. "Five among the unChosen. More of the very young, but until they mature . . ." Adrius wheezed vigorously at that, likely, Aryl decided, imagining the trouble his already infamous great granddaughters would cause. "Few, if any, of our Chosen—understandable, since those of exceptional Power are already Adepts. Those who didn't die in the Harvest—or of it."

"A good start," Tikva claimed brusquely, pushing aside Sian's final comment. "The use of Power to move objects will help everyone."

Yorl rested his chin on a fist, as if deep in thought.

Cetto's palm smacked his chair arm for the second time. "Help! Instead of Adepts, trained and sworn to work for the benefit of all, we would have those with this ability and those without, choosing to do what they will. Do you not see it, Tikva?" He lowered his voice until it vibrated through Aryl's bones. "You would stratify our kind, sort us by the strength of our Power instead of family. You would divide us, when we must stay together."

Tikva made a dismissive gesture. "Power has always varied among Om'ray. Even now, our youngest reach each other over greater distances than before—better shield their thoughts—healers help speed recovery as well as ease pain—"

"This is not the same. You know it isn't. Those are Talents that bring us closer, help us communicate, one to the other. An ability like this?" Cetto reached as if for something far overhead, then brought his hand down as a fist to wave at the Adept. "To be able to have a thing in your hands, without climbing for it? How long before it becomes the ability to take a thing, without right to it?"

"You are old, Cetto. Old and old-fashioned; our people will die of your ideas."

"You would have them battle each other because of yours?"

PEACE!

They quieted, but Aryl flinched as anger spilled over shields. The ability to *push* an object had seemed almost trivial, but the passions regarding its use were, she realized with dismay, anything but. What she'd done, using Power to move Bern and now her thoughts through the *other place*? If they knew, would they argue about its use like this—or would it be worse?

Best, she glanced at Taisal's expressionless face, never to find out.

Morla, for it had been her sending, spoke aloud. "It's time to hear from all. I call a vote on Yorl sud Sarc's initial proposal. Shall we, as Council, prepare Yena to leave the canopy and seek safety elsewhere? All must agree."

Aryl kept very still, hoping to continue unnoticed. A Council vote? Only Councillors and the Speaker attended such. It would be full of ceremony, she knew. Dignified. The result was vitally important . . .

Adrius staggered to his feet. "To the Lay with everyone

else!" This with a spew of droplets that just missed his fellows. "I'm dying in my chair." With this, he sat, wheezing soundlessly to himself.

"Parth votes no," Morla said, giving the older Councillor a weary look. She rose. "Kessa'at votes—no." She gestured apology to Yorl and Cetto as she sat.

Sian and Tikva, however divided on other issues, voted no.

"You doom us," Cetto said when it was his turn. "Yes. For what it matters."

Leaving Yorl. He rose to his feet, standing as tall and erect as a much younger Om'ray. The weakness Aryl had sensed might never have been, except for her own now. He spoke with passion and resolve. "We sent our best from Yena to save their lives. Our future, loose on the wind. Do you remember that day, my friends?"

A pause during which he studied the others, including Aryl. She made herself gaze back without flinching; she thought she saw a familiar warmth light his eyes before his expression turned implacable again.

"We told our grandsons and great grandsons there was hope away from here. All of us agreed that was so. All of us."

There was no answer to this.

"I will not abandon that hope," Yorl insisted. "We will not." He gestured gratitude to Aryl, included Taisal, then flattened his hands over his chest. "Sarc votes yes. We should follow our unChosen and soon." He sat.

"Council is not agreed," Morla concluded, rising to her feet again. "Your proposal is not accepted. Yena will stay and wait for the next M'hir."

Yorl closed his eyes briefly. Aryl glanced at Cetto. He showed no reaction. She sighed with relief, as inconspicuously as possible. The mere idea of leaving . . .

Morla bowed her head to the others. "Firstnight approaches. I suggest we end here for today."

"Wait," Tikva stayed seated. "I ask a vote on my proposal. Let the Adepts teach those capable the Talent to move objects—to begin immediately."

"No vote without debate," Cetto insisted, his thick brows in a frown.

"Which I can start and end with one question to our Speaker," Sian offered smoothly.

Morla hesitated, then returned to her seat. "Ask it."

He gestured gratitude, then looked to Taisal. "Speaker—when the Tikitik see pods floating through the air into Yena nets—what will you tell them?"

Tikva scowled as Taisal stood, the fingers of her right hand drifting across her pendant—to remind herself or her elders, Aryl wondered.

"I need tell them nothing," her mother began. "They will see for themselves the Agreement has been broken. They will have proof for the Oud that Yena Om'ray have adopted a new and potent ability. Such reckless change will disrupt the peace across Cersi, a peace that has held longer than any memory. You would doom not only Yena, but all Om'ray."

She'd begun to see her mother as powerless and vulnerable, least among the others. Aryl sank deeper into her chair, understanding at last that Taisal di Sarc was none of those things.

"What would they do?" Morla asked, her face bloodless.

Tikva's eyes locked with Taisal's. "What could they do?" she countered acidly. "The Agreement is clear. The three races share the world in peace. The Tikitik and Oud may not like the Om'ray gaining Power. They can't do anything to stop us."

"And you believe that?" Aryl knew that note in her mother's voice; it didn't bode well for Tikva.

"I do."

"Then let me remind Council exactly how we three share this world. May I?" She reached for the mug in Tikva's hand;

the other Adept gave it to her with a puzzled, not-yet-angry look.

"Cersi," Taisal named it. She tapped its polished wood with a fingernail. "The Tikitik." Another tap. "The Oud." A final tap. "The water beneath us, the sky above, all that grows between."

Aryl swallowed, unsure why she suddenly felt afraid. Unless it was something from her mother she sensed but couldn't name.

With a violent sweep of her arm, Taisal dashed the mug to the metal floor. Aryl jumped as it splintered on contact, fragments sliding in all directions, connected by a spray of dark liquid.

Taisal walked to the mess and bent to touch a fingertip to the liquid. "This," she told them, straightening to hold up that one dark speck, "was the Om'ray.

"Om'ray are the shape of the world," she continued, the flat calm of her tone more chilling for what it said. "But we are not what binds it together. We are not needful to this world. Om'ray exist at the whim of Oud and Tikitik. If either of those races fails, we fail. If either abandons us, we fail."

Tikva looked defiant. "You assume the worst. The Tikitik haven't cared that we speak mind to mind over greater distances. Why? Because they care how much we harvest, not how we do it. Think the Oud care we can better heal ourselves? It's the number able to work that matters, not why they're healthy. This new Talent will be no different, mark my words."

"You'd risk our lives on their indifference?" Cetto growled. "I need proof."

Yorl's mocking laugh startled Aryl and tightened Taisal's lips. "What proof do you expect from Adepts?" he said. "They can't agree how to tell if the other races are real, let alone if they have the ability to detect Power or its use."

"They'll detect this." Taisal swept her long white hands

together. In answer, the splinters and spilled liquid hurried back to the point of impact with muted, urgent slurps, until only a small, messy pile marred the Council Chamber floor.

Aryl was not surprised when Morla Kessa'at declared the debate and Council session over.

Taisal di Sarc escorted Aryl to the massive doors leading to the bridge. Neither spoke. Aryl didn't know what to say. She suspected her mother's thoughts were of other things besides her errant daughter.

When they arrived, she was relieved to find the rain had stopped. The climb home would be easier; she was still weary. Overhead, the canopy was more gray than green, with long shadows reaching beneath. Morla had been right; firstnight was close.

With a wave of her hand, Taisal dismissed Pio di Kessa'at from her post. The old Adept gave Aryl a curious look before she left.

As for Aryl, she hefted her bag over one shoulder, happier to take it home unopened than to reveal the full extent of this disaster to her mother, and waited patiently for Taisal to open one of the doors—however an Adept accomplished that feat. With luck, she'd escape without the scolding she deserved. Never meddle in the business of any Chosen, she reminded herself. Especially her mother's.

Instead, Taisal hesitated with her hand on the door, staring at her. Aryl did her best not to squirm. "Do you understand what happened?" her mother asked after an agonizing pause.

Memories, too many and too fresh, tumbled through Aryl's head: the smashed mug that was the world, the alarming notion to abandon their homes, the Cloisters traded to the Tikitik, never being able to summon her breakfast with a thought.

She, Aryl thought with some self-pity, now knew far more than any unChosen should and it wasn't anything to help her sleep at night . . .

"You mean Yorl," she said at last, recognizing the bewilderment in Taisal's eyes. "No. But," she added, "he wasn't trying to hurt me. He asked for my help." Taking it before she could answer, she finished to herself.

A flash of anger. "All so he could stay for the vote. Stubborn, opinionated, difficult . . . his only virtue is being harder on himself than anyone else. Still," the anger faded, "I'd rather keep him around than lose him. Thank you, Daughter. He would have happily died trying to make his point—you did help him survive that misjudgment." Taisal touched Aryl's wrist, sending a flood of warmth and caring.

Aryl's eyes filled with tears. She hunted for words to send back, to tell her mother how proud she was, but Taisal withdrew her hand too soon. She looked angry again. "Don't think that I approve of what Yorl did, Aryl. Or for that matter, of your coming here without permission, then interrupting a Council session instead of going home as you were told!"

"I knew something was wrong," Aryl said truthfully, clamping down her shields. She could only hope Taisal had been distracted enough by the afternoon's events to overlook the discrepancy between her daughter's sending and her daughter's arrival. The knowledge of one's place granted by sensing other Om'ray didn't involve counting one another. Not usually. But she had no idea what her mother, as an Adept, could do.

"Something was wrong," Taisal admitted. "The moment I saw Yorl today, I knew he was in trouble." She looked up at the canopy as if hunting something, then her gaze dropped to Aryl again. Her mouth turned down at the corners. "He hides it, Aryl, but he can barely climb anymore. He should be living here all the time, yet won't. But today, this—it was the worst

I've seen him. He denied it; refused to listen to me, refused to admit weakness before the others. When he started self-healing, I felt the drain on his body grow beyond his control.

"It's a trap, Aryl, using your Power to heal yourself. It's like trying to make a ladder from one rope. You can unwind the braid and make two ropes from the one, but the ladder's only half as strong. Stealing strength from one part of the body to help another weakens the whole. No Adept would attempt it unless there was no other recourse."

"So Yorl stole strength from me instead," Aryl concluded. She still felt weak, though not as much as before. The sense of betrayal was worse. The head of their family was supposed to care for her, protect her . . .

"You said he asked for your help," Taisal said gently.

"I thought he needed help to get out of his chair!" Having made her protest, Aryl gestured apology. "It's all right," she admitted. "He knew I'd give what I could to him."

"You gave him his life." Her mother sighed. "You're young and strong. What you gave him—what he took—you'll replace with a night's rest." This last with distraction, as if Taisal's mind was worrying at other, more difficult topics. "Go home. And this time stay there." She touched the door and closed her eyes briefly.

The massive curve of metal sighed away from its partner, leaving a gap sufficient for Taisal's hand to wrap around the edge and turn the door open. Aryl peered down the empty bridge. If Till was at his post, she'd have to explain the still-full bag. . . .

Aryl sighed and pulled it off her shoulder. "I brought these for you," she confessed.

Taisal took it and looked inside. Her mouth quirked, then she closed the bag. "My room here is bare. Thank you. Reminders of home are welcome."

"I—" hadn't thought of that, Aryl almost said, torn by unexpected guilt, but stopped herself in time. The result was what counted. "—I'm glad you like them."

"I always have," her mother commented lightly.

There was an ease between them, and Aryl finally knew what to say. "In the meeting. I may have saved Yorl," she told her mother, "but I think you saved all of us."

Taisal's smile faded. "I prevented a vote," she corrected. "Today. Tikva's not going to give up—and she's not alone in her belief that Yena should have greater use of their Power. All we can do for now is keep Forbidden Talents secret. Imagine the temptation, if all Yena knew abilities like mine existed."

"I wanted breakfast in bed," Aryl admitted ruefully.

That drew a chuckle. "That I can arrange without breaking the Agreement—granted I get home tonight. Which is where you belong, youngest."

Then, as if Aryl was a baby, her mother kissed her on the forehead and pressed two fingers over the warm spot, *sending* her love.

Aryl was halfway across the bridge when she realized her mother's sending had contained something else, something Taisal hadn't intended her daughter to share.

Dread.

Interlude

THE OUD HAD LEFT THE TUANA village as they'd come, their vehicles etching a second set of lines through the dust. There'd been no more surprises.

One had been more than enough, Enris thought, kicking a tread mark.

"Hey!" Ral jumped sideways. "These are—were—clean boots, cousin."

Enris gestured apology. "I'm in a foul mood," he admitted. "You shouldn't bother with me."

Ral laughed and clapped the other on his shoulder. They'd had breakfast in the meeting hall, a usually lighthearted gathering to host those taking Passage. Tradition abounded during Visitation. "How can you be grumpy today?" he protested. He spun about, holding his hands from his sides to show off his new shirt. "Do I not look fabulous?"

Enris' lips twitched involuntarily as he considered his cousin. It was, to be fair, a fine shirt and Ral looked ridiculously blissful in it. Still . . . "She hasn't Chosen you yet," he cautioned. Gelle Licor was one of Naryn's ilk, in his opinion, full of her own Power and herself.

"A mere detail." This with an airy wave. "She filled my cup twice!"

"Well. That says it all, doesn't it." Enris somehow managed a straight face. Besides, what did he know of Choice? No Chooser-to-Be had offered to fill his cup. "Congratulations." And he meant it. Several couples had left the meeting hall last night with soft looks at one another. All during breakfast, Traud and Olalla had touched fingertips under the table when they thought no one could tell. Mind you, she'd hiccupped each and every time.

He should be grateful this morning had been calm and civil. There'd been a threat to the look and feel of Mauro Lorimar and his friends at the end of last night. They hadn't taken Irm's being picked for Passage well; they took Enris being "spared" as a personal insult. Only the watchful eye of the Speaker had kept them from saying what they felt.

Or worse.

"It'll be my turn to congratulate you soon, Enris," Ral said magnanimously. "That is, when you . . . when there's more . . . next time . . . I mean—" He coughed at some dust and then laughed. "You know what I mean."

"Not a clue," Enris grinned. "But if it has anything to do with letting me get to back to work sometime today, I'm happy."

The two stopped outside the shop. It was locked against the night; Jorg hadn't arrived yet.

Enris wasn't surprised. The Chosen weren't expected to attend the breakfast and they'd stayed up late, he and his parents, trying to make sense of the Oud. Jorg wanted to go to Council even if it meant revealing they'd had commerce with the Oud earlier. Ridersel wanted the strange object away from her family and forgotten. Returned to the Oud. Tossed in a field, if need be.

He'd—Enris sighed. He'd wanted to keep it a while longer, to puzzle at it in secret. Maybe not the best or wisest course, but his mother had given him that too-keen look, the one she used to see right through him, and agreed.

"I'd help you fetch the leavings, Cousin, but . . ." Ral indicated his new shirt. "Gelle would never forgive me."

Enris laughed and waved him on. "See you later."

To save time, he didn't bother unlocking the shop but went around to the side where he parked the cart each night. It was a long, thin alleyway, protected by the overhang from the potter next door. Enris was in its cool shadow before he noticed something wrong.

The cart had been turned upside down.

He ran the rest of the way, stopping with his hands on the wheels. They were priceless, virtually irreplaceable—and intact, he discovered after checking them carefully. He let out a sigh of relief. Whoever had done this hadn't been thorough fools.

They'd been angry. At him.

He didn't need to be an Adept to figure that out. Or to know who. There were footprints everywhere he looked, footprints made by fancy, hard-soled boots. Mauro Lorimar and his friends. He should have realized why they'd been all smiles at breakfast; it hadn't only been the company of their Choosers-to-Be.

Enris shook his head. None of that mattered. The Oud who brought the new day's leavings expected the previous ones to be gone. He was already running later than he liked—it would take most of the afternoon to empty the bins.

The cart was made of thick metal, built for heavy loads and rough terrain. On its big wheels, it could be moved with ease, even fully loaded. To flip it like this? He guessed there'd been five of them, maybe more.

Help would lead to questions. There were, Enris decided glumly, too many of those already.

He stood back, concentrated on the cart, and *pushed*. It was easier than shoving the bench. Once in the air, the cart moved without resistance. He turned it over and lowered it. Slowly. Slowly.

"Nice trick."

The cart thudded to the ground. Enris groaned. Had he damaged the wheels? He plunged to his hands and knees to check, ignoring Naryn.

She came closer, kicking dust. "Did you hear me?"

He rocked back on his heels and gazed up at her. "The wheels are fine." *No thanks to you,* he added to himself, keeping his shields tight.

"Wheels—? What do—" She seemed to collect herself. "So this is why you wouldn't vouch for me. You wanted to show off yourself!"

Enris got to his feet, brushing dust from his pants. "I'm not the one who ran to Council and the Adepts," he pointed out.

"I have every right to use my special Talent."

"No," he said calmly, "you don't. Not if you make a display of it where the Oud could find out." He wrapped his hands around the handles of the cart and heaved it into motion. "If you'll excuse me, I'm late." She didn't move; and he was forced to stop. "Naryn—" with exasperation.

"You didn't pick anyone last night. Why?"

Enris stared at her. "What are you talking about?"

"You know what I'm talking about. You aren't—" this as though she'd made a startling discovery "—stupid."

"Thank you. Now get out of my way."

Naryn put her hands on the cart. "Not until I get an answer."

"I could *push* you out of the way," he suggested almost idly.

She arched a shapely brow. "You could try."

For an instant, Enris ached to do just that, to pit his Power against hers, to make her stop behaving like the spoiled child she was. It was more than frustration, more than anger. Something deep inside, something he'd never felt before, wanted . . . was trying . . . trying to . . .

To answer . . .

"You!" he accused, dropping the handles and backing away. "What are you doing?"

Naryn tilted her head, as if she needed a different view of him. "How—interesting," she said, running the tip of her tongue over her lower lip to taste the word. "I suspected. Oh, yes. There was always something about you, Enris Mendolar. Annoying. Addictive. They're much the same, you know." She eased out of the cart's path, but only as far as the wall of the shop. She leaned back against the brick, stretching her slender right arm languidly over her head as if daring him to reach for it. "Go."

Enris wrapped his big hands around the cart handles and left her there.

By the time he reached the Oud tunnel, he'd almost stopped wanting to go back.

Chapter 15

WITHIN THREE FISTS OF THE M'hir's weakening, the afternoon rains returned with a vengeance, deafening and deadly. They pounded walls of water between buildings, obscured bridges and ladders. It was impossible to find a grip to climb while they fell; they left every branch and stalk slick and treacherous, encouraged slimy growths that puffed a choking black dust if touched. The brief morning respite swirled with mists and swarms of returning biters. It was, in Aryl's opinion, the worst season of all.

Council had ended the desperate hunt for dresel pods. There would be none left to find, none whole, that is. They'd done what they could; the precious extra stores were now hidden within the Cloisters. No Tikitik had ever set foot there, though if Yena fortunes held their course, they might.

Aryl made a wry face. Not something to say out loud, even if she dared admit having heard Council debate that very thing. It was too easy to be afraid of the future. She didn't need to be told how important it was to keep trying. To keep working. If they were to survive as a Clan, it would be because no one gave up.

At least she need no longer worry about those on Passage from Yena. There were no more isolated glows of Om'ray life; all who'd survived had reached their destinations, their presence merged into the larger glow of their new clan. With an effort of will that surprised her by growing easier with time, Aryl resisted the temptation to *reach* for their identities. She now understood the reasons to be wary of new Talent. It was enough, she told herself, to know these Yena lived.

To know Bern lived.

She wished them joy.

Over the past fists Aryl had discovered, also to her surprise, a talent for coaxing along Costa's greenery. There had been more sweetberries and, she thought proudly, a quite remarkable set of yellow-and-black gourds—type unknown—continued to ripen on the floor by one window panel. Maybe she'd paid more attention to his work than she realized.

"You'd probably grow without me," she told the rustling leaves. Her main task was keeping each growth from overwhelming all the others—that, and providing rain water to those pots not under a leak. A drop landed on her head and Aryl glared upward, suspecting her brother had made strategic holes in the family roof.

Costa . . . falling . . . screaming . . .

Taisal told her the sharp bite of loss would fade, that she'd be surprised by its pain for M'hirs to come, but no longer overcome. She wasn't there yet, Aryl thought helplessly, tears rolling down her cheeks. The world still stopped when she remembered he was gone. Each breath had to fight through her throat and . . .

"Aryl?" softly, from the doorway. "Are you all right?"

There were distinct disadvantages living with someone whose range of accepted Talents included an unsettling sensitivity to the emotions of others. Aryl rubbed her eyes and tried to keep irritation from her voice. "I'll be fine, Myris." She didn't try to lie; if shields hadn't protected her privacy, words couldn't. "I was thinking about Costa."

Myris took this as an invitation to enter, though she moved with caution. Her skin had produced a painful rash in response to one of Costa's captives. Not knowing which, her only choice was to avoid them all. It wasn't easy. The rains stimulated growth in the canopy—apparently even that indoors. An entire table had disappeared.

"Ael went for our supper," Myris told her, tactfully concentrating on the gourds. She pointed at the nearest. "Has anyone decided if we can eat those?"

"First Scout Haxel saw climbers eating a broken one she thought looked the same. She—" Aryl coughed slightly. "Seru told me Haxel chased them off so she could try it herself. Said it wasn't bad. The Adepts are watching her for signs of poison."

"Haxel is—" Myris broke off, her face flushed. "There's no respectful way to say this, Aryl. Anything she'd try, well, no one should. Trust me. No one. She has the sense of a flitter who's hit a tree once too often."

Aryl had to chew her lip to stop an equally disrespectful grin. Then, she stopped trying and chuckled with Myris. "How did you do that?" she spoke without thinking.

"Do what?"

Aryl took her turn pretending to study the gourds. They were as long as her arm and starting to thicken. If she squinted and imagined slices, maybe fried . . . they looked like food. Sort of.

"How did you change how I feel?" she asked finally, quietly. She glanced sidelong at Myris. "Through my shields."

The other Om'ray half-smiled. "You're too strong for me to influence, if that's what you think. But you know I'd never do that, even if I could."

"Then how?"

Myris reached out and gently tugged the lock of hair that

always escaped Aryl's binding. "You and Taisal. Always thinking about how to use your Power, your Talents. You want to change things. Do things. Me?" That mischievous look Aryl knew very well. "All I do is feel. Nothing more complicated. If there's Power in that, I don't know how to explain it. I feel what those around me feel. It took Ael a while to get used to it, believe me." The mischief became something dreamier and distracted.

Sending to her Chosen, no doubt. "You do more than that," Aryl insisted. "You changed how I felt, just now. You can't deny it."

"I didn't intend to—" The other hesitated, then sighed. "It's not something I control. But if I'm near someone in pain, sometimes I—sometimes I can ease it."

She was seeing Myris, really seeing her, as she hadn't before. This was why her aunt's expressions were always changing. Some weren't hers at all. There were those who could use their Power to accelerate a body's healing, but this? "The Adepts must value your Talent—" Aryl stopped at the flash of misery she couldn't help but sense. "I'm sorry," she said, unsure what she'd said.

"It's all right, Aryl," Myris said sadly. "They do. But I've more limits than use. I can ease the discomfort of close family—I do little or nothing for anyone else. I've tried." This last came out so utterly bleak, Aryl was afraid to ask.

"That's why you and Ael came to live with me, isn't it?" she guessed, shaking her head. "Here I thought I was taking you in."

Myris had a smile that could outshine the glows. "And we're grateful. Especially me." She swept up her arms in a grand gesture that just missed the purple vine draped over the glowbead string. "It's nice being home. This was my room, you know," as she caught Aryl's mystified expression. "I lived here until your mother Chose that handsome rascal Mele first and claimed the right . . ." her voice trailed away. "*Aie*. What am I saying? Poor Taisal."

That grief belonged to them both. Hers had faded, Aryl realized with a faint guilt. Or maybe newer pain had more strength. "What's past is past, Myris," she offered clumsily. "I'm glad you're here. So is Taisal." Their eyes sought the doorway at the same time, then they looked at each other. "Ael's back." Aryl stated the obvious. "We should eat." Her stomach gurgled agreement.

Myris laughed. "Glad someone has an appetite these days," she said. "You'll need a good breakfast before today's climb." Her hand reached out as if to touch Aryl's arm, then sketched gratitude instead.

Aryl followed her aunt to the main hall, bemused to think she'd been the one to comfort anyone else.

Not my fault . . . not my FAULT!!! . . .

Aryl winced and tightened her shields, already sorry she'd agreed to take Seru's youngest cousin with her this morning. Seru wasn't feeling well—she rarely was, these days. Being a Chooser newly ready for Choice was difficult enough. Having no unChosen in reach? Until she settled, Seru was, to put it mildly, difficult company.

Besides, it had seemed a golden opportunity. Aryl's bag was filled with her latest fiches, as she now thought of them. With the child along, she had a good reason to stay within the home grove instead of foraging during the rainless morning, and climb the sort of straight, open stalks she needed.

NOT MY FAULT!

Aryl winced again. "Will you hush?"

Joyn's black hair stuck through the gauze of his hood in every direction, making him resemble a startled flitter. Now he gave her a puzzled look. "I didn't say anything, Cousin Aryl."

"You're sending again," she sighed. His maturing shields were at that awkward stage, new and tight enough to damp most emotions, so he could be allowed away from his parents, but not yet under his conscious control. They should have been barely permeable to mindspeech. Should have. There were a handful of truly gifted Yena children; none were remotely as precocious or strong as Joyn Uruus, barely past eight M'hirs and already giving adults—and her—a headache. No wonder his mother, Rimis, had been doubtful of Aryl taking him.

"Oh!" His blue eyes brightened an impossible amount. "You could hear me? I was thinking about—" His expression fell. "It—"

"Wasn't your fault," Aryl finished wryly. Had she ever been this worried about something so trivial as cracking a bowl? Hard to imagine. She gave the thin rope between them a gentle shake. "Pay attention to where we are, little one," she suggested. "Your parents will not be pleased with me if you—" she caught herself unable to use the everyday Yena expression . . . "drop into the Lay" . . . and substituted "—if you're lost in the M'hir."

"Can that happen?" His eyes were wide. "Can the great wind sweep me away?" With the easy balance of the young, he let go of the stalk and stood tiptoe on the narrow frond, flapping his arms like a flitter caught in a gale. "Where would I go? What would I see? How would I get back down again?" this dubiously, with a look past their feet. "Would I fall?"

Falling was a game to Om'ray children, taught to climb as soon as they could crawl. Aryl remembered the willing tumbles, the snatching for holds, the laughter and shrieks, not to forget the ire of any parents who caught them. There would usually be a lecture on how only caution and care would keep them safe. But they played, she remembered that too, because they feared to fall. They felt safer having dared it to happen. Why wait on fate?

Children, she thought, had a special wisdom.

"Save your arms for climbing," she told him. "Once we're as high as you can go, I've something to show you."

I can go HIGH! I can go higher than anyone! This sending was accompanied by interwoven images of his age-mates, their faces filled with awe.

She'd never, Aryl decided, been that young. She shook her head and started to climb.

Joyn was a good climber; moreover, as a child he received all the dresel his body needed. Aryl set the pace more to husband her energy than his, though she was careful to choose a route suited to his shorter reach and small hands. All the while, she pointed out signs of danger, whether a weakened strip of bark or lurking stinger, waiting for his nod of understanding each time.

It had become a habit by now to gather what could be eaten. Joyn helped. As they filled a net, she'd leave it hanging to await their descent. They were in the lean season, when white fruits appeared in great numbers from the vines draped everywhere on older rastis, but these were hard and small, too bitter to eat. In the past, the Yena left them alone, knowing by the end of the rains they'd swell and ripen. When that happened, the fruits produced a scent that attracted flitters and climbers in great numbers. That was the harvest the Om'ray wanted, and their nets would fill with meat in short order.

This M'hir, they couldn't afford to wait a season. The unripe fruits weren't nutritious but, when added to other food, they improved appetite. It was becoming harder and harder to convince the older Om'ray to eat what they should. Aryl couldn't remember feeling hungry. What food they had would do no good if they couldn't bring themselves to eat it.

They were becoming thin, even the harvesters, now given slightly more dresel per day. Last fist, Council had declared all the strong climbers—all those left—to be harvesters. It gave Aryl no joy to be one of them at last, only purpose.

When she thought of her childish outbursts at being passed over last M'hir, of her blind envy, she was ashamed.

"Why are you sad?"

"Don't *sense* others," Aryl snapped, reaching for another hold, then shook her head again. How many times had she been scolded for the same ability? He was younger than she'd been, too young to understand. She glanced down. "Do your best, Joyn," she said firmly but with sympathy. "I know it's difficult. I had to practice and sometimes I still sense more than I mean to."

Easy to *sense* the child's state of mind—an interesting blend of unconscious pride and very aware contrition. He hadn't meant to pry; he did care why she was unhappy. He had, she decided with a rush of affection, a good heart.

Just as well. There was more Power in that tiny frame than in most adults; Aryl tightened her shields. "You're right," she admitted freely. "I am sad. It's all right. It's not about you, or being here."

"I understand. Everyone's sad," he said matter-of-factly. "And scared."

Little more than half her age, and growing up too fast. They all were. Maybe, she thought wearily, they had to. Aryl hooked her leg over a branch. At this indication they were to rest, the child did the same. "Do you know what history is, Joyn?" she asked, offering him a drink from her flask.

Neither wore their gauze hoods over their faces, so she could see his freckled nose crinkle with disgust. "The stories grandparents tell you when you've been bad. About your parents when they were children. They aren't," this with profound feeling, "fun."

"True," she chuckled. A flitter—the blue-and-red kind—landed nearby. It bent its head to turn one, then the other of its large green eyes at them, as if gauging how dangerous they were. Apparently satisfied, it began snapping at the cloud of biters that had settled over the branch at the same time as the two Om'ray. A good neighbor. "But I mean stories that are about all the Om'ray in a Clan, not just a family."

He looked astonished. "Do the Tuana have stories? The Vyna? The—"

Aryl interrupted what was sure to be the full list. "Every Clan has its own. That's another reason Passage is important. Those who come here tell us their stories and any they've heard from other Clans. Those who," she took a breath, "leave Yena take our stories with them."

Joyn frowned. "I hope they didn't take my grandmother's stories."

Her lips quirked. "Not that kind. Bigger stories. And those stories are put together into the history of all the Om'ray, of the entire world. We're in one of those stories, you and I, right now."

He gave her a suspicious look. "We're in a rastis."

Aryl gazed back, nonplussed. "I thought children had great imaginations," she said finally.

"For playing," Joyn informed her with great dignity. "We aren't playing. You," he clarified, "are too old to pretend."

"Maybe I am," Aryl agreed. "But this is a story, Joyn. One that will be retold everywhere there are Om'ray."

"What's it about?"

Death and disaster? She shifted the bag at her hip. "It will be about the brave Yena Clan," she began. "How everyone was a little sad and a little afraid—because we faced a time of danger and trouble, worse than any before it, worse than any to come. Every other Clan will know."

Joyn grew still. "How does the story end?"

"That's the good part," Aryl assured him. "It ends with the

best Harvest ever. We'll have so much fresh dresel cake that everyone could eat themselves sick—but they won't—" that for his parents, "—and there'll be a party that lasts until the next rains. Everyone will be happy."

He smiled, just a bit, then rolled his eyes. "You made that up."

"I thought you said I was too old," she responded archly. She shooed away biters. "Time to go."

They climbed in silence to the next whorl of fronds. As they eased past more thorn-shooters, Joyn spoke again.

"You don't believe our story will end that way. With everyone happy."

So much for shields against this one, she told herself ruefully, not that it couldn't have been simple perception. Somehow, though, she doubted it. Joyn was going to be a force to be reckoned with in future M'hirs. He was now.

"I don't know," Aryl said honestly. "No one does. But that's the ending I want."

I want everyone happy, too . . . I want everyone happy, too . . . I WANT EVERYONE HAPPY, TOO . . .

She didn't try to silence him.

She did, however, wince.

"Fiches," Joyn repeated, frowning in concentration. He held up two. "And I throw them?" this eagerly.

"No! Not yet," Aryl ordered, making sure he obeyed before turning back to her own preparations.

These fiches were a far cry from the first crude versions she'd tossed from Costa's window. Much of the change lay in their construction. At night and during the rains, she'd taught herself to braid threads teased from old clothing. Sore fingers later, she could reliably produce miniature ropes, strong yet light, that could be tied using a needle.

When dipped in vine sap and hung to dry, the tiny ropes became solid rods—perfect for bracing pieces of dresel wing. The wing itself was her limit. She'd found only one more, almost shredded, and her fiches shrank in size as she was forced to use smaller and smaller sections. Aryl had tried to sew or glue wing material together, but failed.

The rest of the change was in the design. Because of the small pieces of wing, the fiches were made of several supported pieces tied together. Through trial and error, they'd lost their simple triangular shape, becoming bent and angular. From a certain direction, Aryl squinted at one, they could be wastryls. She now had fiches that would soar in a straight line until hitting something—and there was always something. She needed open space to learn how far they really could fly.

As for landing? "Remember you asked me how to come down from the M'hir?" She turned over a fich and showed Joyn the tiny hooks dangling from its underside. "This is how. The hooks will catch on branches and hold."

"So it won't fall into the Lay."

"So it won't fall into the Lay," Aryl repeated firmly. It wouldn't be a soft or safe landing. But the fich wouldn't vanish beneath the canopy and drop to sure death.

Nor would a rider . . .

She focused on today.

They'd climbed as high as Joyn could. Aryl had watched him slow as his inner sense responded to the contrary tug of his bond to his mother. He didn't feel it as a leash; it was the awareness of *far enough* natural to an Om'ray. She imagined the edge of the world, beyond the outer Clans, would feel the same. This was, she thought with satisfaction, far enough for her as well.

This old rastis wove its fronds through the branches of an upstart nekis. The other plant was bare this season, its topheavy burst of leaves shed and new growth swelling in buds at every twig tip. Aryl had marked it before. The upper third away from the rastis was open to the sky.

And thick with twigs. She'd wasted time clearing them from her chosen perch, using her longknife to trim that growth as well as a hearty crop of thorn-ready thickles. Everything loved the sunward side. Joyn had cheerfully joined in, using his small blade to hack at a lump of bark that wasn't remotely in their way. But it kept him busy. The end result was a natural platform, broad enough for the two of them.

Aryl was satisfied.

From this vantage point, the canopy top flowed down and away like a green-brown sheet tossed over a lumpy mattress. The expanse ended where the Sarc grove rose, its larger, full stalks blocking any view of the lands beyond. Aryl had hoped to show the child the smallness of the world; perhaps, she thought, he didn't need to know quite yet.

Joyn had been impressed enough, particularly when he spotted flocks of flitters below, wheeling through the air. He'd wanted to send a fich flying after them, unaware how the open air tricked the eye with distance.

Aryl found herself enjoying his enthusiasm. At least, during those brief moments when Joyn kept it inside his own head and not hammering against her shields like the pending afternoon rain.

He was, she sighed, trying his best. She felt an unexpected sympathy for her own mother.

"Now?"

"Let me test the wind." The M'hir had finished, but there was a perceptible breeze flowing over the canopy. Aryl turned her face until the sweat on her forehead began to cool. "That way," she pointed, then added quickly, catching at his arm. "When I say and not before."

The sky wasn't the brilliant blue of her memories, but a more sullen hue, as if it harbored a grudge against the clouds already building toward Amna Clan. Those were tall and white. Joyn noticed her attention. "Buildings! Sky buildings!"

"Clouds," she corrected absently. "Where rain comes from."

The child fell outwardly silent. Inwardly, his mind was a frenzy of questions. *Who lives there?* He also wondered what they ate . . . *was it air?* . . . *how did it TASTE?* . . . and how often they went to—

"Joyn," Aryl interrupted, before too many details developed. "It's time to launch the first one. Just like we practiced with the twigs."

They both cocked their arms back, then threw them forward, releasing the little models at the extent of their reach. Aryl's throw was longer and more powerful, but Joyn's achieved a better angle as he let go. The two fiches floated off through the air.

"Look!!! Look at them!!!"

Aryl did, her heart in her mouth. The tiny craft caught the breeze and actually rose higher. At the same time, they traveled away, their easy flight mocking the full day's journey along bridge and branch that lay between them and the Sarc grove—

She shook off the wonder of it and began paying closer attention, noting the tilt and self-correction of Joyn's fich, how hers, a slightly different design, shuddered as it moved.

If they descended, it was imperceptible at this range. Soon, they were specks, eventually disappearing against the dark green of the grove.

With the power of the M'hir, she thought, they could fly across the world.

Joyn's small hand slipped into hers and Aryl gazed down at him in surprise. "Can we throw another one?" he pleaded.

She smiled. "That's why we're here."

They went through her bagful of fiches, all but one flight cheered as a resounding success—that one involving a too tight grip by very small fingers. He'd been so painfully sorry to break it *SO SORRY,* Aryl had to tease the child back to cheer or be unable to think a coherent thought the rest of the day.

She was crouched over her bag, digging out the last—having promised Joyn he could fly it—when she felt his sudden excitement.

"What is it?" Fich in hand, Aryl swiveled on her knees to look.

He pointed to the sky. "My fich! My fich is coming back, Cousin! It's one of mine. I'm sure it is. Look! I threw it, so it comes back!"

MINE! LOOK! MINE! LOOK!

HUSH! she threw against the joyful babble in her head. Joyn's mindvoice disappeared; he whimpered. Aryl gestured apology, but didn't lose her concentration. She tried to make sense of what she saw moving through the air. The child was right, it was coming in their direction. "There are sky hunters," she began to explain, then paused. "But that's too fast—"

Light slipped over a curved surface . . .

The fich dropped from her numb fingers. Aryl swept up Joyn and ran the wide branch back to the trunk. The child took hold without question, wrapping his arms and legs around her body to free her hands and arms. She kept moving, jumping to the branch below, then the next, and next, following the natural spiral of the nekis to put the massive trunk between them and what flew as quickly as possible. They crashed through leaves and vines, were whipped by twigs.

Finally, Aryl stopped, her back to the solid comfort of the trunk, and took shallow, silent breaths.

Safe? a whisper in her mind.

No. She stayed waiting and still. Joyn did the same, holding tight. This was the earliest training, to freeze at danger and trust the adult. Aryl brushed greenery from the hair sticking from his hood, wishing she felt like one.

Or was the calm assurance of her elders nothing more than this? she wondered suddenly. An outer shield, as effective as the inner at hiding fear and self-doubt.

Somehow, that wasn't a comfort.

Biters found them. One of her leaps must have planted her right leg in the midst of a thickle, judging by the needle-stings coursing up and down her calf.

After a few long moments of nothing more threatening, Aryl became restless. And curious. What was it doing?

"Stay here," she told Joyn, who obediently climbed down and took her place against the trunk. His eyes were dilated but calm. "I won't leave you," she added, startled by the intensity of her own promise.

To see it at such distance, she told herself, it must be larger than the device that had exploded during Harvest . . . much larger . . . but that glimpse? She'd swear it was the same design.

After pulling her hood's gauze over her face, Aryl bent to strip off her boots. They were protection and grip on flat branches, but for this, she needed her strong toes. She pressed her body to the trunk, reaching out to explore the ridged bark, finding and avoiding areas soft with moisture and rot that would crumble under her fingers. Once her hands had found a solid grip, her feet did the same.

In this way, slow and careful, she climbed around and up the trunk. She kept to the shadows and, when she reached the branch below the one where they'd stood to launch the fiches, she laid herself on it. Pacing each move with a pause, keeping those moves random, she crawled forward. Biters feasted on her feet and ankles. At least, she thought wryly as she crushed a familiar plant beneath her, she'd already fired this thickle's stock of weapons.

The shadow's edge, where the sunlight first reached this

branch and prompted a cluster of bud-tipped twigs, was her destination. From there, she should have a view of the sky, without being exposed herself. Aryl eased her hand forward.

The shadow grew.

Instantly, Aryl flattened against the wood. Her hand crept to the hilt of the longknife at her side and she tensed.

Instead of the fierce cry of a hunter, she heard something else.

Voices.

Chapter 16

VOICES? ARYL SLOWLY TURNED her head to look up, straining to see past the obstructing branch and the plants growing along its sides.

Two voices. One low and steady, that reminded her of Cetto's deep tone. The other was lower still. Every so often there'd be another sound, as if pieces of metal clicked together.

Something was wrong with those speaking. The cadence of sound, its complexity, suggested words. But the result was gibberish, as if flitters tried to repeat odd syllables of overheard speech.

The Tikitik communicated something to one another with incomprehensible hisses, she thought, entranced. Were these almost-but-not familiar sounds words of another kind?

The Tikitik—Aryl's whirling thoughts kept coming back to them, the only non-Om'ray she'd met. Their Speaker had claimed the device belonged to strangers from another world.

What other world?

Her stomach lurched at the concept, and Aryl turned her attention to seeing who spoke.

She dared crawl into the new shadow. Once there, she found

herself looking at the underside of a silvery metal platform, curved yet not all that strange—unless she considered that it was floating in air.

Aryl pulled the gauze from her face and head, dislodging a few biters who'd hung on in hope. The metal of the bottom wasn't smooth. She longed to touch it, but it was too high above her. She counted six open tubes, evenly spaced, and noted a series of long bumps sloped from one end to the other. Between the bumps were small clear domes with moving parts within—proof, if she needed any, that the device spying on the Harvest had been made by the same hands.

If they had hands.

The voices had continued their utterings. From the changing volume, they were now closer to the trunk than she was. Aryl cautiously rose to her feet, poised to hurry back to Joyn at any sign she'd been discovered. But she had to see.

The second vine she tested took her weight. Aryl climbed hand over hand until she reached the swell of the branch. Its bark was too smooth to grip, but an empty stinger nest offered support for one bare foot.

Hopefully empty.

Her toes found their hold and she pushed upward, slowly. Slowly. She had to slide her head and shoulders through rootlets, then twist to avoid coming too close to a round dark hole that probably housed a nesting brofer or two. They wouldn't bite unless disturbed. Hopefully, she repeated to herself.

At last she could see the rest of the flying machine.

Like a platform, the upper surface was open to the sky, but this wasn't designed for standing or walking. There were seats, two of them, and an area behind those with some disappointingly ordinary boxes.

Though they weren't, as far as Aryl could tell, made of wood or metal, but of something slick and white.

A sharp crack made her ease back down until she peered

through twigs. The voices were returning to their craft. The giant branch vibrated, as if to the footsteps of something much heavier than an Om'ray. Something familiar passed by—her bag, swinging in the grip of . . .

Somehow, Aryl didn't move or let out a sound.

Her bag was suspended from the dainty tips of an immense black claw—easily the size of Joyn. She knew better than to attract the attention of anything with that kind of armament. The claw, and her bag, continued past to the flying machine; the branch continued to complain until she worried it might snap.

She couldn't make out more of the creature. Its back was a huge dome of gleaming black, completely blocking her view.

The owner of the second voice was approaching. Aryl held her breath, wondering what kind it would be.

A boot appeared in front of her nose. A black boot that might have been leather, with fastenings of metal. Her eyes traveled up a loose tube of brown fabric, finely woven, then stopped, riveted by four fingers and a thumb that carefully held a small object.

Her fich.

Held by a hand twin to hers.

Another boot and leg moved by. Then she was staring at the back of an Om'ray.

Someone on Passage? Aryl's foot pushed against the nest as she hurried to climb up. At the same time, she instinctively *reached* to discover who this could be, wearing such clothes, keeping such company . . .

Nothing.

To her inner sense, the Om'ray standing above her didn't exist.

The wrongness made Aryl dizzy, and she grabbed desperately to keep from falling. The rustle attracted attention at last. The not-real Om'ray turned and looked in her direction. The giant black creature left the flying machine with disturbing agility, its pair of claws snapping in the air as if seeking her throat.

The resulting violent sway of the branch drew a cry of protest from the other and knocked Aryl loose.

She plummeted.

Her hand shot out and wrapped around the vine she'd climbed before; her other hand joined it and she half-slid down to the safety of the branch below. Then, she was running.

Behind her, voices rumbled and spoke in urgent tones.

Not one word made sense.

Joyn asked no questions. Ready the instant Aryl reappeared, he launched himself into her arms, settling against her chest. She couldn't carry him for long, but she didn't think of detaching him here.

Not when that—that abomination was still close.

FEAR.

She didn't protest, quite sure her own emotions were under no better control. But her movements had to be, and Aryl finally slowed just enough to plan the best path through the nekis to the old rastis and down.

Could the flying machine follow?

A question she couldn't answer.

Her back and legs were already burning. Aryl looked at the black-haired head nestled against her chest. "Joyn," she said reluctantly. "We have to go quickly from here. Can you do that for me? Be fast?"

A flash of proud assurance. He let go at once, his blue eyes bright. "I'm too fast," the child boasted. "My mother says so."

"I'm sure she does." Aryl's hands wanted to shake as she

reattached the line between them. "Don't go too fast for me, please. You know I'm old." She glanced up through the canopy. No sign of the machine.

No voices either.

They went down, Aryl keeping the pace to Joyn's ability. Down was harder on them both. She used the line to lower him where she could, carried him where the best handholds were too far apart for a child. It wasn't the way home—not directly. She couldn't risk being followed there.

All the while, she fought to understand and failed.

Only the dead were silent—even the Lost had a presence that could be *sensed*, minds to receive instruction. But the silent Om'ray hadn't been dead. He had walked, spoken, been curious about her fich.

All while not being real.

When at last convinced they weren't pursued, Aryl stopped to let them both catch their breath. They were, she judged, a tenth's hard climb from home.

She glanced at Joyn, sitting at her feet, and revised her estimate. His eyes were half closed, and he gave little hiccups of misery. Two tenths—maybe more. Worse, the air was ominously heavy. The afternoon rains would arrive long before they were safe.

Aryl considered the problem. Rimis Uruus, Joyn's mother, would know exactly where he was. They were to be back soon. She'd worry, perhaps *sense* her child's agitation despite the distance. At any moment, if she hadn't already, she'd follow her bond to her son.

So Rimis and whoever came with her would meet them halfway or better. There was safety from some threats in numbers; to others, they presented a more appetizing target.

"Let's go." Aryl rubbed the child between his thin shoulders. "Here—I saved you a bit of cake." It was hers, but he'd need it more. She was right. Joyn pushed it into his mouth with both hands, gesturing his thanks as he chewed. "Drink. Not too much." When he handed back the flask, she took a long swallow, then left it hanging. There'd be rain to drink soon, or they'd be beyond thirst.

Either way, extra weight was their enemy. She'd learned that lesson retrieving the pods. Aryl continued divesting herself of what she could do without. Her boots from her belt. Her longknife—after sober consideration—joined them. As Joyn watched, wide-eyed, she shed her waterproof over-jerkin and its hood, though she left the gauze wrap on her arms and legs. Some bites could end their journey and, thinking of that, Aryl left the thorns in her leg. If she pulled them free, they'd bleed and attract worse trouble.

"I can take off my clothes, too." He was already pulling at his belt fastening.

"You need yours," she told him. "Tough old skin, remember?"

Joyn gave her that by now familiar doubting look, but stopped. If they were caught in the rains—when they were, Aryl corrected, tasting the air—he'd chill too quickly without the waterproof layer.

They began to move again. This time, Aryl sought the straightest route. Fortunately, they were now at the level where the largest branches leaned and crisscrossed into roadways for nimble Om'ray feet. The problem lay in what else liked such easy paths.

Stitler traps were the greatest threat. Several times they were forced to retrace their steps and go around patches with that ominous glisten of mucus. Strips of dried skin and wisps of flitter wing bore mute witness to the appetite hiding in shadow.

Aryl made note of each. If they made it back, she'd tell Haxel. The scouts didn't tolerate stitlers in Yena territory, but the creatures took full advantage of the rains' lessened patrols to sneak closer.

Joyn's steps grew slower and less sure. Sooner than she'd hoped, he staggered and would have fallen but for her hands under his arms. The sense of exhaustion the contact sent through her made her want to drop down and sleep for days, too. She crouched to let his small arms wrap around her neck, then helped him put his legs around her waist. He sighed and burrowed his head into the hollow of her neck, half-asleep already.

Afraid to trust his grip, Aryl wound the line that had connected them around them both and knotted it. It would help if he lost his hold.

It was easier going at first. Aryl moved at her own pace, no longer confined to paths suited to a child. Joyn's warmth fought the chill starting to go through her; as the first tentative drops of rain fell, his clothing shielded the front of her body. His trust—that renewed strength she didn't know she had.

But he was a solid weight, sapping her energy and shifting her balance. As Aryl climbed, she added this now-nightmarish journey to her list of grievances against those in the flying machine.

Whatever they were. She could only hope one day they'd have to—

Mother! HERE HERE HERE!!!!

Aryl almost slipped at the power of that sending. "Hush," she whispered urgently, lips against Joyn's hair. "She knows." But she lowered her shields, hoping Rimis really was close.

Closer, not close. And lower. Aryl frowned as she understood. Rimis must be frantic to reach Joyn. They were taking the summer bridges, faster, yes, but dangerously close to the now-high waters of the Lay. Council forbade their use during the rains and had scouts remove the ladders.

None of which counted against the bond demanding these two be back together.

As if to make her life perfect, the rain chose that moment to go from gentle downpour to deluge, erasing most of the world.

"Wh—here are we?"

"Dry, for now," Aryl told the sleepy child. She strode to the edge of their shelter. *Tooks* were rare; only their giant upturned leaves could withstand this flood from the sky. They'd been lucky. She'd known one was somewhere near, but found it by virtue of blindly blundering into its shelter.

Shivering, she waved to discourage the mass of biters who'd taken refuge with them, and tried to make out anything through the lines of rain.

"My mother!" This with outrage as Joyn came fully awake. "She's not coming!"

"I know," Aryl said. She'd sensed their rescuers' retreat. "It's not safe in this, Joyn. They've found shelter, too." She hoped. Without *reaching* more deeply—and failing her promise—she couldn't contact them to be sure.

I have to go! I HAVE TO GO!!

"Oh, no, you don't." Aryl caught the child as he lunged to his feet and tried to run past. "Are you a baby, to crawl off a bridge after a toy? Look outside. Look!" as he struggled weakly, then gave up. "We don't have a choice, Joyn. We wait out the worst of it. So must Rimis."

He leaned against her. "I'm eight."

Aryl couldn't tell if this was to impress her or explain. She put her arms around Joyn anyway and held him tight.

Aryl opened her eyes, at first gradually, then abruptly awake. Her first conscious thought was fear. The canopy was no place to take a nap. Falling asleep here was a sure way to be a meal for something else. She hadn't meant to sleep. Hadn't dared . . .

Her second thought was that they weren't alone.

The rain above must have ended. Sunbeams sparkled through the slow, steady drip from leaves and fronds.

They sparkled improbably along the knobby circles that served the Tikitik as skin.

Joyn! The child woke in her grasp; warned by Aryl's sending, he did no more than open his eyes and tense.

Three of the creatures stood looking at them. Though much taller than Aryl at the shoulder, their heads hung below the edge of the leaf. She stared at what passed for their faces. Their eyes weren't all locked on her. The smaller front pairs kept watch, darting in random directions on their cones of flesh to survey their surroundings.

In the hush, she could hear the sound this made, moist and sharp, like raw flesh being tugged from a bone.

Their larger hind eyes were fixed on her. They appeared to be waiting for something.

Aryl staggered to her feet, helping Joyn rise as well. Her leg was asleep and protested, the other starting to swell painfully around each embedded spine. "We see you," she said, guessing what they expected from her. Om'ray were supposed to take time to grasp the reality of others. After the creatures from the flying machine, she thought, these no longer seemed as improbable.

The finger-things around the mouth of the centermost creature writhed for a moment, as if tasting the air. Aryl put her hands on Joyn's shoulders. Then, all four of that Tikitik's eyes focused on her. "Yes. You are the witness. Come with us."

"No!" Aryl protested. She backed a step, pulling Joyn with her. She deliberately set him behind her and repeated more politely, but as adamantly, "No. We're on our way home. To Yena."

Its head bobbed twice. "Yes. You are the witness. That is not in dispute. We require you. Come."

"What do you want with us?"

Silence for a moment. Then, "You are to come. Not the youngling."

Leave Joyn alone in the canopy? For a heartbeat, Aryl let her Power touch the *other place,* desperate enough to consider sending him through the Dark . . . where? Her thoughts scattered.

Just as well, she realized, calming down. There would be nothing worse for all Om'ray than demonstrating that Talent to Tikitik. Then she remembered her mother, bargaining with the Speaker. The creatures weren't completely unreasonable. Hadn't Cetto thought to trade with them?

"Let me take him home first," Aryl pleaded. "Then I'll go with you." Once back at Yena she could let Taisal take over. And would.

That double nod. She was beginning to fear it had nothing to do with agreement.

"Our puzzle to solve. You will come."

Her mother's words.

The flanking Tikitik bent lower, their flexible arms reaching in—

"Joyn!!!" That shout didn't come from a Tikitik. Aryl sagged with relief. Joyn, with blithe disregard for strange creatures or danger, pushed by her and ran out between the Tikitik.

HERE HERE HERE!!!

The joyous flood of welcome and reunion mean Rimis was out there, near enough to take her missing son in her arms, somewhere behind the Tikitik. Aryl felt three other Om'ray as well and didn't hesitate to learn who: Joyn's father, Troa sud Uruus. Haxel, First Scout. Ael.

"I'm going home," she told the Tikitik firmly, and started to walk by them, too.

Like the wastryls' strike, they grabbed her, their three-fingered hands fastening like claws on Aryl's arms and legs, lifting her into the air. Before she could draw breath to scream, a hideous face pressed against hers, its gray writhing finger-things racing over her cheeks to find and enter her mouth.

She couldn't breathe!

The world dimmed and disappeared.

Interlude

"'BEST IS.' " ENRIS SHOOK HIS head in disgust. "Huh."

The mysterious cylinder sat on the turntable, mocking him, its secrets quite safe. Frustrated, he stood and kicked his stool under the bench. The heat should be shunted back to the melting vat soon anyway, and there was always sweeping to do. They didn't waste a shaving, not here.

But his steps slowed and stopped before he reached controls or broom.

Enris turned, caught again by the puzzle. "What are you?" he whispered. Not that he'd be overheard. These days, he woke well before dawn and made his way to the shop through the fields rather than the road. It let him work in privacy on what shouldn't be in their shop at all. Jorg and Ridersel understood.

That this clandestine approach also let him avoid Naryn S'ud-laat was something he didn't share with his parents.

He went back, pulling out his stool to sit, his eyes locked on the cylinder. A sophisticated device—no doubt of that. A tool, not an ornament. But how to discern its function without power? He'd tried touching an Oud cell to its exposed inner workings. While those ably fed the ubiquitous strips and beads of glows, the cell had had no effect on this.

The materials of its manufacture were equally unhelpful. Yes, the outer case was metal, but the kind? It defied everything he'd tried, and he'd tried everything short of tossing it into the melting vat. Tempting as that seemed at times.

The object might be safe from him, but Enris feared his failure to understand it. Not because of what the Oud might do if it returned before he had an answer for the creature—though his father was sensibly anxious on that point—but because he was sure the cylinder held a meaning important to Om'ray, not Oud.

Three fists since the Oud left the cylinder and, beyond the leaving of those on Passage and the arrival of two others, nothing had changed. As for the Oud? Some seasons, the Visitation drums sounded but once; in others, the Oud seemed obsessed with the village, and their Speaker reappeared so often nothing could be accomplished for days at a time. They hadn't returned yet, but there was no way to predict or understand them.

They hadn't made this.

"Who did?" Enris asked softly. Someone with incredible skill. Someone, he knew, who could teach him more about metalworking than he could imagine.

And maybe more about his own people than they knew.

"Not if I can't—" His eyes narrowed in thought. If this was made by an Om'ray . . . someone like himself . . . there was one way to possibly learn more.

If only a name . . .

His fingers hovered over its surface as if asking for permission.

Nothing else had worked, he reminded himself, licking suddenly dry lips. And he was alone.

Feeling thoroughly foolish, Enris let a strand of Power reach toward the cylinder, as if the metal was something he'd made and given his name. Let Power *touch*.

His lips parted in wonder as unheard sounds flooded his

consciousness . . . they were words that made no sense, uttered by a voice he'd never heard before . . . another voice . . . another . . . some different, some the same . . . until it was as if everyone in the meeting hall spoke at once . . .

He tried to isolate one, follow it, but the words . . . they were noise . . .

Disturbance! Something was twisting his Power. Something that rebuffed and snatched for it at the same instant, as if compelled to consume what it knew was poison.

Enris broke free, his head spinning until it was all he could do not to retch.

An Oud.

That much he realized as the nausea faded beneath waves of pain, each new onrush worse than the one before. If he didn't know better, he'd swear there was a vise being screwed over his temples. By no friend either.

He fought to think . . . being too near certain Oud when using Power caused an unpleasant reaction. Every Om'ray knew that.

This was "unpleasant?" He'd have laughed except the movement would likely remove his throbbing head from his shoulders.

What, he knew. But how? He was alone. There'd been no drumming. The Watchers would never let an Oud enter the village without that warning.

An Oud had brought the device—had handled it. Had the creature imprinted its own version of Power, its name, into the metal?

Something for Adepts to pick at, not a metalworker.

Enris made his way to the sink, put his head under the tap, and turned it on full. Clenching his teeth at the cold, he kept the water pounding against the base of his skull until he felt able to stand. Which he did, after a fashion. His hands gripped the solid, rounded rim of the sink and his arms braced his shaking body so he didn't collapse. He stayed that way and stared, trying not to think, watching drips from his face and hair vanish into the torrent swirling to the drain.

After a few moments, Enris took a deep breath and turned off the water. He eased himself straight, the muscles of his back burning as if he'd pushed a full cart all day. One hand swept still-wet hair from his brow.

Instinct made him *reach* for those around him, to reassure himself with his own kind. But each speck of warmth was distant, as if he had been pulled away from them without moving at all. Even the Call from Tuana's eager Choosers was dimmed and strange.

Shivering now from more than his wet hair and shirt, Enris *reached* farther, intent on reestablishing the world and his place as it should be.

It was as if his Power was smothered by sand or blankets. He could, if he wanted, lift his hand and point to Yena and the other clans. He couldn't feel their existence as richly as he should.

If this was why the Adepts cautioned every Om'ray to keep shields tight around the Oud, he was more than willing to obey. As for how long he'd be affected? Enris didn't dare flinch, but his heart sank. It was said to be worse depending on a person's individual Power.

"Wonderful," Enris muttered. He might not share Naryn's craving for an Adept's robe, but he knew his own strength.

He didn't need Power to work. That was the truth. He forced himself to the furnace controls and disconnected the village shunt, keeping a steadying hand on the wall as he worked. The edges of the vat doors began to glow.

There were four in total. The first, the mouth they called it, was close to the door and had a ramp that allowed the cart to be pushed up and its load dumped. Through that opening was the vat's fiery heart, where Oud metal leavings were quickly melted into liquid. Farther along the vat, itself twice as long as any shop bench, were two lower, small doors that opened into troughs. The troughs were of stone, like the vat itself, and as impervious to the immense heat. They led to the assembled molds for the day's pour, some created by Jorg and Enris, others older than any memory of their making. Once the streams of molten metal began to flow, every window and skylight would have to open to keep the shop bearable.

The fourth and final door was outside the shop and could only be opened by Oud. They supplied the heat that melted their own metal, as well as warmed the Tuana village by night. They kept the manner of that heat secret, like their power cells, like their glows, like all other scraps of technology they doled out to the Om'ray above them with as much charity as a sandstorm. Cells that failed were replaced with new ones. Over time, the melting vat would fail as well and the Oud needed access to its interior to restore its function.

For all they knew, Enris scowled, the Oud collected something of value only to themselves from the vat, using the Tuana to do the work.

Once sure the vat was heating properly, Enris turned open the upper windows. It was still too dark outside to open them all and risk lopers. Then he went in search of the cylinder, finally locating it under his father's bench within a curl of shavings. He found himself loath to touch it, and had to force his fingers to hold the cool shape.

They slipped, naturally, into those five indentations. He was as startled as if this was the first time. In a way, it was, for now he had a glimmering of what the device could be. Each indentation was softer than the rest of the outer case; the pressure of a finger was enough to push a spot further in or release it. Controls, he decided. The positioning of it in his hand? It was easy to lift and hold it near his mouth.

As for what he'd sensed, before being hit by whatever remnant the Oud had left behind?

"A voice keeper," Enris exclaimed.

"A what?"

He slammed tight his shields and slipped the precious cylinder beneath his shirt before he turned to face the intruder. "A rude interruption," he snapped, "by someone who should have better manners."

The young Om'ray standing inside the door gestured apology, but his eyes were bright and curious as they gazed around the shop, then back to Enris. "I didn't mean to startle you. But my room went cold. Someone told me you control the heat?" This was offered with caution, as if the other felt the brunt of a joke. He came farther in, ignoring Enris' warning scowl. A sudden wide grin split his face as he came closer. "I don't believe it! You do! This is the first warm place I've been since I arrived." He gave an exaggerated shiver despite wearing not one, but two heavy coats.

Enris relaxed at the other's delight in the heat radiating from the vat doors, recognizing one of the newcomers recently arrived on Passage. A stranger. "Try working here during the day," he suggested. "Then you'll want to be anywhere else. I'm Enris Mendolar."

"I'm good with a broom," the stranger offered, taking the one near his hand and waving it about. "Yuhas Parth, at your service."

There'd been a Parth who arrived two generations ago; those vivid green eyes were now part of Licor heritage. Enris, though his Power waxed and waned uncomfortably with the effort, could sense nothing but goodwill through Yuhas' weak shield. Goodwill and a dark, terrible grief.

Enris withdrew, somewhat surprised to discover himself already nodding. He shrugged. "If you like," he said. "There's a place—" he pointed "—by the back wall for anything you sweep up. We don't waste metal."

"Who does?" Yuhas took off one coat, putting it on the hook Enris indicated, but kept on the second. As he got to work, he said over his shoulder, "There's more in this room than is owned by my entire clan—outside the Cloisters. Not that there's much call for metal in the canopy."

Enris had gone back to his bench, waiting for an opportunity to put away the cylinder. Now he looked at Yuhas with greater interest. "That's right. You're from Yena."

"Called halfway across the world by the lovely Caynen S'udlaat." This was said with that wide grin Enris now suspected was the other's mask. "Her family has given me permission to lay my heart at her feet. We're having supper tonight. I don't suppose you could turn up the heat in their home before that?" A comical look of dismay.

"Not really. I can turn it on or off," Enris admitted. "The Oud built the underground pipes that heat the floors. Some buildings have more than others. You'll get used to it."

"If you say so," Yuhas replied, clearly doubtful.

Both were silent for a time after that. Enris busied himself wrapping the handle of a new carving blade, glancing at his new assistant once in a while. Yuhas plied the broom with such intensity it threatened to wear away the flooring, but he didn't comment.

The heat continued to rise, now joined by rays of sunlight. Since he couldn't strip off his shirt while it hid the cylinder, Enris opened the remaining windows, grinning to himself when Yuhas, far from objecting to the sudden cool draft, shed his final coat. Beneath, his muscular arms were bare, since he wore only a body-covering tunic of white-and-black fabric, belted over what appeared to be tight leggings of a gauzy material. No wonder he'd been cold last night, Enris thought, rather amused.

Otherwise, Yuhas appeared ordinary enough, with a strong frame that rivaled Enris' own. He began to seriously consider the advantages of an assistant who could push a full cart—after all, each stranger would need to find a workplace once Chosen and part of Tuana.

But first . . . his attention was caught by what hung from Yuhas' belt. "May I see those?" he asked, indicating the unusually long knife and hook.

"Of course." Yuhas leaned the broom against a bench and

handed Enris the knife first. "It's Tikitik," he said with a note of apology. "Yena don't make things from metal like you."

"It's fine work," Enris said sincerely, surprised by the lightness and edge of the blade. He'd never seen such—no surprise, he'd never met a Yena before. The hook was next and he turned it over in his hands, trying to imagine what it was for, then shook his head. "What's this? To help with climbing?"

Yuhas took it back. His lips quirked oddly as he settled the big curve of metal against his palm. Without warning, he leaped from the floor to the cluttered benchtop in one easy move, the hand with the hook continuing that upward motion in a smooth overhead sweep as if to capture something hanging from the rafters. The metal flashed in the light.

Enris opened his mouth to protest, closing it as he saw the Yena Om'ray balanced on the very edge of the bench, using only his toes. With another too-quick move, Yuhas was on the floor again. He looked, if anything, less confident on that flat surface than he had in the air.

The hook landed in the pile of shavings beside the broom. "Of no use here," Yuhas said, his voice flat.

He meant himself, too. No need to touch the other's deeper thoughts to know. They were close in age, but Enris had never felt anything close to the black despair leaking through the other's best efforts. The Adepts—Council—would have read the memory of Yuhas' journey here. They would have listened and recorded any stories he brought concerning his kind. But those weren't always shared with all of Tuana. "What happened to you, to Yena?" he asked, sinking to his stool.

Bitterness now. "Why do you care, metalworker?"

"I—" Enris checked that the door was turned closed. It was early for anyone else to be about; nonetheless, he lowered his voice. "My brother went on Passage three harvests ago. I—I have reason to believe he went to Yena. That he died there. Alone."

"Kiric Mendolar. You look like him."

He hadn't wanted to be right. "How did he die?" Enris asked heavily.

"His Passage was slowed by flood. When he arrived, the Chooser he sought had Joined elsewhere." Yuhas paused and shrugged. "Now that I see your part of the world, I understand why our Speaker said our way of life killed him as surely as that loneliness. Yena do not set foot upon the ground." His voice grew husky. "Death waits."

"Tuana don't set foot below ground—not without permission." Enris searched the other's face. "Kiric's why I care what happens to Yena—what may have happened. He died there, yes, but he went willingly, full of hope for the future. He wanted to become one of you as much as I—" He stopped there, unwilling to say the rest and offend his visitor.

"As much as you want to stay here," Yuhas finished for him. "Don't look surprised, Enris. I didn't want to take Passage either." Hard strokes of the broom sent shavings and hook into the collection pit. When done, he leaned his crossed arms on top of the handle and gazed at Enris, his face bleak. "So much for what any Om'ray wants."

Chapter 17

ARYL SCREAMED.

The echoes were strange and deafening. She tried to cover her ears.

Her hands . . . she couldn't move them! Couldn't move her arms . . . her legs . . . her . . .

Swallowing another scream down her raw throat, Aryl made herself stop struggling. Where was she? The darkness seemed to press against her face. She blinked to prove her eyes were open; that nothing covered her face. It was still dark.

More than dark. There was no light at all. Was she in that *other place*?

No. This was nothing more than the absence of light. Being in the *other place* was like being in the M'hir—to stay still, to stay yourself, you had to hold on. She took a breath, reassured by the sound of air moving in and out of her body.

Alive. In the dark. She tested her body with more care. Something held her arms against her body. Not painful, but snug. Her legs were slightly apart as if she stood naturally, but immobile. She could rock her head forward and back, but her body . . . her body . . . a scream tried to force its way out.

Calm down! she told herself. Think. Her body wouldn't move, though she could take deep breaths.

And those breaths . . . Aryl closed her mouth and sniffed, then gagged. "I know that smell," she whispered. Her voice echoed, as if there was space overhead. The smell was what mattered. Damp wood. Rot. Water.

The Lay Swamp. Why would the Tikitik . . . ?

They'd kidnapped her! "Let me go!" Aryl shouted. "Let me go!" The echoes were harsh and punished her ears, but she didn't stop. "You've no right to keep me here! Let me go!"

She was blinded by a circle of light and lifted her face to meet a rush of fresher air. Her triumph lasted as long as it took something like hooks to grab the corners of her mouth and force it open. *Something* was pushed into her mouth, then the hooks, light, and air were gone.

About to spit, a wonderful, familiar taste changed her mind. Fresh dresel, sweet and ripe and moist. She chewed slowly, with relish, and licked her lips when done.

Not killing her, she told herself, faintly surprised.

Aryl closed her eyes and sought her inner sense, *reaching*. No others were close; she was relieved at first. They hadn't taken Joyn or the others.

But no others were close at all.

The cluster of Om'ray that must be Yena was appallingly dim and distant. She could barely tell it from that of Pana or Tuana. When she tried, she couldn't sense *who* anyone was.

Had the Tikitik taken her to the edge of the world?

She concentrated, pouring all her Power into a frantic sending. *Mother . . . I'm here . . . Mother . . . !*

And reached no one. The perfect time to discover her limit, Aryl scolded herself weakly.

There was another way.

Without giving herself time to hesitate or doubt, she threw open her thoughts to the *other,* seeking the feel of Taisal's clear, ordered thoughts within its wild current, doing her best to remember her mother's face.

It wasn't as easy as before. The inner *darkness* threatened her, pulled at her. Desperate, she refused to stop, feeling the drain as though blood poured from her body.

Here.

With the word, an easing of effort, as though their meeting in that Dark formed a bridge. Across it poured a torrent of worry, anger, fear . . .

Mother! Aryl drowned in emotion: Taisal's, her own. All she could think for a moment was that she wasn't alone—no matter how far they'd taken her—she wasn't alone.

Where are you, Daughter? I can't find you. Sudden, overwhelming dread. *Are you still within the world?*

A question too close to Aryl's initial fear for comfort. *I'm all right, Mother*, she hastened to send. *I've been unconscious—I don't know how long. When I woke—Pana's as far. Tuana. But I can barely sense Amna from here.* She fought panic. *Or home.*

It has been two days. A burst of images and sensations, as if Taisal sought to tell her too much at once. Or did their strange connection allow more than words and emotion through? Did it grant access to memory, too?

For Aryl might have been there at the interruption of a Council meeting . . . might have seen Ael's face as he gasped the news of her kidnapping. She might have been Taisal, demanding the right to see where it happened . . . insisting on leaving at first light . . . overriding every argument . . .

She might have shared the exhausted pain of muscles no longer used to hard climbing, the desolation at its end . . . made the decision herself to continue despite protests from her companions . . . been determined to follow Haxel, for the First Scout had never left her captors' trail, leaving markers behind . . .

Aryl might have come face-to-face with the weary, returning First Scout, frustrated to lose the trail in the waters of the Lay, and now sincerely furious to be responsible for Yena's Speaker and others so close to truenight . . . watched lengthening shadows while curled within a makeshift shelter high in a nekis, with only strings of glows for protection . . .

The images stopped there. Either her mother had found a way to stop them spilling free, or Aryl had pulled away, shocked by what she'd learned.

Her mother had spent truenight in the open?

You shouldn't be here, she sent, startled by her own anger. *What if the Tikitik Speaker went to Yena? Who would speak to it?*

Her mother sent an image of the Speaker's Pendant, hanging free in front of what had to be a scout's thick tunic. *If it wants conversation, let it find me. Let it explain why the Tikitik have taken my daughter!*

The fury was matched by determination. Taisal di Sarc might be away from Yena's protection, but Aryl sensed no fear.

That was fine. She felt more than enough for them both.

You must go home.

Not without you! Her mother's sudden desperation disturbed the *other,* weakening their link. *I can't lose you, too!*

Aryl fought to keep them connected. She projected confidence, hid her fear. *Don't worry.* She sent the taste of fresh dresel, careful to avoid thoughts of being pinned in the dark. *They're taking care of me. I'm safe. I'll get home.*

The link firmed as Taisal calmed, but only slightly. *Come home. Now. The way you sent Bern.*

Aryl opened her eyes and stared at the real darkness. *You can't mean that.*

I do. Come home! I know how you've reached me, where we are. You control the Dark, *Aryl. Use your gift!*

The urgency to escape, to be home, ripped through her like pain. Aryl tasted salt on her lips and blinked away the rest of her tears. *Even if I knew how—even if I dared,* she sent at last, *I can't. Where I am—it's someplace impossible to leave. If I make myself disappear, the Tikitik will know it must be by Power. The mug will break.*

Aryl thought her mother gone then, so faint did her presence become.

Then, their connection was restored.

Restored, but with a difference. Taisal's anxiety for her was gone, replaced by cool satisfaction. *My trust was not misplaced, Daughter.*

A test?

Aryl found if she bent her head forward as far as it would go, she could rest her forehead against something hard, that crumbled slightly but held. *Is that why you climbed after me, Mother?* she asked, feeling something inside crumble too. *Did you risk truenight to save me—or to stop me saving myself?*

If she'd thought she'd felt Taisal's determination before, that emotion was nothing to the wall of will that surged across their connection. *What makes you think those are different?*

Many an otherwise peaceful night's sleep had been disturbed by the incessant *chewchewchew* of the various crawlers that ate their way through wood. They didn't appear to care if they were snacking on a living rastis or the floor of a house, though the Yena certainly minded the distinction. Hunting them out after the rains was a task for all.

Having wept herself to sleep, Aryl woke to that familiar annoyance. It took her a befuddled moment to realize she wasn't home, had slept standing up, and the sound came from something in front of her face.

She was being chewed? "Help! Hel—"

Light burst against her eyes. Squinting through the tiniest slit of her eyelids, Aryl saw it came through a steadily enlarging hole. A hole in . . . she squinted harder, eyes tearing . . . wood?

It was so ordinary a material that she sagged in relief. She hadn't wanted to admit, even to herself, that she'd harbored a nightmare of being inside one of the Tikitik's great beasts.

More light, but her eyes were quickly adapting. She was inside something, Aryl grasped with amazement. But not a beast.

She was *inside* a rastis.

"Hello?"

Whatever widened the gap didn't reply. Aryl fell silent, wondering what was next. Should she open her mouth? She was in favor of eating; just not the hooks.

The opening grew larger than before, its edges falling away. Release? Rescue? Aryl's entire body throbbed with hope.

Then, what was opening the hole came into view.

"Help!!!!! Help!!!!" she screamed. "Please! Help me!"

It was a creeper, its eyes gleaming at her as it used its sharp mouthparts to bite away her protection. Another appeared overhead, upside down, long black feelers tapping at the wood as if assessing its partner's progress. Together, they kept at their task. Soon, the hole would be wide enough for their bodies.

After that, she'd start to die. Creepers cut into living flesh with those terrible jaws, making an entryway for the hordes of hungry offspring who rode their parent's back. Trapped like this, she was a banquet.

An Adept could have *pushed* them away.

Aryl didn't know how.

She only knew she wanted those things *gone*. She sobbed, so terrified she could hardly breathe. A feeler brushed her forehead . . . another tapped her right eyelid closed.

Self-preservation won. Aryl tried to concentrate . . . to send them to the *other place*. She'd seen them attack a nesting aspird, knew how quickly they moved, she could hear their now-frantic chewing to reach her. She couldn't think through her fear, not even to send herself away.

A loud hiss sent the creepers scurrying. A shadow crossed the hole as something, someone, outside looked in. "Are you damaged, Om'ray?"

Aryl blurted, "No thanks to you!" Which made, she decided in the next instant, no sense at all, since obviously the Tikitik had saved her. "I'm not hurt," she told it, not quite ready to be grateful either. "Please. Let me out."

"You leave tomorrow. Tonight you must remain where you are safe from all danger."

Had it forgotten the creepers? Maybe Tikitik didn't consider being eaten alive as posing danger to an Om'ray. Her head, already throbbing, hurt even more. "I don't like being in here."

"You leave tomorrow. Tonight you must remain—"

She leaned her forehead against the crumbling edge. "'Where I am safe from all danger,'" she finished numbly. The creatures were predictable—if impossible.

"To ensure your safety, I must restore this chamber. Do you wish nourishment first?"

More dresel? She didn't hesitate. "Yes. Yes, please."

Once its shadow left the opening, Aryl's right eye could see outside. She blinked, eager for any clue to where she was, beyond a simple grove of young rastis.

But this was no simple grove. She blinked again and tilted her head from side to side to try and see more.

Within her narrow arc of vision were the lower stalks of six rastis, rising on slender buttress roots. At this stage, they had no spools of great leafy fronds, but bore all their green growth atop the crown. The rest of the stalk was normally smooth and sleek, no wider than four Chosen Om'ray would surround with their joined hands and arms.

Except these stalks were different. Costa would have loved to see this, Aryl thought, studying what she could. The lower part of each expanded outward, like a round gall on a damaged branch, but this growth was smooth and regular, its dimensions matched to the Tikitik who moved between the plants. The surface of each bulge bore intricate designs, either carved or painted with ink, Aryl couldn't tell.

What had the Tikitik called it? A chamber.

Each chamber had a door. Or rather, wood had been removed from a tall, narrow oval on the outside of each bulge and replaced with a blue material. Aryl rolled her eye around to check the edges of the small hole the creepers had left. She could make out small bits of wood, mixed with some dull blue substance. She could testify it was hard.

The chamber directly across from her wasn't fully sealed, having a large round opening near the middle of its "door." She watched, puzzled at first, as a Tikitik approached with a large bowl. Then a cluster of familiar gray protuberances appeared in the opening, wriggling like eager fingers.

They imprisoned their own kind? She shuddered.

The outside Tikitik scooped its fingers into the bowl's contents and proceeded to offer the one inside what looked like mouthfuls of fresh dresel. Aryl licked her lips. After three such offerings, it put the bowl aside and began to use its own mouth protuberances to pat new material into the opening in the rastis. It worked quickly and efficiently. She could have sworn she heard it hissing contentedly to itself. In short order, the opening was completely sealed. The Tikitik collected its bowl and moved to the next rastis.

An eye filled Aryl's view, then pulled away. She stifled a shriek, somehow managing words instead. "What do you want with me?" She thought that came out remarkably well, under the circumstances.

"I've brought you nourishment."

She tilted her head back in panic. "Wait! I can *umphf—*" The hooks, which turned out to be Tikitik fingers, ended any discussion. Aryl let herself be fed, receiving two chokingly large—and utterly delicious—mouthfuls for her trouble.

As expected, the Tikitik began resealing her hole, spitting blue and bits of wood, its gray mouth-fingers working quickly to pat those in place. Too quickly, for the number of questions Aryl had. "Wait," she begged. "I need to know—"

To her surprise, it stopped and drew back. "What do you need to know?"

Everything, she wanted to wail, including what to say to be freed. Instead, she asked the first thing she thought it might answer. "Who are in the other chambers? Why are they imprisoned like this?"

A small eye filled what remained of the hole, as if the question made the Tikitik curious about her. "Only the Sacred Mothers are worthy of the rastis' life gift. They await birth under our care." A pause and the eye retreated again. She could see it shift uncertainly on its cone. "You are not worthy, of course, nor one of ours, nor in any way I can tell pregnant. I don't know why you deserve this gift."

Most of this meant nothing to Aryl, but she grasped the last part. "I don't. Deserve it. You could," she suggested, "let me out."

"I will keep you safe until they come for you tomorrow. A chamber is the only way I know. Om'ray are," another pause, "as tender-fleshed as newborns. You will rest. I will watch."

With a series of spits and soft busy pats, it sealed Aryl and her questions in the dark.

She did rest. The dresel coursing through her system satisfied a craving she'd had so long, she'd forgotten. Knowing she was being treated with the same care lavished on Tikitik mothers was—if not reassuring, for Aryl didn't know what that meant—at least sounded better than being a prisoner or food in storage. Rather than strain her eyes against the darkness, she closed them. Really, it wasn't that bad standing up inside a stalk. The bindings were rather comfortable, in a limb-numbing way.

Aryl.

Taisal's sending was strained, as if she used all her strength. Aryl immediately sent her own thought flying to meet it, the result a sure, solid link within the wild darkness of the *other*. She was too grateful to be alarmed by her growing control, grateful not to have been abandoned. *Here.*

Then she sensed enclosing walls, a steady light. Her mother was at ease, though her legs ached. *You've returned to the Cloisters.*

A moment's discomfiture. *Haxel insisted. Her scouts will watch for any Tikitik, to summon their Speaker.*

No one was coming for her.

Aryl fought an irrational despair. She understood. No one could come. Yena's resources were stretched to the breaking point. There was no one to spare. The distance was too great.

She'd given her mother—which meant Council and the Adepts—a way to watch her from safety.

She understood that, too.

What do they want?

The Speaker, preparing for negotiation. Her mother did love her, Aryl thought, rather numb. There were simply priorities attached.

I saw the strangers, she sent.

Startlement. Clearly, this wasn't what Taisal had expected.

Aryl's lips twitched in a half smile her mother couldn't see. Probably, she decided, just as well. *Did you think they took me because of what I did to Bern?*

The hollow feel in the *other* was answer enough. No wonder Taisal had been frantic to find her, and Council willing to risk its Speaker. They must have believed the worst. Aryl found herself without sympathy.

Who did you see? Where?

Words weren't enough. Aryl deliberately let her mind dwell on those moments high in the nekis, her glimpses of the black creature and the one who wasn't Om'ray—yet was. She felt the images leap from her mind.

An answering shock flashed through the *other*. *How are you doing this?*

Her next-to-be Forbidden Talent? Aryl kept the thought and its suddenly bitter taste private. *It doesn't matter. These are the strangers, Mother,* she sent. *They must be. They have a flying machine like the device at the Harvest. The Tikitik must plan to ask me questions about what I saw.*

A waiting stillness. They remained linked, mind to mind, within the *other place*. Then, with an underlying reluctance, *Or the Tikitik assume this Om'ray-seeming stranger is one of us. You were in the same grove. They may suspect you share some connection.*

One of us? He wasn't real, Aryl reminded her mother. Perhaps the memory hadn't been complete.

Taisal must have felt her incredulity. *Pay attention, Daughter. Not all the world is defined by Om'ray. There is a secret task set Adepts when they accept the 'di' and that is to watch for change in our neighbors as well as ourselves. We listen for their Power; we taste their reaction to ours. That is why we believe the Tikitik cannot sense our inner presence. As they are unreal to us, we are unreal to them.*

It was like the long, confusing arguments about the source of Power and the shape of the world her mother used to have with her father at truenight. They'd trade obscure phrases until Aryl wearied of pretending to listen and went to bed. But she wasn't that young anymore. Somehow she knew her mother—no, the Yena Speaker—was trying to educate her quickly, give her what she could to help understand those who'd sealed her in the nekis.

They can't tell us from the stranger? she ventured.

They can't tell the stranger from us. Foreboding. *Whatever he does, the Tikitik could blame on Om'ray as well.*

Aryl finally felt some empathy for the old ones on Council. Not only did they have to worry about the future of Yena while concealing a growing number of Forbidden Talents from their own kind, as well as the Tikitik—now they faced a new kind of being they'd never imagined existed.

Taisal had shared this, and her reply held an undertone of laughter. *I doubt they feel as ancient as you think them, Daughter. Now rest—it's almost truenight.* Concern. *Will you be safe?*

Would she? The chamber seemed to press in on all sides; the lack of light a danger signal to any Yena. If she thought about her body, it itched and ached in so many places she'd lost count. Still, the Tikitik viewed this as a safe place and she could hardly argue. Where was safer than inside a rastis?

I'm safe. The word should have meant sitting at the finely polished Sarc table . . . listening to wysps through the gauze . . . Aryl sighed with longing.

Then, *sleep, little one. It's late. I'll get you home.*

With that, their connection was severed. Her mother's skill within the other was growing, too.

Sleep? Nothing was further from her mind. Frustrated, Aryl struggled to free herself but succeeded in nothing more than growing warm and aggravating one shoulder. However she was wedged or tied in place, it wasn't coming loose without outside help.

She could shout—the Tikitik seemed attentive. She could claim an injury. Certainly she needed a bath. She drew breath to call the creature and then hesitated, unsure why.

Something. Some sound.

She leaned her head forward again, and held still. Slowly, her heart settled.

It was like soft rain, at first. But the beat—it was more organized, almost rhythmic. It came closer, grew louder. Like feet running down a bridge, only more feet than were possible at once.

More and more. An unending procession of hurried steps, as if their owners couldn't delay, couldn't wait.

Then the first screams came, muffled through the wood.

Aryl jerked back, her eyes wide in the dark.

It must be dark outside as well. Truenight. When the Lay's most dreaded hunters swarmed from the water in their millions, to climb every buttress, stalk, and trunk.

They were climbing her rastis. She could hear them. Thousands upon thousands of feet. The worst death she could imagine was a layer of Tikitik spit away.

Her mother's party had had glows, Aryl told herself. They'd been high. Too high for the swarms. Haxel knew how to survive. They'd have watched for aerial hunters, but they'd been safe from swarms.

While she had Tikitik spit.

The laugh burst from deep inside her.

The sound, strained and too loud, scared Aryl more than the drumming feet. She pressed her lips together, used her teeth to hold them, tasted blood and kept biting. She couldn't lose control. Not over her mind.

She wouldn't.

The lonely battle. That was what Om'ray called it, this struggle with oneself.

Children were taught its methods; unChosen practiced them into habit. The Chosen learned ways to accommodate that mind forever Joined to theirs, but this war was always fought alone. A race able to share thoughts was only as sane as each individual mind. There were reasons the Adepts cared for the Lost or the mind-damaged. Only their Power could control that of another. Only they had the strength and training to protect the inner whole that was Yena.

Aryl struggled to focus on the here and now, however frightening. To retreat into the false comfort of memory, or worse, let *what-was-Aryl* be lost in the *other place* would be defeat. There was no one here to pull her back from either abyss.

Instead, she counted heartbeats. She counted distant screams. She imposed order on the world and insisted on being part of it.

When at last she unclenched her jaw, swallowing blood, and licked her swollen lips, she knew she'd won. She was terrified—but she had sane reason to be. All that remained was to stay calm until dawn, and hope the Tikitik were prompt in unsealing her.

Truenight had never seemed so long.

Chapter 18

"IS THIS YOU?"

Facing the light as if she were one of Costa's plants, Aryl squinted at the silhouette of a second Tikitik. The first had removed more than half the door sealing her within the rastis—to her great relief—before standing to one side for this sudden question. "Is what me?" she asked, trying to see what her visitor held.

The creature moved to block the brightness. Now she could make out the strip of white cloth between its hands, inscribed in black with one of their symbols. No. Aryl's eyes widened in surprise. It was the tiny curve and dot she'd put on her drawing, rendered larger. "Yes," she said, wondering that the Tikitik had understood her intention. "That's—it means something I did."

"Good." Tucking the cloth into a belt, it took a blade and approached. Aryl tensed, but all the creature did was cut her arms free from whatever had held them against her body. She hissed in pain as her arms flopped loose and useless; eight eyes riveted on her immediately.

"I'll be okay," Aryl told them, hoping it was true.

They had kept her safe, as promised. She'd listened to

screams until falling asleep; was roused by the drumming of feet as the Lay's hunters returned to the water with their mouthfuls of flesh.

It hadn't been long after that—though time seemed to move oddly—before the first holes had appeared before her face, streaming with glorious light. She'd never imagined being glad to see something so ugly and strange as a Tikitik.

Now the new one took her right arm by the elbow, gently lifting it. Aryl watched in fascination as it neatly wrapped the ink-decorated cloth around her forearm and wrist so the symbol was displayed, slipping the loose ends under a fold to secure it. "What is this for?"

The Tikitik showed her the cloth around its wrist, the symbol much more ornate. "You are no animal, to go unnamed." It backed a step back to allow its fellow to continue breaking open the chamber "door," a process involving its fingers. The blue material crumbled away with deceptive ease. With that grip, she judged, they should be able to climb anything.

But there was a more pressing matter. "Go where?" Aryl asked anxiously. She was far enough from home now. "Are you taking me back to—oomphf!" this as a final restraint gave way and she fell forward, every muscle in her body locked in spasm.

The Tikitik were ready, catching her in their dry, cool arms. Aryl trembled helplessly, horrified at their touch, expecting at any moment to have one of the creatures force its flesh into her mouth and send her into unconsciousness again. They merely lifted her to her feet, her body and arms in a strong but gentle hold, and waited for her to be able to stand. "Th-thank you," she managed, blinking away tears. She was free!

As Aryl began to regain control over her body, she felt the *other* suddenly close; Taisal, wanting contact. She risked a quick *Later*—afraid to be distracted.

"Do you need nourishment?" A third Tikitik approached, carrying a bowl of dresel large enough to feed three families.

Behind it, Aryl could see the other chambers remained sealed. Or had been resealed. How long did the "Sacred Mothers" endure captivity?

And why?

She pulled at her arms, and the creatures released her. "Yes." Gesturing gratitude before dipping her fingers in the bowl was likely pointless, but she felt better for the courtesy.

Two left as she licked her fingers. The one who'd given her the cloth band remained, all its eyes on her as she stretched with care. Aryl finished by bending forward to rest her palms on her feet, then rolled her back upright again. She wanted to groan with relief, but was acutely aware of her audience. "That's better," she said.

"You recover quickly," it commented. "Good. We will go soon." It hesitated, then bobbed its head twice. "The other cloth you wear. Is it something you need?"

Surprisingly tactful. "I need to be clean," she said, making a face. Filthy as she was after a day trapped, she'd rather be naked in the rain; it wasn't a choice, not with biters that liked Om'ray already making their presence known. "Is there water I can use? To wash my clothes and myself?"

A long, knobby arm reached past her to point. Aryl half-turned. Behind her rastis, the ground slipped into still black water. Water that wasn't still for long, as something beneath its surface surged hopefully up and down again.

"Not that much water," she clarified breathlessly.

The Tikitik gave its soft bark. "There will soon be much more than this, Om'ray. But I understand." It beckoned to another of its kind. "This humble one will wash you."

From the way its small front eyes rolled, the "humble one" wasn't any happier about this than Aryl.

Are you sure you're all right?

Aryl considered several possible replies; none suited the moment. *Yes. They're responsible hosts and respectful. I've no complaints.*

None that she'd share. The Tikitik's wash had produced admirable results. Her skin was so clean every bite and thorn hole showed in exquisite detail. Her hair, free of soil, was free in truth. The braided net hadn't been returned and the result flew loose around her head and in her face. Her clothes? The undertunic was clean and intact, for what it was worth, since it went only to her knees. The wraps for her arms and legs had disappeared. Those, the Tikitik could replace and did. Their cloth was finer in weave, so those were an improvement.

Otherwise? She really and truly didn't want to know any more about the cold, flat, and thoroughly slimy creatures the Humble One had slapped over every part of her naked body. They'd pulsed and scraped and giggled to themselves as if she'd been a feast. When Aryl had tried to pull them off, the Tikitik had quickly prevented her, saying only the "wash" wasn't done.

When it was, the giggling stopped and the creatures dropped to the ground around her feet. The Tikitik had carefully collected them in a bag.

Where are they taking you?

Aryl collected her thoughts. *I don't think the Humble Ones know. The leader isn't back yet.*

Is it the Speaker? With a rush of anticipation.

I didn't see the pendant. The others take its orders.

Those others sat to either side of her on the damp ground, large eyes closed as if they slept. Their small eyes, however, were wide open. These bent on their cones as often to gaze at her as their surroundings. Guards or protectors—the result was the same.

Send to me when you know more.

Aryl felt their link thin; Taisal was leaving her. Involuntarily, she *reached. Don't go*, she pleaded. *Not yet.*

Taisal struggled, but Aryl's hold was too strong. *Release me!* With the command came a distress close to fear.

She relaxed her grip at once, horrified at what she'd done. *I'm sorry. I didn't mean—*

I know. Her mother was still there, though her mindvoice was distant and cold. *But have a care, Aryl. Do you think it's easy for me in the Dark? Do you think it's safe?*

She hadn't, Aryl realized guiltily, thought about it at all, too grateful for a familiar voice. Taisal had almost been Lost. Having felt the almost irresistible pull of the *other,* its lure to dissolve herself in its darkness, she should have understood how hard this was for her mother.

Her hands gestured apology, even as she let Taisal's mind slip away from hers.

The Tikitik on her right opened its hind eyes, its neck bending to orient its face toward her with stomach-turning ease. "Do you require something?"

"I need to walk around," she said truthfully. "Stretch my legs. Do you understand?"

That bark. "I understand that my legs need to not stretch for a change. Do not go far."

A joke—or at least humor she could grasp. Aryl got to her feet and stood looking down at the two creatures.

They had no more weapons than she. Their knobby skin was thicker, affording more protection from small biters, but hardly a barrier to anything with teeth. They couldn't have stayed outside through truenight and survived the Lay's swarms.

Could they?

"You are not walking around," observed the Tikitik. "Do you require something?"

"Where were you last night?"

A drop landed on its face and four eyes blinked together. Another hit Aryl. She didn't bother looking up. She could smell the rain above.

"We were here," it said at last. "Our place is with the Sacred Mothers. There are many dangers." It tapped the back of her hand with one finger. "Om'ray know of fire."

Aryl couldn't tell if the cryptic statement was a warning or simple fact. She did wondered if Taisal had known why Tikitik couldn't tolerate fire within the groves, or if her threat had been a lucky guess. "There are many dangers," she agreed, "including what comes from the water in the dark." She pointed toward the Lay, its waters too close for any peace of mind. "I heard—I could hear the swarms climb."

The one with two eyes shut barked.

"As they should," said the first. "They have their work to do."

"Work?" Aryl repeated, sure she'd misunderstood. "They kill everything they find!"

Its head lifted as if in surprise. "Of course. The swarms clean the groves of what would harm the rastis. That is their function. By so doing, they protect both the Harvest and our Sacred Mothers. Why else would we have made them?"

She took a step back. "What do you mean . . . 'made them?' "

Both Tikitik barked, their eyes open, as if she entertained them. "We made everything here, little Om'ray. Did you not know? Our needs." An expansive gesture. "All this."

Rain began to rustle its way through fronds and leaves, big drops thumping against the ground, splashing in the swamp.

Aryl stared at the Tikitik. "You didn't make us."

One hissed. The other raised its head sharply, the fleshy protuberances of its face flailing about as if it wanted to smother her again.

"You didn't make us," she insisted, unsure why that mattered so much to her. They could be teasing her—making fun of a stranger. Why believe the creatures anyway?

But she did. With a sense of her world shifting into something unutterably alien, she did.

"No. We did not make you." This was followed by a long, venomous-sounding hiss. "We endure you."

She eased back on her right leg. The rain plastered her hair against her cheeks, produced puddles at her feet. The Tikitik endured that, too, she noticed numbly, their skin easily shedding moisture, their eyes blinking more quickly.

In an instant, the rain became deluge, erasing the creatures from view. Aryl spun on her heel and sprinted for the nearest stalk, hands out to find and take a grip. Four strides, slipping through the mud and debris. Five. Six. Let her climb—they couldn't catch her. She didn't care what else did.

Three strides short of her goal, she slammed into something huge and warm, something that grunted in her face with righteous indignation and awful breath as she rebounded to fall on her back.

Something that lifted her into the air before she could scramble up to run.

Interlude

YUHAS PARTH, NOW YUHAS SUD S'UDLAAT, waited to take over the cart five steps inside the tunnel mouth, an accomplishment Enris was careful not to praise. Natural good humor and a willingness to work let Yuhas fool everyone but his thoroughly smitten Chosen, Caynen.

And Enris himself.

Each day he watched the former Yena force himself deeper into the mold of Tuana. Yuhas studied how others took slow strides to cover the hard dry ground and walked slower. He saw Tuana clump up stairs one at a time and did the same, though it wasn't natural to a body with perfect balance, easily able to leap five stairs at a time. But once Yuhas had noticed that his graceful, careful movements caught everyone's eye—some admired, while Mauro and his ilk sneered and made mocking noises with their boots—he'd worked hard to change.

And now wore heavy boots.

Yuhas worked well in the shop and Jorg was pleased. Other than a tendency to spend as much time as possible near the melting vat, he'd noticed nothing unusual about their new helper. Enris hadn't told his father how Yuhas had panicked his first time within the Oud tunnel, falling to the floor, then half crawling, half running in his desperation to reach daylight. He kept to himself Yuhas' vow—to overcome his aversion, to take his turn pushing the cart.

Each day, Yuhas walked one step deeper into the world of the Oud, trembling and shaking like one of the giant leaves he'd tried to describe to Enris. It was an achievement of such magnificent will, Enris knew himself privileged to be the only witness.

"A good load," Yuhas complimented breathlessly, hefting the handles as he pushed.

A scrap tumbled free, and Enris caught it before it hit the sand. "Not bad," he agreed, tossing it back in as he walked alongside the cart. "Should fill the vat. Good thing. We've seventeen cutting blades to pour. Geter ran over a *joop* mating line and half the blades snapped."

"The joop—whatever it is—can't have liked that." Yuhas' voice eased the moment the sun hit his face. It was the light, Enris decided. There wasn't enough below for him—for some reason, Yena feared the dark.

They made their way along the still-quiet road. Enris chuckled. "Oh, they probably didn't notice. Joop are almost impossible to kill—they're shelled, you see. If they'd die above ground, we'd collect them for bricks, but they only come up to mate. Almost the size of the cart," he nodded at it. "They tuck themselves between the rows. I've heard of forty hooked together in one line." A grimace. "It doesn't take that many to be a nasty surprise for anyone operating a harvester."

"You use these machines?"

From the sudden intensity of Yuhas' green eyes, this wasn't a casual question. "Of course. Oud-built, but we make replacement blades. There are tillers as well as harvesters. Don't you?"

"This *nost* you grow," the Yena said instead of answering. "Is that for the Oud or for yourselves?"

"Only an Oud could stomach the stuff," Enris assured the

other, making a face. "We grow our own food—which I've noticed you like well enough. Why?"

Yuhas shrugged and leaned into the handles. "Lucky for you," he said obliquely.

About to pursue the issue, Enris spotted someone waiting outside the shop. Recognition slowed his steps. "What does she want?" he muttered.

Yuhas chuckled. "The same thing she wanted yesterday. And the day before that. You really should give up, Enris."

"You Chosen want everyone to be like you," he complained, not without cause. His cousin was equally unrelenting in his zeal to improve Enris' love life.

It's a good thing, my new brother, to find someone to complete you. You've seen my joy.

It was the first sending Yuhas had tried with him. Faint—he wasn't Powerful—but characteristically warm and generous. Enris had to smile. "That I have," he said aloud. "But—" his smile faded "—trust me when I say that's not what she wants."

As surely as he knew how to work the Oud's metal, Enris knew Naryn S'udlaat was drawn to his Power, not him. Worse, her ambition had nothing to do with the making of useful, beautiful objects, or even friendship. There would be nothing of him left in Enris sud S'udlaat.

He wouldn't risk it, despite the helpless desire that grew each time she came near.

"I'll take this inside," Yuhas offered.

"Oh, no, you don't!" Enris gently but firmly shouldered the other Om'ray from the cart. "Do me a favor. Go tell her how wonderful your Chosen is—that should send her running for the Cloisters." No secret that Caynen S'udlaat, Naryn's cousin, hadn't been expected to catch the eye of the exotic, handsome stranger in their midst. But it was a good match, Enris thought, happy for his friend. There was no hiding the contentment the two had found in each other. Tunnels or no, Yuhas would be fine.

"Naryn!" Yuhas called, easily outstepping the cart. Despite the new boots, his every move made Enris feel clumsy and slow. He did his best not to grin at Naryn's suddenly fixed expression at Yuhas' babble as he pushed the cart past her to the shop. She was obliged to listen politely to Yuhas—Chosen were adult, after all, however new that state—but she didn't have to like it. That much was clear from the glare she sent his way.

Enris smiled.

Jorg was inside. He waved an absent greeting to his son as he swung open the vat, eyes assessing the cart's load as Enris pushed it through the wide door. No doubt Jorg knew to the blade how many they could pour this morning.

Enris was a step inside, about to start the cart down the ramp to the vat when a hand clamped over his bare wrist.

ENRIS!

The sending struck like a blow. He staggered back into the door's frame, the cart tipping its load over the ramp with a resounding clatter. He could hear his father's running steps. Yuhas was shouting. Louder by far was the voice in his mind.

ENRIS!! COME! COMECOMECOME!!!

The summons beat against him. He couldn't see, could barely remember to gasp for air. He had no strength to pull free of the now-light grip. Instinct made him throw his free arm over his head for protection. Useless. This attack came from within, but his shields were useless, too. All he could do was resist. At that resistance, the summons turned to *pain* . . . waves and waves of *PAIN* . . . He heard a scream . . .

"Enris!? What's wrong?" His father. "What are you doing to him?" This a shout. "Stop!"

Somehow, he began to force the other out, to wrest control of his senses from her—for it was *her.*

"Nar—Naryn—" he managed to whisper.

She was *pulling* him. As he struggled, a darkness rose behind his eyes, a churning emptiness that sang with delirious joy and fear. It seemed a *place,* somewhere he could be safe . . . if he only let himself fall apart, the pieces would flow *there* . . .

PAINPAINPAIN—!

As suddenly as if cut by a knife, the pain and pull were gone. Enris found himself slumped against the wall, breathing in great sobbing heaves as though he'd raced uphill with his cart. His hands . . . he stared at his hands. They couldn't be his. His hands had never trembled before. "What . . .?"

"Yuhas threw her into the street. The Adepts are coming, my son. Stay here. Listen to me. Stay here."

I'll never leave. He tried to say it, tried to send it, but the darkness was coming back.

This time, he fell.

* ✷ *

"You're to leave, Enris Mendolar."

He struggled to sit up in an unfamiliar bed, pulling at the constriction of a strange shirt around his shoulders. "Why?" He fought to see through the dark.

"You're to leave. When you are ready. Which won't be today."

Sleep.

It was a command.

* ✷ *

"I want to see my family." Enris reared up in the bed, tossing the blanket aside. "I want to see them now!"

The Om'ray with the tray didn't react. He said, as he had said for the last two meals Enris had been served, exactly and with each syllable the same: "Here is food. Eat what you wish."

One of the Lost.

Enris rubbed one hand over his face, feeling a fool. He pressed two fingers into the corners of his eyes, hard against his nose. There was pain still. Not overwhelming. Not even real.

Not his. *Imposed*. How had she done it?

"Here is food. Eat what you wish."

He sighed and dropped his hand in order to take the tray. Otherwise, the Lost would continue to repeat his message, over and over.

He knew the face. This had been Sive sud Lorimar. A harvester. A friend of his father's. With the death of his Chosen, he'd been brought here. To stay.

The Cloisters. Enris shuddered inwardly as he watched the Lost walk from the room. He'd wanted, once, to explore this place—see its ancient metalwork for himself, explore the many mysteries supposedly hidden behind its bold arches and smooth walls.

Now, he wanted home. He stared helplessly at his impeccable meal and wanted Ridersel's sweetpies.

The voice had said he had to leave.

Had he left already?

Was this his destination?

It could be. His thoughts felt thick, unsettled, more so than the disorientation left by the Oud trace. The Cloisters was the refuge of those too mind-damaged to live with the rest of Tuana.

Naryn's *gift*.

Enris threw the tray and its contents against the far wall.

Chapter 19

"IS THERE SOMETHING YOU NEED?"

Aryl kept her eyes on her hands, trying to ignore that her hands gripped a shoulder-high leather-wrapped post, and that post was embedded into the back of . . .

. . . impossible to ignore sitting on top of a room-sized mass that grunted and stank and ate its way over a world that . . .

She squeezed her eyes shut in denial. "What I need," she said bitterly, "is for the edge of the sky to stop moving."

"It's called the horizon. It isn't moving. You are. The feeling will pass."

Her stomach didn't care about the distinction. The Tikitik and their beasts had taken her from the rastis grove to where the rain no longer fell as it properly should—deflecting in all directions from the tips of leaves and fronds, half mist, half heavy drops—but instead hammered straight down as if she'd stood under the cistern's open tap. Every identical drop stung exposed skin. She'd had to bend over, her head between her arms, simply not to drown.

Almost worse, the terrifying rain had ended as no rain ever had: quickly, as if shut off from above. She'd opened her eyes in shock to find herself in a place she'd never imagined could exist. It had taken until now for her curiosity to outweigh the nausea.

Aryl eased open her eyelids.

The sky she knew. She'd seen its ripped blue amid the clouds before. But the land beneath had been erased by a smooth flat sheet of water.

Not the black water of the Lay, though some of that churned around the feet of their mounts as they lumbered through the plant-thick shallows, grunting to themselves. This expanse was the color of her grandmother's failed eyes, a soft gray that no longer remembered blue. Nothing disturbed it beyond the ripples and silt of their passing. It stretched to meet the sky in a straight line, like the end of the world.

It wasn't. Though Yena grew dimmer to her with every step, Amna and Rayna, distant Vyna, grew brighter. No wonder so few arrived on Passage at Yena. Aryl couldn't imagine how long it would take to skirt this all-wet place.

She turned her head the other way. A green wall rose alongside their path, abrupt and solid, crowned by the familiar vegetation of her canopy home. Its feet stood in the black flood, that boundary fringed on this sunward side by a dense growth of short, thin plants that rose from the water. They were bent, as if to an unfelt wind.

Her mount lurched as it lowered its great head—again—to snatch a green mouthful, yanking the plants free by their dripping roots. It munched as it continued wading. Munched and grunted. Those of the Tikitik didn't take such liberties, Aryl noticed glumly.

There were dozens of the beasts ahead in straggling lines and, when she dared turn—holding on for dear life—even more behind. Only their five had riders. The rest seemed accidental companions, following the plants they liked, grazing as they moved. All had at least one post rising from their backs. Some had two or three.

"We call them *ossts,*" the Tikitik told her, as if noticing her interest. It was the first time it had volunteered information. Perhaps, she thought, it was at ease here. It looked comfortable, sitting with one leg hooked around the post as if it were a branch, the other crossing to lock the first.

Aryl copied its position, at once more secure. She dared release a hand to trace the post to where it vanished within the osst's thick coat, digging gingerly into the coarse dark hair with her fingers. She couldn't find the end or its skin. "How did you do this?"

"The posts are inserted at birth, whenever possible. By the time the young are weaned, they are large enough to object."

She'd object at any age, Aryl thought, awkwardly patting the hair flat again.

"If you require nourishment, your osst will provide." The Tikitik twisted a leather cap from the top of its post to reveal a metal disk. Removing that, it bent its face over a tube protruding from the post, its mouth-fingers flattening to its cheeks as though getting out of the way. Aryl could see its throat convulse and relax all the way up to the shoulders.

Its eyes bent on their cones as if to watch her reaction.

Calmly, Aryl twisted the cap from her post. The disk took a bit more doing, because she couldn't bring herself to loose both hands, but came off eventually. She put her lips over the tube and sucked.

It was blood, hot and rich. Though she'd expected it, her abused stomach wasn't happy. Deliberately, Aryl took one more swallow, then replaced the disk and cap. So much for all the canopy dwellers who'd taken her blood without asking.

"Convenient," she told the Tikitik, who'd also finished.

"Yes. Though the inner tube must be replaced several times. Its lining stops the first wound from healing, but eventually wears away."

There were biters who left always-oozing holes in flesh.

Om'ray died from those. Aryl found herself patting the osst again, though it gave no sign of noticing her or the multitude of small brown flitters that walked across its horned head, themselves preoccupied with the assorted small biters dining on the osst's naked ears.

By the symbol on its wristband, she guessed this Tikitik was the one who'd come this morning to give her her own band. A leader, as she'd told her mother. Someone who should have answers. "How do you make such things?" she asked.

"Make what?"

"The osst."

"Who told you I did?" It was amused—of that she was suddenly sure.

"The Humble Ones—after I was washed—" a now thoroughly redundant process given the rain, "—they told me the Tikitik made the rastis, the swarms, everything." Aryl waved her arm at the wall of green beside them. Everything except Om'ray, but she didn't add that.

"You believe this."

Aryl hesitated. From her mother, this would be a challenge to some childish presumption. From a Tikitik? She felt vulnerable. Could she back down? Should she? Or was that the mistake. "I mean no disrespect," she said after a moment. "Is it true?"

"It is true that what the Oud accomplish with their loud machines and metal tools, we Tikitik accomplish with life. It is true, we do not hide it, that we were greater once."

"Once?" Aryl frowned. "I don't understand."

"No," it replied. "You would not. For Om'ray, there is only now. The world is as it has always been and will always be. I'll tell you an important thing, little Yena. For Tikitik, there is an endless span of befores and weres and perhaps-one-days—" As if sensing her growing confusion, it stopped, mouth-fingers moving restlessly. "It doesn't matter. In this now, we can do many things, but we cannot create a new living creature. Did we, in the before? There are those who believe so."

"Do you?"

A barking laugh, but she noticed its eyes tracked away from hers. "Most of those who do will also tell you the Oud were a mistake made by our ancestors, and those long-dead Tikitik were condemned to seal the sun each night within a rastis chamber and open it by day. Thus, darkness reminds us not to be wrong again."

It was Aryl's turn to laugh. "The sun goes to Grona Clan. Everyone knows that."

The Tikitik barked twice. "And how does it get back again, without being seen?"

She glared at it, nonplussed.

"You don't know," it stated.

"The Adepts teach what we need to know." The words fell flat—when had she ever been satisfied with their explanations? When had she glibly swallowed what was told without seeing for herself? Too often, it seemed. Aryl flushed. "It's our way," she finished, determined to defend her people. And ask more questions.

"They don't teach you to read."

"Only Adepts need to read." Her lips twisted in a grimace. It had found a sore point. "It doesn't matter," she threw its words back. "Reading isn't something they could teach. Only those worthy can receive that skill. It's given—it's not taught." She didn't know if Tikitik understood how Adepts were trained, how they delved through the memories of those of greater knowledge to acquire what they needed—or if it even should.

"Anyone can read." The Tikitik held out its arm to show her the symbols on its band. "This," it drew a fingertip along a wavy pair of lines, "stands for 'traveler.' This," now a trio of widening circles, "for 'thought.' We are named for what we are. Thus, my name is written as 'Thought Traveler.' These," it indicated the rest, "are the most important names and tasks of kin-groups through which my line has passed. Each part has a meaning."

"The markings always mean the same thing?"

"Always."

It was, she warned herself, probably Forbidden. New things were—and she'd certainly never heard of anyone being taught by a Tikitik. Or imagined it. Her hands itched to copy the symbols in ink, to repeat them over and over so she would never forget them. She heard herself ask, "Would you show me more?"

Another bark. "Show me your name."

She opened her mouth, then realized it meant the marking on the cloth. "It's not a name," she admitted, offering her wrist. "I like how this looks, so I put it on all my drawings. Among Om'ray, my name is Aryl Sarc."

"This has meaning, intended or not. The curve, like a bowl. It means 'everyone.' For you, all Om'ray."

The world, she thought to herself, amazed something so simple could convey so much. "And this?" She eagerly touched the dot above her "bowl."

"Shown there, the meaning is 'apart.' Does 'Apart-from-All' name you?"

Besides uncomfortably apt? "It will do," Aryl admitted. She made herself gaze out over the empty water. "Does this have a name?"

"Lake of Fire."

It hadn't barked, but she was wary of another Tikitik joke at her expense. "It's water. What kind of name is that?"

"Do Om'ray eyes see so poorly? Do you not see its smoke?"

Aryl held back a retort and looked more intently. For what, she had no idea.

Then she saw what Traveler meant. What appeared to be

tendrils of cloud were rising in the middle of the lake, from the water's surface. Smoke? Each spiraled, slowly, higher and higher, but stopped in midair well before real clouds began. Some tendrils were thin; one was fat at its middle.

"It can't be smoke," she decided out loud. "It rises too slowly. And there's no bright flame underneath."

Traveler's head shot up. "You've seen fire?" No mistaking the threat in its voice or posture.

"Lightning struck near the Cloisters," Aryl explained quickly. "All of us went to see." It had been terrifying—and beautiful. So was this "lake."

"Are there rastis on the other side?"

The Tikitik lowered its head in slow stages, all eyes on her. "Oud are on the other side," it said at last. She wasn't sure how this answered her question, but it seemed to think so.

Aryl studied the lake, growing more curious instead of less. The Oud had machines to fly—this water should be no barrier to them, though she didn't know how long their machines could stay in the air. Longer than a fich. She leaned as far as she could over the side of her mount away from the Tikitik, holding the post with one arm and leg. She tried to see through the swirling silt, afloat with vegetation torn loose by the ossts ahead. "Are there hunters here, like the Lay?" she shouted from that position. When the Tikitik didn't answer, she pulled herself up again. "Are there?" she repeated.

"Where the reeds grow, yes. Farther in—" its eyes focused on distance, "—see the line where the surface begins to sparkle? From there, the Lake of Fire contains only water, without bottom, without life. We give it our dead. And those who disappoint."

Not a casual explanation, Aryl judged, both hands on the post as her mount lurched after another mouthful. Tikitik might be invisible to her other sense, but this one, at least, was expressing itself perfectly.

She was being taken somewhere for a purpose of theirs. Whatever it might be, she'd heard the cost of failure.

They rode through deepening shadow, the sun touching distant glints from the Lake of Fire as it sank below the canopy. The clouds turned yellow, then pink. A line of darkness began to climb from the horizon. Aryl hadn't made up her mind if it was beautiful or frightening, to see the sky's changes firsthand.

She did know how this time would be within the canopy. Yena would be heading for shelter. Glows would brighten, forbidding the swarms.

Aryl closed her eyes and *reached* gently, without insisting. *Mother* . . .

But Taisal wouldn't allow their minds to link. Aryl stopped trying, guessing her mother was in a Council meeting or with other Adepts; neither would be good times to be interrupted.

She didn't, she sighed to herself, have anything new to say.

Aryl clung to the osst's post as the insatiable beast lunged for another bite. It never stopped eating. For some reason, that made it easier to sip its blood, for that was the only food or drink the Tikitik offered.

Home. Myris and Ael would be sharing their scant ration of dresel powder over supper. Talking about her, maybe. A little concerned, but wasn't Aryl on a kind of Passage? Maybe they'd think her famous, the first Chooser-to-Be to leave her clan.

After all, her mother would have told them she was safe.

No, Aryl told herself, abruptly certain, Taisal would not.

The Yena Speaker would keep her secret. She would never reveal being able to contact her daughter over such a distance, let alone her use of the Forbidden *Dark*. To do either would only encourage Tikva di Uruus and her supporters, risk the Agreement her mother cared so much about.

Taisal would let Myris and Ael, Seru, all the rest of her family and friends, think her dead first.

Aryl sniffed miserably.

Interest.

What? She shook her head. Nothing. Still, Aryl concentrated, opening her inner awareness.

Yes, there.

A wisp . . . a *hint* of another presence in her mind. Lurking. Hiding from her in the *other.*

It wasn't Taisal.

Aryl *threw* herself at it, like a hook through air.

The *hint* disappeared before she could touch it. That *hint.*

Another in the roiling *other,* the merest glimpse, as if she'd seen something almost break the surface of the lake. As if her attention startled it, it was gone. The Dark sang its tempting song, luring her to forget herself, to let herself thin and be consumed.

Aryl pulled free with an effort.

Spies? Set to watch her . . . or her mother. The Adepts?

Or was it something much worse.

She stared out at the line of monstrous beasts, splashing their mindless way between grove and lake, the froth from their steps gleaming briefly before disappearing.

Where, she wondered with a shiver, did the minds of the Lost go? What was left of them? Were they fragments, swept and spun by those remorseless currents, or something more, something that clung to, if not consciousness, then purpose?

Did they hunger for their own kind? Was that the source of the lure?

Aryl couldn't stop shivering. Taisal had been right to warn her against the Dark. She—

"Do you require something?"

Startled, Aryl glared at the Tikitik. "Yes," she snapped, her fear turning to anger. "I need to know why you've taken me from my home. To know where we are. To know where we're going. To know why—" her voice cracked. "What do you want from me?"

Its head reared up and back. The other four Tikitik, so silent till now she'd almost forgotten them, broke into agitated hisses.

"You asked," Aryl said in a voice that sounded thoroughly sullen even to herself. Oh, she was handling all this well.

But it wasn't fair. She was supposed to be home, in her bed. Not sitting, her legs cramped and backside numb, on a creature she hadn't known existed before today. All she'd wanted to do was see the sky for herself.

And now even that was disappearing, swallowed by the dreadful black of truenight.

As for the connection to her mother, her one link . . . did she dare touch the *other* again, given what might be watching?

"Are you ill?"

Not for an instant did she dare believe it kindness. Nothing her mother had ever said about the Tikitik offered that hope. Self-interest, perhaps. She had a role to play—Thought Traveler was involved in that role, whatever it was.

"It's almost truenight," Aryl told it. "Am I safe?"

Its head lowered back to normal, its shoulders hiding it in shadow. "What do you fear?"

Where would it like her to start? Aryl asked herself, but settled for, "The swarms, for one. You said they could reach here. Last night you sealed me inside a rastis. Don't tell me being on top of an osst will protect me." Or the osst, for that matter. She'd seen the remnants of what the swarms did to large, furred creatures who didn't or couldn't climb beyond their reach.

"You are safe. They cannot tolerate light."

"What light?" The clouds had lost their color; the lake itself vanishing gray into grays. "The sun's almost to Grona. Do you have glows?"

"The Makers will rise." In the dimness, she could see its left arm pointing up and ahead. Traveler sounded supremely confident.

She'd probably sounded just as sure to Joyn, knowing nothing of what was to come. Thinking of his small trusting face, his warmth wrapped around hers, Aryl was overwhelmed by longing. All she wanted was to be home—away from the stench and unceasing movement of the osst, her bewildering surroundings, and above all her helplessness.

Had those on Passage felt this way?

Had Bern?

She lowered her face into the crook of her arm, shutting it all out. Maybe she should wish for the Tikitik to be wrong, and swarms to consume them all. Make an end to it . . . Bern might hear, one day . . .

"Apart-from-All. Look."

She didn't obey at once; having her head down was unexpectedly comfortable. But curiosity, morbid or otherwise, couldn't be denied.

She rolled her head to the side and opened her eyes.

Then Aryl straightened, slowly, her eyes growing wider.

The clouds had retreated to become pale gray walls of their own, exposing the sky over the lake. That sky was now the deepest blue Aryl had ever seen, almost black at its edges and where it met cloud tops. Holes in that blue let through sparks of light, like glows through leaves. Stars.

Brightest of all were two that sat exactly where the Tikitik had pointed, one larger and so white it hurt to stare at, the other a warm gold, its surface marked with dimples and swirls. Their light didn't just puncture the sky, but spilled over the lake in two endless lines that never crossed, the sum bright enough to pick out green from the tops of the canopy. Bright enough to send the swarms hunting within the darkness deep under roots and stalks, not out here.

Cersi's moons.

She'd heard of them; she'd never imagined being out in truenight to see them with her own eyes. "What did you call them?" she asked. "The 'Makers'?"

"Some believe everything on Cersi was made by beings who now reside within those orbs. The Makers. They say we see their lights because the Makers never cease their labors to make this world perfect for Tikitik."

"What about the Om'ray?" Aryl demanded without thinking, then shut her mouth.

The Tikitik was a silhouette; it might have been one of her kind—save for its height, the depth of its voice, and the lack of a head between its shoulders. As well as not, Aryl thought firmly, being *real*. "Those who populate the moons with powerful beings consider the Om'ray no better than the Oud. A flaw."

She shivered, though the air wasn't cold and the osst shared its heat. Taisal should be here, not her. This wasn't a conversation for an unChosen. She suspected the only reason for Traveler's frankness was exactly that. She wasn't important. He could indulge his version of curiosity by getting her reaction.

Aryl scowled at the Makers in the sky, knowing one thing for sure. The Om'ray weren't a "flaw." "We trade with you," she said, pleased at the calmness of her voice. "We harvest the dresel you need. There's no harm in us."

"The dresel you supply is nothing. We gather a thousand times more for ourselves. What—" Traveler continued when she sat silent and stunned, "—did you think your contributions were significant?"

Her grip on the post was painfully tight. "Then why did you take most of the Harvest?" she asked finally, her voice unfamiliar to her ears. "We're starving. Some of us will die—some already have!" Bern, the rest on Passage . . . for nothing?

A bark. "I am gratified."

Aryl stared at its dark form. "Because we're dying?"

"Be at ease, Apart-from-All. I am gratified because I recognized your value from the beginning. Now you have told me something I need to know. Thank you."

"You didn't know we were starving?" Aryl wanted to hit the smug creature. "Why?"

"Much like Om'ray exist in Clans, my people are divided into factions. By ideas, not place. There is a faction that looks to the moons for guidance. Others who mourn our past or fear the future. Most care only for what is important for the survival of our groves and our kind, season by season. The Yena live within the influence of three different ideologies: one faction continues to honor the Agreement; one wishes to avoid that duty, but dares not; and one . . . from you I learn that this one does so dare, doubtless inspired by the arrival of the strangers."

Not curiosity. By the moons' light, at the edge of the Lake of Fire, she, Aryl Sarc, was being given information vital for all of her kind. Factions? Strangers? Feeling woefully inadequate, she licked her dry lips and tried to think like her mother. What would the Speaker ask? "Which—which faction are you?"

"Each has its Thought Travelers, like myself, who move between to gather and share information. This is how Tikitik decide what to avoid—to stay away from any course likely to be wrong. Thought Travelers are neutral and act only to better understand a situation. I have an opinion, of course."

"An opinion."

"The Agreement was made for a reason. Our races are together, here, for that reason. Until we know what that is, my opinion is that only a fool would break it. And you?"

"Me?" Aryl hesitated. "What about me?"

"Do you honor the Agreement that arranged the world as it is?"

It didn't seem a safe question. Not that silence was an

option. She took advantage of her osst's loud series of pained grunts, something the rest were now doing as if to keep better track of one another in the dim light, and tried to *reach* Taisal.

Nothing.

When the creatures quieted, Traveler repeated his question. "Do you honor the Agreement?"

"Yes," Aryl said carefully. About to say "as do all Yena," she thought of Haxel and substituted the more truthful, "Our Council makes such decisions. Most of us worry about survival, too." She ran her hand up and down the leather wrapping. "Can you help us?" she dared ask. "Can you tell your Council what's happening? That the Yena have been put in danger?" It would all be worthwhile, she thought with abrupt, fierce hope. All of it. Even Bern. "We need more dresel; more glows and cells."

"There is no Tikitik Council," it replied. "I tell other factions what I learn, not what each or all should do about it. Om'ray are resourceful. Yena will survive."

Bitterly disappointed, she almost didn't answer. But it wasn't this Tikitik's fault. By feeding her for days, it had unwittingly provided more for those at home. She sighed. "We will try."

"If you succeed tonight, I'll send what I can with you. It will be what we have left. I can't do more."

Back? She'd be going home? Aryl hadn't realized how sure she'd been that this was a one-way trip, that she was already as good as dead, until relief made her dizzy. And supplies? About to thank the Tikitik for its offer—any supplies would help—the rest of what it said sank in. "Succeed at what?"

"You will solve this puzzle. You will learn if the strangers did interfere with a Harvest. Such an act is offensive to all Tikitik. The faction who tolerates their presence here will no longer."

As well fly over the lake, she thought. "I don't understand. How can I do that?"

"Search their belongings for a device like the one you drew. I require this confirmation. I am sure—" it said with a bark, "—you will find it, Apart-from-All. Be sure to take nourishment."

Aryl had never felt less like sucking blood from an osst. Or anything else, for that matter. "The strangers are here?" She looked up at stars and darkness. How would she spot their flying machine?

"Look to the right of the Makers, low on the horizon."

She did, finally spotting a group of white-and-blue stars, twinkling like the rest. Or were they? "Glows?" she hazarded, realizing they were in front of the clouds.

"Yes. The strangers dared settle on the Lake of Fire. We'll be there by the time the sun returns from its visit with the Grona Om'ray. Shall we watch for it, Apart-from-All? Discover how it sneaks past Yena every night before dawn?"

It made fun of her. From an Om'ray, such teasing would be an attempt to lighten her spirits. From Thought Traveler, she decided gloomily, it was because she'd revealed herself to be ignorant, like those it disdained for making up incredible stories to explain what they couldn't. "If you know," she challenged, "tell me."

"Ah. This isn't reading, Apart-from-All. You couldn't comprehend."

Aryl frowned. "I'm not stupid."

"I don't think you are. Describe the shape of the world."

Automatically, Aryl *reached* to locate her kind. She nodded to herself in satisfaction. "Amna," she pointed, "then Rayna with Vyna beyond, Grona, Tuana, Yena, and Pana. With," she added magnanimously, given her newfound experience, "the sky above. Amna," this in case it lacked her sense of distance, "is beyond your Lake of Fire."

"And beyond Amna?"

Churning darkness . . . Aryl forced it away. "Beyond Amna? Nothing."

"Interesting. I wish you could travel with me, Apart-from-All, so I could see your reaction when you learn otherwise."

Otherwise? It tried to trick her. She deliberately ignored this, having no intention of spending more time with any Tikitik. "How do you think the sun returns to Amna each morning?"

"Perhaps it turns off its light, to sneak past us in the dark."

"I'm not a child!"

"I meant no insult." A pause. "Om'ray are never lost. We know this from those on Passage. You are never lost, because to you the world is not a physical landscape, but a living one. I envy you that perception, Apart-from-All, but I can't feel it—just as you can't feel my perception of this world, its sun, those moons and stars. I can't help you understand. I can't describe other worlds or their suns to you. Be content with yours. Its sun and mine will be up all too soon. Rest if you can."

They proceeded in mutual silence for a while, except for the grunts and bellows of their mounts.

Finally, Aryl had to ask.

"If the strangers are on the lake," she ventured, "how do I get there?"

Chapter 20

THE ANSWER TO HER QUESTION arrived with the earliest hint of dawn from Amna.

"You're sure the osst can take me there." Ignoring her first horizon-spanning sunrise, Aryl regarded the distant speck in the glittering water with dismay. Nothing about her mount suggested it could swim. She certainly couldn't.

"It will manage." In the steadily growing light, Thought Traveler appeared less and less familiar. Its mouth-fingers moved restlessly, and its small eyes divided their attention between her and the activities of its companions.

Those Tikitik were busy consolidating supplies from the gourds on their mounts into fewer. They appeared to want two emptied. The reason thus far escaped her.

She was sure she wouldn't like it.

Aryl pushed a sweat-damp lock of hair from her eyes. The night had been warm; riding the osst, rank with sweat itself, had been like standing out in the hot sun. If it weren't for the cloudiness of the water beside them, she'd have been sorely tempted to try and wash.

But Traveler hadn't recommended it, this close to shore.

Where it wanted to send her—not close enough, she thought. "There has to be another way."

"If you have a suggestion, Apart-from-All, I would be glad to hear it. The strangers pretend we aren't here. Shouting doesn't bring them closer. You must go to them."

Aryl shivered. "And the osst will bring me back again?"

All the eyes turned to her. "They will return you. We've seen their behavior when a flitter lands on their platform. If it doesn't leave on its own, they catch it and use their machine to fly it back to shore, unharmed." A pause and a bark. "They don't behave similarly with biters."

"Who would?" she said, almost to herself. Still, Aryl perked up, things were looking better. A chance to fly in their machine—to learn how it worked?

She wondered if they'd show her how to control it. She could ask, couldn't she?

"Here."

All the osst grunted explosively as their riders insisted they move closer together. For the first time, Aryl saw the Tikitik use pointed sticks, applied like prods, to control their mounts. She held her nose at the result—this was not going to help her first encounter with the strangers.

"Here" referred to the pair of now-empty gourds. They were about her size. The four Tikitik stood on the wide backs of their osst, balancing without difficulty, and carried the gourds over to hers.

Confirming their climbing skills, she thought dourly.

"These go under your arms," Traveler explained as the gourds were positioned beside her. The Tikitik, hissing unhappily to themselves, nonetheless gently rigged a harness of sorts around both gourds and her body. When her osst heaved in protest over its five passengers, it was prodded to be quiet.

Aryl, in the midst of it all, sympathized completely.

When they were done, the Tikitik returned to their mounts,

leaving Aryl puzzled, her upper arms resting over the empty gourds. Her legs began to cramp.

Thought Traveler came close again. "The Lake of Fire is without life in its heart, but there are hunters where the water first deepens. You must stay on your osst there, or die."

Aryl managed to bend her arm so her hands could grip the post. "It knows what to do?" she asked, eyeing the beast doubtfully. It hadn't seemed overly bright to this point.

"It knows to flee."

With that, three Tikitik gave their throbbing shriek and leaped to Aryl's osst, plunging knives deep into its hide. As the beast bellowed in pain and lunged away, they scrambled back to safety on their own, leaving the hilts embedded amid growing patches of blood.

After that horrified look, Aryl found herself too busy to care. Her osst was heading straight out, its instinct to run from danger taking it away from its now-agitated fellows. Its powerful movements drove it through the water, deeper and deeper, water that crashed over its shoulders and into Aryl's face.

Then, the heave and push of muscle beneath her changed to something more rhythmic and outwardly peaceful. Long hair spread out around them.

It could swim. Loud huffs of air from the osst's dilated nostrils measured its effort. Aryl began to enjoy herself as the place of the strangers drew closer and closer. She could see details now. It was a floating platform, not that dissimilar from those in the Lay beneath the Yena meeting hall. Larger than she'd have guessed, with an entire building at one end, the other boasting a tall series of ladders joined to form a tower. There! She spotted the flying machine, then was surprised when it seemed to grow smaller.

Until she realized her osst, perhaps finally aware it had left the safety of the herd, was gradually turning around. Aryl kicked it, making no impression at all. The stupid creature began swimming toward shore with strong, methodical movements. They should have given her a stick, not tied her to gourds.

So much for the Tikitik's plan, she thought, casting a longing look over her shoulder at the platform.

The osst shuddered, like a tree lashed by the M'hir.

Again.

It let out a piteous bellow and turned back toward the strangers. Aryl hung on, confused until she saw the stain in the water. Something—some things—were attacking the osst from below.

Another shudder, another cry. She patted it, weeping, unable to imagine anything that could save it, despairing for the first time in her life for something mute and helpless.

There was a terrible jerk. The osst screamed!

Then she was underwater.

Somehow, Aryl kept her mouth closed, remembering not to breathe until she surfaced. If she surfaced . . .

The gourds tied to her body saw to that. They popped out of the water and lay on top, with her hanging helplessly between them. Aryl gasped for air, then looked frantically for any sign that she was to be prey next.

The chill water around her was free of blood and so clear that the dawn's light slanted down until it faded into shadow. She might have been flying in midair, instead of floating on a lake.

The harness cut into her waist and made it hard to move. She struggled to stretch one, then both arms over the gourds. This pulled her head high enough to see her surroundings.

She was closer to the strangers' platform than ever. Aryl twisted her neck to look back and wished she hadn't. She was too close to where the water was torn by splashes and spurts of red. The osst, mercifully silent now, was being ripped apart.

She couldn't see by what. She didn't want to.

This had been the Tikitik's plan all along. For all their ability to talk and reason, they were outside her understanding. That was plain.

She hoped for better from the strangers.

What other choice did she have?

Interlude

THE TUANA CLOISTERS rose above the plains and town, its rounded roof easily twice the height of any other building. Had Om'ray needed a beacon to guide them at truenight, its rings of soft light would ensure none were lost, for the flat land of the Oud stretched well beyond Tuana territory. But only those on Passage traveled there.

And those who left on Passage did not look back.

Enris leaned on the wide solid rail that encompassed the Cloisters' uppermost tier and watched the moons rise. He wasn't curious where they'd been until now. He didn't care that the sun had abandoned the day or how. He only knew that the light of moons and sun fell on places he didn't want to be.

As Yuhas had said. "So much for what any Om'ray wants."

Tomorrow, he'd be leaving in truth. On Passage. Council had made its decision. For Naryn's sake, he must go beyond her Call. Where? That was why he'd come outside, to try and find a direction that wasn't away from everything he cared about.

As if such could exist.

"Shields, Enris." A cane tip smacked against the floor. "Any grimmer and you'll give the Lost nightmares."

He straightened and turned, gesturing respect. "Grandmother." There was, he checked, nothing sloppy about his control over his thoughts and emotions.

No surprise. Councillor Dama Mendolar had always been able to read him without using Power. And his father. She admitted to difficulty with young Worin, complaining he took after her daughter too much. Ridersel's lips would tighten at such comments, restraining a response. Theirs was a tumultuous relationship at best; at more than a few family gatherings, the two managed not to speak at all.

Dama came to stand in front of him, moving ably with her canes' support. An accident before Enris was born had ruined her knees; an accident involving unsettled Oud and a section of street collapsed with no warning.

"Unfair," she said now, in her dusty voice. "Unjust. Good words?"

"With respect, they are pointless ones," Enris replied, stiffly. "Choosers never leave."

"Naryn S'udlaat is an abomination."

Surprised, Enris gave a bitter laugh. "Everyone else tells me how desperate she must have been, how drawn to me, how impetuous in her love. Her drive as a Chooser overwhelmed her senses. Surely I'd wanted to respond . . ." He leaned back, elbows against the rim, and stared at the softly-lit arches behind his tiny grandmother without seeing them.

"Didn't you?"

That got his attention. "I'd rut with an Oud first."

"Hush, Enris. My delicate ears." But her thin lips curved, wrinkles cascading over her face. "I do hope a better option awaits you."

He shrugged. "The Adepts can't be sure—did they tell you?"

"That there was injury they couldn't repair? Yes. But also that you may heal on your own. In time."

"Or I may never be able to Join at all. No one's tried to force Choice before."

"That we know." Dama tapped her canes against the strange yellow flooring, one and two, one and two, paying careful attention to their tips as if this were some task of note. Then her gaze rose to meet his, clear and cool. "What I tell you, son of my daughter, goes no further."

"Who would I—" he began.

"Hush," she said impatiently. "No further. Understand me? Good," at his nod. "To protect the Agreement, we prevent change, say we Forbid it. Bah! A scandalous lie. We cannot. There's no hope of it. We ride a storm, Enris." Taptap. "Each generation afflicts us with children of new Talent. Each shows an increase in Power among all, however slight. The Power itself may be changing its nature."

"Matters for Adepts, Grandmother." Enris raised a skeptical brow. "What do they have to do with me?"

"Everything." She edged closer, looking from side to side as if she wouldn't trust her inner sense that they were alone on the platform. "We have kept secret something else. Power can affect a Joining."

He flinched as if she'd touched an open wound. "I don't—"

"Listen to me. It's true. Those weak in Power have always Joined with ease. But those with great strength . . . sometimes there are difficulties. An Adept must be called, quietly, to assist. There is a drug, a drug that eases—"

"I will not!" The harshness of his voice startled them both. Enris gestured apology, but he didn't back down. "You called her an abomination. You can't imagine I'd try to Join with her. Not after this."

"An abomination we have to keep." In that moment, Dama looked every one of the Harvests she'd seen. "I fear the consequence, Enris. There are more like Naryn to come. Those who care nothing for risk to others or even themselves—only their Power and its use. You could be a good influence. As her Chosen—"

"No."

"You wouldn't have to leave." Lightly, Dama tapped her left cane against the side of his shin. "Your father needs those strong legs."

"He has Yuhas."

She frowned, her eyes all but disappearing. "That one? He still carries the weight of his former Clan, though safe and Chosen and one of us. Ungrateful, I say."

Despite her shields and complaint, Enris sensed sympathy for the Yena Om'ray. "He has reason to fear for those he left behind, his family and friends." As her frown deepened into a scowl, he added gently, "It's not unlawful, Grandmother, to care about those you leave." He took a deep breath. "I know I will." There. It was done. Somehow he felt safer, just saying the words aloud.

"We," she said haughtily, her small frame stiff, "will forget you. That is what must be. You go to a new life. Find joy."

Seeing the glisten in her eyes and the way she fought her trembling lips, Enris simply nodded. "Yes, Grandmother."

* * *

There was no ceremony when Enris left on Passage, no feast or gathering of well-wishers—Council wanted no witness. No new shirt to wear for his Chooser-to-be, lovingly given by his family—they would learn he was leaving when distance faded him from their inner sense and no sooner. No landscapes or other useful memories had been set in his mind—the Adepts remained cautious of his still-damaged state. There was only this hurried departure from the Cloisters after moons set, the light cut off as doors were turned closed behind, so he made his way down dark stairs to the empty street.

Well enough. Enris shrugged the pack given him over his broad shoulders and started walking. He hadn't found a Chooser's Call to lure him in a particular direction. He hadn't tried.

Oh, he had a goal, of sorts. The Om'ray device might be locked in its hiding place at the shop, but it haunted his thoughts. Who could have made it? None of the Clans he or his father knew.

Suggesting the one Clan no one could claim to know: Vyna. There had never been a Vyna unChosen arrive at Tuana, not in the memory of any Adept he'd asked. Nor had other clans claimed one. Beyond Yena, Vyna was past distant Rayna as well. Some said a broad and dangerous sea lay between, or unclimbable mountains. The Adepts had smiled at him, and told him not to be tempted. Pana was closer, the largest clan other than Amna. Both would offer more Choosers-to-Be.

But it was toward Vyna that Enris now *reached* with his inner sense, making sure of its direction. One mystery called to another. Perhaps the device belonged to these unknown Om'ray. If not, perhaps their Adepts would recognize its description. If not?

He brushed his fingers over the token affixed to the upper left of his leather tunic, aware of the irony. It wasn't the one he'd kept. They hadn't allowed him back for his things. The Tuana Speaker, Sian, had produced another, possibly even Yuhas' own.

He'd use it and keep it, he vowed. A token meant freedom. If he didn't find the answer he sought with the Vyna, he'd leave them for another clan, and another after that. It wasn't Forbidden. Why would anyone want to leave his new Clan and Chosen?

Someone who would never let Choice or a Chooser dictate his life, Enris promised himself.

The air was still and cool. While he could wish for his favorite longcoat, they'd given him warm gear. Farmer's gear. He tried not to think whose it had been. He could hear lopers scurrying in the shadows, their occasional giggles as they found something to their liking, their high-pitched snarls as that something became the object of envy. Otherwise, Tuana slept under the stars. He looked for the set he'd taken for his name. They lay low on the horizon, the faintest one straight ahead.

A favorable sign, he decided, stretching his legs to cover more ground. He needed what encouragement he could find. Hard, these first steps away from his home and family. Like starting a full cart upslope, he told himself. One step at a time and don't stop.

Dim light picked the low oval mouth of the Oud tunnel from the night. Enris gave it a worried look, but there was no sign of life. He disliked leaving the device in the shop. Worse was the thought of his father left to explain to the Oud why they'd made no progress. He consoled himself that he'd had no say in the matter, that even if he could, taking the cylinder would risk setting the anger of the Oud against Jorg and Tuana itself.

What was that?

Enris hesitated, sure the faint sound hadn't come from a loper. He stood where the street split around the tunnel mouth, its left fork leading out to farmland, the right little more than a convenient alleyway to the backs of shops. No homes, not this close to the tunnel mouth. No lights but the tunnel's. He could hear his breathing, the pound of his heart, the distant sibilance that was the evening's breeze making its way through the dry, bent stalks of the fields.

Something held Enris still. He lowered his shields enough to send a thread of thought outward, *seeking* . . .

Finding!

Just as he realized he was ambushed, figures spilled from the shadowy farm lane and through a now-open shop door. They moved with quick, deadly purpose. The first was on him as he struggled to drop his pack and free his arms, a blow to the head sending him to his knees, another striking his shoulder, another a kick to the ribs. He managed to rise to his feet again, arms flailing, but they struck from behind, tripping his legs. This time he landed hard on the packed earth, losing most of the breath from his lungs. Kicks struck his legs, his side . . . he tried to protect his head and get to his feet again. They grabbed him. He *sensed* their rage and was afraid for the first time.

They were losing control. What might have started as a parting lesson to someone they despised was turning into something far worse . . . something no Om'ray should have been able to do . . . Enris spat blood and struck out himself, his powerful arms and hands landing heavy, bone-cracking blows. But there were too many . . . they evaded him, took his arms, his legs . . .

"Yahhhh!!" The furious shriek didn't come from his silent attackers. Their grips fell away, and he dropped to the dust.

Yuhas. The Yena stood over him, brandishing his . . .Enris blinked his eyes clear . . . his broom.

It didn't matter that it was a homely weapon. Yuhas was clearly accustomed to fighting with whatever he could put to hand. Whap! Someone fell with a scream. Whap! Down went another. The shadows, always dim and faceless, melted away into the darkness, dragging their fallen comrades with them.

"Cowards!" Yuhas bellowed. "May your living flesh be stripped from your bones by the swarms! May your bones drown in the Lay!"

Sounds messy, Enris sent, unwilling to test his mouth yet. He didn't try to stem the flood of gratitude and affection that went with the words.

"You don't have anything dangerous here," the other complained mildly, bending down to offer a hand. "Is that why you fight each other?"

Enris swallowed a groan as he stood with Yuhas' help. He could move—nothing broken, though his ribs argued the point. He spat more blood and wiped a stream from one eye. "We don't," he muttered absently, staring into the darkness. Mauro Lorimar. If he made an effort, he might put names to some of the others. It wasn't worth it. "You'd think—" spit, "—having me leave would be enough."

"On Passage. I know."

Enris couldn't see the other's face, it was too dark for that. "You were waiting outside the Cloisters. Why?"

"I've seen what happens when a Council has a problem it can

remove with its unChosen. Did your Adepts finally tell you? Yena sent ten of us on Passage. All there were."

"I—" Enris couldn't think of anything to say to that. "I'm sorry." He reached for his pack. It took two tries to bend that far. "You told me this season's Harvest had failed. That you worried there'd be enough to eat."

Soft and bitter from the dark. "There was enough, barely. But our neighbors aren't so gracious as yours, Enris, and they eat what we must. The Tikitik took almost all we had, leaving us to starve. The unChosen—we were sent away because only those on Passage can move freely. Our Council gave us a chance to escape, to survive. But they were wrong. They should have let us stay. After the Harvest—we were the best hunters—the best gatherers—Yena had. We could have—" a violent whistle-*snap* as Yuhas broke the broom against the ground. Then, quietly and in pain, "We should have helped."

"Maybe you did," Enris offered, finding the other's shoulder with his hand. "Fewer to share what's left has to help. And, no offense," he added as lightly as he could manage, "but there have to be other Yena who can hunt and gather better than you. I've seen you work."

Through their contact, Yuhas sent a remembered image. It was of people, dozens of people, most older, a few very young, all standing on a bridge of some kind that looked much too fragile and slender to hold them. They looked sad and afraid.

Within the group, though, was one who was neither. She looked back at Yuhas—for this was his memory—with determination written in her large gray eyes and slim, erect body. There was someone who wouldn't give up, Enris decided. Ever.

Yuhas snorted. "Aryl Sarc," he identified, having followed the thought. "You're right about her. Bern worried she'd—" he stopped, a tinge of embarrassment quickly hidden. "It doesn't matter."

Enris had been testing his legs. Shaky and sore—he'd have livid bruises—but not much worse than the last time the cart had tipped and dropped on him. He'd made his way home then.

Not home. Not this time.

Then something made him squint at his friend. "You're out in truenight. In the dark."

A shaky laugh. "Don't remind me. Now, can we please head indoors?"

His right shoulder and side protested the weight of his pack, so Enris shifted it to the left. "You've been a good friend, Yuhas, and I thank you," he said. "But nothing's changed. Naryn's still here; I still have to go."

"You Tuana are all the same," Yuhas said with amusement. "You realize you're dripping blood. Even I can smell it."

Enris wiped some from his eye. "Nothing that will slow me down." Much, he added to himself.

" 'Slow you—!' " A laugh. "I don't care how fast you move, my friend. The instant you leave these hard walls of yours you're prey. Blood draws hunters. If you want to live till the dawn, wash it off, cover any cuts, change to clean clothing. Or you won't."

"I have my knife," Enris protested stiffly.

"You'll have no time to use it. Come, Enris." A flash of impatience. "How many Yena unChosen do you think survived their first truenight on Passage? You might want to listen to one who did."

Enris wavered, staring down the long street. Slowly, he shook his head. "I'm listening. It's good advice. I don't doubt it. But—Yuhas, I can feel her," he confessed what he hadn't to anyone else.

"Naryn? Enris—that's not possible. She's not here."

"The Adepts think they control her—" the words tumbled out, urgent and desperate, "—that she obeys Council. It's not true. Somehow . . . somehow she's found a way around them all." That darkness. Naryn was *there*. "I still hear her. She doesn't care what the Adepts or Council says, Yuhas. She'll never stop Calling me. If

I stay any longer . . ." . . . if he dared open his inner sense to that *place* . . . if he allowed her touch once more . . . she'd have him.

And he wouldn't even care.

"I can't stay," Enris said bleakly.

The Yena shrugged. "Fine. Then take the tunnels."

"You hate the tunnels."

Yuhas made a rude noise. "I'm not the one bleeding like supper on the table," he pointed out. "You wear a token—Oud have to allow you Passage, don't they?"

His hand flattened over the disk; it hadn't been torn loose in the fight. Enris gazed at the tunnel mouth, surprised to find himself considering the idea. "By the Agreement, yes," he mused aloud. "But no Om'ray has taken that route. The fields—overland—"

"Where there are things with teeth, remember? You've talked to an Oud—Jorg told me. You aren't afraid of them. It's not as if you could get lost." This last with unconscious superiority.

Yuhas made it sound easy. He'd yet to see an Oud. He didn't know, Enris shivered inwardly, how strange they were, how quick to react. But was there another choice? He was already fighting real shivers—pain was settling throughout his body, pain and reaction. He wasn't a violent person. No Om'ray was . . . or had been. The tunnel . . . he need only follow it till morning. Rest a bit in safety. Nothing said he'd encounter an Oud at all. Runners did it all the time.

"I'll do it," he heard himself say.

"Better you than me." Under the levity, a swell of concern and grief.

Yuhas had said good-bye to everyone he'd cared about, yet made room in his heart to care for him, as well. Enris sent his own regret and worry, adding: *Be careful of Lorimar and his ilk. They won't forget you helped me. Or forgive.*

A gentle push on his shoulder. "You planning to wait till daylight? Go. Caynen wants me home." Underneath, grim and sure, *I remain Yena. Let them be careful of me.* Aloud, "Find joy, Enris Mendolar."

There was nothing left to say. Enris turned away from his friend, his Clan, and everything he knew, to limp into the Oud tunnel.

And began his journey to its depths.

Chapter 21

ARYL DIDN'T NEED TO UNDERSTAND the words to recognize an argument with her at its heart. The strangers may have worked together, and quickly, to snag her harness with long hooks and pull her alongside. They'd cut her free of the gourds and helped her up stairs of metal from the water, opening and closing a gate in a formidable railing that ran around the entire floating platform. From its tips of outward-bent spikes, they were well aware of what lived in the Lake of Fire.

From the gestures and angry tones of the three now in front of her, they didn't agree on much else.

Two she'd seen before. The Om'ray-who-wasn't talked the least, his eyes hidden behind pale green ovals that wrapped around the upper part of his face. The huge creature, neither Oud nor Tikitik, talked the most, its voice like the thunder rumbling in the distance. Tall and wide from front to back, it had round eyes enough for a dozen Tikitik, all busy moving between two halves of black gleaming shell. Its body was covered in more shell, but fasteners had been drilled into it to hold what were either ugly ornaments or an assortment of unknown tools. Or both. It snapped the larger of two sets of claws for emphasis as it bellowed.

The third was new to her. Pale-skinned and fragile-seeming, it leaned toward whomever spoke, as if physically displaying agreement with one side or the other, or hard of hearing. Leaning was easy; its body was so thin Aryl wondered how organs could fit inside. Its hairless head was long and thin as well, with a pair of large eyes on each side of a prominent, hooked nose. The mouth was prim and disturbingly Om'ray-like. It wore, like the Om'ray-who-wasn't, pants and a loosely-hanging shirt of that fine, brown fabric. No boots—but its long four-clawed feet would never have fit inside them. When it spoke, it sounded petulant, like a child too long without a nap, and waved its two sticklike arms in agitation.

Shivering, Aryl tried to make herself less conspicuous, staying hunched and quiet where they'd left her. She hadn't understood if they'd wanted her to stand or sit—she'd sat anyway, too shaken to trust her feet so soon. Her hands explored the unusual surface that made the floor. Water from her dripping tunic and hair had soaked into it immediately, yet she felt no holes or porousness to the stuff. A cautious inspection from under lowered eyelids showed the same material in use for what she could see of the strangers' . . . what was this? Too small for a village, too permanent for a day camp. Something between, she decided, sneaking a look at the metal tower. Maybe they thought themselves safe here, while they explored. Her eyes fastened greedily on the flying machine at the tower's base—likely the same one she'd seen before.

"Who are?"

Real words? Aryl gaped, her eyes flashing to the shell-stranger. Real words had come out of it, from somewhere between its eyes. "I'm Aryl Sarc of the Yena Om'ray," she said eagerly. "The Tikitik sent me. Who are you? What are you? Why—"

A claw raised slightly and she closed her mouth. "Seekers, we." This with a sweep of the same claw to indicate the others.

Real words, but—Aryl frowned—not used properly. "Can—you—understand—me?" She spoke slowly and with emphasis, as if to her almost deaf great-aunt.

A noise came from the Om'ray-who-wasn't that sounded exactly like a laugh. It—he—removed the ovals from his face. It was, Aryl saw, a perfectly normal Om'ray face, though older and starting to wrinkle around the eyes and mouth. Brown eyes, a normal smile. A nice face—

With *nothing* underneath. She flinched back involuntarily as her inner sense repudiated what she saw. "You aren't real!" she declared, wrapping her arms around her body. "Go away!"

The smile disappeared. He glanced at his companions. The shell-stranger snapped its claw lightly this time, making a bell-like ring. "Real are," it said. "Afraid, don't."

"Don't be afraid," she corrected, guessing what it meant. She wasn't—not that she'd admit, anyway.

Another snap. "'Don't be afraid.' Better is?"

Aryl tilted her head and considered it. Several eyes clustered to consider her in turn. For all its armor and natural weaponry, it didn't seem threatening. "Better," she agreed. "Why do you talk like that?" A breeze riffled over the lake; it stole what warmth she had left. Her teeth chattered as she spoke.

"Cold is." More real words, this time from the mouth of the stick-stranger. They were oddly slurred, as if its teeth weren't quite right. "Back go. Back go!"

It couldn't mean into the water, Aryl hoped fervently.

"No." This from the Om'ray-who-wasn't. He gestured to Aryl, a beckoning. "Come." His tone and expression were kind.

Like the flowers that lured biters close, she decided. The kind that snapped shut to devour their helpless prey. She rose to her feet and edged closer to the shell-stranger. She couldn't take her eyes from the Om'ray-who-wasn't. "What *are* you?"

The stick-stranger rattled off a stream of angry-sounding syllables. The shell-stranger interrupted with more of the same, much louder and low enough to vibrate through the floor. Aryl quickly stepped away from them both, glancing with dismay at the nearness of the railing and the water beyond. She looked back at the Om'ray-who-wasn't. "Om'ray," she stated desperately. She put her hand on her chest as if to reassure herself. "Om'ray." She thrust a finger at him. "Not."

His lips twisted up at one corner. Not quite a smile. "Om'ray, not." He repeated her gesture, putting his own hand to his chest. "*Human*, me. *Human*."

Meaningless sounds. She shuddered as much from frustration as chill. Why didn't they talk in words that made sense?

He frowned and beckoned again, the gesture indicating she go to the building. The stick-stranger began shouting something incomprehensible, clearly unhappy with this decision. Aryl winced.

"Responsibility, mine," the Om'ray-who-wasn't said firmly. This silenced the other. An inner lid closed over each of its eyes, giving it the look of something dead. As if this expressed some final opinion, the stick-stranger walked away, swaying from side to side like a tree that had forgotten to fall.

Under any other circumstances, she'd have laughed.

"Responsibility, yours," agreed the shell-stranger, but Aryl thought it sounded amused. "Better, how?" it said with a sly swing of several eyes her way.

"Better?" Belatedly, she realized it was asking her to help it speak. Which was ridiculous, since everyone knew how to talk from the moment they were old enough for their parents to give them words. Still. These obviously weren't Om'ray. Maybe—Aryl took a wild guess—maybe for some reason they had to learn words, the way she had to learn the Tikitik's writing. Why was another question. "It's your responsibility." This with the barest nod to the one calling himself Human as she said "your."

"It's *your* responsibility, *Marcus*!" The shell-creature appeared to delight in adding emphasis to its words. And words of its own.

Aryl rubbed her bare arms, starting to warm from the sun despite the breeze. Two could play the learning game, she decided. " 'Mar-cus?' " she echoed, making it a question.

The Om'ray-who-wasn't bowed his head to her and touched his finger to a line of small symbols on his shirt, reminding her of the Tikitik when he said, as if reading, "Marcus Bowman. Triad First." Then he pointed to himself. "Marcus." Then at her, his eyebrows rising as if in question. "Arylsarc?"

"Aryl," she corrected, unsure if she should fear her name in his mouth or not. But it was, she decided, civil behavior. As her mother would say, that was a start. "My name is Aryl."

"Welcome, Aryl," boomed the shell-stranger. It tapped its bulbous head with a claw, producing a dull thud. "My name is Janet Jim-bo Bob. Triad Third."

"Your name not," said Marcus quickly. He was, she noticed with astonishment, blushing. "Mistake was."

The shell-stranger patted Marcus on the back with its great claw, making the other stagger. "It's your responsibility." Then it gave its booming laugh.

The two acted like friends, Aryl thought, despite their physical differences. Marcus made a face, just as Costa would have done when teased.

Marcus wasn't real, she reminded herself, aghast at how quickly she'd begun to ignore her inner sense.

"My name is Janex Jymbobobii, Aryl." This with another tap of claw to shell. "Janex."

They both seemed to be waiting for something. All she could think of was to copy Marcus' bow and repeat their short names. "Marcus. Janex." How peculiar, to move her lips around totally new words. She tried another. "Human. Both?" she asked, pointing to each.

"Human, yes," agreed Marcus, seeming pleased, then nodded at Janex. "Human, not. *Carasian*. Om'ray, you?"

Aryl sagged with relief. Despite the awkward phrasing, the meaning was clear. She couldn't sense this Marcus as an Om'ray because he wasn't one. He was this "Human"—some other creature altogether. There were many mimics in the canopy; some so perfect only a knife could tell them apart. Perhaps, she told herself gleefully, his blood was blue instead of red.

All she had to do was keep reminding herself he wasn't what he appeared to be.

"Aryl. Come, please. Cold, not."

The unexpected courtesy surprised her almost as much as Marcus' worried frown. She took a step forward, a gesture he understood, for it brought a quick smile and wave toward the building.

Aryl walked between the two of them, the Carasian doing an excellent job of blocking what wind rose from the lake. It moved quietly on what looked more like balls than feet. When Janex noticed her interest, it paused and leaned to afford her a better view. "Rocks, good," it informed her.

She eyed its bulk, amazed it had managed to walk along the nekis branch.

Did they recognize her? Could they?

Aryl wondered about this only until they reached the door, which was like no door she'd ever seen. There was no spindle on which it could turn open, nor handle to grasp. She looked at Marcus questioningly and he indicated a light green square of metal on the wall. He laid his palm against it.

The door moved itself out of the way.

Startled, Aryl stepped back. As quickly she moved forward

again, her hands exploring the exposed doorframe. The door hadn't disappeared. It had gone inside the hollow wall.

She flushed, angry with herself. Of course the strangers had unfamiliar technology. That was why she was here—to confirm whether they'd sent the device to disrupt the Harvest. The Tikitik were waiting for the answer.

Her hosts didn't appear in a hurry to deliver her back to them.

Hopefully Thought Traveler would wait, she told herself, stepping through the strangers' door.

"You're not touching me." Aryl kept her back to the wall as she glared at the stick-stranger.

"Safe are!"

She eyed the object in its twiggy hands—an object it had tried to press against her bare skin without permission—and shook her head. Hair tumbled into her eyes. She was a mess. And cold. And hungry.

And this thing persistently got in her way. If she wasn't afraid it would snap in two, she'd push past it and out of this odd little room where they'd left her. "Stay away from me," she ordered.

A stream of incensed babble issued from its lips. It tossed the object on the smooth white table that was the room's only furnishing where it lay, blinking like a glow about to fail.

She smiled in triumph. "I'm glad we understand one another."

"Aryl?" The Human, Marcus, stood in the doorway, one hand on the frame. After a look, he said some of their words to the stick-stranger, who answered with more of the same in a surly tone, giving an unmistakable glare at her in the midst of it.

"Om'ray don't touch one another without permission," she

said, knowing it wasn't being fair. She waved at the object. "What is that anyway?"

The Human eased to one side to let the stick-stranger leave, which it did with relieved speed. He came into the room and picked up the object.

"No, you don't," Aryl said, ready to defend herself. But all he did was hold it out to her. When she reluctantly took it from him, he pushed up one sleeve and offered his arm.

The object seemed harmless. There was no sharp edge to any of its flat sides, merely a play of rather lovely lights over one surface, the other—she turned it over—being featureless and polished. "Try," Marcus said, standing quite still.

Aryl brushed hair from her eyes, then used both hands to hold the object. She approached the Human as the stick-stranger had tried to approach her, stopping short of touching him.

"Try," he urged. "Safe, is."

What was he? This close, she wasn't sure anymore. Aryl stared into eyes that lied with their familiarity, her nostrils flaring at a faint, not unpleasant new scent. She could feel the warmth of his body across the small distance between them. Not that she was wearing much.

She watched with interest as he swallowed once, then again, color blooming on his cheeks. "*Bioscanner*," Marcus said in an odd voice. "Try."

Of course. The object. She looked down at the smooth underside of his forearm. It was soft and rounded, like the palm of his hand. The Human, she realized with an inner shock, had probably never climbed a rope or stalk. Did he rely on machines for everything? She put her arm next to his. Muscle and veins wove like cords from wrist to elbow; over that, her tanned skin was patterned in white scars. Cuts, the deeper attentions of biters, nothing much of note.

She wasn't the only one comparing. "Strong are," Marcus observed, his other hand reaching as if to touch her.

Aryl jerked her arm away. "I'm Yena Om'ray," she said proudly. "We don't fall."

"Fall?" He frowned. "Means what?"

To distract him, she took the object—the "bioscanner"—and put it on his arm.

Two things happened.

The first was that the lights changed position and became a flock of moving symbols. She was almost fascinated enough to miss the second.

Almost.

The second was that she inadvertently touched the side of her smallest finger to his skin. And through that tiny touch, slowly, then more quickly, she could *see*.

His mind was *real*.

Though the Human was not Om'ray to her inner sense, with contact she could *hear* incomprehensible words she somehow recognized as his thoughts. Nothing was shielded. Should she wish, Aryl realized, she could explore every level of his mind. Were she Adept, she might even understand what she found. Still, she tried, using her *sense* to chase tantalizing images. Memories. Vast dark spaces. Depths. Confusing mosaics of light and shapes. Places. Other beings.

Emotions. *Goodwill. Curiosity. Admiration*. A growing discomfort—not pain yet, but its precursor. Her presence in his mind wasn't sensed, but it was felt.

Aryl pulled her inner self back. At the same time, she lifted her hand from his arm and gave the Human a real smile. "Bioscanner," she repeated carefully, pretending to examine the symbols before passing it to him. "What does it do?"

"Do?" Marcus repeated. He appeared to search for words,

then nodded as if to himself. "Sick. Sick not. Food best. Food not. Bioscanner, all."

A device to detect what food her body should have? If she was ill? Aryl looked at the small thing incredulously. How could it do that? She thrust out her arm, eager now to see it work.

Marcus applied it. All she felt was the coolness of metal, quickly warmed by her flesh. His fingertips brushed her skin, but she restrained her curiosity. He meant no harm toward her—she owed him the same.

The device blinked and produced symbols that looked, to Aryl's disappointed judgment, to be exactly the same. But the Human made a pleased sound and tucked the device into a fold in his shirt. "Aryl good."

She laughed. It sounded like something a young child would say, though this was no such simple being. "Thank you." She made the gesture of gratitude. He seemed to know it was important, and copied the movements of her hands. "Good," she said, then got straight to what mattered.

"What do you eat?"

"Good?"

The scrutiny of those dancing black eyes was hard to ignore, but Aryl had done her best. The Carasian, Janex, was apparently fascinated with her. Or her eating habits, Aryl thought.

"Good," she agreed, though most of their food was bland by her standards. There was a dark, hot drink she liked, bold and bitter, as well as a tangy green froth within a bowl, though Janex had removed a bright red swirl from the top before handing it to Aryl. There was no dresel, nor did they appear to understand the word. If this food didn't supply its equivalent to her body, she'd have to return home before too many days passed and she weakened.

Aryl wasn't in a hurry. The marvels of this place multiplied by the moment. After the bioscanner had been a very small room, no larger than her outstretched arms, called a *fresher.* She'd stood inside and first been sprayed with warm, fragrant foam that had tingled over her skin and through her hair. Then, a wind, warm and soft, blew the foam away, leaving her clean and as refreshed as if she'd slept. The rest of the facilities were disappointingly normal—she supposed sinks and toilets had practical limitations—though she couldn't tell where water or wastes went.

There had been clothes as well. She was now dressed like Marcus or the stick-stranger, though she'd doubted the pants at first. Once on, they'd proved softer and more comfortable than they looked. With luck, the garments would last until she was home. Yena weavers would be fascinated.

Now this, an eating place with a window like those in the Cloisters, fitted with something hard and clear. Beams of sunlight passed easily, patterning the otherwise plain white floor with shadows. Through it, Aryl could see the glittering expanse of the Lake of Fire. No mysterious smoke now. Only hard reflection, hiding what might lie beneath. It filled the view, as if there was no other landscape in the world.

She sat with her back to it at one of four round tables, on a comfortable-enough chair. The stick-stranger had its own, the seat designed for the challenge of its posterior, not hers. Food came on trays from a slot in an otherwise ordinary wall. She'd wanted to look though that, but the Carasian had been too quick to remove her tray and bring it to the table for her.

The Carasian's own repast had consisted of a bowl of the dark drink, consumed tidily, if noisily, by pouring large amounts into a cavity in its claw, then lifting that to a space between its eyes. The ensuing slurp made her smile.

Aryl tucked her hair behind one ear—again. She'd been unable to explain the need for a hairnet and consoled herself that no one here knew about such necessities.

"Better?"

Janex was unrelenting in its efforts to improve. Aryl found it frustrating. The shell-stranger had an ample store of real words. Putting them together in a sane order—that was the problem. At least it learned quickly.

"Your food," she said carefully, using the utensil they'd given her as a pointer, "is good. Thank you."

" 'Your food is good.' "

That wasn't right. Aryl frowned in thought. "I say that," she clarified, indicating herself. "You say: Our food is good."

Janex gave that booming laugh. "Our food is bad."

Making perfect sense. Aryl grinned and lifted her cup gesturing to Janex's empty bowl. "Not all of it. I like this."

"*Sombay*. Our sombay is good, yes. Better is?"

"Is this better?" she corrected, though suspicious she was being teased. "Yes, that's better. You're good with real words."

"Real." The eyes settled, every one looking at her. The Carasian said, "Is this real?" and uttered a few of those incomprehensible sounds.

Aryl shook her head. "No. These are real words." She touched her own mouth, then gestured to the other. "Those are not real."

A moment of silence, then, "Your words, real you. Our words, real us." This last with a sweep of a claw around the room. "All words, real both. Words," a shrug that rattled its tools, "new. New words is good—are good. Is this better?"

Aryl found herself on her feet. Janex remained still, as if not to alarm her further. "Everyone uses the same words," she insisted. "Everyone in the world speaks the same. Om'ray, Tikitik, Oud."

"Oud words, us," Janex offered promptly, in a pleased tone.

"Teach all. Expert, I. Aryl is Om'ray. Oud words, different pattern. Om'ray complex. More meaning. Good."

Strangers, the Tikitik called them. How strange, she hadn't fully appreciated until this moment. Their food threatened to leave her stomach, and Aryl closed her mouth tightly, breathing through her nose.

"Aryl not afraid, please."

She'd *seen* remembered images of the reclusive Oud, knew they followed the Agreement, communicated through a Speaker with the other races, allowed Passage across their lands. She knew little more—had cared to know nothing more about them. What could they matter to a Yena who would live her life high in the canopy? She would never meet an Oud.

The Carasian had. More than met—if she understood what it said, the strangers had learned the language spoken by all on Cersi from the Oud.

Aryl sank back down on her too-solid chair, in a building of strangers, on a platform in the middle of the Lake of Fire, and realized anything was possible now. "I'm not afraid," she said as calmly as she could. "Tikitik and Om'ray use words as I do. The Oud—" What had Costa said? "—the Oud use as few words as possible. They can be difficult to understand." She thought that a tactful hint to the other.

"Difficult? Aryl kind." Janex pounded the table, threatening their plates. "Oud difficult, us. Confusing talk. Now we difficult, Aryl? Sorry," this said with what appeared a sincere regret. "Rules I hunt. Rules for words. Oud use no rules."

She had to smile. "You're a Speaker, aren't you?"

"Speaker, me?" Janex's eyes milled around briefly. That note of amusement was back in its voice. "Good, is. Janex Triad Third. *Recorder* and *comtech*. Talk, talk, talk. *Pilip*, Triad Second." The stick-stranger looked up at this, strands of blue hanging from its mouth, then muttered something unpleasant-sounding through that mouthful before looking away again. "Janex is Carasian. Pilip is *Trant*. Better?"

"Better," affirmed Aryl, trying to fix these new names in memory. At the rate they were multiplying, she feared it was hopeless. She didn't have the Carasian's obvious Talent with words. "Marcus is Triad First," she said, proud to have remembered that. Whatever it meant. A rank, she guessed. Like the scouts.

"Good!" The Carasian clicked its big claw. "Pilip *scantech. Finder.* Marcus, Triad First, *Analyst*."

Different names, an entirely different—if she understood correctly—set of words. Their technology—and the Oud involved? She didn't think Thought Traveler would be pleased, not pleased at all. As for Yena Council? Aryl decided not to think about them.

"Are there others here?" she indicated the room. "Oud?"

The giant creature's head rocked from side to side. "Oud, no. Others?" She thought it hesitated, as if it didn't want to reveal how many they were. Aryl wasn't sure why the answer would matter. "Others." This with a large claw raised overhead. "Others." The claw pointed through the window.

That wasn't helpful. Aryl decided to assume they came from somewhere else—from exactly where being a question she wasn't in a hurry to have answered. "You're on Passage?"

"Understand not."

Already a habit to correct it. "I don't understand."

" 'I don't understand' Passage."

Aryl leaned back in her seat, more thoughtful than shocked. "When Om'ray go from place to place," she mimed walking with her hands, "it is called Passage."

"Aryl is on Passage."

No, she'd been kidnapped and dropped into the lake to spy on them, but as this explanation couldn't lead to anything but harder questions, Aryl settled for, "I'm looking for something."

"Seekers, we also," announced Marcus, sitting beside her. "Food good?"

"I liked the—sombay," Aryl said, finally recalling the name of the drink. "Seekers." Were they scouts of some kind? "What do you seek?"

"Show Aryl?" The Human jumped back to his feet.

All three strangers were looking at her now, Marcus with an expression that, on an Om'ray face, would be hopeful. Why?

There was, Aryl sighed inwardly, only one way to find out. Maybe she'd find the Tikitik's answer at the same time.

She rose to her feet, her new boots making a faint shhhh on the floor. "Show me."

Chapter 22

ARYL . . .

Aryl didn't stop walking at the inner touch, but her attention was no longer on her surroundings. She'd been waiting for privacy to contact her mother. To be honest, she'd been waiting for courage too.

It seemed Taisal could no longer wait, so Aryl opened her mind to the *other*, making the link. *Mother.*

Her mother's sending was colored by emotion; a residue of anger mingled with concern. *What has happened? Are you all right?*

Mother . . . we're not alone here! As if forming the words made them true, Aryl could barely contain her fear, torn by the urge to somehow look beyond their link into the seething darkness. What—who—might she find?

Almost scorn. *We're never alone here, daughter. This is the hollow between minds, where the dead linger and the Lost hide. Don't be afraid. They're harmless unless you follow or answer them. Don't look for anyone. Those here . . . they're no longer Om'ray. They are shadows. Nothing more.*

The voice of experience? Aryl shuddered. *I won't. I won't.*

Tell me where you are.

With the strangers. Aryl sent her view of the lake and platform.

Something hard gripped her around the waist, shattering her concentration and the link.

"What do!??"

Aryl blinked and found herself suspended in the air in one of the Carasian's great claws. Its eyes moved aside to reveal two knifelike jaws as long as her arms. Aryl squeezed her eyes closed and tried not to scream. "What do!?" it roared at her again.

"Careful, Janex!" Marcus cautioned. Aryl peered down at him, hoping for rescue, but he frowned at her, not the Carasian, before uttering a string of his own words.

Janex, its focus never leaving Aryl, answered—mostly—in real words. "*Grist!* Aryl grist different. Better now." The last word was calmer, as if Janex had taken time to think something through and been relieved. Sure enough, the claw eased Aryl back to the floor.

She smacked the claw the instant it released her. "Don't do that!" she scolded, as furious as she'd been scared. This was the stranger she'd almost trusted. Now? Aryl backed against the wall, her arms tight around her waist, though it hadn't hurt her.

It could have. She'd underestimated the strength of that unusual body. And maybe something else. Had it somehow detected her connection to Taisal? Aryl tried opening her inner sense, to feel anything from the Carasian's mind.

Chaos!

"Ouch!" she exclaimed, retreating behind the tightest possible shields, her eyes wide.

Janex, if it were possible for a creature built like a machine, looked smug. "Grist, me," it said. "Good smell, Aryl."

Aryl sniffed cautiously. The fresh lake, something musky from Pilip's direction. "I don't understand."

Marcus looked from her to his companion. "I don't understand," he agreed.

"Problem, not." Janex waved a jaunty claw. "Go on. Show Aryl."

Aryl, equally willing to avoid the topic of what grist smelled like, or what it was, continued walking.

They took her to the roof, up a winding solid ramp that suited the Carasian's bulk and maneuverability, though it wasted too much of the building's interior to Aryl's way of thinking. Pilip, on the other hand, clung desperately to a railing until they were again on a flat surface. She tried not to pity it.

The roof itself was cluttered with more of the plain white boxes, but most of these bore some kind of symbol, the lines sharper and more angular than the Tikitik's. A few larger boxes had doors, implying they were more than boxes, but these weren't, apparently, what she was here to be shown.

Around a pile of loosely coiled ropes—Marcus and his companions were, Aryl judged, remarkably sloppy for all their technology—she found herself at a step that led to a raised solid circle. Around its rim were six identical stalks, plantlike in that they were topped by something else. The something else was like a box, but this time with metal twigs and balls sticking out at all angles.

Not decoration. Aryl was reminded of the poles that protruded from the stalk of the Cloisters.

There were obstacles in the way: folded white petal-things that they had to walk over or around. Aryl bent to touch one. It looked like window gauze, but felt hard and strong.

"Cover," Janex explained, doing a fair job with its smaller claws to pantomime the petals rising up to protect the circle and its stalks.

Aryl . . .?

Seeing the immediate swivel of eyes her way, Aryl sent a

hasty *later* . . . then made herself smile at the Carasian. This could become, she warned herself, a problem. "Cover," she nodded.

"Aryl," Marcus called from atop the circle. Pilip followed him, going at once to one of the metal stalks. Aryl stepped up, feeling the floor shake slightly as the Carasian did the same. The Trant made a scolding noise. Odd. Why would this floor shake, and no other?

Aryl controlled her curiosity. Marcus was eagerly waving her to one of the stalks. When she came closer, cautiously, he gestured. "Seeker. Look."

She wasn't sure if he meant to look at the lake surrounding them, or at what appeared to be a larger version of the colored panel of the bioscanner device. Marcus, guessing why she hesitated, indicated the panel. "Watch."

He spoke to Pilip in their words; the Trant did something to its stalk. Aryl jumped as a round disk rose from amid the mass of boxes on the roof to hover directly over them. She craned her neck to study it, recognizing features she'd captured in her drawing. The device from the Harvest!

Her triumph faded. Thought Traveler had been right; it had been the strangers. She had its proof. But knowing that wasn't enough, not anymore. Not to her. They had names. Marcus, Janex, Pilip. They had a place, here. Above all, they had a purpose—and whatever else, it wasn't harmless. Those who had died, she reminded herself grimly, had had names, too.

This close, she could see inside the device. Its components were suspended within a clear material; none had a function she could guess.

It floated away, over the roof railing, to hover in midair above the lake. It seemed to wait for instructions.

"How does it fly?" Aryl asked.

Marcus shrugged, another familiar movement. "Pilip?"

The Trant glanced at her from its stalk, pressing its lips shut in a thin line. Meaning no, in any language, Aryl thought. She scowled back.

"It is tool," rumbled Janex. "Seeker tool."

The Tikitik wanted her to connect the strangers to the device. Much better, Aryl thought, to learn why it had been at the Harvest in the first place. "What does it seek?" she asked. Her voice was strained to her own ears; none of them seemed to notice. After her initial reaction to the bioscanner, maybe they expected her to be uncomfortable around any of their technology.

She didn't care about their opinion.

"Look. Here, look."

"Look here," she said and obeyed Marcus' summons to direct her eyes at the panel. "What—" Aryl closed her mouth, concentrating on what she saw.

Instead of blank, now the panel was a window showing this roof. She considered the view—too high, too far—and turned to point at the hovering device. "From that?" she asked.

The Human looked astonished. Aryl frowned at him. What did he think? That an Om'ray, used to seeing images from other minds, couldn't grasp something so obvious? "It looks this way," she told him dryly, gesturing her meaning. "I understand."

How it looked was probably as secret as how it flew, but now she was more concerned with the possibilities. It was a spy. That was clear. What wasn't clear was why it would spy on the Harvest—why it would interfere.

A breeze ruffled her hair against her cheeks as she looked at Marcus, at a loss. How to ask such questions?

"Aryl, where?" This with a gesture to the panel. "Look."

It was a place to start, though she was unsure what he wanted. This time, the image was of a distant shoreline, moving past quickly. A quick glance at the device showed her it was now higher and had turned. She looked back at the panel.

"Can it go closer?" she asked. Pilip muttered something, but the shore leaped toward her.

Not where she'd ridden the osst—that was immediately apparent. This must be the far side of the Lake of Fire, beyond their view. Lifeless stone rose in great steps from the water. At the top? Aryl blinked in amazement. The top was a different land altogether, flat as far as the image showed, covered with an even growth of brown hair. Not hair, she realized in the next instant, grasping at the distances the device so effortlessly revealed. Plants—all the same plants, with thin leaves that moved like water in the wind. "Oud," she said. Her inner sense confirmed the direction of the device had turned. "Pana," she pronounced, pointing away from the panel. She shaded her eyes with one hand, able to see only a line on the horizon, below building clouds.

" 'Pana?' " repeated Marcus, looking where she indicated. "Pana, Aryl?"

"No." She snorted with exasperation. "That's Pana." A stab of her finger. "Amna." Aryl turned and pointed again. "Rayna, Vyna." She continued to turn and point, "Grona." Back almost to Pana. "Tuana." Then, with an ache in her heart, she faced home. "Yena. I'm from Yena. There."

The strangers appeared paralyzed, as if she'd grown another head.

"What's wrong?" she asked finally. Had they no idea of the shape of the world?

"Vy, Ray, *So,* Gro, *Ne,* Tua, Ye, Pa, Am," Marcus said, quickly and easily, for some reason dropping the final half of each clan name while keeping them in order by place and adding two of his words. He was smiling, not at her, but at the other strangers. He continued, his voice growing stronger. "*Nor, Xro, Fa.*" More words she didn't know.

"Vy-NA, Ray-NA!" this a triumphant bellow from the Carasian. Even Pilip appeared cheerful for once, its twig fingers wiggling in the air and eyes bright.

She must have shown her bewilderment, for when Marcus looked at her, his smile faded. "Sorry, am. You don't understand. Seekers, we. Seek these words: Vy-na, Ray-na, all. Thank you." He made the gesture of gratitude, imperfectly, but close enough. "Thank you."

If they were sane, something on which she reserved judgment, then they had found something in the clan names of greater meaning than an Om'ray knew. But if Cersi wasn't their world—Aryl shivered despite her new, warm strangershirt—how could that be?

"What is?" Pilip indicated its panel. Marcus, after giving Aryl a worried look, went back to his.

"Aryl?"

Feeling numb, she looked at a closer image of the Oud shore. The device had found a tall narrow building of stone, a tower, with still-dark earth piled haphazardly around its base as though it had thrust through the soil overnight. Light glinted at her from the upper level. Windows like the strangers? "Looks like yours," she commented.

"No." The image slid along the coast. There were more of the towers. Many more. "What is?"

Not theirs? "Oud," she guessed. She could only imagine one reason for new towers with windows overlooking the Lake of Fire. "To watch you."

"These also watch." Janex said something to Pilip and the image flickered, then changed to show the lush growth of a more familiar shore.

"Tikitik," Aryl identified, nodding to herself. Osst grazed in the shallows. Tall figures moved among the shadowy buttresses. "They're waiting for me. I have to go back." She indicated herself, then that shore.

"No!" Marcus looked shocked and said several things in his words before catching himself. "Saw, Aryl. Look!" He did something to switch the image. It became a strangely lit vision of the osst struggling in its pool of blood, her clinging to the gourds. Her mouth was wide open; she hadn't remembered screaming.

Aryl closed her eyes, waving at him to get rid of it.

"Back, no," he said firmly. "Aryl, stay. Safe."

Stay?

She looked at the Om'ray-who-wasn't, this Marcus Bowman, and took a deep, steadying breath. Kindness or suspicion or something unique to Humans? Any created a problem she hadn't anticipated. Thought Traveler wouldn't wait forever. Tikitik plotted and planned—she'd seen that for herself. Traveler would have seen her rescued by the strangers. That was part of its plan, but the longer they delayed her return, the more likely it was the Tikitik would realize she'd managed to communicate with them—that Aryl herself was now part of whatever game they were playing.

It wasn't, she told herself with significant pity, at all fair.

Before she could think of an argument, Marcus spoke again, this almost a whisper. "Aryl. Look."

What now? She turned to the panel, already hating the thing.

Another view of the past. She and Joyn, on the sun-kissed branch, launching their fiches into the open air. They looked almost in the sky themselves, she thought longingly.

That image flickered into another. Aryl held herself still as the machine showed her its version of the worst moment of her life. The wings in the M'hir, beautiful and wild; the webbing and its riders, the flash of arm and hook. She was there, holding to newly-bare stalks, staring up with wonder in her face.

Costa. There was Costa . . . with her.

A blur of black and white as the wastryls attacked . . . a brilliance that overwhelmed the panel and made her flinch . . .

Then nothing at all.

"They fell," Aryl finished, because they had no way to see

what she could, and always would, see. "They fell with the wreckage of your device, burning, impaled on stalks. The luckiest died on the way down. The rest fell into the waters of the Lay and were eaten alive. My brother—" Her hands flattened over the blank panel, obscuring it. "We lost those we loved." Her eyes found Marcus. "Can you understand me?" Could he? "You harmed Yena. My people may all die because of your machine. Was it worth it, Seeker? Did you find what you were after?"

The Human's soft hand reached toward her face. Aryl drew slightly away, then stopped to permit the touch, let it brush her wet cheek. As she held his brown, too-normal eyes with hers, she willed him to understand, to move past the barrier of words despite his solitary mind. She didn't use Power, not deliberately, hoping there was something else in her that could reach him through that fleeting contact of finger to tear.

Marcus paled, his eyes dilated despite the bright sun pouring through the clouds. "Sorry," he said after a moment, his throat working. More of his words, replies from Janex, Pilip. She let them talk, waiting. Then, "Sorry, all. No harm mean. Accident. Aryl, safe. Please."

If words were all they had, Aryl thought, these were good ones. Point of fact, she doubted these three would swat a biter. Well, maybe the other two would, after arguing the matter, but not Marcus. She'd felt his thoughts, even if she hadn't understood them. There'd been compassion as well as curiosity.

"Why did you send your machine to the Harvest?" Aryl asked then. "What do you seek?"

Marcus nodded back. "See!"

Not the panel, she complained to herself.

It wasn't. Instead, Marcus asked something of Pilip and the circle on which they all stood startled her by turning underfoot. It came to a smooth stop once Aryl and Marcus were opposite the still-hovering device.

As if that had been a signal, the device plunged into the water. Startled, she leaned forward to watch the splash settle into froth. The others didn't appear worried.

Once the ripples calmed, the Lake of Fire's clear water allowed her to follow the descent to the limit of sunlight. She thought she'd lose the device there, but it began to give off its own light. She watched that light grow smaller and smaller with every heartbeat, like a fich tossed from the top of a rastis.

No rastis was this tall, she reminded herself, wondering what that meant about the depths beneath this platform.

"See what is," Janex offered. "Here."

It could still send an image? Of course. That smooth clear casing protected it. Aryl joined Marcus in front of the panel, this time eagerly.

What was the underwater world like? At first, she was disappointed. The panel's image had a lot in common with a mist-bound window at home, revealing nothing but diffused light. It could have been worse, she consoled herself. The Tikitik put their dead into the lake—what if their bodies were floating around, uneaten?

"Is there nothing alive?" she asked, after a moment more of this.

The Carasian had left its panel to stand behind her. "Life, no," it rumbled. "Wait."

Wait? For what? Aryl eased her weight from one foot to the other, impatient with standing still.

When the image changed, she froze. "What is that?"

"That" was a curved shape, touched into reality by the device's light. The curve led to another, and another. A straight line crossed behind. Another, no, three more, rose behind that. More shapes, all perfect, free of silt or debris, extending in every direction. At this improbable depth, beyond sunlight, the still-clear water of the Lake of Fire revealed its secret.

Aryl had lived her life high in the canopy. She understood

the tricks perspective could play with the eye and realized at once what she saw was immense.

And what she saw had been made.

"Who built this?" she demanded, wrenching her eyes away. "You?"

"No." Marcus gazed at the panel. His hand hovered nearby, as if wanting to stroke what it showed. "Old, this. Oldest."

"Who would live underwater?"

"Lake, new," stated Pilip. She hadn't noticed the Trant nearby until it spoke. "Land, once."

Aryl started to laugh, then realized the strangers were serious. For all their amazing devices, perhaps they were not well educated. "The world is as it has always been," she informed them. "The Agreement means it cannot change."

Marcus frowned at her. "Worlds, change always."

Not world. Worlds.

It was true, then, she thought, feeling as though the strangers' solid platform moved with the water after all.

" 'Agreement.' What is?" This from Janex.

Those from other worlds—if she let herself believe, for now, in other worlds—were patently outside the Agreement, which named only the three races of this one. "Tikitik, Oud, and Om'ray share the world," she explained, as much to herself as them. "This world. Cersi. That is the Agreement."

"Cersi, yes." A claw brushed by her to point at the panel. The device was now moving sideways, sending images of more underwater buildings, each complex, strange, and flawless. "First, them. Seek, we. What was."

"Cersi, Vy, Ray, Tua, Ye, Pa, Am." Marcus tapped the panel. "Words, theirs."

The existence of other worlds, places that might be real despite having no Om'ray, was suddenly the easiest part to believe. A lake—she looked out over the vastness of the Lake of Fire to remind herself—a lake that hadn't always been?

Aryl groped her way around the concept. It was true that the waters of the Lay rose and fell with the seasons. Puddles formed and dried with each rain. She found she could imagine, though with difficulty, a lake this vast not always being here.

As for the buildings—anyone so foolish as to build on the ground risked losing their homes to flood, not to mention the swarms within. Yena knew better. So she could imagine such a disaster befalling these buildings.

Thought Traveler had talked of "before." Was this what it had meant?

Aryl could imagine all this. But that these strangers could know words used by whoever had lived down there, be they Tikitik, Oud, or Om'ray? And that those words resembled the names of Om'ray clans?

Her skepticism must have shown in a way Marcus could read. "*Hoveny Concentrix,*" he said to her, saying the new words slowly and clearly. "Know this?"

"No."

"Hoveny old, their worlds—" he indicated Janex and Pilip, "—old, many worlds. Triads, seekers are." His inability to communicate more fully frustrated him. She could see it in his face.

That was fine; what little she grasped frustrated her. She felt as if she tried to see something hidden behind too many leaves. Aryl pointed to the image. "Hoveny made this?"

"Proof, no," this from Pilip. Its fingers tapped against one another. "Hope, maybe."

Marcus scowled, launching into something long and passionate in their words. Aryl didn't have to understand to know he defended a position against the Trant. She looked to Janex, who'd been silent longer than usual.

The Carasian's eyes settled on her. "Come Cersi, hope is." A pause. "Many Triads seek. Many worlds, hope is. Proof?" Clawtips closed, the barest distance from touching. "So.

Words, few. Buildings, less. Hoveny Concentrix, important is. Seekers long, we."

Why? Aryl wanted to know. Who had these Hoveny been? People like the strangers—people like herself?

Why were they gone?

They'd probably broken an Agreement of their own, she decided grimly. It seemed all too easy to do.

These were matters for Adepts. She'd go home and gratefully give it to her mother and the Council. Costa's plants would need watering by now. These strangers were interesting but obviously harmless. Let them stare into the water for the rest of their lives.

She was done.

"Take me back," Aryl ordered, pointing to shore.

Aryl sat at the top of the strangers' metal tower, back against a support, and kicked her feet back and forth, back and forth. She couldn't wait to argue with people who could argue back.

Not that the strangers couldn't communicate. Oh, they understood exactly what she'd wanted—to be returned to shore and the waiting Tikitik. They didn't care. They had more questions for her. Many more.

When it became plain she was their captive—well fed and treated—but a captive nonetheless, Aryl had left the pointless debate to climb their tower.

From here, the strangers' floating camp was a small cube of white beneath her. She'd ignored their shouts and pleas; none of them could, it seemed, climb after her. They'd sent their device—or its twin—to spy on her. Though tempted to stick out her tongue, Aryl ignored it, too. They'd taken it away, doubtless to seek more interesting images.

She admired the view. From this vantage, the Lake of Fire

stretched in all directions. Behind the gathering cloud—it would rain soon—the sun was on its way to Grona. The flat land of the Oud, stretching across Pana and Tuana, disturbed her, so she faced Yena, imagining herself closer than she was.

One moment the air was heavy, but dry; the next, it filled with rain. She'd never get used to the suddenness of it, Aryl thought. She pulled the loose shirt over her head, drew her knees inside the same shelter. No reason to climb down. She'd been wet before; there were no biters. Lightning was the only risk, and there was no sign of it, or thunder.

She needed time away from their questions and contradictions.

Time, she admitted to herself, to recover her balance, badly shaken by their claims of other worlds and long forgotten races. She'd let herself grow comfortable with them; in return, they'd threatened the foundations of her understanding.

Aryl let her inner sense expand outward, reestablishing the world she knew as real. No need for machine "eyes." No need for searching or questions. That which was Om'ray surrounded her—was her. She relaxed, having found her place.

She dared *reach* farther. Yena was a tight glow; all were home and safe. There were a few solitary sparks toward Amna and Pana—newly on Passage, she thought, feeling for those lonely travelers. She'd never think of them as strangers again. No Om'ray could be. Not like the three below.

They were trouble. What they'd found was worse. Aryl didn't need the wisdom of Council to know that. The Tikitik gave their dead to the Lake of Fire; they used it to punish their failures. They were concerned—or whatever word applied—by the presence of the strangers here. Enough to enlist her to learn more.

The Oud's new towers? No coincidence. Their teaching these strangers real words was a deliberate act. They had an interest here as well.

Making her wonder what the Tikitik and Oud knew about what lay below the surface.

Her hair dripped; the shirt had soaked through. Resigned to such minor discomfort, Aryl locked her legs around the rounded metal beam. A Yena could sleep thus. She should stay up here until she starved to death, she thought morosely. Leave the strangers a corpse dangling overhead to remind them not to meddle in the affairs of her world.

She gave a bitter laugh. The only problem with that plan? Unless it possessed incredible eyesight, Thought Traveler wouldn't know it was *her* corpse. The Tikitik would continue to believe his Yena "scout" wasn't coming back for some other, more sinister reason.

And the strangers wouldn't take her back. Even if she could swim, Aryl shuddered, she wouldn't dare—not in these waters.

Which left her sitting atop their mysterious tower. Its purpose eluded her. They didn't need it as a lookout. It was topped with a small ball of the white material they were so fond of using. She'd dismissed the tempting notion of trying to pull it off; it was never wise to disturb a nest when you didn't know what might be home.

The *other* was something else she chose not to disturb. Taisal had shown she could *reach* her at will. Until Aryl had something worth saying, she was happier out of that ominous darkness.

Something moved through the rain.

Aryl lunged to her feet, putting the tower's struts between herself and the approaching dark shape. It was larger than she was, larger than the strangers' flying machine, and made no sound other than the tinny pound of rain against it. She relaxed slightly at that, realizing the rain must be striking an artificial surface, not a living one, then tensed as whatever it was moved closer and closer.

It touched the tower, metal claws grabbing a crossbeam to

hold it in place. She blinked away rain, trying to see it better. Was this Oud?

Light cracked along a horizontal seam. The upper half lifted straight up to become a roof protecting those inside. Not Oud.

More strangers.

Aryl counted four: three seated and one standing to stare at her. That one looked like a giant wingless flitter, with plumes covering its body and an immense green eye on either side of its head. Its mouth was more like a stitler's, bony and pointed. If she'd met it in the canopy, she'd have climbed out of reach. Quickly.

Now? Aryl instinctively glanced up for an escape route, hand over her mouth to breathe through the heavy rain, then looked down. The tower's metal would be as treacherous as a wet branch. There was nowhere to go.

One of those seated came to join the flitter-stranger. Another Om'ray-who-wasn't, like Marcus, equally *not-there* to Aryl's sense. Another Human. This one shouted something. She couldn't make out words over the rain. He beckoned impatiently to her.

New strangers. A new, more elaborate flying machine.

Aryl eased herself through the tower to the side of the machine and climbed inside, avoiding the hands that reached out for her.

Maybe, she told herself, shivering for the first time, they'd come to take her back.

The machine closed its protective cover and began to move.

Interlude

ENRIS TOSSED A STONE. Iglies skittered from his path, flashing alarm, only to turn and lurk in the shadows that fringed the tunnel. They watched him with a bold, disquieting interest he'd never seen before.

He'd never seen a tunnel like this either—the floor rough and loose and glowstrips hanging from occasional supports. It looked unfinished, as if freshly dug. He dropped his pack in a brighter area than most and eased himself down, hissing between his teeth. The iglies made their wet-smack noises, as if agreeing with his bruises and aching rib. Ignoring them all, he took a deliberate sip from his flask, then resealed it. There'd been none of the Oud water taps, or even a puddle, for the last few tenths. Best not to assume he'd find more water soon.

Had he made a mistake, taking whatever turn went most directly toward Vyna? It had seemed easy, at first. He'd ignored tunnels with upward slopes, gambling on another stretch free of Oud, willing to go deeper to elude anything more dangerous than iglies. He'd made reasonable time, despite a limp and the need to rest more and more often. The bleeding had stopped. He was safe. Wasn't he?

Not if this tunnel was about to be reshaped. All Enris had to go on were runner stories—and who knew what to believe from them? He'd always heard the Oud left behind their technology, simply shutting off power before destroying what was there. What if the runners were wrong, and some tunnels were stripped by the Oud first, lights left on so they could do whatever they did to collapse ceilings and move walls . . . ?

He got up, doing his utmost not to feel the press of earth above him. There was no room to panic, not down here. "One step at a time," Enris told himself, his voice startling the iglies to flight. "One step."

It was several steps later when he thought he heard something moving behind him, something much larger than an iglie. When he turned to look back, all he saw was empty floor, scattered with stone and shadow. "Bad as Yuhas," Enris muttered to himself, almost wishing the other—and his broom—were nearby.

Almost. He was alone and hoped to stay that way. The jitters were normal. He picked up his pace as best he could on the uneven footing, searching ahead for any sign of an intersecting tunnel, preferably one leading above ground. Down here too long, Enris decided, if he was hearing things.

Another sound, not imagined. As he looked over his shoulder, he realized with dismay the strange clattering wasn't coming from behind him at all. It was coming from above his head.

Enris looked up and found himself staring at an Oud.

Despite its bulk, the creature looked quite at home. It ignored him, busy doing something to the ceiling of the tunnel. Enris took a few slow, careful steps to move from directly beneath it. He could smell it now, that mix of old oil and dust. Unlike the ones who visited Tuana, this wore no clothing. The revealed body was faintly ribbed down its entire soft length, with patches of darker pigment where a spine might be.

It moved abruptly and he backed another step, but the Oud had merely gone forward to a new patch of ceiling. Where it had been was now smooth, any imperfections in the stone polished away. The clattering noise continued. It was, he realized with amazement, trimming the rock away with its appendages. Somehow, the creature must collect any dust or fragments inside its body, for nothing fell loose.

Om'ray had wondered what machines the Oud employed to build their maze of tunnels. Was this at least part of the answer: that they used their own bodies? He wished he could tell his family, his Clan.

They wouldn't listen to him. Once on Passage, an unChosen couldn't be welcomed back by his own.

The creature went about its business, either oblivious to him, or respectful of the token he carried. Enris gave it one last look, then kept walking.

He encountered more and more Chewer Oud, as he came to call them. All were busy nibbling away the roughness of ceiling, walls, and floor; none reacted to his presence in any way he could tell. After a while, Enris ignored them, too, walking around those who blocked his path as he sought an exit.

So he was astonished when he went around the next turn in the tunnel to have one pour itself from the ceiling to confront him.

"Where is?" it demanded, rearing up to expose its talking appendages.

Thinking it meant the token, he reached for the disk, only then noticing this wasn't like the other Oud—its body was draped in fabric.

And if an Oud could be familiar, he had a horrible feeling this one was. "Where is what?" Enris replied, hoping he was wrong.

"Metalworker, is."

Not wrong. Somehow, the same Oud had found him. Enris swallowed, wishing he wasn't tired and sore. Better still, to be clever. Or brave. The truth was all he dared. "I'm not a metalworker now. I'm on Passage. The device is still in Tuana, with the other metalworker."

"Best are," it said, rearing higher. The clattering sounds from other Oud nearby paused, as if they eavesdropped. "We decide other!"

"My father is the best," he said, desperate to calm the creature. "Om'ray go on Passage when Council decides, not Oud. That's the Agreement. It's my turn. You must let me pass."

"Badbadbadbad."

He couldn't argue with it there. "Please. Let me leave."

It loomed over him; Enris didn't dare move back. "Strangers and Om'ray, together, are," it said, clearly upset. "Badbadbadbad."

All he asked was sense from the thing. Was that too much? "I don't understand," Enris said. Strangers? "What strangers?" he demanded. "The unChosen?" The two from Yena, Yuhas and the quieter Tyko? Was that what disturbed it? Unfamiliar Om'ray?

"Not Om'ray. Strangers. Strangers! Want device. Where is?" The Oud reared violently, bashing into a support. The wood groaned and a glowstrip attached at one end fell to the floor, its light extinguished. "Where is!? Where is!!?? Find it NOW!!!"

Terrified for his father—for his Clan, if the Oud went to Tuana in this state—Enris took off his pack and dumped its contents on the tunnel floor. "See? I don't have it!" he shouted desperately. "You didn't tell me I had to keep it. You told me to find out what it is! I did. Do you hear me. I know what it is."

Mid-rear, the Oud paused, its many limbs folding together.

Enris hoped this was an improvement. "It holds voices," he said. "There were words in it. Sounds an Om'ray can sense inside. Do you understand me?"

It lowered itself slightly. "Our words?"

He froze.

"Our words?" the Oud persisted, as if devices to hold voices were normal, as if his ability—an Om'ray's ability—to somehow hear those voices had been expected.

Why else, Enris thought suddenly, bring the device to him? "You knew what it was. You knew—" He caught himself, unsure why he didn't want to suggest the device *was* Om'ray. Maybe it was his growing suspicion that this Oud had tried, somehow, to use its own version of Power and failed, that its attempt had left that disorienting trace. "How did you know I could use it?" he asked instead.

"Probable. Possible. Maybe. Metalworker, start. Skills, some." It tapped impatiently. "Answer! Our words? Other? Answer!"

Enris slowly bent down and began repacking his bag. The Oud leaned over, as if attracted by his movements. He tried not to shake. "Let me leave," he said, standing again. "And I'll tell you."

"Yesyesyesyes!"

"I don't know about other words," he said, choosing his with care, "but what I 'heard' didn't sound right. I couldn't understand any of it."

"Other words." He could swear it sounded smug. "Other words." Then, too quickly to avoid, the Oud lunged forward to tear the disk from his tunic. "Leave now."

"How?" he protested. "Give that back!"

"Find, no." Its many small limbs quickly ferried the small thing out of sight below its body. "Mine now."

What was it talking about? The token?

Or him?

Chapter 23

THEY'D GIVEN HER MORE of their food, dry clothes, and a place to sleep. Aryl had wanted to refuse all of it, to keep arguing until she was understood. Instead, she'd accepted in silence, like a child helpless to prevent the well-meaning interference of a parent.

Why? Because it was clear something had happened. Something important. The strangers had put her aside, politely but firmly, while their voices rose in excited conversation. She ate while they ignored their own meals, watching how they smiled or twitched or clicked at one another. Some consulted plates of flowing symbols, none shown to her. She slept, or tried to, with the thud of footsteps and moving equipment coming through the walls of the small room they'd given her. The heavy tread of the Carasian, Janex, was easiest to identify.

So much for imagining the new flying machine had come to return her to her rightful place.

When the noises finally ceased, Aryl sat up, her eyes on the door. After another long moment of silence, she eased from the bed, a flat platform too soft for her taste.

She'd watched how the door worked; now to see if their

technology would obey her. The stranger who'd brought her here had dimmed the light within her room, not turned it off. She went to the square on the wall. With a confidence she didn't feel, she placed her palm against the square as she'd seen the strangers do.

The door slid aside without a sound.

Aryl slipped out, immediately breaking into a run. She kept on her toes, careful not to brush any wall. The hall was dim too, implying they all slept, or whatever such creatures did. Shadows emphasized the odd lines of the strangers' building; they offered hiding places. Her skin crawled. It wasn't right to move in near darkness. Every bit of Aryl's training said she shouldn't be here.

And everything she believed said she must, that this could be her only chance to determine her own fate.

Her too-brief ride in the strangers' machine had proved there was no hope of taking it for herself. The stranger operating it, yet another new race with shimmering scales instead of skin, had pressed a number of round markings on the panel in front of it with bewildering speed, as well as used a small stick for some other purpose.

Aryl didn't know how to open its door, let alone duplicate any of those mysterious moves.

But there was a device she had seen used.

No one stirred as Aryl ran up the ramp to the roof. Once at the door, she fumbled, trying to find its panel. She'd been preoccupied with the Carasian and hadn't seen Marcus open it. Finally, she discovered a simple-enough latch and let herself out.

The rain had ended; the sky was a blue-black dome, pierced by white specks. She stepped outside and found herself bathed in the soft light of the—what had Thought Traveler called them? The Makers. He'd named her as well. Apart-from-All.

Aryl rubbed her eyes, tired of tears.

The moons hung in the sky, their reflections tripping over

the deceptively peaceful lake. She went to the railing and looked out, hunting the shore. There, she thought. An irregular line without stars, as if the sky's darkness folded at its edge. Better still, unless her eyes were playing tricks, there was a tiny patch of light that wasn't a star. The Tikitik? Using glows against truenight? To read? Aryl could only guess, having spent her nights with them sealed inside a rastis.

She knew where they were, though she couldn't get there.

With luck, she wouldn't have to.

Aryl went to the round platform, staying as much as possible within the moons' light. She went to the metal stalk the Trant had used and studied the reassuringly few bumps and sticks below its blank panel. She summoned her memories of Pilip's hands moving over these controls. The operation of the strangers' spy device appeared straightforward. She didn't need images, anyway.

Feeling as though she stepped on an untrustworthy branch, Aryl put her fingertip on the raised square she believed summoned the device and pushed. Without a sound, one of the round spies lifted from the roof and took a position overhead, waiting for instructions exactly as it had this morning. Its surface glittered like water in the moons' light.

She let out the breath she'd held.

Now, to send it. Keeping her finger on the square, Aryl used her other hand to slide a narrow bar forward and to one side. A quick glance showed the spy moving toward the Oud shore of the lake. She pulled the bar back and to the opposite side, relieved to see the device reverse its direction and pass overhead. It crawled through the air. Her fiches, she thought with disgust, flew faster.

Still, it was heading more or less where she wanted, toward what she guessed was the Tikitik camp. If she could land it there . . . Aryl looked at the controls and shook her head wistfully. Odds were she'd crash it into an osst or Tikitik. This was good enough. As long as it stayed within the moons' light, they should see it. Once seen, Thought Traveler would have its answer. The fragment from the ruined Harvest came from the strangers. She was sending him the proof.

More than that, Aryl couldn't explain without being there.

"What do?"

She remained in front of the control stalk as she turned, hoping Marcus hadn't seen his device take flight. "The moons are up," she said glibly, flinging her arm skyward.

The Human's hair stood on end and, though dressed, he looked rumpled, as if he'd fallen asleep in his clothes. But there was nothing vague or sleepy in the way he checked the roof, nor mistaking his alarm when he spotted the gleam of the device heading toward shore. With a muffled cry, he rushed for the controls; defeated, Aryl stepped out of his way.

Only when the device was safely back on the roof did Marcus pay attention to her again. "Why?" She could make out his frown, if not his eyes.

"You won't let me go," Aryl said, nodding to the distant shore. She didn't care how much he understood. "They want to know if it was your fault. It was."

"They," his hand waved in the same direction before running through his hair, "try kill Aryl."

"No. They sent me—" Aryl shrugged, giving up. They'd been over this too many times. Either Marcus didn't believe her, or the Tikitik had crossed some code of behavior. The result was the same. "It doesn't matter."

But he surprised her. "Tomorrow. Day. Go."

"What?"

A glint of teeth. He was smiling. "Yes. Tomorrow." An extravagant gesture toward shore. "Good."

Having got her wish, Aryl was suddenly uneasy, a feeling that grew as Marcus led her back to her room. "Sleep," he urged, once there. "Tomorrow busy."

He needed the rest more, she judged. She stopped in her doorway. "What's happening tomorrow?"

The dimmed lighting revealed little of his face. "Aryl safe. Don't be afraid." With that, he reached for the panel; she had to step back as the door closed.

When she tried the control panel on her side, it no longer responded. She wasn't surprised.

Aryl climbed into bed, determined not to worry about Marcus' "Tomorrow busy."

Determination didn't help.

"Aryl."

No mistaking that deep rumble for any other voice. Aryl cracked one eye open to stare at Janex.

"Aha! Awake!" the Carasian exclaimed joyfully; it seemed anything was cause to celebrate. She opened her other eye, trying not to frown at its enthusiasm. Not the creature's fault she'd fallen asleep. "Hurry. Eat!"

She shoved the blanket aside and sat up, only then realizing the room was full of an appetizing aroma. One of the creature's large claws gripped the edge of a tray, a tray bearing a steamy bowl of something yellow and brown, and a cup of sombay.

Tomorrow had arrived. Aryl was overwhelmed by impatience to be gone, to return to the canopy and home. Where she belonged. It was all she could to do muster a gracious gesture of gratitude and say "Thank you."

The Carasian put the tray on the end of the bed. The small room offered no table or chair, though it did boast a clear window that presently revealed thick mist and nothing more. "Ready soon. We go!"

It turned itself around, managing more by luck than plan to

avoid bumping her knees or a wall. Aryl reached for the cup, despite having no appetite.

Janex stopped before the door. "Forgot, me!" It turned again. "For you." It held out her fich, the one she'd seen Marcus take from the branch. Was it only three days ago? It could be four, she realized, unsure how many truenights she'd spent in the rastis.

Aryl took it, her hand trembling. The homely shape and materials, in this place where everything was strange, stopped her voice in her throat. She looked into those unfathomable eyes, wondering if the creature had any idea how she felt.

"I am sorry," Janex rumbled, as if it knew very well. Then, "Wish sweet grist Aryl home. Better. Listen not. Triad Third, only," with a dismissive click of its claws. "I am sorry."

This scramble of words, some in good order, most not, made too much sense. "Where are they taking me?" she demanded, rising to her feet. "Where?"

"Discovery made," Janex replied, willing, if unhelpful. Its eyes were busy, moving from side to side at seeming random. "All go. Understand you not. Keep you more. Longer. Do you understand? You go. All go." Its great head tipped from one side to the other. "Eat."

With that, the Carasian turned and left her alone.

Dressing was a matter of pulling on the stranger-pants they'd given her—she'd slept in the new shirt—and putting on her new boots. Aryl avoided looking at the tray. The once-appetizing smell turned her stomach.

She understood what mattered. The strangers were keeping her, for whatever reason. Marcus' promise of "go tomorrow?" They were taking her with them, rather than leave her here.

Which meant taking her away from their locks and building.

On that thought, Aryl tied the loose ends of her too-large shirt around her waist, tucking the fich inside. She retrieved the curved metal implement from the tray, pushing that within the waist of the pants. When she couldn't break the cup, she left it. Was this all she had?

No. Putting the tray on the floor, she removed the blanket from the bed. Using her teeth, she worried a small opening along one edge; from that beginning, she could rip the fabric. When she was done, she had five long thin strips and two shorter and wider.

Sitting cross-legged on the bed, humming under her breath, she braided the longer strips. The result she used to secure the tightly folded remainder of the blanket around her middle. Next she took one of the shorter strips, laying it flat beside her. The cup became a scoop, to dole the driest parts of her breakfast onto the material. She rolled that, tying it in a knot. Into her shirt it went.

Last, but not least, Aryl took the final short strip and used it to bind her hair out of her way.

She had no idea what the strangers would make of her preparations, but she'd done what she could with what she had. First Scout Haxel, she thought wryly, would approve.

Now, to hope for opportunity to escape.

Aryl had dreamed of flying. The model pressing into her ribs had been her first bold step beyond dreams. Now, in the strangers' *aircar*, as they called it, she knew herself a fool.

The aircar entered the sky as she'd leap from branch to branch, the embodiment of assured, confident speed. It sped forward under its own mysterious power. The morning mists curled away from its clear, hard roof as if acknowledging a master. Pilip was at the controls, its twig-fingers almost casual.

Aryl had no idea how any of it worked, except that this machine could ignore everything she'd so laboriously learned with her fiches. Her plan to save the unChosen? Her dreams of giant fiches, able to carry Om'ray safely over danger?

Pathetic, she decided glumly.

This aircar carried the four of them. Janex's bulk filled most of the space behind the front paired seats where Marcus and Pilip sat, looking forward. She was squeezed into a makeshift arrangement of blanket and box beside the Carasian. Behind them were, she decided, too many boxes for a short trip.

The other, larger machine had left first, taking more boxes and the new strangers. She hadn't spoken to them, though they'd stared at one another. The flitter-stranger couldn't form proper words at all with its hard mouth. A second voice came out of a white tube it held in front of its face, overlapping its utterances with a sound more like those made by the Humans. It didn't trust her. Aryl was sure of that much, given the way one of its huge eyes stayed fixed on her if she was near, no matter what else was happening.

The scale-stranger—who reminded her of Myris though its face was nothing like her mother's sister's or any face she knew, for that matter—hadn't looked at her at all. What this meant, Aryl couldn't guess, yet it moved and spoke its incomprehensible words with a gentle grace she found appealing.

The other two were more Humans. One was like Marcus, though larger and quicker in his speech. The other was like a Chosen Om'ray in having mature, feminine curves to her body and face, but her black hair barely covered her ears. Worse, it hung as dead as a Lost's. From her alert expressions, she wasn't mind-damaged. Did Humans deliberately disfigure their Chosen? Aryl found her disturbing.

She'd seen enough of them together to know that, while they'd argued as much as conversed, all deferred to Marcus for decisions. A relief in one way, Aryl thought, since she'd *tasted* his goodwill toward her. A little too much goodwill. Even now, he looked over his shoulder at her and smiled encouragingly. She made herself smile back.

Such attention worried her. No Om'ray wanted to be of interest to those in charge. Obey and respect Council and the Adepts, of course. Come to their special attention, no. Aryl had learned that lesson. Already, Marcus' interest had tangled her life, possibly beyond repair. She could only hope he wouldn't become interested in the rest of Yena as well.

Janex snicked a claw near her ear. "Goodgoodgood. Lake gone," it proclaimed. "Too young for pool, me." This drew a laugh from Marcus.

While the comment made no sense, when Aryl looked out she discovered that mists no longer obscured what lay below. For the moment, she forgot her worries, content to see her world from the sky. The Carasian was right. They'd left the Lake of Fire. If she looked back, she could see its flat gray appearance and just make out the strangers' floating place. The shore itself was already hidden behind towering stalks.

The canopy. From this unique perspective, straight down, it appeared fragile and thin, torn by gaps filled with either the vivid green of dense young growth, greedy for sunlight, or the black consuming flood of the Lay Swamp. It was impossible to see the truth, that the canopy was a strong, safe passageway, lush with its own life. Safe, Aryl reminded herself, for those who understood its nature.

It was where she belonged. Her longing was so great, she touched Marcus on the shoulder, careful to keep her shields tight. When he turned, she pointed outside, then put her hand on her chest. "Home. That's my home, Marcus. Please. Let me go."

He dutifully looked out. The side of his face she could see grew pale, as if what he saw frightened him.

"Home," she insisted. "Take me down."

Instead, he said something to Janex, who rumbled back what seemed argument. Aryl clenched her hands together, hoping the giant creature could convince its companion where she couldn't.

Sure enough, Marcus spoke their words to Pilip, who muttered but moved its fingers on the controls. The aircar began to descend!

Aryl didn't say a word, but her head snapped toward Yena, so much closer than before. She didn't try to reach for Taisal, not yet. When they stopped at a branch—that's what they would do, she was sure. Let her be free first, and away from their curiosity.

They dropped to barely below the height of the tallest rastis, but no farther. The aircar resumed its forward motion, now weaving between those giants.

"What are you doing?" She couldn't help the outburst. To be this close . . . "Stop! Please!"

"Aryl, peace." Janex laid its large right hand claw on her lap. "Fly low, better you see home. Not go home. We go all. There." The claw lifted to point ahead, almost to Grona. "Sorry."

Nothing was straight ahead. Nothing but rock, where mountains stopped the groves. "No," she whispered.

"Sorry," the Carasian repeated, taking back its claw.

Marcus put his arm on the back of his seat to twist and face her. "Sorry too, Aryl," as if he meant it. "Home later. Promise." As if he could.

Aryl turned to look outside, blinking away tears.

So she was the first to see the figures swarming through the branches of the nekis ahead. They moved faster than Om'ray, differently, staying near the main trunk. There had to be hundreds, she thought. Then, with a shock, she realized *who* she saw. "Tikitik!" she cried. "Look out!"

The strangers had spotted them, too, now busy talking in

their stupid words and paying no attention to her warning. To Aryl's horror, the aircar slowed and began to descend. The strangers' curiosity was taking them too close. "No!" she cried.

She grabbed for Pilip, for Marcus. Janex stopped her, saying words, words, more words, holding her in her seat. Aryl wouldn't listen. She struggled against what felt like a piece of metal across her chest. They were in danger and taking her with them.

"Stupid strangers!" she shouted. "No!"

A web of massive vines, the kind Om'ray used to build bridges that would last M'hirs, slammed over the clear roof. More stretched in front. Caught, the aircar slewed wildly to one side, making the first noise she'd heard from it, a shrill metal on metal complaint. It jerked the other way . . . back again. Aryl clung to Janex's claw with all her might as Pilip fought to steer them free of the trap.

For that's what it was. Aryl could see Tikitik running across the vines toward them, balancing as surely as any Om'ray, faster than a nightmare. They might have only knives against the metal machine, but the aircar kept dropping, each plunge sickening and quick. More vines landed on top, pulled taut by the machine's fight.

Aryl had watched brofers trying to escape webs like this. Watched them try and fail.

Fail and die.

But the strangers weren't done yet. The roof went from clear to opaque. Aryl jerked her arm away from the side as it grew hot. A vibration rattled her teeth. Then they were moving!

The roof cleared, though now it was streaked with black. The instant Janex let her go, Aryl swept around to look back.

Vines burned in midair. Tikitik fell. Some clung to the

scorched remains of branches or the ends of other vines, fighting with one another so that more fell. There was fire.

It was the Harvest . . . the Harvest . . . Aryl shoved her fist into her mouth to keep herself quiet.

It wasn't the Harvest, but it was.

This time as the strangers sailed away, leaving carnage in their wake . . .

They took her with them.

Chapter 24

SOMETHING WAS ABOUT TO change. Soon. The *taste* was strong, as when she'd sensed the coming of the M'hir. Whatever it was, she knew it would be bad. Very bad.

Not that this moment was much better, Aryl thought. Marcus and Pilip conferred in anxious tones, the Trant's twig-fingers now locked on certain controls. The Carasian had begun talking into a tube like the one the flitter-stranger had used, its voice a monotone, repeating the same sounds over and over. Beneath the voices, the aircar whined and groaned, shuddering more and more often.

Aryl provided the only help she could, keeping still and quiet. Janex spared some eyes for her once in a while, but otherwise, she was ignored.

Out the window, through the smudges she realized now were traces of burning, she watched their progress over the canopy. Pilip hadn't taken them any higher; in fact Aryl judged they were steadily, if slowly, descending. She didn't take this as hopeful.

The canopy was changing. Yena Om'ray did come this far, to tend the Watchers, or, if on Passage to Grona, to pick their way through the rock cuts between mountain ridges. Climbing the mountains themselves was, Aryl had been told, impossible. A bleak and inhospitable landscape.

The reality she could see past the Human's head was worse. Huge sloping walls of brown and red-streaked gray rose in front; the closer they approached, the less sky was visible above. Clouds appeared, snagged on the rocks like dresel wings caught on branches.

How tall were mountains? She wondered this for the first time in her life. It explained why the M'hir roared, if this was the barrier it had to overcome first.

The aircar began to climb. Did they have to cross, too?

The shudders and vibrations continued. Aryl thought of her fich, dropping from the sky, thought of falling, thought of . . .

Suddenly, it was calm, silent. Before she could sigh with relief, the aircar tipped forward and plunged toward the ground.

Pilip let out a cry, fingers working frantically. The plunge slowed, but didn't stop.

Then everything did.

The first thing Aryl noticed was the smell. Not of growing things. Of the dead.

She fought her way to full consciousness; short of that, she realized she was pinned in place, unable to move. She pushed with all the strength fear gave her, gasped, and pushed again. Again.

Her arm was free. A shoulder. She pushed harder, sobbing with effort, and light blinded her as something shifted loose above. She paused, trying to see, then smelled something else. Smoke.

Desperate now, Aryl shoved and squirmed. Her clothes tore. She left skin behind. But finally, she was free of what held her.

Who.

The air was thick with fumes, smoke only part of it, but Aryl could see well enough to know Janex was the weight she'd struggled against. The slick black of its body and claws were scraped, fasteners broken off, but none of that looked serious. Yet its eyes drooped, motionless and dull.

She eased to a shaky stand—the roof, and most of the aircar itself, was missing—and found the reason. A huge shard of metal was wedged into the side of the Carasian's head, cracks from that terrible wound leaking soft yellow flesh.

Had Janex not thrown itself over her, the shard would have gone right through her body. Aryl pressed her hand against the creature's chill shell. "Thank you," she whispered.

A groan drew her attention to the others. The sound came from Marcus, slumped in his seat. Pilip was—what was left of the Trant was thoroughly broken and the source of the odor competing with the smoke. Aryl scrambled over the ruin to reach the Human.

His eyes were closed beneath a mask of blood. As red as an Om'ray's, she noticed with a calm that astonished her. Her quick inspection was a relief—nothing worse, that she could find anyway, than shallow cuts on his face and through the cloth to lightly score his chest.

Aryl finally found the courage to look at where they were.

Jagged gray rocks, the smallest larger than her body, surrounded them on all sides. They looked as though they'd slipped from a great hand to lie in a vast even sweep that continued as far as her eyes could reach. The mountainside. She'd feared as much. Well away from the first pass that led to Grona. She looked toward Yena. From this height, the great rastis groves looked like the surface of the Lake of Fire, flat and featureless.

Aryl didn't know what lived here. She'd never cared before. Now, she worked quickly. There was nothing she could do about the corpses—they would attract hunters. She almost laughed. Hunters who were in for an otherworldly surprise.

"Enough of that," she scolded herself, knowing the only chance she had was to keep a clear head.

That they had.

Decision made, Aryl worked to free the Human's legs, presently trapped in a spongy white substance. It pulled away easily. She didn't wish harm to him, despite what he'd done with his meddling. He might even be of help, though she had her doubts on that score.

Marcus groaned again when she was done, but didn't wake, not even when she shook him roughly. Not giving herself time to doubt, Aryl placed her hand on his forehead and lowered her shields. She'd given strength to Yorl for his healing; she didn't have that Talent herself. But she could rouse the Human. Or try.

If he didn't wake, she'd have to abandon him. That was the cold truth.

His thoughts were dazed and full of pain. Aryl concentrated, sending his name into that unfamiliar mind. His name plus her image of him, all she knew of him, everything she felt. That couldn't be helped. It was what Om'ray did when summoning a mind back. It was what she had to do.

"*Set—nam*?!" He gave a violent shake that dislodged her hand. Aryl moved to give him room, checking their surroundings as she did.

She hated the rocks already. The perfect cover for an ambush or lurker, they obstructed every path, adding time to walk around. Time—she looked at the sky—time they probably didn't have.

"Ar-yl?"

She turned back to Marcus. "We must leave. Now. This—" her fingers brushed the Carasian's shell, "—there will be hunters. Do you understand me?"

Under the blood, his face was stricken. His hands shook as he stood at last, shook as he touched first the Trant, then, with an anguished cry, the Carasian.

Was it a difficult thing she asked? Aryl wondered. An Om'ray would walk away from the dead, feeling grief, but no connection to the flesh once the mind was gone. Did a Human feel the same?

They were so different. How could he trust her?

Because he must. The swarms might not threaten them in the dark; Aryl was quite sure something would. It was the way the world worked. "Come, Marcus," she said gently, taking his hand. "We need a safe place before truenight."

She was relieved when he nodded. "First. Comtech—" then a rattle of his words, which he stopped almost at once. "Find what need first," Marcus managed to tell her. "Quickquick-quick."

Quick she approved. And if there was anything left in the wreckage of use, she was willing to look for it. While Marcus fumbled around the area where Janex had been, she looked everywhere else.

Her search took her outside the remains of the aircar. Pristine white boxes lay everywhere. Aryl didn't like how visible they were. Her gaze kept returning to the groves below, alert for the signs of pursuit.

The Tikitik wouldn't leave them alone. That, more than night hunters, drove her to search for anything that could be a weapon. But the aircar had been made of tough materials, and she found no broken pieces small enough to carry though many were sharp. She settled for a length of flexible tube, scorched and hollow. Whipped through the air, it would deliver a substantial blow.

"Are you ready?" she asked Marcus, having spent all the time she dared.

He supported himself on one hand, shaking his head. He'd

wiped most of the blood from his face. The deeper cuts still dripped—a significant problem they could do nothing about here. He had a bag with a long strap over his shoulder. She reached for it, and he shook his head again, the movement causing him pain.

"I'm stronger," Aryl reminded him.

"Comlink, bad. Stay here, us." With a pat on the ruined aircar. "Help. Help come. Here. Comtech, good." A gesture to Janex's body. "Call help. Safe soon."

"Not soon enough." She pointed down the slope. "Look."

Flickers of movement where the vegetation met rock. She'd seen them for a while before recognizing what caught her attention. These were cautious, deliberate moves. Not hunters or grazers. Tikitik. Never out where they might be clearly seen, but Aryl felt no doubt, only a quiet dread. "Tikitik," she told her companion. "The ones who tried to trap us in the air. Do you understand, Marcus?"

"Understand who. Not understand why."

Seeing what appeared to be honest bewilderment, Aryl shrugged. "You killed quite a few. They aren't the sort to forget that." She took pity on the Human and made it simpler, with gestures. "You killed them." This was no time to mention what lay beneath the Lake of Fire, or the other Harvest.

"Accident."

"You have too many," Aryl said bitterly. "Come."

Taking his bag despite his protest, she secured it over her shoulder using the braided blanket strip around her midsection. She started walking, her choice to cut across the slope at first to test the footing. It would test Marcus' ability with this terrain as well, knowledge they'd both need.

After a moment, she heard him follow.

The Tikitik stayed down, within the grove, their moves furtive and disturbingly quick. The sun, on its way to give day to Grona, soon hid its brightness behind cloud. The rocks surrounding them flattened in that diffused light, confusing the senses. They had to work their way around and between the largest, some the size of the strangers' building, most taller than they. If Aryl hadn't been able to *sense* exactly where she was, she'd soon have been as lost as the Human appeared to be.

"Where we?" The same plaintive question. He didn't have breath to spare for it. Sweat soaked his torn shirt, spread the bloodstains. She'd driven them both; as she'd feared, Marcus wasn't used to physical exertion.

She hadn't expected him to endure it as well as he had. "Where are we?" she corrected gently. "We are close to the Watchers. We can rest there."

"Safe?" He'd noticed her preoccupation with any view downslope, toward the edge of the grove. He'd begun to watch himself. Now his voice cracked on the word.

"Better." Aryl sighed inwardly. In the coming dry season, they would have met scouts and Adepts, as well as those who came to clean the Watchers and prepare them for the next M'hir Wind. Now, if she *reached,* the rock-littered slope ahead was empty of Om'ray. They were alone.

Aryl had tried to contact Taisal again and again without success. She tried now as she slipped between two flat-sided rocks that might have cracked, one from the other, leaving this cool, shadowy gap. The same result. Taisal was there; for some reason she wouldn't connect through the *other* with her daughter.

Best guess? Taisal was in another Council meeting, or with other Adepts.

If ever there was a time not to be careful, Aryl thought ruefully, it was now. A shame she couldn't explain that to her mother. But she didn't bother trying to force that link.

They came out of the shadow and she halted in dismay. A giant blocked the straight path, its slanted surface pitted and worn. It looked like a minor mountain itself.

"What are . . . Watchers?" Marcus asked, a hand on the nearest rock.

"You'll see." She assessed his condition and the barrier ahead. They'd have to go around it. Which way, was the question. It was more than kindness to spare the Human extra steps; there was only so far will could safely carry him. Push a body too far, Aryl knew, and the clumsiness of fatigue became the greatest risk of all. "Wait here. Here," she pointed to the cool shadow, when he didn't move at once. Marcus turned to put his back to the smooth wall of rock and slid to the ground, his relief obvious.

She removed her stranger-boots to free her toes, eyeing the huge rock.

"What do?"

"You'll see that, too," she told him, her lips twitching into a half smile.

It was a different kind of climbing, not difficult. The slant of gray-and-white rock was easier than any rastis stalk; her fingers and toes fit into its fine cracks as easily as they'd fit cracks in wood. The footing was rough, but secure—once she learned to avoid depressions filled with loose pebbles. Aryl remained instinctively wary of the few deep crevices in its surface; such could have inhabitants to object. She had a great respect for even small things that could bite.

The reach and pull, the extension of muscle though sore and tired, exhilarated her. It was a moment's work to reach the top and stand.

Finally, she thought. A decent view.

The mountainside ahead changed its nature. Instead of an even, downward sweep of rubble, it turned into a maze fractured by sharp, irregular drops. Beyond these the slope ended in a chasm that cut deep to disappear into the mountain's own shadow. Or was this the join between two mountains? she wondered, unable to discern the top of the opposite side amid the lowering clouds. Regardless, she knew what she saw. The first pass to Grona. A hard road, according to those who made it through on Passage, and a hard place to live, trapped between rock and sky. She'd dismissed it thus, Aryl realized, without comprehending what that meant.

She lowered her gaze to the mouth of the pass, where the grove claimed a foothold between mountains. She could see the bare crowns of rastis mixed with the tips of nekis past the rocky edge. From there, she followed the rise of rock until she found the Watchers, their outline familiar from images shared mind to mind.

The reality was oddly smaller. If she hadn't known what she would see, Aryl might have missed them completely.

The Watchers looked like holes near the top of the sheer cliff that began not far from where she stood. The cliff itself rose to slice the side of the mountain, scarred along its length by other holes, most larger and less regular. At its base was a wide ledge that ended in another plunge of rock, its end hidden within the canopy far below.

Aryl squinted up the slope, trying without success to see where the Watchers began. Cloud obscured the upper reach of this mountain too. Not just cloud, she worried. Mist was beginning to trail through the rock around them, fingers of it sliding up from the great groves themselves. It would soon be thick enough to hide the Tikitik, should they venture from that shelter.

She licked condensation from her lips and stared at the thick, lush green. When had it become a threat, instead of home?

Turning, she considered her return climb. Her gaze lifted, reluctantly, to look for the wreckage of the aircar.

Aryl tensed.

She knew where they'd been. If she needed proof, the litter of white boxes from the crash showed the way. But the aircar itself, its broken pieces, were no longer in sight.

Something was wrong. She frowned, unwilling to believe her eyes, then ran to the far edge of the rock for a better look.

"Oh, no."

From that perspective, the wreckage—what remained of it—was again visible. She hadn't seen it not because it had been moved, but because the rocks around it had changed their position. They were now crowded around, some on top, crushing the bodies beneath. Amna Om'ray buried their dead, she thought numbly.

This wasn't a burial. The rocks—which weren't rocks—were feeding.

Suddenly, the last place Aryl wanted to be was on top of the largest one on the slope.

She ran more than climbed down, jumping free as soon as she could, her bare feet scattering pebbles. "Marcus!" she shouted. She'd left him between two "rocks," Aryl realized with horror. What if . . .

"Here." He stood nearby, looking better for the rest, if alarmed by her tone.

Aryl looked past him, at the paired rocks. Was it her imagination, that the gap between had narrowed? These things, whatever they were, could move too slowly to catch in action. As scavengers, such might not be a threat during the day, but at truenight, when she and Marcus would have to stop? If they were attracted to blood, she thought worriedly, plenty of it coated them both.

If the "rocks" were hunters? They could work together—build traps for those foolish enough to wander between them.

Was this why the Tikitik hadn't left the grove?

"We have to hurry," she told the Human, feeling trapped already.

They raced truenight through the maze of living rock, Aryl's nerves growing more and more frayed as the shadows deepened. They were spared rain, though it fell in the canopy and fed cold mists that slithered around their legs. In their brief but necessary pauses, she could hear the grind of stone against stone over their ragged breathing. Hunters, then, she decided, as if it made any difference.

They had to reach the Watchers.

She'd done her best to explain to Marcus why they had to hurry; there was no sign he understood. But he didn't argue. When he began to stagger more than walk, Aryl undid her makeshift rope from around her waist and pressed it into his hands, holding the other end. When he began to shiver, she wrapped the section of stranger-blanket over his shoulders, amused by his startled recognition.

It wasn't until they literally stumbled out on the wide, flat ledge that she believed they'd make it. "The Watchers," she announced with relief.

There was more light, away from the rocks. Aryl didn't know why there were none below the cliff, unless there was some inexplicable danger to them here. She'd never heard of the things, but Yena came here from the canopy, not the slope. For a moment, she let herself face where the vegetation burst from the chasm, breathing in the heady aroma of real living things. There would be bridges and ladders reaching to this place, leading back home.

There would be Tikitik. As far as she could tell, some, perhaps many, had matched their course along the mountain, still staying within the groves.

Aryl sighed and turned back to the now-impressive cliff, assessing their next steps. Deep in shadow, it towered easily the height of ten Om'ray here. To the right, it reared skyward before dropping straight into the chasm, but that wasn't their goal. Not yet.

"There," she told her companion, indicating those openings above their heads.

"Oh."

The dismay in that wordless syllable caught her by surprise. "What's wrong?" she asked. "We'll be safe. Om'ray stay there. There could be supplies." Her stomach growled its complete approval.

"You go." Marcus reeled where he stood, as if too stubborn to fall. "Aryl stronger. Climb good."

Aryl snorted. "Trust me, Marcus. You can do this." She gave the rope they both held a gentle tug. "Let's go."

"Help. Help comes." Weary, rather than convincing.

"Your help is late." She saw him wince and relented. He'd been unable to explain either his hope for help or its lack of appearance. "If we're safe," she said as persuasively as she could given her impatience, "help can find us."

A nod, followed by a frankly terrified stare at the cliff.

"You'll see," she told him, tugging the rope again.

They entered the cliff's shadow together, both shivering at the sudden chill. Water stained its front. Condensation from the mist, Aryl guessed, since there was no sign of water anywhere else. She licked a drop caught on her finger; the acrid taste made her spit. They continued along the cliff until she found the place that matched the image in her mind. "Wait here," she told Marcus.

"Not l–l–leave," he chattered through his teeth, clutching the blanket.

Aryl handed him her boots, then began to climb. Her target was an oval opening, three of her body lengths above. Not far, but this wasn't like her other ascent. The rock was wet and smooth, its surface unlit. She relied on touch to find tiny cracks; it took her remaining strength to wedge her fingertips and toes into them for a grip. Carefully, slowly, she made her way up.

By the time her hand hit the edge of the opening, Aryl was gasping with effort, but that solid grip was all she needed to pull herself up and through. She lay flat for an instant, then stood, leaving Marcus' bag on the ground. Yena came here annually, to clean and prepare the Watchers. As she'd expected, there was a sturdy ladder rolled inside, ready to drop.

Letting it fall, she hurried down it herself. "Your turn," she told Marcus.

Although he brightened at the sight of something more manageable than the cliff, and started with enthusiasm, Aryl treated the Human the way any Om'ray parent would a child. She followed close behind, so close his back pressed against her chest, and braced her arms each time he released a handhold and reached for the next.

Just as well. He began to slow, then tire. The last few rungs were agony for them both, as Aryl did her best to support his weight, and he did his best to keep moving.

"Close, Marcus," she urged. "One more."

At the top, she put her shoulder under his rump and shoved, throwing him forward and out of her way. While he gasped for breath, she pulled the ladder up behind them.

Just as well. "Look," she said.

He rolled over. Aryl could see the gleam that marked his eyes. "What is? Help?"

"Not help," she snorted.

With sunset, the cliff's shadow had grown to lap over what had been the first of the rocks. Had been, for where she and Marcus had stood to look up at the cliff was now well-populated. Small ones, large ones, some atop the others. Nothing moved; several things had.

"Not help," he agreed, making a strained noise she decided might be a laugh. "You know these?"

"No." She shrugged. "Many creatures have their seasons. Om'ray only come here before the M'hir. Until now," she added ruefully

"Good."

It was Aryl's turn to almost laugh. "Rest, Marcus. Then we continue."

"Here stay?" A pat on the stone. "Safe is."

She shared the longing to rest in his voice, but knew better. "Not really. Wait here."

What she hunted should be at the back of this hole. It was too dark to see, so she moved with her hands held out, her bare feet feeling their way along the grit-covered, though level floor.

Suddenly, she could see.

"Better?" Marcus asked, one hand pulling his bag over his shoulder, the other leaking light through its fingers.

Aryl restrained any mention of how she could have used it sooner. Considering she'd assumed anything he'd bring would have no practical use, that wasn't fair. "Thank you." She continued searching with the Human and his glow at her shoulder. "There," she exclaimed in triumph as the light revealed a door.

Not any door, she frowned, making the connection, but a beautiful metal door, twin to those guarding entrance to the Cloisters.

At least this didn't need an Adept to open. Aryl reached to the top and, remembering what she'd been taught, pulled the correct sequence of four latches to unlock it, ignoring the fifth, which would lock it again. The door turned open obediently. Beyond was dim, but welcoming light. "Through here," she said, glancing around for Marcus.

His free hand stretched toward the door, not touching it.

The light from his other hand revealed an expression that, on an Om'ray, Aryl judged, would have signaled severe indigestion. "What is?"

The obvious answer died on her lips. "This is the way to the Watchers, Marcus. It belongs to my clan, the Yena Om'ray. There's no harm here. Safe," she resorted to the word he kept using.

"Old, is."

That again. She scowled at him. "Of course it's old. Come or stay here." She suspected her smile was the thoroughly unpleasant one Taisal used when required.

It had the same effect. Marcus mumbled something to himself, but followed her.

The construction within resembled the Cloisters as well, with the same yellow material underfoot and on all sides. The lighting, barely adequate, came from the joins in the tall tube-like wall. Aryl led the Human up wide steps that circled a central pillar, grateful herself not to climb anymore. She'd offered to carry his bag again, now curious what might be inside. He'd refused, hugging it to his chest.

Something was bothering him. From past experience, Aryl thought wearily, best she didn't learn what.

At the top was a landing with an identical door, opening on a flat, arched space within the rock. As she locked this door behind them, Aryl was almost too tired to reconcile the images in her mind with what she saw.

Close at hand, a homely pile of Yena flasks and slings hung from hooks on the wall. No beds, but mattresses leaned below the hooks, ready for use. A table and six chairs. Comfort for the caretakers.

Their charges filled the rest of the space—the Yena Watchers, their smooth surface agleam with polish. They descended from the ceiling to within her height of the floor. To the right, they passed through the wall to where, unseen from this vantage, they opened their mouths to the outside world. To the left, they rose in long parallel curves, the floor and ceiling climbing with them, until all disappeared in the distance.

If they walked—or, rather, climbed, for there were ladders—the length of the great tubes, they'd arrive just below the mountain's upper ridge. There, the Watchers gaped, ready and waiting for the M'hir to howl down their length, producing the alarm to rouse the Yena to Harvest.

Aryl pointed to the nearest before Marcus could spout "what is?" "A Watcher. When the M'hir Wind comes over the mountain, it blows thus." She cupped her hands together in front of her mouth, and blew through them. It produced little more than a *whoosh*, but he nodded.

"Watchers," he replied. "Loud." This with a grimace.

From his reaction, he'd heard them. Implying he'd been close to the Harvest, Aryl realized. Something else she didn't care to think about.

"Supplies," she suggested, hoping she was right about that. If not, they'd have to leave at dawn to search for water and food. She doubted the Tikitik would be gone.

On the bright side, the living rocks might be.

Interlude

THE OUD WAS TRYING TO KILL him. It just didn't know how.

Only possible explanation, Enris assured himself. He imagined he could hear someone snickering. Probably Mauro and Naryn, having a last laugh at his expense. He couldn't blame them. The not-quite death of Enris Mendolar was a joke on them all.

"Faster. Faster." The Oud dropped back to the floor and humped away.

"I can't go faster!" he shouted after it. How long had he been running after the creature? Half a day? A full fist? Time had no meaning below ground. Too long. The Oud disappeared around a bend, and Enris staggered to a jog. Always the same. The monster insisted he keep up, yet couldn't comprehend that Om'ray had only two legs.

"Two legs!" he bellowed. "Two!"

He'd argued with it, thrown rocks at it, laid down and ignored it, desperate to rest. Such futile protests ended the same way, with the Oud looming over him and a clawlike appendage seizing him—by what didn't matter—to drag him along in the dirt until he moved on his own. Enris had quickly learned to protect his head; the Oud, not so quickly, learned not to grab him by a leg.

He'd dropped his precious pack. It wouldn't let him retrieve it. He'd found a water tap and had thrown himself in front of it, drinking in great gulps. It wouldn't let him finish. In final insult, the Oud was leading him away from Vyna.

"You . . . want . . . to . . . kill . . . me," he panted. "Try . . . a . . . rock."

The Oud covered ground with incredible speed; it knew this landscape. Still, Enris would have chanced trying to escape down another tunnel but for one thing.

The token.

Without it, he was already dead. He couldn't move on his own through Oud territory. He couldn't enter Tikitik. It was doubtful another Clan would admit him. His own . . .

"Give it back!" he begged the mass of gray ahead of him. In answer, it humped away faster.

Why take it? In his coherent moments, he wondered if the Oud was supposed to carry it for him, if he had an escort—albeit one completely ignorant of the physical limitations of Om'ray. At others, he worried this was a homicidal game, the true end for all who left on Passage, that the Oud led him to a pit where he would fall, fall and land on the bodies of those who'd just left, Irm and Eran, bodies atop a pile of the bones of other unChosen.

It said a great deal about his state of mind that he preferred either to the alternative, that the Oud was sane and had good reason for this panicked flight.

* * *

When the Oud finally stopped, Enris didn't. Half asleep, he collided with its back end with enough momentum to send him flying to land on his. He sat there, blinking away dust, and waited to see what would happen next.

"Here are."

"Here" looked like everywhere else they'd been. A newer tunnel, with lighting, heat, and water, the walls and ceiling ready for Chewer Oud to polish them smooth. He wiped his sweating face against his sleeve and kept waiting.

Another Oud approached them, naked and moving with its body pressed to the floor. It stopped alongside the other. His Oud—not that Enris wanted the creature, but he'd started thinking of it that way—reared and smacked the newcomer with its front/head end. The blow wasn't light; the newcomer tumbled over and over until it struck the wall.

It immediately scuttled back on its little legs to take the same position as before.

His Oud, still half reared, patted it. The other quivered as if in joy. Enris looked away, fearing this was the prelude to Oud sex—a subject Om'ray knew nothing about. He had no intention of being the first.

"Things, yours."

The voice startled him awake. Sure enough, the newcomer Oud held out his bag. Enris grabbed it, digging inside for a flask. Only once he'd had a good, long drink, then another, did he bother to look at the creatures again.

And was just in time to see the newcomer take the token from His Oud and convey it down to wherever they stored things. "Wait!"

Too late. The newcomer rose to the ceiling, took hold, and scurried away, upside down.

Now he was to chase *that* one? Maybe his was worn out. Enris forced himself to his feet, though he'd lost feeling in them some time ago, and cursed the Oud. He shifted his bag to one shoulder and started walking.

"Mine now," His Oud exclaimed. "Token other. Find no. Safe."

He stopped moving before it could seize him. "I don't understand."

"Strangers and Om'ray. Come."

"Let me rest first, " he begged, beyond shame. "Please. I can't run anymore."

"Not run."

He should have specified no dragging, Enris thought, tense as the creature came closer.

It moved beyond him to the left-hand wall, then disappeared. "Come!" he heard.

Dead or dreaming, he assured himself, but curiosity brought him stumbling to the wall.

Which wasn't a wall, Enris discovered. Or, rather, there were two walls, identical and overlapping, which gave the illusion of one. The gap between had to be a tight fit for the Oud, the end of which he watched disappear again.

Keeping a hand on the stone, Enris followed, this time not surprised to find His Oud had simply turned itself right around to move through another gap between walls. The Oud version of an alleyway? A shortcut between neighboring tunnels? How many had he missed . . . ?

He stepped out into what wasn't a tunnel, though the entrances of several met here. Light—real sunlight—poured from above. Enris looked up to find himself standing at the bottom of an immense tower, one wall broken by windows of irregular shape and size, the other four solid. There were Chewer Oud clustered around the topmost windows. From this distance, he couldn't tell what they were doing. The construction was of uneven stone and earth, as if the Oud had done little more than hollow a mound from within. How such a pile could be strong was a mystery.

Like everything else, he thought, staring at those pieces of sky with a longing that made him tremble. He *reached* and felt some relief. Pana was closer than Tuana, Yena and Amna almost as near. Vyna? He turned his face to it. Not so distant now. The Oud had done him a favor.

If he survived the kindness.

"Come." His Oud was waiting beside another tunnel mouth, tapping impatiently. "Comecomecome."

Enris walked across the broad floor, fine dust isolating every length of sunbeam. He shuddered at the relative darkness of the tunnel, for the first time understanding Yuhas' horror of such places, but didn't dare hesitate.

This tunnel was another of the rough type, with only a few loose glowstrips. The light from those was soon overwhelmed by brightness ahead. The tunnel became a ramp. Enris found himself walking more and more quickly, despite the slope and his exhaustion. This had to lead outside.

And it did, though not to any view he'd expected. Enris stopped with his Oud, gazing at a confusion of vehicles, most in motion. Some were the platform type, bearing Oud dressed in the fabric and clear head domes he'd last seen in Tuana. Others bore long oval shapes of metal, resembling mechanical Oud. He dodged back and coughed at the dust as one of these swept by too near and quickly for comfort. There were some with sides taller than two Om'ray, and small round ones that could pass beneath the others. He couldn't keep track. The sound of treads and scraping metal was a constant din.

All this within a great walled circle, penetrated by ramps, and domed by sky.

His Oud was on the move again. Enris followed, staying as close as he dared. They went around the outer edge, to his relief. There was no discernible order to the traffic, and collisions were frequent. Those involved merely backed and tried again to pass one another. An Om'ray wouldn't last long.

A loud roar preceded an overhead shadow. Enris ducked instinctively before gazing up in wonder. A flying vehicle. Everyone knew the Oud had vehicles to travel through the air. Such made regular passes over the fields, though at a considerable height. He'd never seen one this close. It looked impossible, heavy and thick, with ridiculous little wings. Nothing, Enris vowed to himself, would make him trust his life to *that*.

His Oud stopped, rearing to speak. Three small vehicles changed direction hurriedly to avoid it, slamming into one another. "Om'ray fly. Goodgoodgood."

Almost nothing.

* * *

The long, dark machine raced and bounced along the empty field, going faster and faster and faster until, abruptly, a final bounce left the ground behind. Enris watched openmouthed as the machine tipped and swerved its way through the air, straightening out just as the clouds swallowed it.

Not encouraging.

Another waited for them, its top half open in an invitation he would have declined if he could. Being surrounded by Oud who rattled and reared menacingly didn't make that likely. There'd been a crowd waiting with the flying machines; from what little Enris could read of the creatures, these were opposed to either his presence or his Oud's. Or both.

His Oud, either because it was superior to the others or oblivious to their posturing, didn't react at all, moving to the machine. By that, Enris judged himself safer in its shadow, although wary of sudden moves on its part.

He was startled by a loud voice, very different from the low husky tones of Oud. He couldn't make out the first words, other than that they were urgent and harsh. The rest were drowned out as the dozens of Oud around them tapped to themselves. It had sounded Om'ray, but wasn't. He sensed no one else near.

"Stranger calls," his Oud said, moving forward with its body half reared. It was an awkward position, from the way the creature lurched, but apparently it must talk to him before they reached the side of the machine. "What means? Badbadbadbad. Om'ray best."

What "stranger?"

His Oud gestured with three black limbs to the side of the

machine. Enris tossed his bag in, jumped to catch the edge. His rib did nothing more than grumble—only bruised, then, though the rest of his body argued against moving at all. It wasn't worth tempting his Oud to do it for him. Most of his bruises were new.

His arms were in the best shape of all, and he pulled himself up and over without too much effort. Over, and into a featureless metal box that reminded him of the inside of the melting vat.

The voice again. The "stranger." It came from the front of the machine. Enris jumped and grabbed the top of the barrier between, pulling his head and shoulders up, gaining support from an elbow.

The front of the machine was larger. It had to be, to house two Oud plus his. The floor, what he could see of it, was covered in what looked like levers and taps and other control-type objects. It was from there the voice was emanating.

No wonder he couldn't sense the Om'ray who spoke, Enris thought, fascinated. No wonder his Oud had understood the device it had found—or stolen. The creatures had technology to carry a voice over distance.

The voice had continued, "—lost!"

"Where is?" his Oud replied.

"*Site Two*."

What did that mean? Enris wondered.

"We come." This with a heavy nudge to the Oud next to it.

Enris let himself drop back down. Just in time, for Oud outside the machine began laying curved metal sheets over the top—a roof, he saw, each piece sliding into the one before.

He was really going to fly, he realized. In the air. In this thing.

How bad could it be?

* * *

Flying was more terrifying than he could have imagined, with the added joy that Oud didn't feel the need for padding or light. Enris sat on the metal floor of what was basically a box now too low to stand in, left to interpret agonizing vibration and random noise as best he could.

The sitting part, that was good. Very good. After a while, when nothing worse happened than a sudden short drop that sent his teeth through his tongue, he put his pack under his head and stretched out flat. That was better.

Nothing he could do about knowing where he was, Enris thought queasily. Though he tried to ignore it, his inner sense informed him exactly how far above other Om'ray he was, not to mention how quickly he was moving away from Tuana.

Eventually, on the reasonable assumption Oud were no more interested in crashing than he was, Enris slipped into, if not sleep, a state of blissful uncaring.

He didn't know how long it was before the vibration and noise shot to the point of pain, the machine doing its best to slide him from side to side. Forgetting the low ceiling, Enris stood to brace himself, managing to bump his head, hard. He cried out, but didn't bother asking questions. If they were falling from the sky, he'd know soon enough.

The machine steadied, though tipped toward the front. Going down was inevitable, he reminded himself, hoping the Oud were better at this than they were at getting into the air in the first place.

A jerk threw Enris against the back of his box, driving most of the breath from his lungs, followed by a regular thumping sound.

Blissful silence. Maybe they were all dead, he half-joked to himself in the dark.

"Come!" his Oud commanded as the roof panels were tossed aside, letting in light and raindrops. Enris lifted his face to both as he eased to his feet, then looked around as he climbed from the Oud machine.

Solid ground, he decided, felt wonderful.

Ground that tilted mere steps in front of him, falling into a black abyss?

Enris stepped back from that edge, no longer sure how wonderful this was. Or where . . .

Shared images of streams and rock came to him then, helping to settle the vast sloping gray into perspective. Mountains. He was on a mountain, or at least the side of one. The sun was setting behind him, rain clouds hastening truenight, but there was still plenty of light. The Oud machine had landed on a long flat strip that looked to have been recently cut from the rock. He didn't want to consider the skill required not to slam into the mammoth cliff that rose up from the strip to the clouds.

The strip wasn't the only cut. Another, the height of two Om'ray above him, dug deep into the heart of the mountain. Part of it was flat, with unfamiliar white structures, like small buildings, surrounding a tower of metal. Part met where the rock had washed away on its own, exposing . . . what?

Enris wiped the rain from his face, trying to understand what he saw. An immense curved something was stuck into the mountain, or rather erupted from it. Other, smaller curves showed to either side, their shapes emphasized by long shadows. A straight piece aimed outward from the top, ended in midair with another at right angles. None of it, from here, appeared damaged or broken. Lost, he judged. Forgotten.

Now found.

"Who is?"

Enris turned in the direction of the voice, expecting it to come from the machine. Instead, he found himself facing an unknown Om'ray in strange clothing. Relieved, he *reached* for the other's mind.

To find nothing.

What had Naryn done to him? He tried again, opening his perception as wide as he dared, this close to Oud.

There. Enris glanced to his right. He could see nothing past the rain-shrouded slope, but he knew one Om'ray was that way, alone. Beyond was the glow of Yena and Grona. Here? He stared at the creature wearing the flesh of his kind, and shuddered. What was this?

"See? Om'ray." His Oud reared up beside him, seemingly unaffected. "Find." This with confidence.

Because it knew what was going on, Enris realized. This must be what it had called a "stranger." And there were more. Others moved on the upper ledge. There was even, he stared, another machine coming down from the sky, different from the Oud's, flying without wings or sound.

"How?"

The demand snapped Enris' attention back to the stranger. If he ignored, for the moment, his contrary inner sense, he might have thought this an older Chosen. Worry lines creased the high forehead and edged the light, almost blue eyes. A scar, old and puckered, crossed one dark cheek. There was personal power here, though not any Power he could feel. And pain.

The eyes looked him over from head to toe and back. They weren't impressed.

He drew himself straight. "I am Enris Mendolar, of—" could he claim a Clan? "Tuana," he said firmly, daring his Oud to correct him. "Who are you?"

"Enris," with renewed, if calculating interest in the eyes. "Tyler Henshaw. Triad First. Help us, you?"

"To do what?"

He wasn't answered. Tyler-stranger looked to where the stranger flying machine had landed, needing no flat strip at all, its roof folding back inside itself. This display of superior technology wasn't reassuring. Enris wondered what the Oud thought of it.

Along with many things—starting with how the Oud knew these beings and ending with why he was here at all.

He watched as others stepped from the machine, their clothing similar to that of the Tyler-stranger. Those wearing clothing, Enris noted. Two were of the Om'ray-but-not type. The third was feathered instead of dressed, and looked like a flitter who'd learned to walk on two legs and carry tools. They spoke as they approached, as if what they had to say was too important to wait.

What they had to say was gibberish. As well try to understand the conversation of iglies, Enris thought, dismayed.

"These words?" Low and quiet, for his ears only. He'd forgotten about the Oud. "Same hold-voice?"

He listened more intently. Were these the words he'd somehow "heard" from the device? Difficult. The strangers were agitated, their words quick and urgent sounding; they swarmed around Tyler-stranger, faces anxious—the ones Enris could read—and he answered in kind.

"Not the same," Enris judged aloud, though how could this be? There was this world and its words. He could accept, with an effort, that the tapping of the Oud conveyed something between them. And that strangers might sound like Oud.

But unknown words?

He couldn't deny what he was hearing.

Was the world not what the Om'ray knew?

Tyler-stranger broke away from the others. "What do?" he shouted.

Enris winced. Never a good idea around Oud.

Sure enough, his Oud reared violently, banging against its flying machine. The others, still inside, began tapping furiously.

Enris held up his hands. "Don't shout at it," he warned, keeping his voice as gentle as he could.

Tyler-stranger, who'd stopped dead in his tracks when the Oud reacted, nodded. "Sorry, am," he said, more calmly. In all likelihood, Enris thought, the stranger was more used to the Oud than he, needing only the reminder. "Help, Enris. Find other you."

The wording was awkward; some of the meaning clear. They wanted him to find another Om'ray. The Oud must have told the strangers he could. What wasn't clear? "Why?" he demanded.

"Truenight," said his Oud, folding down to a more relaxed height. Its black limbs fluttered.

"*Aircar* down," added Tyler-stranger, pointing along the mountain. "*Comlink*, broken."

"Aircar" must be their flying machine. Enris didn't know what a "comlink" might be, though a likely guess was a voice device like the Oud's. As for why an Om'ray would be in one of the strangers' aircars? He shook his head in grim amusement. Who'd just flown with Oud?

What was truenight like here? Cold, damp? Was it dangerous? He didn't know. Would he do worse if he located this Om'ray for them, or if he left him alone?

The Om'ray-not strangers were frowning at him. The flitter-stranger had hard mouthparts it could snap together, and did. Likely, Enris thought, expressing the same feeling. They were worried and impatient for his help.

The same question.

Why?

Chapter 25

ASLEEP, THE HUMAN RESEMBLED an untidy pile of laundry. A foot protruded, like a discarded boot. Otherwise, the only difference was that this pile snored. The chance to relax against the curled inner wall of the Watcher had been all the encouragement necessary. Marcus had burrowed into his own clothes like a brofer into its nest, succumbing to exhaustion in moments.

Aryl closed her eyes, but not to sleep. She *reached*, this time refusing to be denied. *MOTHER!*

Taisal was there, their link solid. *Here.*

Yena's in danger! Aryl sent. *Tikitik attacked the strangers—the strangers fought back and killed them.* Images flashed from her mind to her mother's: the vine trap, the appalling skill of the Tikitik in the canopy, flames and death.

The darkness turned deadly cold. *What have you done?*

Not: are you safe, Daughter?

Aryl didn't care, worried more about holding their connection despite Taisal's fury. Her mother—the Speaker—had to accept her warning. *You must protect Yena.*

Against what? Your companion? This stranger?

My—? Taisal had seen more than the past in her mind. Aryl tightened her shields. *He isn't the threat.*

He? Taisal's outrage was a storm, crashing through the *other*, stirring it into a maelstrom. *It is not* he. *It is not real. Kill it! Kill it now!*

Aryl found herself on her feet, knowing she was about to snap Marcus' neck. It would be easy . . .

NO! She staggered back.

Easy . . . save Yena . . . SMOTHER IT!

NO! She pressed her back against the Watcher's wall, stared down at the helpless figure. *NO!*

Push it out . . . make it FALL!

NO! Aryl didn't know where she found the strength to resist her mother's will. All she knew was that her mother tried to *force* her body to obey and she would not allow it.

The instant that pressure eased, Aryl threw more memories like weapons at her mother: the words of Thought Traveler . . . the Tikitiks' pursuit . . . the chamber and the swarms . . .

The link between them suddenly faltered, as if Taisal tried to flee; quickly Aryl reinforced it, gripping her mother's mind with hers. *If the Tikitik come to Yena, don't trust them,* she pleaded. *Don't believe them. You are the Speaker, Mother. You must protect us.*

The *other* churned and seethed, their link a slender bridge over utter madness. Taisal's mindvoice came as a whisper.

What have you done?

Then silence.

"More?"

The Human grimaced. "No, please." He handed back the pouch of dried dresel. "Awful, is."

More for her, then. Aryl took a careful pinch to put on her tongue, then sealed the pouch and tucked it inside her stranger-shirt with her knot of blanket. She'd lost the piece of metal and her fich. There'd been supplies in the Watchers' inner sanctum—flasks of water, dresel, dried fruit and meat, rope—but no fresh clothing. "Yours is awful," she countered. When she'd wakened him to share her meal—when she'd finally calmed enough to want to eat—Marcus had offered a handful of what he called *emergencyrations*. Wood tasted better.

He laughed. They had that in common, though Aryl remained disconcerted by the familiar sound coming from such emptiness.

They were in the middle Watcher. There were doors underneath each, an important access since wastryls liked to nest in the mouths. Aryl had pushed a pile of twigs out and over the cliff. The smooth interior of each Watcher had to be cleaned before the M'hir.

They should put gauze over the opening, she told herself restlessly. It kept out biters—it might discourage something larger. A suggestion she'd bring to Council.

If she was ever home. If they'd listen. If . . . if her mother hadn't tried to make her . . .

"Where Yena? Show me?"

For a being with a dead mind, Marcus had an uncanny knack for reading hers, Aryl decided. She went to stand beside him. He gave her a still-tired smile, the skin below his eyes smudged with shadow. He already moved with exaggerated care; she worried how stiff he'd be by the morning.

A breeze, dry and bitter cold, pulled at her hair. The Human had no idea how vulnerable he was, she thought abruptly. No idea how dangerous she was. The violence of her mother's command still shook her. Had she not been able to resist, his body would be feeding the rocks below.

Aryl couldn't blame Taisal for fearing the Human. To kill what wasn't real—it was something hunters did daily. Trying to force her to that act—she shuddered and hugged herself.

"Aryl?"

"You want to know where Yena is," she said, and looked out.

The rains were late today, or they came late here. The remaining sunlight struggled to reach the groves—already, the vegetation looked more gray and black than green. She raised her hand to point without hesitation. "There. Where are your people? The other strangers?"

Marcus shrugged. "Know not."

She frowned. "Why don't you know?"

He regarded her quizzically. "Lost are. Aryl and Marcus, both. Lost."

"Of course not. We're here," she objected, patting the metal side of the Watcher. "Om'ray there." A quick *reach* and she pointed to Grona, Rayna and Vyna, Amna and Pana, then Tuana, behind them.

Then, unexpectedly, her inner sense found something else. Someone else. "And there," she said, forgetting who or what she was with. Another Om'ray on the mountain. Who could it be? With sudden hope, she *reached* deeper. But this was no mind she knew, no rescue. An unChosen, doubtless on Passage, perhaps from Grona, though he was well away from the pass. Seru, still waiting for Choice, would be happy.

She wished him luck passing the Tikitik.

"Always know?" Marcus pressed, his voice with an edge.

"Don't you?"

"Here, know," he continued, staring at her. He patted the smooth metal tube. "Not been before. How Aryl know?"

Aryl hesitated. If the most ordinary ability caught his attention, what would he think of other Om'ray Talents? She couldn't know what would be new—possibly Forbidden—to a Human. "I was taught," she said cautiously. "We all learn about the Watchers, so we can care for them."

Satisfied by her explanation, or needing to think about it,

Marcus eased down to a sit again, his back against the curved wall. He stretched out his legs, hissing as they straightened.

Aryl copied his position, gazing outward.

Truenight was near; it edged the horizon beyond the canopy in dark blue, swallowing more of the sky every time she looked. The rains were moving past, leaving a fresh dampness to the air. The mists hugged the grove and played among the now-abundant rocks on the flat ledge below. More than abundant—they formed a growing pile beneath the hole where she and the Human had entered the cliff, as if able to follow tracks or scent. She gave them a worried look. There was no other exit.

And they couldn't stay here.

There weren't enough supplies, even if they shared their "awful" food with one another. His bag had contained objects she'd recognized as coming from Janex, a ring from Pilip, and a flat box he'd tapped with a mournful look, called *vidrecord*. The hand-carried glow was the only useful item, but she didn't say anything. "We'll leave in the morning," she told him. "Try to find your people."

"Morning," Marcus echoed in a tired voice. "Thank you, Aryl." he added.

If he understood gratitude, the way an Om'ray would . . . Aryl crossed her legs and sat up, gazing across the opening of the Watcher at the Human. "I helped you," she affirmed, trying for simple words, using gestures he should be able to follow despite the dim light. "To thank me . . . you—all strangers—must stay away from Yena. From all Om'ray. From the Tikitik. From the Oud. Away. Do you understand me? There is an Agreement among us. A peace here. Do you understand 'peace'?"

Marcus' eyes were bright. He nodded. "First," he said, confusing her, and "*Commonwealth. Trade Pact.*" At her frown, he held up his hands, spreading the fingers. "Peace we. All we.

Carasian, Human, Trant, Tolian. Many, many. All peace. Understand you." He put his hands over his face, pantomimed looking through his fingers at her. "We hide. Stay hide. Contact no."

Aryl's frown deepened. Did he think her a fool? "You've been in contact already. Who taught you real words?" she accused.

"Oud," readily. "Good. Better soon. Hide, Om'ray."

Could the strangers be that ignorant of the world? What he said next confirmed her worst fears. "Talk machine, understand? *Years*. Talk. Invitation. Seekers, we." He spoke with great satisfaction, as if coming here was an accomplishment . . .

. . . instead of a disaster. "The Oud," Aryl informed him grimly, "don't rule Cersi. They can't make their own Agreement with strangers. Do you understand? You put us all in danger. No peace, Marcus. No peace with Humans! Go away!"

He was silent, hopefully thinking. She let him be, too shaken by the audacity of the Oud to know what else to say. Inviting the strangers? No wonder the Tikitik were on edge, suspicious of what was happening. Taisal had been right. The balance of power on Cersi had never included Om'ray; its peace was not their doing. To be caught in some struggle between Oud and Tikitik? Over what . . . a drowned ruin?

Aryl found her voice. "What's so important under the Lake of Fire? What do you seek, Marcus, that the Oud want found and the Tikitik do not?"

He clasped his knees, resting his chin on top. "No." Terse and low.

Not: I do not understand.

" 'Thank you, Aryl,' " she threw back at him. "I deserve an answer, Human. This is my world, not yours." There, she'd said it. Because she believed it at last. They were too different in every way to have come from the same place. "Tell me what you seek that's worth all this death!"

Another, longer silence. Then, "Morning. Home, me. Aryl help."

She made a noise her mother would not have approved. "No. I can't. I don't know where your home is."

The Human looked troubled. "Why? Aryl knows where, Yena, all Om'ray. Why not people mine?"

He thought she could *sense* Humans, too, she realized abruptly. From his side of things, she supposed it made sense. Aryl stood more slowly. "It isn't like that," she explained reluctantly. "Om'ray are—" What? Nothing was right anymore. Om'ray weren't the extent of the physical world. They didn't speak the only words.

Her universe grew larger at the expense of her own kind.

Aryl studied the Human, his face, his shape, his expressions. Nothing was unfamiliar.

Even the Om'ray form was no longer special.

"I can only feel Om'ray. Those like me," she admitted. "If you can't show me where to look for your people, more Humans, I—" she swallowed once, "—I'll take you home, to Yena." Past the waiting rocks and Tikitik, to bring her people a walking nightmare her mother most definitely wanted dead.

As plans went, Aryl told herself wearily, it was the worst she'd ever had. She wished she could tell Bern.

"Take me, Yena? Do that?" She'd startled him somehow.

"I can't leave you here," she snapped, then gentled her tone. They were both afraid, both sore and well past exhausted, but the Human had his own burden. "I'm sorry about Janex and Pilip."

"Thank you. Sorry, Pilip. Triad Second. Good. Janex—" Marcus leaned his head back against the Watcher's curve. His exposed throat worked for a moment. "Special, she," he managed at last. "Friend, long time."

"She saved my life," Aryl offered.

"Special," he repeated, seeming unsurprised.

They were both quiet. Abruptly, the Human yawned, another disquieting similarity. "Sleep now?"

"I—" About to agree, Aryl closed her mouth and stood, motioning him to stay still.

Something had just changed.

The Om'ray she'd *sensed* earlier had moved. No, not moved, she realized as she *reached* to better locate him. He was in motion toward her, but too quickly and . . . from above?

With sudden comprehension, if not understanding, she scanned the darkening sky for an aircar. "We'll sleep later," she told Marcus.

Then she smiled. "I think help's found us."

His name was Enris Mendolar, of Tuana. He was filthy, wore bloodstained rags, and rebuffed her one attempt to speak mind to mind. She couldn't tell the color of his thick hair through the dirt. Stretched out on the opposite seat of the aircar, having fulfilled his task of bringing rescue to hover right in front of the Watcher's mouth—much to Marcus' joy—he was now snoring. Loudly.

Aryl couldn't claim to be any cleaner, wearing her version of the strangers' clothing—liberally stained with whatever had oozed from the Carasian's head—and was too tired to care. Enris was Om'ray, real and solid, and by his existence pushed the strangers aside. Not much older, she decided, studying the face beneath the dirt. A heavier build than any Yena, with big hands and wide shoulders that probably moved things better than they climbed. He looked to have gone hungry and without sleep. Bruises and scabs showed through rents in his clothing.

He was Kiric's brother.

She knew, having *tasted* his identity. To Aryl, there was a resonance between close kin, a similar flavor to their presence. She wondered vaguely if Enris knew what had happened to Kiric, or if she was supposed to tell him.

Not that she should speak to a stranger, without Chosen Yena present.

Aryl giggled.

His eyes opened at the sound. They were dark brown, wide-set, and presently more than a little dazed. "Wha—"

"Sorry. I was thinking of my grandmother's caution—about talking to strangers."

His lips quirked in a smile. It reopened a small cut and he caught the drop of blood with a finger, then wiped it on his pants. "Took her good advice to heart, I see?" This with a deliberate flash of distrust past his otherwise tight shields.

Aryl bristled. "You're flying with Humans, too."

He didn't apologize, but looked more awake. "'Humans?' Is that what they call themselves?"

"The ones who look like us, but aren't? Yes. There are others." She sagged a little. "Too many others."

"Why are they here?" he demanded. Before she could open her mouth to answer, he went on, each question sharper, louder. "What do they want? Where do they come from? Wh—"

"Aryl?" Marcus looked up from his slouch in the rearmost seat. She'd thought him asleep, too. He nodded his head at Enris, his expression unreadable. "Loud, him."

"Human," Enris said, the word an accusation. The two locked stares for a moment, then the Om'ray sank back in his seat, throwing his arm over his face.

Marcus glanced at her. "There soon." As if she'd find that reassuring.

As if words from a Human, an Om'ray-who-wasn't stranger, could matter more to her than the perfectly reasonable passion of her own kind.

Confused, Aryl closed her eyes on them both.

Their flight was over so quickly, Aryl wondered if she and Marcus could have walked to this camp of the strangers after all. Though she might have dozed for part.

Enris had that grumpy look she remembered from Costa in the mornings. He'd managed only enough sleep to be truly exhausted, she decided. Hopefully, he'd be easier to talk to once rested.

The other strangers took Marcus away, exclaiming in their not-real words. The Humans patted his back and arms with their hands, as if needing to touch him. The others—a blur of feather, scale, and odd shapes—added their voices to the din. She and Enris might have been forgotten, but one Human stayed by the aircar to take them in charge. Aryl recognized her. The not-Chosen, not-Om'ray female with dead hair.

Luckily, Enris was too tired to pay attention. Or else he was unlike other eligible unChosen of Aryl's experience, who would, she was sure, have been struck dumb by such a living contradiction.

"Wash. Rest," this Human said to them with a smile. "Come."

Truenight, already upon the rest of the mountain, was held at bay here. Aryl was relieved by the sensible lighting as they followed the Human from the aircar. Stalks with too-bright glows at their tips marked the edge of the long, sharp ledge they used for their machines. She'd taken a quick assessing look over the side. Climbable, just. Which meant dangerous after dark.

Their goal was a second, higher ledge, up a short cliff that presented no challenge, especially where it sloped at one end. Aryl tried to notice such details, remember them, though the contrast between intense light and black shadow made it difficult. More glow stalks marched up a wide ramp carved into the rock; so did they.

Enris limped, favoring his right leg and side. Aryl factored that into her—it wasn't a plan, she admitted, more the preparation for one. If the chance came to escape the strangers, she wouldn't leave him here; his limp meant certain paths open to her were out of the question. That was all.

Maybe he'd heal overnight.

Look.

Aryl raised her eyes from the junction of ramp to upper ledge, seeking what Enris wanted her to see.

The mountain had been eaten away here, its outer flesh of stone stripped to reveal giant bones. Aryl gasped. Familiar bones. She'd seen the same massive shapes, the same building designs through the eyes of the machine. But those lay under the deep waters of the Lake of Fire. These were exposed to the air.

And accessible.

Her eyes narrowed. She didn't care what technology the strangers had, it must take time to dig so much stone. She remembered the urgent excitement of the visitor strangers—was it only yesterday?—enough to draw Marcus and his companions from their own place. There had to be something else, something new.

A change.

"Come, please." This from their guide. Aryl gestured apology for stopping to stare, not that the Human would understand it, and started walking again. Their goal was a cluster of three buildings, each a copy of the one on the lake platform. Marcus and his group were ahead, entering the centermost. How had the strangers brought all this? she wondered.

The curves and angles erupting from the cliff loomed overhead as they approached. Darkness enclosed them from the other side, erasing the world they knew. The strangers had claimed this much of Cersi for their own, Aryl decided, and shivered.

Their guide walked faster, as if eager to rejoin her companions. "You've seen this before," Enris said, his voice quiet and quick.

"Not this." Aryl kept her voice low, too, though she would have preferred the security of mindspeech. "The strangers have another place, on the Lake of Fire. It floats above ruins like these."

"Ruins?" They passed through a bar of shadow, masking his face, but Aryl heard his surprise. "These were buried in the mountain, but they aren't ruins. Do you see any marks of age, any damage?"

She looked to the side, tilting her head to better see up the cliff. He was right. The structures being freed were perfect, without crack or weathering. "How can that be? They are old," she whispered. "Marcus—the Human—said so. And the Tikitik talk of a 'Before.' Who made these? Oud?"

Enris shook his head. "I know more of the Oud than I care to—this isn't their work." He staggered, catching himself with a heavy hand on her shoulder.

A ploy. Through that touch came a flood of memory. Aryl saw a device . . . somehow heard *words* from inside it . . . felt Enris' astonishment at how well it fit his hand . . . his conclusion.

Om'ray? she sent, not holding back her disbelief. *You think all of this, everything the strangers seek—what they found—was made by Om'ray?*

"Who else?" he said out loud, attracting a startled look from the Human.

Aryl had no answer to that she'd care to have overheard.

Om'ray?

They made almost nothing of their own. Had almost nothing. Were almost nothing.

Strange how the realization of her people's insignificance made her sad instead of bitter. This Enris—he didn't feel that way. She'd tasted his fierce pride; she envied it. But Om'ray, responsible for these marvels? Easier to believe the Tikitik sealed the sun away at night.

They were approaching the first building, Aryl losing herself in visions of the strangers' wonderful "fresher," when the sending struck.

DANGER!!!

She bent double and cried out, hearing Enris do the same.

DANGER!!

They straightened as one, to look out into truenight. Toward Yena.

The Human, who'd stopped when they did, raised her hands. Perhaps she said, "What is?" but neither Om'ray responded.

DANGER!!! A third sending, this time mixed with *DEATH!*

There was no time to think, no time to ask herself if she could do it.

Aryl only knew she must.

She grabbed Enris by the hand. *TRUST ME!* she sent, flooding his mind with all the Power and need in hers.

Then she pulled him with her into the darkness that marked the cliff . . .

Chapter 26

. . . *THE DARKNESS SWALLOWED THEM whole . . . flung them . . . they were wings in the M'hir . . . she couldn't breathe . . . couldn't feel him . . . only knew where they had to be . . .*

. . . HOME!

Aryl choked, fighting for air, fighting to see. Why was it still dark? Hands closed on her, big hands and strong. *Enris?* she sent, finding it easier to think than speak.

Here. A surprising burst of humor. *Wherever here is.*

She drew strength from him, managed words. "Home. My home. Yena. I *pushed* us here."

DANGER! DEATH! DEATH!!!

Aryl tightened her shields until she barely sensed Enris, fighting to think past the screaming in her head. It wasn't only in her head, she realized, her heart pounding. It was coming from all around them.

Her eyes grew accustomed to the darkness and she moved toward what faint light she did see. "This way."

Her next step slammed her into the table. She warned him with a touch, then strode with more assurance to the door.

Where were the glows? Why weren't they lit?

Aryl turned the door open and stepped outside.

The faint light came from inside the meeting hall, where she could sense the Yena gathered. The homes—hers, her neighbors, all other buildings —were dark, their windows torn, their roofs ripped open. The bridges . . . two were lit their entire length, but the rest disappeared into the dark of night.

Truenight.

"Aryl," Enris said urgently. "Look. Over there. Something's stealing the glows." Without waiting for her, he began to run, taking heavy, limping steps along the main bridge. "Stop! Shooo!"

Were Tuana insane?

As she followed, Aryl hoped he didn't realize he was running along thin strips of wood high in the canopy.

Above the Lay.

Above the swarms.

She ran faster.

Something dodged past her on the bridge, tiny and quick. A second . . . a third . . . ahead, Enris paused to kick something small out of his way. "Iglies," he announced, letting out a relieved huff of air. "That's all?"

She had no idea what he was talking about. What mattered was ahead. She knew that shape, that abrupt speed. Tikitik were stripping the glows from the bridge, tossing them down. They hissed to themselves as they worked.

Enris reached them first. He grabbed one. Though taller, it didn't strike back or protest, going passive in his hold. Beyond, a dozen more kept working. More than a dozen. Aryl could make out their forms on the roof of the meeting hall, see them everywhere.

"Leave it," she shouted, taking Enris by one arm. The Tikitik scampered away with a bark. "They aren't the danger," she told him. "We have to have light, now. Fire. Can you make fire? Lots of fire!"

Please, she pleaded to herself. Please.

Enris reached inside his waist and drew out a small box. A soft *shhh,* and a miniature flame appeared in his hand. He touched it to his bag, holding that out by a strap. The flames licked over its surface like a beautiful rot.

The Tikitik noticed. Finished with the glows on the bridge, they turned and leaped away. The ones on the meeting hall hissed and worked faster. They were pulling away the pod halves that formed its roof, reaching in to steal the glows from inside.

All around, Aryl could hear movement, clicking, snarls, the myriad sounds of the swarm climbing toward them.

"We need more," she said. "What burns?"

"In this wet?" Enris pushed past her. "Back inside." He rhymed a list as they hurried to retrace their steps. "Wood, cloth. Do you have fuel for cooking or heat?"

"What? No," Aryl replied, hurrying with him. "We use power cells and ovens. The Tikitik don't allow burning."

"Cooking oil?"

"A little. If Myris didn't—" Saying a name sent Aryl into a panic. She *reached,* desperate to know where everyone she loved was . . . were they safe . . . ?

STOP.

Aryl started to protest, then understood. Enris, running with fire licking at his hands, kept her from a fatal distraction.

She dodged ahead to turn the door for him.

The bag flew past her, skidding to a stop against the wall. It burst open, sending flames running up the panels, across the floor. It was too bright now. It made a sound. A roar. Aryl flinched.

"Oil!" Enris shouted. He tore the gauze from the first window with one easy motion, then the next, and the next. As Aryl rushed through cupboard after cupboard—Myris had moved it . . . why would she move it—he ripped free the nearest cupboard door and smashed it against the table, gathering the pieces. "The oil!"

"Found it!" She grabbed the wooden cask and took it to him.

He was wrapping gauze around the end of each long piece of wood. "Pour it on the cloth," he ordered, handing her the first done, making another. "Not too much. We have to get it hot before it will light."

Hot wouldn't be a problem. Aryl ducked as flames found the storage slings among the rafters, sending smoke and scorched fragments of clothing down. She kept pouring oil, refusing to regret the destruction of the Sarc home.

If it would save Yena? Let it burn.

When the cask was empty, Enris grabbed a wrapped stick, oil dripping to the floor. "Like this," he shouted. He pushed the gauze end close to the fire on the wall; she did the same with another. Nothing, nothing. It felt as though she was suffocating, the skin of her face about to fall off. Just as Aryl was about to pull back, fire seemed to leap to the gauze. She raised it, amazed.

"Let's go."

They ran, each with fire in one hand, a second stick in the other. Enris shoved the rest into his belt.

The bridge heaved and moved in front of them. The swarm was already here, clinging to every surface. Aryl held out her fire and the creatures fled with wild clicks, most falling off the bridge. But they didn't leave.

"We have to— No!" A door had briefly turned, spilling light from the meeting hall. Someone knew what they were trying to do, came to help. *NO!* she sent.

There was too much darkness between. Darkness that *moved* . . .

The screams went on and on. When Enris tried to go, she held him back, tears on her hot cheeks. "It's too late. We have to save the rest. The swarm hunts until just before dawn. Only light will keep them back."

"That will help, then."

"That" was her home, now burning on the outside. The light flickered all the way to the main bridge. "We have to burn them all," she said.

"Not at once. Fire's a hunter, too," he cautioned. "It's going to be close."

Aryl felt strangely calm as she gazed at his face, a mask of soot and red. "I'll burn the canopy itself, if that's what it takes. Show me how."

A flash of white teeth. "Let's start with that place over there."

They burned the lowest homes first, buying time by keeping the swarms below. All the while, Aryl fought the ceaseless hammering against her shields—Yena desperate to communicate with her, to know what was happening, fear—enough to overwhelm her if she let it. She assumed Enris struggled, too, despite his powerful shields.

The bridges were too wet to burn, but they could fall. Each time they torched an outlying building, the braids of rope connecting it to a bridge would burn, then snap. Throughout Yena, bridges that had been roads for Aryl and all her kin faltered and dropped, leaving fewer and fewer. They were already less, Aryl thought, remembering like a dream how Sarc had outlasted so many others.

She focused. Enris relied on her to know which to spare. They could, if they weren't careful, burn their last escape.

The Tikitik were gone, or had retreated too far to be a threat. For now. While they waited to start the next blazes, Aryl leaned against Enris—or he leaned against her—to watch the outer ring of Yena spark and smolder. The wavering light was losing; they'd have to fire the remaining homes next, then move to the warehouses, closest to the meeting hall. She didn't know what they could do after that. Though the rastis fronds curled and blackened above each of the burning roofs, they refused to catch fire. The stalks so far seemed impervious, not that it was easy to see them through the smoke. The Tikitik chose their chambers well.

"Aryl Sarc." Enris said her name as if it surprised him. "That's where I saw you." He was pointing at the main bridge, before the meeting hall. It was free of the swarm now. Bones still bound by flesh hung from a rope rail.

"How did you manage that, Enris of Tuana?" Her voice sounded unfamiliar, hoarse with smoke.

"Yuhas Parth shared the memory. Now sud S'udlaat." A pause to cough, something they were both doing. "Handy with a broom."

Aryl didn't laugh, but only because her throat was sore already. "Good. He's— Thank you. That's good news."

"S'long as he never finds out I helped burn his home." Enris left her to choose another wrapped stick, setting it beside a burning one to ignite. "Speaking of which—"

Aryl pointed to his next target, walking away to her own. How could he make jokes? she asked herself. What kept him limping from home to home, saving those he didn't know?

She glanced back at him as she opened the next door, then turned and entered, forgetting to put her fire first to scare away any of the swarm that might be hiding inside. She knew her mistake when the first small jaws locked on her ankle, her shin. She made it worse—frantic to brush the foul things off, she dropped her burning stick. As it bounced and fell from the bridge, they were climbing her body, their jaws seeking her flesh.

Enris!

Here! Light blazed into her eyes, light and heat and help. He reached past her to set the nearest curtains afire—more light—

only then coming back to help pull off the ones too intent on chewing to scurry away. Aryl sobbed in silence, furious with herself, at how close she'd come—

"That's all of them," Enris said, brushing the hair back from her face with one hand. "You all right?"

With a final angry hiccup, Aryl ran her hands quickly over her body, assessing the damage. The swarm killed by the number of mouthfuls they could take in a hurry; her attackers had been mercifully few. She'd lost chunks of skin from her shins and ankles, had holes in her stranger-pants and shirt. The small wounds would ooze blood until cleansed, there was no help for that. The pain was no worse than when she'd fallen into a stinger nest. "I should know bet-better," she said at last.

He didn't comment, but when they left that home to fire the next, he wouldn't let her go alone. "We're both too tired for this," he said when she protested. "We'll stay together."

Aryl stepped from the bridge to the outer deck of the meeting hall. The Tikitik had done their work. There was no light through the windows; holes rent the fabrics and roof, easy entry for the swarm. The sendings from within were subdued, now. From the feel, everyone was huddled in the center of the great room. Unless they dared look outside, her people couldn't know who was keeping the swarm at bay. At least they would know two Om'ray lived, where nothing should.

From the smell, someone—she guessed Haxel and her scouts—had doused the deck and walls of the hall with somgelt. She hoped not to find out if it would work.

Day-bright out here, while the empty warehouses burned. Fires' light was different from glows, she thought. Fierce and full of color.

She hoped, with a deep abiding anger, the Tikitik could see it, too.

"You could go in," Enris said, joining her. "I'll stay."

She'd give anything to believe she could walk in there and wait with the rest to be saved. She'd give anything to believe it would happen without her standing here, breathing smoke, surrounded by ruins and flame. Anything, Aryl realized with a faint pride, but those inside. She was responsible for them now.

"Too crowded for me. I think you should go," she said with an attempt to laugh that turned into a long, painful cough. When she could breathe again, she sputtered, "—only just—occurred to me, Enris."

"What?"

"You're on Passage—which Chooser called you—we've three, you know. I can tell you—" she coughed, "—all about her."

A home burned through its supports and broke apart, flames and wood raining down through the canopy. Aryl was sure she could hear scrambling as the swarm fled its light, then again, when that light was extinguished by the Lay and they returned, to wait. Her bites, the three she could touch, were slick with blood. She'd had worse. She grimaced and pulled soot from her eyelashes. They would have been worse, had Enris not come to her aid. That was the thing about the swarm. They kept eating.

He didn't take up her offer; she didn't press the point. Un-Chosen were sensitive. It was unlikely, though, to be her cousin Seru, Aryl decided. No reason, just what she thought. Her brain was wandering. Not a good sign. "You hungry?"

Enris looked at her. "Passed hungry yesterday."

Aryl reached inside her stranger-shirt. She'd lost or dropped everything but the small piece of blanket with her breakfast. "No promises on the taste," she warned, using her teeth to loosen the knot. It smelled like sweat.

Once loose, she unrolled it, pleased to see the paste from the bowl had formed a stick she could break in half. "Here." She didn't bother with a taste, ramming hers into her mouth. If it was at all edible, her stomach deserved it. Enris seemed of the same opinion. It was an unexpectedly peaceful moment, despite the fires burning on all sides.

So when done, Aryl licked her lips and made herself say what she must. "Enris. Before you meet other Yena, I need you—I ask you—to promise not to tell how I brought us here." From her experience with such things, he'd reveal it to his Chosen; she'd deal with her later. Whoever she was. "No one should ask, but—" she thought of her mother, "—if anyone does, tell them we came in an Oud flying machine." Something of Cersi. "Just not the truth. Please."

"Yes, that." His lips quirked again. "I admit to boundless curiosity. I thought you were tossing us from the cliff to spite the strangers. Seemed as good as any idea at the time."

"It wasn't that high," she said stiffly. He hadn't promised yet. He had to. "Please. It's— I did it to help my Clan, but—"

"Which you have."

"Stop interrupting me," she snapped. He was as hard as Costa to talk to about serious things. "The Adepts call it the Dark; it's another *place*. Dangerous. Forbidden. I wasn't to use it again. I wouldn't have, but—we had to be here. If the Tikitik find out what I did—if anyone else finds out—it will cause trouble."

"Worse than this?" he said with a grim laugh. Before she could object, Enris added, "I promise. On one condition."

"Condition? What—"

"You show me how to do it. When we get out of this."

She stared at him. Was this Tuana like Haxel or Tikva, willing to risk anything for Power? "Didn't you hear me? Using it could destroy the peace!" She shuddered, remembering that *place*. "Such Power isn't for us. I won't try it again. You shouldn't want it."

"You're wrong," he countered with equal passion. "You met the Humans, too. Power—what we each can do—it's who we are. It's what we are. Don't deny yourself, Aryl. The Om'ray are too few, and our world—our world's not what we thought, is it?" She felt his mindvoice then, with a swell of dark amusement. *I never thought I'd meet someone with too much conscience.*

You don't know what it's cost.

The firelight was failing. There was nothing left to burn that didn't hold Yena. Soon, truenight would win, and only the eager swarm would survive it.

Why wasn't she afraid?

"If Yena sees another dawn, Enris," she told him at last, "it's because of you. Keep your word and I'll do—I'll do what I can to teach you." With any luck, she told herself, he wouldn't be able to sense the *other place* anyway.

With no luck at all, it wouldn't matter. They wouldn't be alive to try.

They stood in silence, watching the darkness consume the light. The swarm would reach them across the main bridge first, she guessed. Cutting the massive support braids would take the better part of the night and buy, at best, a heartbeat. They had no more gauze or dry wood. Enris had already tried lighting the rope rails around the deck. They only blackened and smoked.

"What's that noise?" Enris whispered.

"The swarm—"

"Not that. Listen."

Aryl held her breath, ignoring the sullen snaps and echoing crackle of what fires still burned. Too quiet, she realized. She couldn't hear the clicks, the snarls and snaps of the swarm. Why?

"That."

A trill, as if three singers competed to see who could make the sweeter sound. Another. A third, more distant.

"A wysp," she told Enris, her voice unsteady. "They sing to greet truenight." She reached out in the dark for his hand, gripped it tightly despite her blisters. "And they sing—they sing it good-bye. Dawn, Enris. Above the canopy, it's dawn."

Sending the swarm back to the waters of the Lay Swamp.

They'd survived.

Interlude

YENA BEGAN TO EMERGE once sunbeams stroked their way through the maze of giant plants and smoke. Enris sat with his back against the comfortingly solid side of the meeting hall, unable to credit he'd spent the night running over thin bits of wood and rope, suspended so high that . . . he swallowed, hard. They were so high, he'd yet to see the ground. Not that there was ground beneath them, Aryl had informed him while they rested, but rather water and mud, home to those not-iglies who'd done their best to overwhelm and eat them alive.

Other things had taken over that job. Wearily, he flapped his hands in front of his face, trying for room to breathe through the hordes of small flying nuisances. Being filthy had one advantage. There wasn't much skin available for their tiny jaws. "Ouch!" Still some. He'd given up on sleep.

"Here." A Yena who could have been Yuhas' twin bent to offer him a wad of fabric. "Wrap this around your head. Like we do."

Enris gestured gratitude and did his best to copy what he saw. The too-fine stuff snared on his calluses and cuts. When he noticed most of the Chosen left their faces bare, despite the insects, he did the same. It was still a relief not to have to defend his neck and shoulders. He noticed other things. Their clothing—what Yuhas had worn at first—freed their arms and legs while protecting their skin. He was sweating from every pore under his heavy tunic and pants. With the sun, the air had become oppressively hot and humid. The light fabrics they wore made, he admitted, sense.

Aryl had rejoined her clan the moment the first stir came from inside the hall, bidding him to rest as long as he could. She'd had the look he remembered from Yuhas' memory, determination rooted in grief. He'd doubted he could stand anyway. She could. Like Yuhas, these were the most athletic Om'ray he'd ever seen, all of them. They moved with that same quick grace. Too thin, though; every face was gaunt. He felt self-conscious, his thicker body a rude reminder of Tuana's abundance.

There were, indeed, Choosers here. He maintained his shields, but that particular summons had its way of being noticed, like the warm smell of supper on a cold night. He might have an appetite, Enris reminded himself. He didn't have to eat.

He'd kept count as the Yena came out on the platform. Most stopped at once to stare in dismay at what remained of their aerial village. There should be more of them, he thought. He and Aryl had burned enough homes to house four times this number. By daylight, he could see more abandoned, beyond the bridge network.

There were three Choosers, some older unChosen—though none male—the Chosen. No children. No elderly. No one weak.

Where were the rest? He *reached* and found part of the answer. There. Not far. But not in sight. Why?

Easing to his feet, Enris limped to the nearest group, a family of four. He was taller, though he doubted stronger, than the two Chosen. The Yena were subdued, their greeting no more than a quiet murmur of names he didn't need. Tears streaked the face of their youngest, though she didn't speak. Shock, he thought. And who could blame them?

"Stranger?"

He bowed awkwardly to the family and turned as two more approached. "Enris Mendolar of Tuana Clan," he said to the new faces.

One was an older Chosen, a scout, by the knives in her belt and scars. To be a scout here—one of those who patrolled the limits of territory for the Clan? Enris made the gesture of respect. That so many had survived until they'd come was no doubt due to this one's skill.

"Haxel Vendan, Yena First Scout." Her voice was smoother than he'd expected. "This is Ael sud Sarc."

Enris nodded to Ael. Family, though no close resemblance. Aryl's eyes were gray, not brown, and larger, slightly slanted to the outside. Her features—what he'd seen under the soot and streaks of ash—were as strong, with a firm jaw and wide mouth. He'd already noticed how still her face could be, like the crust on molten metal that hid the heat beneath. This Chosen had a face as open and full of expression as his young brother's, although now lined with strain.

"Yena welcomes you, unChosen," Ael said warmly. "Though to what—" he didn't need to gesture to the ruin around them.

"It's going to get worse," the First Scout advised, her eyes hard.

Having experienced truenight here, Enris fully understood.

"What can I do?"

Chapter 27

THE SMOKE CURLING UP FROM Yena kept biters to a minimum. Enris didn't appreciate his good fortune, Aryl thought, almost amused as she watched him wave his hands about.

Almost. They'd survived the night. More than that was yet to be determined. She'd spoken to everyone—a few words, a brush of fingertips—reassuring herself they were well, assuring them she was, too. Yena was whole.

Questions and answers. Time for those now.

"Aryl!" Myris hurried toward her on the platform, a small bag clutched in one hand. "I found some seal."

Ael followed close behind. "Who found it?" His hand fell on his Chosen's shoulder as they stopped; Myris leaned into him. They both looked haggard.

Aryl took the seal and squatted down, pulling up her pant legs. With businesslike strokes of two fingers, she applied the thick cream to each oozing hole in her skin, hissing between her teeth at its burn. The seal would harden in moments. She didn't look forward to having to scrape off the result in a few days, but it was dangerous to have open sores. There were canopy dwellers who'd take the invitation.

"One got your neck," Haxel observed, joining them. Aryl pressed seal to the wound on her throat. "That'll scar nicely," added the scout, as if the marks were some honor.

Perhaps, Aryl thought numbly, they were, but Enris deserved the credit. She stood, returning the bag to her aunt. "What happened?"

Haxel offered her hand, callused palm up. "Take it," she told Aryl. "I'm too tired to think of the words."

She wasn't, Aryl thought uneasily, but couldn't politely refuse. She wiped the remnants of seal on her shirt, then laid her palm atop Haxel's.

The First Scout was accustomed to giving reports this way. That Aryl realized immediately, as the memory of last night came to her without emotion or interpretation, but more as if she watched from a distance.

. . . The Tikitik had arrived in vast numbers at firstnight, dropping to the bridges from every side at once. They brought no Speaker, or none proclaimed itself. Instead, all had spoken at once, an uproarious babble that understandably horrified the startled Yena. Haxel had confronted one to be told they were here to reclaim property . . . the glows and power cells were theirs, most certainly . . . stolen by other Tikitik, disgraced Tikitik . . . trade to the Om'ray was illegal, void, not their business . . .

The Yena were horrified, but their own Speaker had been calm. Taisal di Sarc had lifted her pendant over her head; seeing it, the Tikitik had grown silent and still, their eyes locked on her. In that hush, Taisal had ordered them to leave in the name of the Agreement, not to return without their Speaker.

And without a word, the Tikitik had vanished into the growing shadows . . .

Aryl felt her heart hammering as she relived Haxel's memory. Her own dismay, or finally some emotion from the First Scout, despite her training?

. . . Arguments broke out. Questions. If the Tikitik dared go this far, what was next? Were they safe in their beds? Haxel had stayed quiet. No one knew the answers.

Infants had cried, giving voice to the fear that raced from mind to mind, fed on itself, and grew.

YENA! The Speaker's powerful sending had silenced that as well. She would take the most vulnerable with her, mothers with infants, children, the eldest. They would race truenight to the Cloisters. As an Adept, she could open that shelter to them; as Speaker, she would defend that decision to Council. But they had to leave, now . . . and they had to run—

Aryl broke the contact to stare at Haxel. "She saved them," she half whispered. Because her mother had believed her warning, or felt one of her own?

"Those she chose to save," the First Scout said, her lips tight. The stripped bones on the bridge had been one of hers, Till Parth. Seru's mother, Ferna, had fled to the Cloisters with her infant. Was she Lost or dead? Aryl was afraid to *reach* and find out; Seru, who well knew she could, hadn't asked. "The Tikitik hadn't gone. They rushed back the moment Taisal and the others were out of sight. They didn't hurt anyone—they simply overran us. Took every glow. Pushed or smashed their way indoors to take the rest. Left us for the swarms.

"If it hadn't been for you and the stranger?" Haxel snorted. "Taisal didn't save Yena, Aryl Sarc. You did."

Aryl didn't miss the irony of Haxel's so-proper reference to Enris Mendolar. As for the rest? "There's not much left of Yena," she pointed out.

"What do we do, Aryl?"

She blinked at Ael's anxious question. Why was he asking her?

Others approached, filling the platform but not crowding it.

Even if all were here, she thought with that constant grief, would there be enough Yena left to crowd it? She spotted Enris nearby, a head taller than the rest. To her inner sense, there was no fear left, only anticipation. They were all waiting for her to speak. Why? Aryl thought desperately. She wasn't the oldest here, or the wisest, or anything more than they.

It didn't matter. Haxel's smile twisted her scar. "Care to save us again?"

Haxel and Ael moved among the rest, brushing fingers to confirm unheard instructions. Aryl hadn't needed to warn them the Tikitik could be hiding nearby, listening.

They weren't attacking. She believed they wouldn't, not directly. She'd gained a sense of the creatures' preferences. Tikitik liked to sidle up to a problem and assess it from safety. If they had a goal, they'd rather have something else take the risk to achieve it for them. Ambush over confrontation.

And always, always, claim to be the innocents.

As for saving anyone . . . there was only a single path left open. They'd hardly, Aryl thought, needed her to tell them what they already knew.

The village was gone; they had to leave.

Like others, Aryl had thought to search the wreckage for hooks and ropes first, to collect any supplies. She'd discovered fire was a rot, weakening floors and walls, ruining what it didn't consume. No wonder the Tikitik abhorred it.

She wished them fire in abundance, when she had time to think about such things.

"What's happening?" Enris hadn't so much washed as dumped a bucket over his head, revealing black hair and a magnificent, though fading, bruise around one eye.

"We'll join the others at the Cloisters. It's a short—" Short to a Yena. Aryl reconsidered what she'd been about to say. "It's not far, but with bridges gone, we'll need to climb. I'll help you."

Instead of the unChosen posturing she'd half-expected, he gave her that quirky smile and gestured emphatic gratitude. "Help would be appreciated. I can see why poor Yuhas found Tuana overly flat. I'd vastly prefer not to fall, Aryl, here or off another cliff."

She gave him a wary look. Enris definitely shared Costa's sense of humor. She'd had trouble deciphering her brother as well. She changed the topic. "Your boots."

He glanced down, then raised a brow at her. "What about them?"

"Take them off."

Home felt like a dream, less real than ink on a pane. Aryl walked behind Haxel, Enris beside her, the last to take the main bridge. She couldn't imagine anything restoring what had been destroyed. As for what remained? Without caretakers, it would disappear before the next M'hir, the stubs of rafters and floor boards home to flowers, the last span of the bridge smothered in vines. Stitlers might live in the meeting hall, luring prey inside. Nothing of the Om'ray would last, here, not the way mammoth structures popped out of mountains or lurked beneath lakes. No future seekers would know they'd existed.

Present-day seekers? Aryl deliberately avoided looking overhead, sure she'd glimpsed something that didn't belong, hovering as no flitter could. She suspected the strangers had sent one of their spies; maybe the tower of smoke drifting up through the canopy had made them curious.

They suffered from an affliction of it.

At the end of the bridge, where it met the first ladder, Haxel turned. "Aryl, do we have everyone?"

The First Scout's expression was studiously neutral; asking a question she could answer for herself was not. "Yes," Aryl answered, aware of Enris' attention. He, she concluded, was overly curious, too.

"Good. Has Ael reached the Cloisters with the first group yet? Come, Aryl." This with precise impatience, as if the other had planned exactly how and when to insist on her Talent's use. To make her expose her secret.

Aryl scowled, but *reached* outward, touching and moving past each small glow of Om'ray until she identified her uncle. Then she drew back into herself. "He's at the Cloisters or close to it. That's the best," she added dryly, "I can do."

"Good enough. Let's catch up to him, shall we?" Haxel jumped to the third rung of the ladder and disappeared behind a whorl of fronds.

"Show off."

Aryl glared at Enris. "I didn't want—"

He grinned and nodded at the ladder. "I meant her."

"Oh."

"Don't look so worried," he added, and flexed one big arm. "I can do ladders. Better than bridges, if you ask me."

"Go ahead," she told him, and stood back to watch, reassured when he didn't attempt to copy Haxel's leap, even more when he tested each step—not too slowly, but careful, particularly of his weaker side. He'd taken her advice, in part, hanging his sturdy, too-stiff boots around his neck. They'd proved to have a softer inner lining which wouldn't hold up for long, but gave his feet some protection.

Biters, Aryl thought, gazing back at the smoldering husk that had been her home, were the least of their worries now.

The climb to bypass the fallen bridges wasn't much, by Yena standards. A spool and a half up, two rastis and a nekis over, down five Om'ray-heights from that. Aryl's experience with the Human made her see it with new eyes, however, and she made no assumptions about the Tuana's ability or perception. She climbed beside him, taking riskier holds to show him the better ones.

When the rain started its faint drumming overhead, Enris froze in place. "What's that?"

"What?" At first fearing a threat, Aryl paused to look around, her hand seeking the longknife that wasn't in her belt.

"That sound." By this point, the first heavy drops were making their way through the canopy.

"Ah," she relaxed. "That would be rain." As if to prove she told him the truth, the showers began in earnest, though luckily not with the drowning power of later in the day. Aryl lifted her face to it, rubbing the soot from her skin.

"Where do we go now?" His hair was a dripping fringe over his forehead. She was surprised to see he looked anxious.

"To the Cloisters. Let get moving." They'd fall farther behind, now, she worried.

"Not to shelter?"

"From this?" she laughed. "This is refreshing. Wait till you feel real rain, Tuana."

They climbed to the next spool in silence, Enris proving a quick learner. When it came to the physical aspect of climbing, Aryl corrected herself. He had no idea what he climbed, so she kept a wary eye out for them both.

"This ability you have," he began abruptly. "Knowing who someone is—"

"I don't want to talk about it. Try that hold. No!" to stop his reach for a tempting hole, doubtless with an irritable occupant. "There."

He pulled with more strength than needful. A Yena would

have relied on that good foothold to push, saving his arms for later. "There are Tuana with that Talent," Enris revealed and Aryl gave him a startled look. "It's true. Our Council doesn't forbid its use. In fact," another grunt of effort, "some charge for the service."

"Charge?"

"Trade. Ask something of value in return. Don't you?"

Aryl stopped. Now she frowned. "With Tikitik. Not each other. What Yena have, we share."

"No one goes hungry in Tuana," Enris retorted, clearly offended. "Our lives—" he glanced down, then closed his eyes for an instant as if to erase the view. "Our lives—" this more slowly, seriously, "—are easier than yours. Maybe too easy, in a way. There are no threats. We have time to spare. Some of us make things. My family . . . I worked in metal. Others hardly work at all. So we trade."

Aryl couldn't imagine it. And right now, she thought, wasn't the time to try. "Enough rest. Keep climbing."

"That was a rest?" He laughed when she least expected it. She wasn't sure whether to join in or scowl; she settled for showing him the next hold for his fingers.

His hand stopped in midreach. *Aryl! Above!*

Aryl's eyes flashed up to find a too-familiar face peering down through the next whorl of fronds. With all four eyes on her.

A long-fingered hand beckoned.

Don't move from this spot, she sent to Enris.

Without him, she could climb the rastis stalk at full speed, and pulled herself to an easy balance atop the frond. The Tikitik looked equally at home, rainwater polishing its knobby skin. "Apart-from-All," it greeted.

Her eyes flicked to the symbols on its wristband, though she didn't doubt who this was. "Thought Traveler. Are you responsible for the attack on Yena?"

Its mouth protuberances writhed a moment. "There was no attack."

Aryl wanted to strangle it. She forced herself to think like a Speaker. "Are you responsible for the decision to take—" as it hissed, "—to reclaim the glows?"

"No. You are."

"I—what do you mean?"

The front eyes wandered. "Your actions have been a provocation. There is dispute among the factions who view themselves as interested in Yena Om'ray. Disagreements. Last night should be viewed in that light. Things have grown more serious."

"More?"

"Now you have used Forbidden technology. Fire—"

"We defended ourselves from the swarm," she snapped. "You can't have expected us to die without a struggle."

The eyes came back to her. "Can you so quickly explain how you arrived here from the mountainside? With fire and this strange Om'ray who bears no token of Passage? Without being seen?"

"Your scouts aren't as good as you think," she replied, feeling cold.

"I think you had the strangers' help. I think they continue to help you and the Yena. Does their device not follow you like a pet-thing? I think together you plan to ravage the graves of the Makers and steal their secrets!"

"I don't know what you're talking about—"

"Shall we push this stranger Om'ray? Shall we throw him to our pets?" The fronds on every side rustled as more Tikitik made their presence known.

"No!" Aryl held up her hands. "Leave him alone!"

Aryl? with alarm.

They'd been shouting, she realized. *Hush, Enris. Stay still.*

"You're right," she said to the waiting Tikitik. She thought quickly. Suggesting the Oud were involved could only make it worse. "We flew here in the stranger-aircar. If they're curious about us, I can't stop them. I know nothing of graves or Makers. I only want my people safe. Our life back."

"I give you one thing, Apart-from-All. Advice. Good advice. You can take it, or not." Its head lowered so its eyes looked up at her balefully. "Do not be here for another truenight."

Then it was gone, moving more quickly through the rastis than anything she'd seen before. Rain filled where it had stood.

She climbed down to Enris, stopping above him.

He was clinging to the rastis with both arms, looking thoroughly soaked and miserable. "What was that about?"

"Where's your token?"

This drew a frown. He tightened his grip, but answered. "An Oud took it."

"Why?"

"I don't—look, isn't there somewhere else we can talk? Somewhere flat?"

"Sorry." He was right. "Here." She climbed below him, and took his left foot in her hand. Tried to take his foot. "Relax!"

"How? I'm going to fall, you know." Costa's words, the voice as deep. For a heartbeat, Aryl felt all the old grief. She focused on placing Enris' foot on a nekis branch that conveniently crossed the fronds.

"Flat," she announced.

"That's your opinion." He tested the footing; he didn't let go of the rastis. "What did it want?"

Persistent, she'd give him that. "Us, gone by truenight. I have to agree."

"Will the swarm come back?"

"They always do." Aryl swatted his leg. "Move faster. Unless you want them to find us here."

Interlude

THE MARVEL OF THE CLOISTERS bridge stopped Enris in his tracks. That, and the desire to heave air back into his starving lungs and ease weight onto his better side. He'd thought they'd been climbing quickly, despite the terrible rainstorm. He'd prided himself on keeping pace with a Yena.

After Aryl's encounter with the Tikitik—who, Enris decided, came a close second in ugly to Oud—he'd realized she'd been coddling him like an infant learning to climb stairs. He'd tried to go faster, but for each move he made, she made five, going ahead, checking behind, guiding his hands and feet. She moved like a restless animal and wasn't, as far as he could tell, breathing hard yet.

She hadn't left him.

He glanced at her through his tousled hair as he poured water from his boots, then pulled each on over the wet liner. From that impatient scowl, she might.

Enris forced a laugh. "Done resting?" he panted.

Aryl rewarded this with a by-now familiar look of exasperation and respect. Enris rather liked it.

He lurched after her as she half-ran along the bridge, drawn as much by the lure of Om'ray ahead as fear of what lay behind. It didn't matter these weren't his birth Clan. The *presence* of so many of his kind—*closest this way*—was too strong to deny.

Though he managed to snatch looks at the bridge's construction. The intricate weave of fine metal strands, more like cloth than chain, was beyond anything he'd seen or imagined. It actually held out the rain. The slats over which they ran—or more accurately over which he staggered and Aryl flew lightly—were ordinary enough, until he noticed they were connected by round flexible fasteners. An admirable way to accommodate any bend or twist, but completely unfamiliar. *Who made this?* he sent, astonished enough to slow down.

A snap of *impatience* was his answer. Enris grinned. He'd felt some curiosity, too.

Abruptly, Aryl slowed.

Easy to see why. Those who'd preceded them hadn't gone through the Cloisters doors after all, though both were turned wide open. Instead, they waited here, most leaning wearily against the walls of the bridge. He spotted Haxel and Ael, other faces already familiar.

"Took you long enough!" This loud complaint came from an old Adept standing in the opening. "Hurry, hurry. I won't leave the doors open all day."

Aryl hesitated. Her shields tightened until she vanished from his inner sense.

Powerful. But he already knew that. He knew something else. She couldn't refuse them. He did his best not to glare at these Om'ray who, consciously or not, justified or not, forced responsibility on an unChosen.

He heard Aryl take a deep breath. Before she could move, he bent and whispered in her ear. "After last night, I expect sweetpies."

She let her breath out in a rude snort and gave him that look again.

Enris smiled to himself.

Chapter 28

THEY DIDN'T SPEAK, THOUGH THEY followed her with their eyes.

They fell in behind her without a word; if Enris hadn't limped beside her, Aryl thought miserably, she would feel the thorough fool. What were her people thinking? Haxel should lead them into the Cloisters. Anyone else should.

Haxel, like the rest, had waited for her to be first. Impossible to argue.

Impossible, she thought wryly, also included having survived truenight.

"Hello, Pio di Kessa'at." Aryl greeted the old Adept and waited to be mocked.

As if infected by the others, Pio politely stepped to one side. "Welcome, Aryl Sarc," she said, then gave a toothless grin. "Interesting clothes." A squint at Enris. "Mendolar. Timing's not a Talent, is it?" Before Aryl could do more than bristle, the Adept gestured sharply to those behind her. "Come through. Hurry up. We're all expected, and I need to lock the doors."

Pio di Kessa'at led Aryl, the rest trailing in silence, to the ceremonial doors. Instead of opening those, she stopped and Aryl gave her a questioning look.

"Council's in session. Don't interrupt your elders," the old Adept ordered. "Manners, manners," she complained to herself. "The young should be taught; adults reminded." Without warning she laid her palm, dry and cool, along Aryl's cheek. Her expression seemed wistful. "There were such expectations."

Then Pio di Kessa'at was away, striding along the yellow-floored hall in a swirl of brown robes, her movements as easy and quick as anyone half her age.

Aryl didn't bother to look to the others. They, like she, could *sense* that most of Yena were on the other side of these doors. Council session or not, that was where they belonged. She turned one open; Enris did the same for the other. Together, they stepped inside.

And into an argument.

"Tikitik politics have disrupted our peace before. We need only wait them out—"

"Never like this!"

"You can't be serious—"

The voices died to echoes as the Councillors seated on the dais stopped to face those coming through the doors.

They brought the reek of smoke and sweat into the beautiful room. It didn't matter. Those already here rose from their seats on blankets and chairs clustered against the windowed wall, rushing forward with glad cries to greet their families. Aryl moved aside, savoring the joy rushing from mind to mind. Those who'd survived the swarm mingled with those who'd outrun it. There was no difference, she thought, in how haunted they looked.

"Impressive." Enris tilted his head back, studying the chamber ceiling. Like her, he appeared content to let everyone else move. Or, perhaps he tactfully avoided being too close to any one of Yena's Choosers, before making his Choice. She spared a moment to wonder what he thought of his sorry Clan-to-be; surely he regretted this end to his Passage.

"It's big," she commented absently, watching Chosen find Chosen, parents reunite over their youngest. Cetto stepped down to greet his son and daughter. Adrius stayed on the dais, but happily wheezed and coughed at his eldest, who climbed to be with him. Families became a blur. Aryl focused on Enris, who had no one else. "Tuana's Council Chamber is the same, isn't it?"

"I wouldn't know."

She'd thought all unChosen were taken to the Cloisters before leaving on Passage, to learn from the memories of the Adepts. Perhaps Tuana followed another custom. If so, credit to Enris for surviving without them. She changed the subject. "What are these sweetpies you want?"

Enris shook his big head at her, eyes now laughing. "And you call yourself an Om'ray . . ." his voice trailed away as her expression changed. "What's wrong?"

Aryl gestured apology, but couldn't speak. She'd spotted Joyn and his family among the rest. His mother, Rimis Uruus, held an infant.

It wasn't hers.

Fearing the worst, Aryl *reached*.

She was right; Ferna Parth was Lost.

Seru. Aryl made the sending as gentle as she could, buried her own pain so it wouldn't make the other's worse. She watched her cousin as she walked through the crowd to Rimis; understanding spread with each slow step, until around her Yena grew still and silent.

Without a word, Seru collected her brother and buried her face in his blankets. His tiny hands grabbed her netted hair.

You saved the rest. Soft, carefully free of pity.

Had she? Aryl sighed and met Enris' eyes with hers. *But not all.*

YENA.

At the summons, heads turned to the far end of the room. The other entrance, Aryl thought, and looked with the rest.

In came the Adepts, not in brown but in ceremonial white. Thirteen in total, they walked one behind the other; the assembled Yena parted to make room. There were no words or gestures of greeting, though the Adepts were also family to those here.

Weren't they?

Aryl found her mother, second from last in the line before Pio. Taisal didn't acknowledge her daughter's presence. Instead, with the Adepts, she climbed the dais and took her position standing behind the row of Council seats.

After the Adepts came seven Lost in their long robes, their faces empty, movements eerily identical. Ferna Parth was not yet among them; Aryl let out the breath she hadn't realized she'd held. Each carried a black woven bag. They came to the side of the dais and stopped, faced in whatever direction they happened to be. Other Yena eased away until the cluster of Lost stood alone.

The Councillors took their seats; Adrius brusquely waving off his family. Aryl, like the rest of Yena, moved closer. Here, she thought, were those who governed them. Did anyone else notice that Morla's hands trembled in her lap until she clenched them together? Did anyone else dare *reach* for their minds and find how tightly they were shielded?

Something was wrong, she decided with dread. Something more. Enris tensed beside her. Though a stranger, he felt it, too.

Morla Kessa'at collected herself and rose gracefully to her feet. "Greetings, Yena," her voice calm and serene. "A joy to be together, regardless the reason. We would hear your news. Who speaks for you?"

Catching Aryl's eye, Haxel tipped her head toward the dais. Aryl pressed her lips together in denial.

The First Scout shrugged and casually stepped on the dais. She held out her hand to Morla. The other Councillors touched finger to arm until all were connected. There was a moment of silent concentration—though Aryl suspected Adrius closed his eyes to nap—while they shared Haxel's report.

Yena waited. They'd seen this before.

Though they'd likely never seen such ashen expressions on the faces of their leaders as a result. Cetto looked ill, once Haxel returned to the floor. Morla kept hold of his hand, her eyes bright with tears. Tikva and Yorl were grim and pale. Sian—Aryl's eyes narrowed. The Adept looked remarkably composed, all things considered. He might have known what Haxel would share—or it didn't matter, Aryl thought suddenly. Why?

Morla rose and made the gesture of gratitude to all, pausing to wipe a tear. "We share the pain and hardship you've endured. With you, we grieve for those no longer here. Above all—" this with a warm smile at Aryl and Enris, "—we are grateful to those who came in time to help—"

"Help?" Haxel interrupted. "Where's the food, Morla? Why did our people spend the night here, on the floor? Where's the welcome?" Her scar flamed red. "The Cloisters must take us in—that is Council's decision, isn't it?" The First Scout curled her lip. "Yena's as good as dead otherwise."

There were gasps throughout the chamber. Aryl supposed most had taken their welcome here for granted. She hadn't, she realized numbly. Maybe it was because her mother had yet to meet her eyes. Maybe it was because so far, she'd had to save herself.

On another level, Aryl admired how the First Scout got to the point. She could *sense* the hope of those around her. Council had to feel it, too.

But not all minds were open.

"Yena's survival is our concern, too, First Scout," Sian d'sud Vendan said smoothly. "We must ensure the village is rebuilt as quickly as possible. The situation must be stabilized. Peace restored."

"Until that time, will the Cloisters shelter us?" Haxel's voice rose to the roar she used when training scouts. "Answer the question!"

Confusion and fear spread, mind to mind. Aryl tightened her shields, feeling a superficial calm descend as others did the same.

"Speaker." Sian gave the summons, not Tikva or Morla. It suggested a shift in leadership. Disquieting, Aryl thought, if so. Sian was difficult to grasp at his most open.

Taisal di Sarc stepped from her place with the other Adepts to stand alongside the Council. "Yena, hear me!" she said, her eyes bright, her voice filling the room. "There is no need for fear. I will negotiate with the Tikitik Speaker. Ask their forgiveness—"

"Forgive *us*?" someone shouted. "What did we do?"

Other voices rose. Passions flared past weaker shields. Children began to add their own distress to minds already worn and scared, their high-pitched cries to the bedlam.

YENA!

The answering silence was almost worse, Aryl thought.

Sian rose from his seat. "Our Speaker will ask the Tikitik to forgive us for failing the Agreement that has kept our people safe throughout time. We believed—I admit it, even I—that there was no harm in the careful use of a new Talent, no risk in children using more Power than their parents. But there was. By encouraging these changes, we've threatened the balance of real power on this world. The Agreement itself is now in peril—not just for Yena, but for all Om'ray. It is our fault." He paused, as if inviting reaction.

Such was the shock in the chamber that no one uttered a word.

"There is a solution," Sian continued, matter-of-fact and confident. "We must purge Yena of further temptation. Those who imperil the Agreement must go."

"What is this?" With that roar, Cetto surged to his feet. "We did not debate such a thing. We would never agree!" Morla looked shocked as well. Aryl noted that old Adrius and her mother's great-uncle sat quietly, the former half asleep, the latter's face set in implacable lines. Tikva might have been in a trance.

"This is beyond a Council vote," Sian informed them in a cold, remote voice. "This is about the future. Yes, First Scout. To answer your impertinent questioning, the Cloisters will provide shelter until the Tikitik agree to rebuild our village. To those who deserve to stay."

Haxel's scar was pale and etched; Aryl saw a muscle jump along her jaw. But she said nothing.

"No," protested Morla, her face turning red. "You can't—"

"Further," as if the Councillor hadn't spoken, "we immediately sanction and exile those who endanger the Agreement and the peace."

"Exile?" "Send to die, you mean!" Nameless shouts from the hall. "Who goes?"

Haxel looked ready to use her longknife. "Who dares decide?"

"The decision is made," Sian shouted twice to be heard. When the startled murmurs died away, he continued in a quieter, but no less grim voice. "The Adepts, on behalf of all Yena, watch over the Om'ray and assess new Talent." He took a step back to fill the space Taisal had left among her peers. Tikva di

Uruus, the other Adept on Council, rose and moved as well, to take the end position.

"We let Yena reach this terrible day," Sian stated. "Never again. We will no longer tolerate danger from within. Yena will endure."

At this, Taisal looked directly at Aryl for the first time. There was nothing to read in her face; nothing to Aryl's *inner* sense, nothing within the *other*. Her mother had locked herself behind an Adept's formidable barriers, even from her daughter.

Aryl didn't try to reach her, thinking she understood. Taisal, with her Talent to recall spilled sweetberries to her tray, her use of the Dark to *reach* her daughter, was one of the dangers to Yena. As an Adept, her disgrace would be absolute—worse, Taisal wouldn't survive without shelter in the canopy.

Could any of them?

"Go," Sian told them, "for the good of the Clan."

Yena flinched aside as the Lost entered the crowd, their steps graceless yet intent. One, Leri, stepped up on the Council dais. She reached into her bag and brought out a token, the same as used on Passage. She gave it to Cetto sud Teerac, who sank into his chair to stare down at what was cupped in his hands. She gave another to Morla Kessa'at, who let out a horrified cry.

Aryl wasn't surprised when something cold and hard was pressed into her slack fingers. She didn't bother to see which Lost had put it there. She gripped it and waited.

Enris tossed his in the air, where it spun end over end until caught with a casual snap of his wrist. Which made no sense, she protested to herself. The Tuana was what Yena needed most: new blood. Or was that a danger, too?

Strange, how silent the chamber. Like the hush at truenight, before the clatter of the swarm; it lacked only the trills of a wysp.

Morla's was the only outward reaction. Yena after Yena

accepted a token, expressions stricken, those of their families numb. Aryl knew how they felt. To survive last night only to be wiped away at the verge of safety, by those who should care for you?

The betrayal was too deep to comprehend.

Finished, the Lost returned to their cluster by the dais. They'd given, by Aryl's rough count, over twenty tokens. Twenty sentences of exile and death.

Not one to an Adept. Not even Taisal di Sarc.

Why?

She could betray her mother. She could say what she'd seen Taisal do. They might doubt her word and motives, but the suggestion, here and now, with emotion ready to win over reason? It might be enough to exile Taisal, too.

Aryl kept silent. There was nothing to gain. She couldn't guess why her mother agreed to this; she couldn't guess why the other Adepts would allow her to stay. But, as a result, someone she loved would be safe.

The hush continued. No one seemed to know what to do next. Even Haxel seemed dazed by what glittered in her hand.

Aryl met Cetto's eyes, read his helpless anger and despair. He'd believed they could leave Yena. He'd hoped for their future somewhere else. Not, she knew, like this.

She found herself breathing deeply, the way she would before a climb—or before an argument. Then, before she realized what she would do, she jumped on the dais to offer her hand to Bern's grandfather. "Come," she told him, including Morla with a somber look.

Aryl then turned to face Yena. That this put Council and the Adepts at her back didn't bother her at all.

"We're wasting daylight," she said, making the words loud and sure.

The echoes followed them out.

Chapter 29

"THEY COULD HAVE FED US first," Enris commented mildly as they assembled before the doors to the bridge.

Haxel heard as she walked by. "And waste food on the dead?" she tossed over her shoulder.

"That bad?" he asked Aryl.

She tapped the token on his chest. "You should go back," she urged again. "Argue you were on Passage, that none of this is your fault. It isn't, you know. You came to help us. It's—"

"Unfair? Unjust?" For some reason, Enris chuckled. "At least this—" his fingers brushed the token, "—will come in handy."

Those nearby looked from Enris to Aryl, then away. She understood their reaction. The Tuana was smart, brave, and strong. It wasn't enough—not in the canopy. They needed proper equipment and supplies to have a chance. All but the two Councillors, Cetto and Morla, had been in the village during the attack. The exiles had nothing but what some had carried to the Cloisters, most of that personal belongings grabbed last night during the panic.

Haxel made a good show of assessing resources—in her

element as First Scout—yet no one but Enris believed it was anything more than show.

Aryl gave her attention to who, rather than what, they had. She raised her chin, a greeting to Ael. Unlikely the Adepts would have exiled him, in her opinion, if he hadn't been Joined to Myris. A partner left behind would be Lost; not just a burden, but a living reminder of guilt.

That both of the Chosen pairs received tokens didn't surprise her. Other decisions did. Taisal wasn't the only one with exceptional Power to remain safe. Joyn and his parents were to stay, while her cousin Seru, with about as much useful Power as a flitter, sat with other exiles by the door. She cradled her brother in her arms and thus far had ignored everything but the task of shielding his desires from others. Alejo, for his part, slept the oblivious, preoccupied sleep of all babies, eyes squeezed tight and mouth working.

There, Aryl thought sadly, was a problem.

Sixteen Chosen all told, though four were too old for strenuous climbing and one, Juo Vendan, awkward with her first pregnancy. Five unChosen, counting herself but not Seru; were they the ones Sian had picked as most able to learn a new Talent? Twenty-three in all, several superb climbers. She didn't understand how Yena could spare them.

Nor, she added bitterly, how they could be let fall, like scraps into the Lay.

"Aryl? We should leave." Myris said quietly. "They're turning the doors."

"I'll—" She'd *sensed* the arrival she'd expected. "Go ahead. I'll catch up."

Other than two Adepts to open and close the way to the bridge, only exiles gathered here, sheltered by the overhang of the great doors. They'd left the chamber like unChosen taking Passage—quickly, as if already gone. A kindness, to give them a chance at composure. Most Yena couldn't shield intense emotion; lingering with their grief-stricken families would have been cruel to both.

Exiles plus one. Aryl waited as Rimis Uruus appeared in the arch, then ran across the platform to join her. Raindrops streaked her fine-boned face, disguising tears. She hadn't come alone; a small figure watched from inside the Cloisters, hands pressed against the transparent material of a window. What did Joyn think of the story now? Aryl wondered.

"Thank you, Aryl." Rimis kept her voice low. "How did you convince her?"

"She didn't have to," Seru answered for herself as she came beside them. "I'm not always a fool, Aunt."

"I'll do my best for him. You know I will."

I know.

Seru opened the blanket to uncover Alejo's sleeping face. She pressed two fingers to her lips, then to his small forehead. If there was a sending, it was nothing shared beyond the two of them.

The baby gave a piteous cry as Rimis took him from his sister's arms and hurried away. Seru turned, her shoulders hunched, and headed for the open doors and the bridge.

Unfair. Unjust. Enris had the right of it.

The *taste* of change she'd felt since the M'hir was finally gone. It had, Aryl realized with a pang, been a warning against her own kind and this moment.

She walked toward the bridge. Most were on it; Enris and Ael waited for her, relaxed against one door. "You like climbing, I take it?" Ael was saying to the Tuana. His keen eyes wouldn't miss how exhausted the other was, nor the bruises and returning limp.

"Climbing's fine," Enris replied with his easy smile. "Looking down's another thing altogether."

"Good thing we don't recommend it." Ael's expression grew guarded. "Aryl," he warned with a gesture behind her.

Aryl glanced over her shoulder. Another figure waited within the Cloisters arch, this one wearing a long white robe, stiff with embroidery.

"Don't climb without me," she told Enris. "I'll be quick."

"Take your time. I'm not in a hurry." He'd lifted his gaze to the arch. He brought it back to her, his eyes wary. *Is this trouble?*

Aryl shrugged helplessly. "It's my mother."

The light in the Cloisters discouraged shadows. It glinted at the edge of the frames on the walls; gilded the meaningless angles and curves of the metal symbols they enclosed. Where Taisal stood was lit well enough to reveal any expression, had she shown one. She didn't speak as Aryl approached. She seemed less real, all of a sudden, than one of the Humans.

Aryl stopped in front of her mother, torn between hope and bitterness. When Taisal didn't speak at once, bitterness won.

"Come to wish me joy, Mother?" Aryl snapped a finger against the token pinned to her stranger-shirt. "That is the role of the Speaker, when saying good-bye to those on Passage."

"I have a question," Taisal said, each word soft and precise.

She felt hope struggling to be born and held it still. "About the strangers," she guessed. "Why they're here. I can tell you—"

"The strangers are not of Cersi. They matter not to Om'ray."

"But what they've found—"

"Hush," Taisal said with impatience, as if Aryl wasted her time. "The Tikitik have their puzzle solved. Let them war with the strangers if they wish. It's nothing to us, which of them kills the other."

"Nothing? Is that why you lied to Council?" Aryl accused,

her hands clenched at her sides. "The Tikitik can't sense our Power in use—that's why you answered me when I was their captive. You knew! Just as you know their attack last night was provoked by the strangers, not any new Talent. Why didn't you tell them? Why did you let this happen?"

"Why?" Taisal lifted a brow. "Council deals with Yena—that's their role. The Adepts must deal with the world. Your strangers?" A toss of one hand. "Flood. Famine. Strangers. Plague. Any one could have pushed us to the brink. We *tasted* this day coming. I tried to warn you, Daughter," a hint of pain in her eyes. "This—" those eyes shifted to look outside "—this was what we feared would be necessary."

"Necessary?" Aryl cried. "Sending twenty-three to their deaths?"

"Twenty-three who would use any means to survive, risk any Talent, however dangerous or unknown!" The first passion on her face, in her voice, but it was cold, cold and harsh. "We won't allow desperation or carelessness to ruin us. Power must be controlled, not only to preserve the Agreement, but for the future of our kind. We know you." Taisal curled her palm, then turned it over as if she emptied a cup. "You are discord."

"I'm your daughter," Aryl whispered.

The words might have been a blow. Taisal's lips parted without sound and her eyes glistened. For an instant, her hands lifted toward Aryl. "All I have," she admitted, a tear sliding down her cheek. "All that's left. Aryl, if I'd trained you as an Adept," her words like an old, worn grief, "you could be trusted now. If you hadn't failed me—" her mother's voice caught, "—if you hadn't failed me last night, you could have stayed. Do you understand?"

"Failed you?" Before Aryl could touch her, *reach* for her mother, Taisal drew herself straight, her hands on the Speaker's Pendant.

"How did you arrive in time to save the others from the swarm?"

This was the question? Aryl stammered "The–the Oud brought us—"

Taisal cut her off, her face gone so white, her eyes were like holes. "The truth—" her Power surged, pressing against Aryl's shields, "—or must I drag it from your mind again? You traveled the Dark, didn't you, as you did when you put Bern on the bridge instead of Costa. You used it."

Aryl flinched. "Yes, but—"

"Now do you see, Aryl?" Her mother's long fingers clutched the pendant, as if it were a ladder to safety. "You can't be trusted. All it took was being desperate."

Desperate.

Aryl remembered the sending from those about to perish, their horror and pain. At that memory, she felt the blood drain from her own face, taking with it every emotion but rage.

"What if I did?" Her voice was a stranger's, stern and edged. "You talk about Yena's future, Mother. What gives Adepts the right to say what that should be?" Rage, she found, could be cold. "What gives you the right to say who gets to breathe tomorrow?"

Rage could offer strength.

"You're right. I can't be trusted. To save my people," Aryl finished with scorn, "I will do anything."

Taisal closed her eyes, lashes sparkled with tears. "I can't save you," she whispered. "I can't."

"I didn't ask you to."

Aryl turned and walked away.

Interlude

CLEARLY, THAT GOOD-BYE HADN'T gone well. Enris straightened from his restful slouch as Aryl crossed the platform. The rest had gone through the open doors to the bridge, fingertips brushing as loved ones exchanged private messages.

Aryl hadn't offered a hand to her mother.

"Ready to go—" The words died as he saw her face. In his nightmares of Kiric, when he'd shared his brother's worst moments of emptiness and despair, he'd seen that same look. He felt strangely paralyzed.

Then that familiar determination firmed her lips and caught fire in her eyes. "Ready when you are," Enris finished, as if he hadn't paused.

"I'm ready. There's nothing here."

"There had to be at least one bed," he complained as he fell in beside her, not having to force the yawn that threatened his grit-filled eyes. "You do realize I haven't slept in—I don't remember sleeping properly since we met. Naps, yes. Bed, no. I need my sleep, Aryl Sarc."

His reward was a lessening of the tension that surrounded her like a cloak, as if he'd drawn her back ever-so-slightly from some hurt. "Here I thought someone your size would have more stamina," she told him. "Come on."

As they passed through the doors, the two Adepts turned them closed with such alacrity Enris felt a breeze. He whirled to scowl; with no target, he admired the colors blended through the metal. It was similar in result to Tuana work, but the technique was new to him.

A bell began to toll, deep-toned and slow, each beat separated by a breath. If this were Tuana . . . he guessed the custom was the same for all Om'ray. A death bell. "Bit premature," he commented, fighting to control his voice. Unfair. Unjust. His anger for these people wouldn't help.

Aryl's lips moved. She counted in silence. "Twenty-two," she said calmly when the echoes of the last peal died away. Her smile surprised him. "Guess you can't be mourned if you didn't officially arrive, Tuana." The smile faded. "Too late to go back."

"I don't want to go back," he told her, gesturing toward the long curve of bridge. The others were at the halfway point. "Although I must say, it's their loss."

Fingertips brushed the back of his hand. *You weren't welcome because of how I brought you.* There wasn't regret, but something of apology.

Yena was never my goal.

Enris started walking, favoring his sore side. Aryl matched his pace. "It's true," he said aloud. "No offense to your Choosers, but I'm on a different type of Passage."

Aryl tilted her head, regarding him from the corners of her eyes. "The Om'ray who make things. And if you find them, what then?"

"When." He left it at that as they reached the first of the other exiles.

They'd caught up? Enris looked toward the end of the bridge, wondering why those farthest ahead were sitting among their small bundles of belongings. Wasn't daylight crucial? He couldn't believe the bells had done anything but stir their anger, as it had his.

A Chosen beckoned to them. "What's the delay, Aryl?"

Enris smiled politely. This was the family who'd greeted him in the village, parents and two older children. Too late to wish he'd paid attention to names this morning.

"I'll go and see," Aryl assured the Yena, then gestured an apology to Enris. "My manners. Enris Mendolar, Syb sud Uruus," she introduced, seeming embarrassed. He refused to feel guilt. "Taen," the mother. "Kayd and Ziba." The children. Kayd showed the promise of height already, his arms and legs gangly though well muscled, as all Yena; Ziba was smaller, but sturdy, her hair pale gold under its net. She gripped her brother's hand, something Enris guessed she hadn't done for a long time.

The bridge protected them from the rain. Enris noticed that only made it easier to see the tracks of tears.

"We've met," he said with a small bow.

"To your detriment." Syb's gesture was more fury than apology. "Their treatment of you shames us all, Enris. To condemn someone who—"

"Aryl!! Aryl!!!" Haxel, sharp and urgent. From the end of the bridge.

With an apology of his own to Syb, Enris went with Aryl as she sped off in answer. He tried, anyway. At a plodding jog, his legs protested the recent climb and his side ached. He promised his body rest if it wouldn't embarrass him in front of all these Yena. Fortunately, the First Scout came to meet them at a run, her steps echoing within the enclosure. The exiles parted to let her through.

The instant she spotted Aryl coming her way, however, Haxel spun about to rush back the other way. "Quickly!" she shouted over her shoulder. To the rest, "Let us by, all of you. Wait here. Stay inside the bridge!"

"This can't be good," Enris panted to himself.

* * *

It wasn't good at all, Enris decided, when the three of them met where the Cloisters bridge opened on the rain-swept wooden platform.

The great rastis that supported the platform was empty. An invitation, of sorts.

Tikitik were everywhere else. They didn't bother to hide behind fronds or stalks. They stood exposed to the downpour, as if prepared to wait forever, their four eyes locked on the Om'ray. There wasn't a path from the platform or the upper spools that wouldn't mean having to push one aside.

Somehow, Enris didn't think they'd let themselves be pushed. If they could be—he hadn't forgotten the wiry strength of the Tikitik on the bridge before it decided not to struggle.

"Witnesses. They expected this," Aryl decided. "Or something like it."

"How?" Haxel looked more annoyed than convinced.

"When Tikitik fail, their fellows toss them into the Lake of Fire to die. This is no different. Yena has failed. They understand the bells. We're—we're being tossed."

"And they plan to help." Enris set his shoulders against the bridge's thick support, inside enough to avoid the heaviest rain. "Wonderful."

"They won't touch us," Aryl disagreed. "They'll watch."

Haxel, ignoring the rain, laid on the platform to look over the side. "Oh, I'd say they're helping," she said as she rose up again. "There's easily ten esask tied to this stalk."

A round of smug-sounding hisses greeted this discovery.

Enris had to ask—he wasn't about to look down. "What's an esask?"

"Appetite with legs," Aryl informed him absently, busy taking a look herself. These Yena, Enris decided, had a callous attitude to being eaten he truly didn't share. "They might have other surprises in mind."

"We'll post a watch on the platform." Haxel ran her hand along a rail. "The glows were stripped before I got here. Tikitiks or our fine Adepts?"

"Does it matter?" Aryl replied wearily.

He'd been here before, Enris realized. With one difference. He wasn't alone. He closed his eyes, *reaching* for the others. The glow of nearby Om'ray was steady and strong, giving him his place. He hadn't realized how much he'd missed the companionship of his kind.

Then he felt a chill. He'd been in this kind of situation before—and some of his kind had waited in ambush.

Eyes still shut, Enris blew out a heavy sigh. "Post a watch at the other end of the bridge."

"They won't let us back in—" Aryl began.

"That's not what he means," observed Haxel grimly. "Is it, Tuana?"

He grunted. "Let's say I've had enough surprises."

* * *

"Aryl, there it is again. What's it doing here?"

Enris cracked open an eye. The flexible metal mesh of the bridge side made a surprisingly comfortable back rest, not to mention the slats of its floor were dry. He'd only meant to rest while they sorted out the watches, to be ready for his turn. Not that they'd asked.

Haxel, ever alert. This time she wasn't pointing to any of the Tikitik, who were still, Enris noted glumly, lurking on all sides. Instead, her outstretched finger targeted a shape hovering overhead, its rounded, transparent surface close enough that Enris could see how raindrops beaded and ran off.

A device of the strangers.

It gained the Tikitik's attention, too. There was hissing and more pointing.

Haxel looked wonderstruck; Aryl's glare should have melted it. "You've seen one before," Enris guessed, creaking to his feet.

"The strangers use them to spy on us," Aryl said bitterly. "I suppose our deaths will be entertaining."

"A machine to watch from a distance . . ." From her tone, Haxel wanted one of her own. Trust a scout, Enris thought, to see the possibilities.

He took a step toward the oddly cooperative machine, blinking raindrops, and scrutinized the varied shapes exposed by its clear underside. Some looked like eyes, which made sense. Some, he judged. "I think it hears, too," he concluded, pointing at something that could be a voice holder.

Aryl didn't look surprised. "He heard the Watchers," she murmured, almost to herself.

"Then he can hear you."

"Who?" Haxel demanded, looking from one to the other. "Hear who?"

"Long story." Enris grinned. "Seems to me time for a trade," he added, looking at Aryl. "You did save his life."

She stared up at the device, her lips twisted to one side. Rain drummed on the platform, collected and dripped from every leaf tip and frond.

It soaked his hair and slid like chill fingers down the neck of his tunic. "What have we to lose?" he coaxed.

"Nothing," Haxel said flatly, an unexpected ally. "We've no retreat. The bridge can't be defended against the swarm. We're trapped. If there's anything this machine can do for us—" she gave it a dubious look.

"I think Aryl knows exactly what it could do." His heartbeat sounded loud in his ears as he waited.

Save them again, he sent then, with all the urgency he felt. *Save us.*

Aryl looked at him; her eyes were wide and wild. "What if the Tikitik then go after the others?" *What if saving us makes it worse?*

"The others," he pointed out dryly, "are behind nice big doors. We're the swarm-bait. Which I might add you've tried for yourself and didn't like." Underneath, he sent, *Too much conscience* and *you think too much.* "It's better than doing nothing while we wait to die a horrible death. Probably won't even work. Feel better?"

Her lips quirked at one corner. "I think you need more sleep."

That made him laugh.

Then Enris held his breath as Aryl walked under the hovering machine and looked up at it.

"Marcus Bowman!" Her call startled a frenzy of hisses from their watchers. Aryl raised her voice above it. "Help us!

"Please."

Chapter 30

TWENTY-ONE LIVES.

Aryl stood in the rain, feeling them behind her, safe for the moment inside the Cloisters bridge. They believed in her. She felt that too, an inner warmth they freely sent mind to mind. She'd arrived in time to save them last truenight, brought light to the darkness. They trusted her now.

Or, her lips twisted, they saw no other hope and, being Yena, were too stubborn to admit it.

Plus one. Enris Mendolar had stood with her, or rather sagged against a bridge support, asleep on his feet, until she'd insisted he go inside to check on the others. Ael had reported the Tuana nodded off within moments of sitting with Myris and was snoring, loudly.

Enris was stubborn, too.

The Tikitik, no less persistent, remained on watch. Most now squatted, their larger eyes shut as if they dozed. The device hadn't moved in four tenths. She chose to consider that promising, though what took the strangers so long?

Or were they waiting, too?

Aryl shivered.

"Your turn inside. It's dry."

So much for Enris getting his rest. "I'll stay."

"Go. They could use your company." That just-awake grumble roughened his voice, but she thought he moved more easily.

The idea of rest—Aryl couldn't imagine it. She motioned to the device. "I have to stay." It was their only hope, now. She couldn't abandon it. "He has to see me." As if she could be sure Marcus Bowman was even looking at the image from the machine.

"The strangers know my face, too, remember?" Enris shrugged and squinted upward, blinking away drops. "How long?"

He wasn't asking about the Human. "The rain makes it hard to tell—maybe a couple of tenths to firstnight." She didn't say the rest: after firstnight, too few moments until truenight. And the swarm.

The Tuana's shields were better than most. Now, he allowed mindspeech, but reserved any emotion behind that barrier. *Can you move so many?*

I don't know. She let him feel her uncertainty. She didn't know what she'd done or could do. This wasn't the way to learn. Aryl wiped water from her face and chewed her lower lip, thinking of her mother, thinking of the dangerous lure of the *other,* of Bern's horrified reaction. *It didn't upset you,* she sent, curious. *Moving through the* other.

He didn't laugh, but his reply held an undercurrent of amusement. *I thought you were tossing us to our deaths, remember. Finding myself still alive in the village was a distinct improvement.*

Aryl didn't argue, but she had a feeling Enris Mendolar wasn't easily dismayed by Power or its use. She sighed. The others would be. "Flying machines—most have seen the Oud's. What I can do would be—" she vacillated between "devastating" and "terrifying," and settled for "—disturbing. I'll try. If nothing else, I'll try."

When, Aryl told herself, aware of the irony, she was again desperate.

"So we hope the Human comes."

"He'll come," Aryl said, as much to herself as Enris. "Whether he can help? That's another question."

"Think he answers to the Human version of a Council?" A short laugh. "Then we're doomed."

She didn't know what to say to that.

"Go." A tenth later, it was Haxel ordering her inside. This time Aryl didn't argue. She could feel the growing anxiety of those within. What she could do about it, she didn't know, but she had to try.

The exiles sat as families against one or the other mesh walls of the bridge, no farther than a few steps from the bridge opening. None slept; none moved other than to shoo one of the many biters who sheltered here as well. Kessa'at, the most numerous, had Morla at their center, looking frail. Uruus had taken in Seru, the sole Parth; their young daughter was curled on her lap. Teerac, without children, listened to the low deep voice of their eldest, Cetto. Vendan, Haxel's niece and her Chosen, listened, too, though Cetto wasn't talking but hummed a weaver song.

Haxel's Chosen, Rorn sud Vendan, stood with Syb apart from the rest. In the gathering gloom they were little more than silhouettes, their strong arms strangely elongated. Longknives, Aryl realized.

They faced away from the opening, down the long curve of the bridge. There was nothing that could come at them from that direction. Nothing but other Om'ray, other Yena.

She'd thought herself immune to shock by now. Seeing this, Om'ray prepared for violence against one another? Her heart missed a beat.

"Aryl?" Myris came up to her. "Is everything—" She gave a nervous laugh. "I suppose that's a pointless question."

"There's been no sign of the strangers," Aryl admitted, aware everyone was looking at her. Cetto stopped humming. She didn't know what else to say.

"What are they like?" Ziba squirmed to sit in Seru's light hold, her eyes solemn. "Are they ugly?"

From the attentiveness of the others, it was a question on everyone's mind.

With some misgivings, Aryl summoned a memory of Marcus when he was smiling. She offered her fingers to Ziba, taking care to tightly shield every thought but the image. Young un-Chosen weren't always able—or willing—to keep out of other minds. Hers, she knew, held too much to share with a child.

Ziba rested her small hand on Aryl's, after a smirk at her brother who was not so entitled. Then she took her hand away. "That's only an Om'ray," she said, clearly disappointed not to see a monster.

"Humans only look like us," Aryl explained. "The way a brofer-sneak looks like a real brofer." It wasn't the most flattering comparison, but among canopy dwellers, mimicry usually involved a fatal trap. A brofer-sneak only borrowed living space from its confused host. Aryl pushed Ziba's hand gently toward her brother's. "Share it for me, please. I should be outside."

Aryl made sure to brush her hand against her aunt's as well, and added a message. *Share with the older ones—this is a being who means us well, but there are other strangers, different in form. I don't know their intentions. We must be aware and stay together.* And, after a moment's indecision. *Myris, they are not real to the inner sense. It will be hard to be near them.*

Myris paled, but she understood. Aryl knew she'd make sure the others were ready. As much as they could be. "Be careful," her aunt told her out loud. Beneath, *I'd ease your pain, but it's become your strength. We need you strong.*

"I'll be careful."

She didn't reply to the sending, unless walking away was an answer of sorts.

Aryl stepped out to find the gloom within the bridge extended outside as well. Firstnight was close, hurried by the clouds. It wouldn't be long before wysps sang through the rain. Aryl gazed over the curve of the bridge to where the Cloisters stood, tall and aloof, its petal-walls upturned to keep its secrets. Then her eyes widened at a glint moving downward through the canopy above it.

"There he is," she told Enris, watching what was, in truth, the strangers' large aircar as it slowly descended.

The Tikitik hissed, rising to their feet, their heads swinging low before their bodies. There was a throbbing shriek from higher in the stalk, an answer from below. Aryl walked to the edge of the platform and stared at the one closest, her hands on her hips. "Tell the rest. Interfere," she said firmly, "and the strangers will use fire."

They could, she reminded herself. Whether they would?

"What's it doing?" Enris asked.

Aryl turned to watch the aircar lazily circle the top level of the Cloisters, once, then again. "Being nosy," she guessed. Before she had to talk to the device again, the aircar's path paralleled the bridge on its way to them.

Finally, the machine came to rest alongside the platform. Intensely bright lights snapped on at the front and sides, their beams slicing through the vegetation. The Tikitik withdrew, hissing their fury. "Handy," Enris commented.

At the least, Aryl thought, she would ask for one of those. Last another truenight.

But she wanted more. "You and Haxel keep the others

back," she said. "They'll be curious, but the fewer who see him . . ." she let her voice trail away.

He made a rude noise. "The fewer who'll feel sick. I'll take care of it. But you're sure you won't need me? We Tuana are great traders."

"I'm sure. Go."

She was alone on the platform when the opaque roof of the machine lifted, revealing Marcus Bowman and the flitter-stranger. The latter immediately fluffed its feathers at the damp and clicked its mouth at her. Marcus beckoned her inside. "Hurry!"

Aryl came as far as the side of the aircar then stopped, her hands on its cold metal. "Thank you for coming, Marcus. I need your help."

"Here, help," he agreed, giving the dark vegetation on all sides a worried look. "Come! Safe!"

Sweat, not rain, beaded his face. He'd either seen what had happened last night or its aftermath. Not, she knew, that he'd ever trust Tikitik again. "All of us, Marcus, please?" she pleaded, pointing to the now-dark mouth of the bridge and then patting the machine. "Take us to the mountain pass. Near the Watchers. Safe from the Tikitik."

"All?" He looked his doubt.

She held up her hands, flashing her fingers to count. "Twenty-three. A few bags. Please. Just to the mountain."

The hissing intensified. Instead of frightening the Human, he seemed to take offense at the sound, snapping a harsh-sounding phrase at their watchers in his own language. "All," this with a brusque nod. He conferred with the flitter-stranger, speaking quickly. The other answered. Marcus held up both hands. "Ten. Understand? Ten come. Then ten. Then three and bags. All safe." His face softened as he looked at her. "Aryl. Promise. All safe. Help you."

She tasted salt with the rain, only then aware she was crying.

"Thank you. Thank you. But—" It was unfair, what she had to ask, but the others would be upset by his not-Om'ray presence. "Two trips, this one only, please?" she indicated the flitter-stranger. "You stay with me, out of sight, till the last." As his face darkened, the Human surmising who-knew-what of her motives, she gestured to him, then to herself. "Not-Om'ray. I understand." She ran her hand down his sleeve, dared touch his hand. Next, she pointed to the bridge. "They don't know you. They don't know Humans." She mimed fear. "You'll scare them more than the swarm."

Like Enris, the Human sometimes laughed when she didn't expect it. Then he climbed from the aircar, pulling up a quite sensible hood against the rain. The flitter-stranger gave a resigned click of its mouth. "Tell *P'tr sit 'Nix* where go," Marcus said. "Hurry, all. Understand?"

Aryl gestured gratitude to them both, quickly. "Hurry" was exactly what they had to do.

First, however, came the slight detail of showing Marcus where he would hide from the exiles—suspended from the platform by their one rope, with only Enris, another non-climber, to help him.

She didn't think either would laugh about that.

There'd been no debate over where to go. Aryl had told Haxel her hope, to use the aircar of the strangers to take them out of danger. The other hadn't blinked; the First Scout had, however, been adamant in her belief that there was only one feasible destination. Without weapons, without food, with truenight close, anything less than secure shelter was pointless. Haxel wanted them taken to Grona itself.

Which would have been fine, had the strangers arrived midday. The first flight of ten had left quickly, none hesitating to enter the aircar, though each paused to brush fingertips with Aryl, a wordless sending of gratitude and renewed hope. But the second flight had left only moments ago. Her fingers still tingled from their touch, her mind still brimmed with emotion.

Including a very healthy amount of fear.

Grona, it turned out, was almost a tenth away roundtrip, even by aircar, so truenight had arrived before the machine returned for its second load of passengers, leaving the rest to wait but not, thankfully, in the dark. Marcus had brought a powerful type of glow. Now it sat, their guardian, where the metal span met the platform. The light carved a safe passageway between the bridge and the aircar. Beyond that safety, the air throbbed with the canopy's normal evening chorus: the distant clicks of innumerable small feet; the screams of the dying. The swarm was at work.

"Safe are." This assertion from Marcus. The four of them crouched within the opening of the bridge. He regularly consulted the stick he called a comlink that produced voices, including this latest reassuring report. Haxel watched with calculation; Enris with curiosity.

"Thank you," Aryl told him, finding a smile. The Human was remarkably cheerful, almost relaxed. Either he had greater trust in his technology than she, or he didn't appreciate how vulnerable they were here, light or no light. It kept the swarm at bay, that was all. Should the Tikitik wish them dead by other means, they were easy prey.

That wasn't all. She was so desperate for sleep it took all her energy to keep alert, but she must. Those in the Cloisters had mourned their deaths, however prematurely. She was quite sure they hadn't expected to feel them live to truenight, let alone rise into the air and fly like wings on the M'hir to another clan.

Hard as it was for Aryl to feel wary of her own kind, she

knew she wasn't the only one. Haxel divided her vigilance between the platform and the empty bridge behind them.

And the Human. The tough First Scout wasn't, Aryl observed with a certain satisfaction, immune to the contradiction of his form to her inner sense.

Enris had no such difficulty. "Why are you here?" he asked Marcus abruptly, as if frustrated by a puzzle.

"Aryl—" the Human began, stopping as the Om'ray held up one hand.

"I mean here, in the world. All of you."

"Seekers, we." The answer he always gave, that caution in his eyes.

Haxel paid close attention to this exchange, Aryl noticed.

"Your technology, the things you make," Enris persisted, indicating the light and the comlink. "They're better than ours. Why seek what's older here?"

Aryl thought Marcus looked impressed by the question. "Things, not matter. Understand, matter. Why this, not that, matter." The Human pantomimed a series of layers with his hands, ending with both hands palm up. "Before this world, before world mine, these makers were. Why not now? Important."

How old was old, to the strangers? How many kinds of people could live in one place, and never know one another? Why would the passing or survival of others matter now? Aryl let the questions tumble through her mind, unasked, unanswered. She had complications enough in her world, without adding those of the past.

Or of the strangers.

Enris questioned, Marcus responded. Aryl let her mind drift, catching what rest she could without sleeping. The two had deep, peaceful voices, though one spoke in broken phrases and the other shortened his, as if this would help understanding.

"You didn't see us leave?"

Aryl. From Enris, with an undertone of warning. Aryl kept her eyes half closed, but now listened intently. Marcus had finally got around to asking how they'd managed to get from what he called Site Two to Yena. The Human wasn't, she grumbled to herself, slow.

Luckily, neither was Enris. "I'm Tuana Om'ray," he said easily. "The Oud fly us where we want. If they understand. Hard to talk to, aren't they?"

She relaxed as Marcus chuckled. "Hard is. Easier, you."

"Glad to hear it. The Oud are like these Tikitik, you know," Enris elaborated, obviously relishing his role. "No sense of manners. Rude. Uncivilized. It wouldn't let us say good-bye—"

She sent a snap of *caution*, hoping he'd pay attention.

"Hush!"

Urgent, quiet. The word drew them all to their feet, eyes on Haxel. She'd shielded her eyes against the glare of the stranger-light, trying to see beyond it. Aryl joined her.

Some thing comes. The First Scout drew her longknife, passing the shorter blade from her belt to Aryl.

Stay behind, Aryl sent to Enris. *Guard Marcus. Watch for Om'ray at our backs.* This last with a touch of shame.

The dark outside the light exploded into a mass of legs and jaws, into thick heavy bodies black and glistening with rain. Stitlers. Out of their traps, doubtless forced here by the Tikitik; they fled the swarm as much as hunted.

Aryl ducked and drove her blade into the swollen pouch dangling below the first, ripping more than cutting it open. As she'd hoped, it was full of still-living prey. The squirming mass dropped to the planking of the bridge, an irresistible magnet to the others. How many others, she didn't bother to count, too busy finding and severing spines as the mass of creatures struggled to be first to eat, Haxel doing the same.

Done. Nothing moved beyond a spasm, or twitch. She turned to check on Marcus and Enris—

"Aryl!" Another stitler launched itself over the rest. Haxel's blow removed a leg, but it kept coming. Aryl readied her short knife, knowing it was nothing compared to the jaws aimed at her . . .

Her attacker was *pushed* into the night.

It had been Enris.

And it had been Power. The hair rose on her arms. A great deal of Power.

Haxel's eyes met hers, her lips stretched in a grim smile. "I like your friend."

There was no time for more. Another stitler met Haxel's longknife. But the next, smarter or more stupid than the rest, snagged the stranger's light box as its prey, pulling it away with great heaves of its legs.

Darkness swallowed them.

She had to trust her Power, now. Always, the *other* darkness was too easy to find, calling to her. Aryl fought to keep her focus on her companions, to keep them with her. Where to go . . . where to go . . . the cavern of the Watchers . . .

Stop! It was Enris. Aryl gasped, eyes opening only to squint against a new, far brighter light. There was a rapid burst of incomprehensible words, answered from nearby.

The aircar was back.

Chapter 31

"WILL HE KEEP HIS WORD?"

Aryl shrugged, wincing as the movement involved a part of her shoulder well past sore. Something she'd done during the stitler attack. Nothing rest wouldn't cure. "How can we know, Enris?" she admitted, eyes locked on the retreating dot of light that carried away Marcus Bowman and the flitter-stranger. "He means well by us. I wish he wasn't so curious."

"If he hadn't been, we wouldn't be standing here," with his quiet laugh. "Welcome to solid ground, Yena."

Surrounded by the few bags that were the exiles' belongings, they stood before another bridge, but this was of stone, not wood or metal, and rose over light, not darkness. Its upward curve offended Aryl's sense of proper structure. The light beneath filled a long, shallow hole—she didn't know what else to call an artificial depression in the ground. Within the hole moved machines of various sizes. Looking down at them, Aryl had yet to see any pattern to their constant movement, beyond that some disappeared into the stone walls while others came out.

"Oud."

"I know," she said, taking a deep breath. She managed not to gag on the dry, dust-filled air. "We'd better go." Aryl reached for a bag.

"Leave it," Haxel ordered, already moving. "Let's join the others first."

The *pull* of other Om'ray was strong and warm. Like Haxel, Aryl was drawn by her awareness of the rest of the exiles on the other side of Grona's bridge. Them, and others. Many others. Grona wasn't as large a clan as Yena—as Yena had been—but all were out to greet the new arrivals. She eased her shields the slightest bit more, feeling surprise, welcome, curiosity. Strongest of all, the bone-deep relief of her people, as their pain and shock began, ever-so-slightly, to ease.

There was, she could finally believe, safety in reach. An Om'ray village. A Clan. From here, Aryl could make out well-lit homes along a wide, flat path. Mountains ridged the night sky, like walls of black. Grona itself sat on the lower reach of one, here a gentle slope discernible underfoot, blissfully free of loose, predatory rock. First of the other buildings on the far side of the bridge, their Cloisters rose on a short stalk, more like an improbable blossom than a beacon.

And everywhere, though she couldn't sense or see them, Oud. They tunneled the mountains, hunting metals and other ores. They were beneath her now. Enris had said so, on their journey here; a turnabout of expertise he gave willingly.

He had said the Oud were unlike the Tikitik, that they asked little of the Om'ray in their midst.

He'd warned they were like Tikitik, in being dangerous if disturbed. That some had a form of Power, disturbing and painful to Om'ray. They should be cautious.

Cautious was fine. Peaceful was fine. Aryl was fully prepared to be the quietest, most peaceful Om'ray ever to walk the world, given she was allowed to rest and soon. She'd asked

Marcus to promise never to contact her or other Om'ray again. Not to spy on them, ever. To ignore them.

She hoped the Oud would do the same.

Haxel was halfway across the unusual bridge; Aryl followed with Enris. The worked stone underfoot also made low walls on either side of the structure, smooth and cool under her hands. Polished with care, she decided, like the Sarc's table.

It wouldn't burn.

Aryl pushed the thought away. There were no swarms here, no other predators. The Grona were like Enris' Tuana, living where only the growing of their own food was of concern, their stone homes ample protection against the elements.

Her people were clustered at the base of the bridge; they were surrounded, outnumbered, by unfamiliar faces and shapes. Someone saw her and gave a glad cry. "Aryl!"

She used the downslope to walk faster, eager to be with Myris and Ael, to see Seru and all the rest, to make sure they'd made the trip by air to this new kind of place without being somehow changed.

It was only when Aryl reached the bottom of the bridge, only when the others, smiling despite their tears, moved aside, that she saw who had called her name and who now waited with the widest smile of all.

Bern Teerac.

"You'll like her." Bern dropped to the bench on the other side of the table, depositing a bewildering array of mugs and steaming baskets between them.

He'd gained weight—or she remembered him thinner. Aryl smiled fondly and took something warm and soft in her hand, too tired to eat or even look at it. Enough that he was here. Enough that they were all here.

All around the large room, their version of a meeting hall, the Grona kept pulling out more tables and benches. Their arrival apparently required a celebration.

She wasn't the only Yena numbed by their hosts' enthusiasm, though the youngest took it in stride. Ziba, for one, had joined a vigorous game of chase-me. Every so often, Aryl could hear an outraged shout from one of her pursuers, less swift on tabletops or at jumping up the stone stairs set, oddly, around the walls. Her elders watched with bemused weariness. Except Cetto and his Chosen, Aryl fretted to herself, having the news from Myris. Husni had been dizzy after her ride in the aircar. They'd insisted she go to healers in the Cloisters; naturally, Cetto had accompanied her. Nothing serious, he'd proclaimed. The wear of events on an older body.

They took their toll on young ones, too, she thought and yawned.

"Aryl? Are you listening to a thing I say?"

" 'Like her.' I'm sure I will," Aryl replied. She gestured apology then leaned her chin in her hand to gaze at him. "It's good to see you."

Not so thin—and no longer Bern Teerac. She'd immediately sensed the other presence Joined to his; it had stopped her impulse to lower her shields to him, to connect mind to mind. He'd been hurt by her refusal. She'd seen it in his face and was sorry. But she wasn't ready, not yet, for that.

For now, this close, the warm bond of *heart-kin* was enough.

"I'd like to say it's good to see you," Bern replied. His troubled gaze swept the crowd, finding it too easy, Aryl knew, to spot the Yena. Oh, they'd been given clothes, a chance to wash. No rest—they'd been told this welcome feast couldn't wait. But the ill-fitting Grona clothes only made their difference more apparent, while washing had exposed the red of cuts and burns, the pallor of exhaustion.

They looked, Aryl decided, like the dead from her nightmare. Skeletons come to the table, with eyes that had seen too much. She shivered. They all shivered. It was bone cold here. "Give us a couple of days," she suggested through her teeth. "We'll be fine."

Bern filled their mugs with something white and frothy from a large jug, downing half of his at once, his throat working. She didn't touch hers. He licked his lips, then gestured apology. "Aryl . . ." His voice shook. "This is horrible. The Tikitik destroy the village . . . you here . . . grandfather, grandmother . . . but not my parents? I don't understand." He scowled at her. "I don't understand any of it."

A blissfully warm and heavy coat descended over her shoulders. "You look like an icicle," Enris announced, lowering himself to the bench beside her. On his face, washing had unveiled a wealth of half-healed bruises and cuts. They didn't affect his wide grin.

"What's an icicle?" she asked.

Bern shuddered. "Be glad you don't know. The mountains will soon be much colder than this—I've seen memories. Do the plains of Tuana know the cold?"

"We get a frost but not every season. You're Bern Teerac? Enris Mendolar."

"Bern sud Caraat," Bern corrected. His eyes lit and his tone grew almost fervent. "The magnificent Oran di Caraat Chose me. An Adept," he added unnecessarily, "living in the Cloisters."

Whatever appetite Aryl might have had abandoned her. She pulled the coat tighter, wishing it covered her legs, too.

"Made Adept, did she? While still unChosen?" Claiming Aryl's untouched mug, Enris tipped it to Bern's. "Quite the accomplishment."

"Oran is powerful." Bern's hand, wrapped around his mug, seemed stuck in midair. Like all the newly Joined, Aryl reminded herself, the topic of his Chosen drove any other thought from his head. "And very Talented."

"Beautiful, I'm sure," Enris supplied cheerfully.

He was doing it on purpose. She'd done the same to Costa. Aryl put her forearms on the table and considered dropping her head to join them. Maybe her companions would ignore her.

Or maybe, she thought, her head for some reason already resting on her arms, on this remarkably comfortable table, she'd ignore them.

A feast they'd barely touched, a night's sleep broken by nightmares, and now this day of polite inquisition. Grona had a right to ask questions, Aryl told herself, rubbing her eyes. It was unprecedented, to have so many from one Clan try to join another. Grona wasn't unwilling; they were cautious.

They could have waited one more day.

"Haxel Vendan."

Her turn would come next. Aryl watched Haxel stand where each of Yena's exiles had throughout the morning, then bow deeper. It was something Grona Om'ray did as part of their greetings. She wasn't sure why. It looked awkward. Perhaps it had something to do with how they tended their fields. Did living on solid ground make it easier to bend over? Her lips quirked. Her guess? There was nothing here to attack them, so they were willing to be helpless. Haxel looked slightly embarrassed when she rose from her version, but Grona's Council smiled at her.

Aryl felt chilled inside as well as out when she looked at Grona's Council, though they seemed placid, pleasant Om'ray. Old, of course, though, being plump, their wrinkles failed to add stern lines to their mouth and eyes. There were no Adepts among them. One wore the Speaker's Pendant on her chest, but a bright woven vest covered it most of the time. They sat shoulder-to-shoulder along a bench at one of the tables in the meeting hall.

A bench with thick, warm-looking cushions. Aryl wanted her own before she sat this long again.

The First Scout didn't offer to share her report mind to mind, instead giving a terse, bloodless summary of what everyone before her had said. Yena had been caught in a struggle between Tikitik factions that resulted in the destruction of their village. Not all could stay. She passed over the role of Yena's Adepts in choosing who would leave, finishing with the truth. There wasn't enough food left for all; by leaving, they hoped those sheltered in Yena's Cloisters would survive to rebuild one day. They had no idea why the Oud would come to their aid and offer transport to Grona, but all were grateful.

The truth, but not all the truth.

It made a heroic end to their story, while erasing betrayal. The Yena would do their best to keep it that way—they would avoid contact mind to mind until established here, keep their secrets. There was no reason for Grona to insist. Outside of family, Om'ray normally maintained their privacy unless there was need. Outside of Clan? They could, Aryl thought, make their own rules for that.

She didn't like partial truth. It had been Taisal's tactic; Aryl knew firsthand how it felt to be so betrayed. But the exiles had no better choice. Admit they'd been exiled by their own? Brought here by beings from another world?

Grona would exile them, too, Aryl thought, her mouth going dry, and checked her shields.

The Councillors rose and bowed as one. A couple were less than steady; they'd heard from all but Aryl, and old bones didn't forgive the hours despite cushions. "Our thanks, Haxel," intoned their Speaker. "Grona accepts your token and yourself with joy. Welcome." Rote words, perhaps, but said with warmth. The others bowed again.

Given the sluggish look of their own First Scout, Aryl didn't doubt the warmth. The only other exile to receive such an enthusiastic welcome had been Enris, not only eligible but a metalworker. Then again, he'd blended with these Om'ray from the beginning. Tuana must live a similar life. He'd feel at home here, within these stone walls.

She would, too, Aryl told herself fiercely.

"Aryl."

Aryl stood and took Haxel's place. She bowed low as well. They looked at her for a moment. She returned the favor.

Efris Ducan, Mysk Gethin, Gura Azar, Lier Haon, Cyor sud Kaar, and, head of Bern's new family, Emyam sud Caraat. Instead of proper nets, all Grona Chosen left their hair free to squirm opinion from under the loosest of caps, something Aryl tried not to notice as she faced those on Council. Cyor and Emyam might have been brothers, so closely did they resemble one another.

Their unfamiliar names grated on her ears. Truth be told, she feared them. It was a new worry, one that had stung like a fresh bite this morning, when she'd awakened in a flat unfamiliar bed and lay there, hearing nothing but the grind of foot on stone. Since that moment, the mere thought made her heart pound. Grona's names.

Efris wore the Speaker's Pendant. The person to ask about the Oud, Aryl decided. She'd done most of the talking for Grona; she did so now. "We've heard from your elders, Aryl. There's no need to burden the young retelling such tragic events. Grona accepts your token and you, Aryl, with joy. Be welcome."

The others rose more quickly than before. They all bowed, two with longing looks at the door.

They were done for the day.

Aryl didn't mind being dismissed as unimportant. In some ways, it made a pleasant change. But she wasn't done.

"I have a question for Council," she told them.

Aryl could feel the immediate attention of the other exiles. They'd stayed in the meeting hall, waiting for the decision of Grona's Council. The youngest were asleep on blankets in a corner. All but Enris. The Tuana had been cheerfully claimed by members of a grandfather's family and whisked away to inspect the metalworker's shop.

She had Bern's attention as well.

He'd sat apart from his former Clan, listening to account after account of the destruction of Yena. The rest of Grona had gone to their fields for the day; if that was his new role among them, he'd ignored it. He was still and quiet, outwardly relaxed enough to rest his heavy Grona boots on a table, but his grief and sullen anger were like a heavy pulse against her shields. Rude behavior from an adult, being too obviously tolerated by those around him. Like Grona, he'd been forced to learn of his family's fate through words alone.

What did he expect? Aryl wondered. No Yena would share memory with him. It would be sharing with Oran as well.

Whether Bern was too upset to reinforce his shields or wanted everyone to know his pain, the result, in Aryl's opinion, was unpleasant and unwelcome. She didn't have sympathy to spare. Now she tightened her shields until the oppressive *sense* of him through their bond vanished.

"A question?" Efris echoed. The rest of Grona Council froze mid-bow, their dismay almost laughable. But they resumed their seats. "And what might that be, young Aryl?"

Aryl took a steadying breath. She had to sound calm and mature; she felt neither. "My cousin, Seru Parth, comes to Grona as a Chooser. Will you support her right to grant that name to her Chosen?"

The dismay increased tenfold and Aryl clenched her hands into fists within the overlong sleeves she wore. She hadn't wanted to be right. They didn't want to deal with this, she thought, not in front of all of Yena. Not now.

She did.

"You're old enough to know the unChosen leave their family names behind on Passage," the Speaker's smile seemed forced.

"Seru is a Chooser, not unChosen. She carries her family's name. Parth."

They looked at one another. After an uncomfortable pause, the silence through the meeting hall as thick as mist in the canopy, Emyam sud Caraat shrugged and spoke. "An important issue, Aryl. Thank you. We will discuss the matter in days to come. You've only just arrived, after all. There's housing to settle. We want everyone to be comfortable."

"And we must get to know one another," reminded Efris. Her cheerful tone might have worked, Aryl judged, if her gray hair hadn't been free to twitch over her shoulders. "There'll be a proper welcome feast in two days to introduce Choosers and unChosen."

At the word feast, the rest smiled and visibly relaxed. "If that's all?" Grona's Council rose to its feet and bowed.

Accepting delay, if not defeat, Aryl bowed back.

"Seru is the only Parth." Aryl kept her voice down. The stone and pressed dirt of Grona's village had a distressing ability to carry sound. "Yena's families must not end here."

Morla Kessa'at sighed. "They heard you, Aryl. Be patient. Trust me—Councils take their time, especially with important matters." The four of them talked as they walked, retracing their steps up and down the straight Grona street. Aryl had noticed she wasn't the only Yena to find it difficult to sit indoors.

"I don't see why it's important," said Husni Teerac.

"They've made us welcome. Why don't we take the names of our new clan—like anyone on Passage?"

"Husni!" They all reacted, even Haxel, who'd so far been quieter than even her habit.

Husni pursed her thin, peeling lips and stared back. She was soft-spoken, to Cetto's loud rumble; as far as Aryl recalled, she hadn't ventured an opinion in years. She had one now. "Parth, Teerac, or Sarc," Husni said emphatically. "Our families will survive us, back home. They're safe. These are kind Om'ray. We should show our gratitude, young Aryl. They've given us a place to live. Work for our hands."

Like the rest, Husni and Cetto stayed with a host family. There was nothing said about separate homes—perhaps the Grona preferred living atop one another. Most exiles were already busy somewhere, learning the tasks required to produce food instead of finding it. Aryl envied the ease with which the others had settled into place.

"What if our families don't—" she began, only to be unwilling to finish.

"Of course they won't," Haxel growled. "They've wrapped themselves in a net and hung it out to dry." She stalked beside them like a hungry esask. She'd been hard to find these last two days. Aryl guessed the former scout had been busy assessing their new surroundings, uncertain of her knowledge now that the familiar threats were behind a mountain. It wouldn't take her long to learn the new ones.

If there were any, she thought. The Grona were peaceful, almost docile. Aryl hadn't decided if she envied their lack of fear, or feared its lack. Surely a village built above the Oud was at risk, always. It was no different from the Lay Swamp. What was below their feet couldn't be trusted.

"Slow down." The plea came from Husni again. Not that the old one couldn't keep up, especially at this easy pace, but the

Grona found Yena too quick. They were all learning to move more slowly. The Grona were methodical Om'ray and took their time with everything, it seemed. "The Cloisters is safe, Haxel. Don't exaggerate."

Morla agreed. "The Tikitik told Aryl they have dresel to share. Yena need only wait for calm. Negotiate for supplies—"

The four paused as Ziba ran by, each quick step kicking dust. She was followed by a pack of young Grona. Without breaking stride, she climbed a shop's stone wall and ran up its roof, disappearing over the top.

The Grona stopped in their tracks, then turned as one to walk away. They didn't look happy.

"Well?" Husni demanded of them, pointing at the shop wall. "What are you waiting for, younglings? A ladder? Get up there!"

Wide-eyed, they broke into a run—in the opposite direction. Doubtless, Aryl sighed to herself, to share this latest Yena oddity with their parents. She shivered, despite wearing all the clothes she'd been given. "We'd better get ready," she said. "The welcome feast starts soon. It will be a good chance," this with all the conviction she could muster, "to get to know each other better."

Haxel studied the deceptively empty rooftops with a knowing eye. "I'll fetch Ziba," she said, a smile twisting her scar. "She's an excellent distraction."

"Child's a menace," Husni muttered, but with a note of pride.

Cold fingers brushed the back of Aryl's hand. *Nothing more about Yena names, Aryl, please.* Morla's sending held an undercurrent of anxiety. *Not today. We're still strangers here.*

"I'll see you in the meeting hall," Aryl replied aloud.

She understood Morla's concern. To survive, they needed Grona's welcome.

But everything inside her warned there could be too high a price.

Aryl shortened and slowed her stride. If she could walk like this, she decided, she could do anything.

Even convince Grona's Council.

Interlude

ENRIS HAD EXPECTED TO FEEL at home. If being treated well and with kindness mattered, if being welcomed by all, especially Grona's anxious Choosers, mattered, if having his skills with metal greeted with joy mattered, he would have.

Drums had sounded. An Oud vehicle rolled down the main street, its treads crushing stone to dust, a cloud of whirr/clicks in attendance. He'd yet to see when the small things attached themselves to the Oud above ground. Perhaps they waited around the mouths of well-used tunnels.

The Oud riding on top was dressed as the ones in Tuana had been, a lump under a shroud, with a dome over the end that went first.

He should really, he told himself, feel at home.

Not an official Visitation, he assumed, given the lack of interest shown by Grona. He'd been told they'd always lived in peace with the Oud. Unlike Tuana. No runners to obtain scarce supplies. No sudden destruction as part of their village was reshaped from beneath.

"Enris? Aren't you going to the feast?"

Rather than answer immediately, Enris considered the clean

boots at the end of his clean new pants, then crossed his legs at the ankles before leisurely leaning back against the wall. This bench was in front of the shop Grona's Council had proposed he take for his own. They had several vacant. There'd been more of them, once. Just like Yena. "I ate already," he said, finally tipping his head back to look at Aryl Sarc.

Different but the same. Three days of rest and comfort had changed them all. Aryl had lost some of the haggardness around her eyes and mouth; he'd stopped limping. She wore as many clothes as she could and was presently buried under layers of woven tunics and coats. Like Yuhas, the Yena were cold away from their steaming canopy, while he went bare-armed, enjoying the nip to the air. And lack of biters.

She'd found or made a net to confine her hair. A shame, in his opinion, but it was their custom.

"It's not about eating." Aryl sat beside him, squirming in her coats until she was comfortable. "You could save me," she admitted after an easy moment. "They're frantic to know anything about you. I'll hardly get to take a bite. And," as if this settled the question, "without you, I'll have to make things up. You'll gain a very romantic past."

"I'm not interested in their Choosers. I don't plan to stay."

"The voice holder." She fell silent; he waited. Then, "Does it still matter?"

"It wasn't the strangers'," he reminded her. "It worked for me, an Om'ray. Yes, it still matters."

"It could be what they seek."

Enris turned his head, looking down to meet that clear gray-eyed gaze that, whether she knew it or not, always puzzled at what she saw, always tried to understand it. "Maybe," he acknowledged. "But what if it's new, Aryl? Something we made? What if there are Om'ray in the world now who don't rely on Oud or Tikitik?"

She considered this. "Where will you look first?"

"Vyna." At her surprised look, he explained. "Think about it. They're the Clan no one truly knows. I've asked here—it's the same. Never been one on Passage. All anyone knows is that there must be an impassable 'pick your choice' landscape in the way. What if there isn't? What if Vyna unChosen don't take Passage so their Clan can keep its secrets?"

Aryl caught her full lower lip in her teeth, a habit, he'd noticed she had when thinking. "Interesting," she said at last.

He pulled the token from its pocket. "I've told Grona's Council I'm being Called there. They're disappointed—warned me of the dangers—but who argues with an unChosen who hears that special voice?"

A sidelong glance. "For the sake of Grona's Choosers, I should tell them the only 'Call' you hear, Tuana, is curiosity."

"You could come with me." The words came out before he'd realized he would say them. "If you're curious, too."

She tucked her nose inside her vests. "Is it warmer?"

"I've no idea."

Aryl pretended to shiver, surely impossible under so many layers. "If you can't guarantee a decent heat, I'll stay, thank you. Besides," with a lightness he knew better than to believe, "I've my people to look after."

"They seem to be settling in," Enris commented. Three days wasn't long, but he'd noticed a few more smiles among the Yena, less tendency for them to cluster together. The young ones ran the street—mostly. The Oud? He'd watched, but seen no sign they cared about the arrival of new Om'ray. They would, at the next Visitation, when the lists and numbers changed. For now, they seemed preoccupied with mining, the rocks of Grona's mountainside being the source of their green metal.

He'd like to know more of that; like to, but not enough to draw their attention to a certain metalworker.

He'd like to spend time with his grandfather's family and ask them where he could find a stream with rounded stones. But not enough to linger.

"Are they?" Aryl said wistfully. "I hope so. They've welcomed us."

"Grona needs you," he observed. "They've barely enough to till the terraces they farm, even with Oud machines. Think they'll refuse a gift of strong, grateful Yena? You did notice, I trust, the lack of questions about your amazing Oud rescue." He grinned. "Your lie suits them just fine. They don't care how you got here. Only that you're here."

She looked offended. "Were you always so cynical?"

Enris laughed and leaned back again. "Were you always so responsible, Aryl Sarc?"

"Maybe not. Now I must be. I've family here, Enris," she said more seriously than he'd expected.

"And Bern." He *felt* her outrage and laughed louder. "I'm not blind."

Her outrage faded. "We were close. Once."

That feeling, he understood. "Choice happens. Doesn't mean you've lost your friend. Think of it as gaining an endless topic of conversation."

"He's changed." His inner awareness of her faded as her shields slammed down between them. Which was, he decided, answer enough.

"As for me," Enris said casually, "I'm leaving in the morning. The Grona tell me storms will close the mountain passes soon. I've no desire to do any more climbing or meet your hungry rocks."

"So soon?" She sounded flustered. "What about my promise? To try and teach you what I—what I did."

Enris gestured to the road and buildings. "You want this, for yourself and your people," he said gently. "I won't ask you to risk it for what might not even work. Besides. If I do have that Talent—" he made himself laugh again, "—I'll figure out how to use it on my own."

Her eyes searched his. "You're sure?"

For one heartbeat, he wasn't. Not about this, not about why he was so set on leaving.

The next heartbeat, he was.

"Find joy, Aryl Sarc. And do me one favor?"

"Anything," she said quietly.

"Don't tell the Choosers I'm leaving until I'm long gone. Please?"

He was glad to see her start to smile, even though he couldn't. "I'll do my best," Aryl vowed. Then her smile widened, becoming thoughtlessly happy as her head turned.

Enris followed her look. The street had been empty of Oud and Om'ray, but now two figures approached them.

Bern with his Chosen, finally out of the Cloisters.

Not being blinded by Choice, Enris didn't find Oran di Caraat beautiful. Her pale face was too austere for his taste, with puckers at the edge of her mouth and eyes that would, he judged, age into lines of temper, not laughter. Her blonde hair hung thick and heavy over her shoulders, its ends moving restlessly, as if she were impatient.

They stopped in front of Aryl and himself, so close he had to look up. Bern seemed preoccupied, as usual. Oran was tall and imposing in her white embroidered robes. Adept. It was rare for an unChosen to be elevated to that rank and Enris doubted she let anyone forget it. Least of all—he glanced at Aryl—her Chosen's former best friend.

He needn't have worried. Aryl still smiled, if not quite as warmly. "Hello," she said pleasantly, rising to her feet. "You must be Oran di Caraat. I'm—"

"Aryl Sarc," the Adept interrupted. "Come with us."

Enris thought Aryl braced herself; he wasn't sure why. "Is it time for the feast?" she asked. "I've been trying to talk Enris into coming."

Bern looked at Oran.

Just that. Normal in all Chosen pairs, an accustomed nuisance to unChosen, left to wonder what was exchanged. Enris had teased Yuhas about it, in what seemed another life. The Yena had claimed it part of being Joined, a joy to constantly gaze at one another. Especially, he'd laughed, with a Chosen as lovely as his Caynen. No secrets.

Bern looked at Oran, and there were secrets between them. Enris felt it, like the chill that slid down the mountain at sunset.

He wasn't the only one. "What do you want, Bern?" Aryl demanded, her smile gone.

Enris was on his feet before he realized he was uneasy. There was something wrong here.

Oran's dark eyes flicked to him. "This has nothing to do with you, stranger."

"Aryl, please," Bern said, breaking his silence. "Just come with us. We want to talk to you."

"Alone," Oran added, eyes still on Enris.

Enris deliberately lifted his hand and brushed the back of it along Aryl's cheek and jaw. *Don't trust them,* he sent through that private contact. *Don't go.*

If I can't trust my heart-kin, she replied, the words tinged with weary grief, *who is left?*

Aryl stepped away from him without looking back. The other two turned, taking positions on either side. Together they walked away.

Heart-kin? It explained a few things. It didn't explain this.

Enris watched until he was sure they weren't going to the meeting hall.

Then, he followed.

Chapter 32

UNTIL NOW, REGARDLESS OF HIS new status, Bern had been happy to see her—she'd known it, seen it. If Bern wouldn't meet her eyes, something wasn't right.

Aryl wasn't tempted to *reach* to him. The physical fact of Oran di Caraat was unpleasant enough.

"Not the feast," she observed after a moment.

"Be silent, unChosen," Oran ordered. Her hair lashed across her face, forcing her to take it in both hands.

Aryl laughed. She couldn't help it. She'd faced so much worse than this opinionated too-young Adept. "I might," she offered mildly, "if you tell me what can't wait until tomorrow. I'd like to enjoy the festivities."

"You don't belong there."

The words came from Bern. She would have dismissed them from his Chosen, assumed an unseemly jealousy. From him? "Why?" she asked, stopping in her tracks to stare at him. "What's this about?"

"You—"

"Hush," Aryl snapped at the Adept. "I'll hear it from someone I know."

From the sour look on Oran's face, she'd never been hushed before. Probably couldn't climb either, Aryl thought uncharitably. "Well, Bern?"

He glanced over one shoulder, then the other. She saw no reason for it; the street was empty. "I listened to the others," Bern said then, his voice low and strained. "I heard what they said about you."

"That I helped save them?" Aryl made herself gesture apology, despite the tension crawling up her spine. "They're too kind. You would have done the same."

He scowled. "When Yena was attacked by the swarm, you were suddenly there, with the stranger. No one saw an Oud aircar bring you."

That? "Of course they didn't see it," she said as reasonably as she could. "The glows were gone. The Tikitik took them."

"Don't bother to lie, unChosen," the Adept accused. "We know what you can do."

By an effort of will, Aryl didn't react. There were no shields between Chosen, except those of courtesy.

She should have seen this coming.

"What do you know?" She stressed the last word.

"You do what's Forbidden," Bern burst out, his face flushed. "You're the reason Yena was attacked—my family destroyed!" Something passed between him and Oran; he sagged and gestured apology.

To which of them, Aryl wasn't sure.

His Chosen took over. "I know you possess a new Talent, one that can pluck an Om'ray from this world and lose him in another, deadly one. Or retrieve him, if you so choose." Oran made the last sound unlikely.

Altogether, Aryl had to admit, a different way of looking at it. She looked at Bern. "When I saved your life. Heart-kin."

Oran didn't like the reminder.

Neither did Bern, whose face took on that angry, obstinate

expression he'd shown his parents when they'd wanted him to work rather than climb with Aryl. "Then prove me wrong, *heart-kin,*" he challenged. "Drop your shields and share your thoughts with me as you once did. Show me how you came back to Yena."

Which would be opening to Oran di Caraat as well. They all knew it.

Why did they care? Aryl wondered suddenly, her eyes narrowing. Bern hadn't wanted to know more about the *other*. He'd been horrified—he still was. No, she decided, it was this young, too-ambitious Adept. They were Joined, but not like Costa and Leri, two halves of a loving whole, each enriching the other. This Oran ruled her Chosen; it was her will that drove them both. Why?

Oran was of Haxel's ilk, but without the First Scout's common sense or desire to help her Clan. This one wanted Power, for Power's sake.

She wouldn't get it here.

"Good-bye, Bern Teerac," Aryl told him, knowing this time, it was the truth.

At first, Aryl stayed on Grona's flat road, keeping to one side as she'd been told, in case an Oud drove by without warning. Though the ugly things were too slow to run over a sleeping aspird.

Walking at her normal pace, she soon passed the meeting hall, bright and noisy with voices. The feast had started at midday. From what she'd been told, a special one like this would last through truenight. Though they didn't call it that, here. There was day and there was night and both, she'd been told, were safe for Om'ray to be out.

Her nerves had yet to believe it.

Aryl hesitated, looking back.

No one in sight. Bern and Oran had sputtered behind her, as if unable to believe she would dare walk away from a pair of Chosen, then been silent. They must have gone inside.

No sign of Enris. Packing, Aryl guessed. The Grona were generous; he'd have all the supplies he'd need.

She'd *listen* for him, she decided. For the first while. Make sure he was all right. Know where he'd gone. A discreet use of Power. Harmless.

No. That was the mistake she'd made before. For all she knew, some Grona could detect her *reach*. Let such a new Talent's use by a Yena be exposed, just once, and she'd as good as exile her people again. Unless the Grona was Oran di Caraat. Aryl's lips twisted. Would she want that for herself, too?

Enris Mendolar would be fine. He was smart and strong. Those who left on Passage were gone to those who remained.

As she would be.

She'd given her token to the Grona Council, so avoided the Oud. It was easy enough; their clumsy vehicles were confined to roads or tunnels. Daylight, rocks without appetite, no rain . . . Once past the last vacant home, she walked along the narrow jagged tops of Grona's terrace walls, balancing without thought.

If anything, Aryl was bored.

Bored was better than anything else she was.

She hadn't dared go first to the room they'd given her. Oran and Bern could be waiting there, this time prepared to insist. Or someone from her host family, not yet at the feast, with questions and honest concern. They'd likely have insisted she talk to Council and their Adepts.

Who, as far as Aryl knew, were all like Oran di Caraat. At

best, Grona's Adepts had brought her among them, in her opinion showing a serious lack of judgment in those supposed to be wise. At worst? She'd seen that side. She wouldn't trust her fate there.

Aryl kept going, jumping the occasional gap in the wall of boulders and pebbles, heading—she wasn't sure where. Away from Grona. Away from Yena. Haxel had mentioned sheltering from the night's cold under ledges or in holes. She'd also noted the Grona carried fire starters with them, though what they burned for light and heat, Aryl couldn't fathom. Their crops maybe.

She didn't have a fire starter anyway. Maybe there were warm holes.

Aryl laughed at herself. Haxel had been right after all. She should have been a scout.

Survive first.

Then worry about why.

"Find a warm hole." Like all advice, it had been easier to give than take. This close to firstnight, walking wasn't enough to warm her; the bulky Grona clothing insulated what it covered, but the now-icy breeze worked through at wrist and ankle. And, Aryl tightened her belt for the second time, it snuck in at her waist. First chance she had, she'd fix that.

She'd passed a handful of Grona Om'ray working in their fields. They hadn't spoken, merely stared as if it had never occurred to them someone could walk on their walls. Others moved along the road, busy at what she didn't care. The feast was well underway behind her; likely no one had noticed her absence. She kept up her shields. There would be time to seek her own kind when she was away from here, and closer to . . . closer to anywhere else, Aryl told herself firmly.

"Something wrong with the road?"

Startled, Aryl looked down to find Enris grinning up at her, a large pack over his shoulders.

At a loss for anything else to say, she pointed. "It's too flat."

"Suit yourself." He resumed walking, as if there was nothing unusual about him being on the road, and her being on the wall.

She had to lengthen her strides to keep up. "I thought you weren't leaving until tomorrow morning."

"I thought you weren't leaving at all." A hint of something dark beneath the words. Anger?

Aryl stopped. Enris walked a few more steps, then stopped as well, turning to look back. "I changed my mind. I couldn't stay," she told him, wrapping her arms around her waist. "I don't like it here. It's too cold."

"They made it impossible for you to stay," he countered, the anger out in the open now. "I was there, Aryl. I heard."

"Heard—?" she repeated numbly.

"Your so-called heart-kin and his Adept." Enris' lips twisted over the word as if it left a foul taste. "They wanted what you can do. And I'm no better." Guilt. He let her feel that, too. "I wanted it. I'm sorry, Aryl."

Aryl jumped to the road and took a tentative step toward him, rubbing one foot in the dirt. "Flat," she complained. Then, before he had to say anything else, "Don't be sorry, Enris. Oran wants to make herself more than other Om'ray. I chose not to help her. That's why I left."

As she came beside him and looked up, Aryl felt strangely shy. "You think of others first. I know that. I promised to teach you and I will, if I can. Do you see a Council here to forbid it? Not," she added hastily, "that I know what it is—yet." She shivered again. "You did bring fire," she said wistfully.

"Yes," with his deep laugh. Then Enris sobered, his dark eyes gazing at her. "And something else, Aryl Sarc." His eyes lifted to look behind her.

Aryl turned, her heart suddenly pounding, and saw figures coming up the road from Grona. More, she choked on a laugh, walked along terrace walls. Without hesitation, she lowered her shields and *reached*.

They were all there. Every Yena who'd come with her, from Haxel to Seru, Myris to Ziba. Even old Cetto and Husni. She *reached* deeper, feeling their joy at having found her, their courage, their determination to be together, always.

Wherever they were to go, Aryl Sarc promised her Clan, *they would be.*

Epilogue

A POD BURST, ITS BRITTLE shell no match for the urgency of life. Rastis seedlings spilled forth in a determined confusion of reaching roots and stalks. This was a race, after all. First to grow meant first to the light. Fail and starve in the shadow of others. These sprouts had an unusual opportunity, for their pod lay on a mountain slope, dropped in a dispute between greedy wastryls. Though they lacked the cover of a wing, nothing grew here to challenge them. Rastis need only a roothold and light to conquer.

But Cersi was a world meticulously divided and ruled. Rastis belonged to the lands of the Tikitik, not in the mountains or plains of the Oud.

Sensing the lush young sprouts, other life roused from slumber and began to move, equally determined. Working together, slow and sure, they smothered the young rastis before the first fronds could open. Over time, they digested all flesh, even the splinters of podwood, until only rock remained. As it must, by the Agreement.

Others would dare trespass. Some quick and hard to corner. Some with strange tastes and unfamiliar machines. Some hidden behind barriers and within walls.

None of this will save them, when their time comes.

The Om'ray of Cersi

(Note: names shown as first encountered in the story.)

YENA CLAN:

Adrius sud Parth (Member of Yena Council)
Ael sud Sarc (Chosen of Myris)
Alejo Parth (Seru's brother)
Aryl Sarc
Barit sud Teerac (Bern's father, Chosen of Evra)
Bern Teerac
Cader Sarc
Cetto sud Teerac (Member of Yena Council, Chosen of Husni)
Chaun sud Teerac (Chosen of Weth)
Costa sud Teerac (Aryl's brother, Chosen of Leri)
Dalris sud Sarc (Taisal's grandfather, Unnel's father, Chosen of Nela)
Evra Teerac (Bern's mother)
Ferna Parth (Seru's mother)
Fon Kessa'at (Son of Veca)
Ghoch sud Sarc (Chosen of Oryl)

Gijs sud Vendan (Chosen of Juo)
Haxel Vendan (First Scout)
Husni Teerac
Joyn Uruus (Son of Rimis)
Juo Vendan
Kayd Uruus (Son of Taen)
Kiric Mendolar
Lendin sud Kessa'at (Chosen of Morla)
Leri Teerac
Mele sud Sarc (Aryl's father, Chosen of Taisal)
Morla Kessa'at (Council Member)
Myris Sarc (Taisal's sister)
Nela Sarc (Taisal's grandmother)
Oryl Sarc
Pio di Kessa'at (Adept)
Rimis Uruus (Joyn's mother)
Rorn sud Vendan (Chosen of Haxel)
Seru Parth (Aryl's cousin)
Sian d'sud Vendan (Adept, Member of Yena Council)
Syb sud Uruus (Kayd and Ziba's father, Chosen of Taen)
Taen Uruus (Kayd and Ziba's mother)
Taisal di Sarc (Aryl's mother, Adept, Speaker for Yena)
Tikva di Uruus (Adept, Member of Yena Council)
Tilip sud Kessa'at (Fon's father, Chosen of Veca)
Till sud Parth (Seru's father, Scout, Chosen of Ferna)
Troa sud Uruus (Joyn's father, Chosen of Rimis)
Unnel Sarc (Taisal's mother)
Veca Kessa'at (Fon's mother)
Weth Teerac
Yorl sud Sarc (Taisal's great-uncle, Member of Yena Council)
Yuhas Parth
Ziba Uruus (Daughter of Taen)

TUANA CLAN:

Caynen S'udlaat
Dama Mendolar (Ridersel's mother, Member of Tuana Council)
Enris Mendolar
Eran Serona
Eryel S'udlaat
Gelle Licor
Geter Licor
Irm Lorimar (Mauro's brother)
Jorg sud Mendolar (Enris' father, Chosen of Ridersel)
Mauro Lorimar (Irm's brother)
Mirs sud S'udlaat (Chosen of Eryel)
Naryn S'udlaat
Olalla Mendolar (Enris' cousin)
Ral Serona (Enris' cousin)
Ridersel Mendolar (Enris' mother)
Sive sud Lorimar
Sole sud Serona (Speaker for Tuana)
Traud Licor
Tyko Uruus
Worin Mendolar (Enris' brother)

GRONA CLAN:

Cyor sud Kaar (Member of Grona Council)
Efris Ducan (Member of Grona Council, Grona Speaker)
Emyam sud Caraat (Member of Grona Council)
Gura Azar (Member of Grona Council)
Lier Haon (Member of Grona Council)
Mysk Gethen (Member of Grona Council)
Oran di Caraat